Series by Julie Johnstone

Scottish Medieval Romance Books:

Highlander Vows: Entangled Hearts Series
When a Laird Loves a Lady, Book 1
Wicked Highland Wishes, Book 2
Christmas in the Scot's Arms, Book 3
When a Highlander Loses His Heart, Book 4
How a Scot Surrenders to a Lady, Book 5
When a Warrior Woos a Lass, Book 6

Regency Romance Books:

A Whisper of Scandal Series
Bargaining with a Rake, Book 1
Conspiring with a Rogue, Book 2
Dancing with a Devil, Book 3
After Forever, Book 4
The Dangerous Duke of Dinnisfree, Book 5

A Once Upon A Rogue Series
My Fair Duchess, Book 1
My Seductive Innocent, Book 2
My Enchanting Hoyden, Book 3
My Daring Duchess, Book 4

Lords of Deception Series
What a Rogue Wants, Book 1

Danby Regency Christmas Novellas
The Redemption of a Dissolute Earl, Book 1
Season For Surrender, Book 2
It's in the Duke's Kiss, Book 3

Regency Anthologies
A Summons from the Duke of Danby (Regency Christmas Summons, Book 2)
Thwarting the Duke (When the Duke Comes to Town, Book 2)

Regency Romance Box Sets
A Whisper of Scandal Trilogy (Books 1-3)
Dukes, Duchesses & Dashing Noblemen (A Once Upon a Rogue Regency Novels, Books 1-3)

Paranormal Books:

The Siren Saga
Echoes in the Silence, Book 1

My Seductive Innocent

A Once Upon a Rogue Novel, Book Two

by
Julie Johnstone

My Seductive Innocent

The best way to stay in touch is to subscribe to my newsletter. Go to www.juliejohnstoneauthor.com and subscribe in the box at the top of the page that says Newsletter. If you don't hear from me once a month, please check your spam filter and set up your email to allow my messages through to you so you don't miss the opportunity to win great prizes or hear about appearances.

Dedication

For Nina Costopoulos McCallum for all the advice, encouragement, and endless listening. You are a true friend and a talent on the rise! I cannot wait to see how bright you shine!

And for Katherine Bone for your knowledge, wisdom, and graciousness in helping me with the seafaring aspects of this book. You are an amazing writer and beautiful soul!

If you're interested in when my books go on sale, or want to be one of the first to know about my new releases, please follow me on BookBub! You'll get quick book notifications every time there's a new pre-order, book on sale, or new release with an easy click of your mouse to follow me. You can follow me on BookBub here:

www.bookbub.com/authors/julie-johnstone

One

London, England
The Year of Our Lord 1820

*N*athaniel Ellison, Marquess of Deering, the fifth Duke of Scarsdale tried to block out the annoying noise flowing from his crowded ballroom into the sanctuary of his billiard room. He gripped his billiard stick and took aim, but it was no use. The second the stick connected with the ball, he knew he was too far to the left.

A deep chuckle erupted from the candlelit corner where his friend Philip De Vere, Earl of Harthorne, reclined in a leather chair sipping on his brandy and waiting to play the winner of the game. "I've never seen you miss a shot, Scarsdale."

Nathan smirked in Harthorne's direction. He didn't mind the jibing. It was a long-standing, good-natured tradition. "You've never seen me give a ball, either. Did you think you knew everything about me?"

"Hardly," Harthorne replied, amusement lacing his tone. "For example, I would have sworn you would never invite the *ton* into your home, but then you astonished me by agreeing to my sister's request to host a ball here. How *did* Amelia talk you into this?"

"Sweetly," Nathan replied. He didn't care to admit that her story about the plight of London's orphans had affected him in such an unusual way. It had made him feel compelled to help, and he rarely felt compelled to do anything.

Nathan's cousin, Ellison, brushed past him to stand in

front of the billiard table. He drained his third brandy of the night before speaking. "If you two are done chitchatting," he slurred, "I'd like to take my turn, so I can wrap up besting you."

Nathan swept his hand toward their game as he stepped back. "By all means, give it your best shot." Ellison was always churlish when he drank too much.

As Ellison leaned awkwardly over the table to line up his stick, Nathan's unwavering and long-established guilt drew his gaze to his cousin's bad leg, which often made balancing difficult for Ellison. When Nathan looked up, narrowed brown eyes met his, and Ellison curled his lip back from his teeth.

Damnation. Nathan fought to suppress his annoyance. The crowd in his home had already obliterated his patience, not that there had been much of it in the first place. He was in no mood for one of Ellison's drunken tirades, but he'd put up with it. The price was nothing compared to what Ellison endured every day with his maimed leg, thanks to Nathan. Nothing had been the same since he'd wrecked the carriage they'd "borrowed" from Nathan's father so long ago and crushed Ellison's leg in the accident.

"Shelve your tedious, never-ending guilt, Scarsdale," Ellison growled before turning and taking his shot. The clank of balls hitting and missing their targets filled the room.

From the corner, Harthorne clapped his hands. "Bravo, Ellison. This little game has shown me I'm not the worst billiards player I know," he teased.

Nathan watched as Ellison gripped the billiard stick so tight that his knuckles turned white. *Hell and damn.* He could feel the heat of Ellison's mounting ire.

As Harthorne rose and strolled toward them, Nathan tried to give his friend a warning look, but the moment Harthorne spoke again, Nathan realized the warning had gone undetected. "Until tonight I thought I was the only one who missed such easy shots," Harthorne said as he clasped Ellison on the shoulder and grinned. "I admit I'm glad to have company in not being an expert billiards player like Scarsdale and my sister's husband, Aversley."

"That's enough, Harthorne," Nathan interjected. Ellison looked as if he was on the verge of exploding with his now red-mottled coloring.

Harthorne's eyes widened in belated realization, and he hastily nodded his agreement, but Ellison slammed the billiard stick on the table and scowled at Nathan. "I don't need a defender, *Scarsdale*. God knows where you developed that loathsome trait. Your father certainly never defended you."

Nathan stiffened at the mention of his deceased father and at the idea that Ellison might think Nathan gave a damn that his father had never taken up for him against his mother's harsh treatment. He may have cared at one point, but he had ceased to give a damn long before his parents perished in the carriage accident twelve years ago.

"You're inebriated," Nathan clipped.

Ellison swayed, even as he shook his head in denial. "I can beat you at billiards most every time, even with this bad leg, and you damn well know it." His sharp words rang in the room.

It was on the tip of Nathan's tongue to flay his cousin for his crass behavior, but then Ellison grabbed his leg with a wince, and guilt slammed Nathan straight in the chest once again. *You did that to him,* his inner voice reminded him. Slowly and with the casual air of one who seemed to be contemplating the assertion, Nathan twirled the billiard stick with his fingers as he stared at his cousin and, in truth, debated exactly what to say to soothe Ellison without him knowing it.

"You can beat me when I'm distracted," he drawled, allowing a bit of the conceitedness everyone expected from him to tinge his tone. Truthfully, Ellison had never won against him of his own accord, but Nathan would take the secret to his grave. Stepping around Ellison and briefly meeting Harthorne's knowing gaze, Nathan took his shot and purposely missed.

Ellison laughed as he swept back the platinum hair that had been hanging in front his eyes and repositioned himself to shoot. The balls clanked together, and Ellison came up grinning as he motioned to the table. The ball he'd been aiming for disappeared into the appropriate hole. "If only my mother would consider her crippled son besting the Golden Duke time and again in billiards an accomplishment, I feel certain she would regard me with the fondness with which she holds you."

"I'm not the Golden Duke, and you *are not* a cripple. And you know as well as I do that Aunt Harriet's esteem is not for me but for my title and the esteem it brings her with all her simpering friends."

"So true," Ellison agreed with a lopsided grin, becoming suddenly affable, as was his typical pattern when he drank. Ellison leaned down beside Nathan as he stared blindly at the balls. His cousin's pudgy face appeared inches from his. "You are a daunting duke, if not golden, and one with a fierce scowl on his face at the moment. There are several easy shots here, yet you are staring as if you don't see one."

Nathan shrugged. "I suppose I don't have the keen eye you do."

"And I suppose you do."

"Do you?" Nathan drawled.

"Indeed. Do you know what else I suppose?"

"I can't say that I do, but I suspect by your serious expression that you are going to enlighten me."

Ellison was the one scowling now. "I propose you are throwing the game and allowing me to win."

"You said *propose* not *suppose*. The words carry different meanings." Nathan parried the truth with drivel, a trick he'd learned long ago from his father when dealing with one of his mother's moods.

"Don't try to distract me, Scarsdale. Are you letting me win the games we play?"

"You give me too much credit," Nathan said. "I'm not nearly that generous or kind."

"I don't think so, either, but if you miss scoring this next point, I'm going to know you have been mollycoddling me.

And the only creatures I've ever seen you mollycoddle are lame dogs. Therefore, I will know you think of me much in the same light as you do that old three-legged hound you rescued some time back. What was his name?"

"His name is Duke," Nathan replied as he decided what shot to take. It would be simple enough to beat Ellison, though he hated to do it. Obviously, his attempt to help his cousin had backfired.

Nathan moved his stick, tilted his head perfectly to line his shot, and ceased breathing. As the stick slid forward, a shrill, earsplitting sound cut through the background noise of the ballroom music, and Nathan lurched, recognizing Miss Benson's obnoxious laughter at once. His stick jerked, the cue hitting the ball too far to the left, and his point was lost. Slowly, he turned his head as he stood and tried to think of a reasonable explanation for missing such an easy shot, but when he met Ellison's accusing stare he snapped his jaw shut at the futility of the endeavor.

Ellison's gaze fell toward his shoes as his fingers traced a line over the billiard table. "It's good to know what you really think of me," he said, so low Nathan almost missed the pitiful words.

Irritation flared in Nathan's chest, but he tamped it down. "Bollocks. You had to see me lose control of my stick just now when Miss Benson snickered so loudly."

"I did not," Ellison insisted in a mutinous tone.

"I saw you," Harthorne assured in his usual helpful way.

"Woo-hoo, Your Grace, are you in there?" Miss Benson called from the other side of the door.

Bloody, bloody hell. He was in no mood to deal with the chit. "A moment, gentlemen, if you please," he said before setting down his cue and striding toward the door. No doubt Miss Benson was loitering in the hope of trapping him alone and somehow maneuvering him into marriage. How the lady could conjure so much false hope from one dance of pity more than a year ago baffled Nathan.

Jesus. Did that make him a sappy defender of the downtrodden as Ellison had accused?

That would mean he allowed emotion to rule him, and he certainly did not. No, that had been a momentary slip when he'd rescued her from the wallflower line. It had never happened before, and he would not allow it to happen again.

His own father was a sterling example of the tragedy that could strike a man who let emotions rule him. His father had fancied himself in love with Nathan's mother, and the poor devil had paid for the weakness the rest of his beleaguered life, married to a woman who, for years, was an unpredictable tempest until she settled into permanent frostiness. Nathan had paid, too, until he'd realized her affection was unattainable. But his father had continued to want her love, despite everything, and she would never give it to him. Not really. She'd give snatches of it, and then she'd become angry and snatch it right back. And her actions eventually drove Nathan's father away from both of them.

Nathan clutched the door, angry he'd let the memory surface. He could see Miss Benson's long, pointy nose and spectacled eyes as she peered at him from the opening in the ajar door. With a sigh, he swung it open, but before she could even attempt to enter his private domain, he gently took her elbow and maneuvered her into the corridor. "Miss Benson?"

"Your Grace, imagine finding you here!"

"Yes, it's quite the leap of the imagination," he drawled.

She blushed ever so lightly and tugged on one of her tight brown curls. "Your house is enormous," she gushed. "I became lost trying to find the terrace."

"Ah, quite understandable," he lied, his cheek twitching. "It's located directly off the ballroom and *outside*."

She batted her eyes and smiled as if she did not understand how ridiculous she appeared. "Do you mind showing me the way?"

"Ah, I wish I could, but I've important business that cannot wait. Follow this corridor back the way you came and one of my many servants will guide you the rest of the way."

"But—"

"Off you go," he ordered and gave her an encouraging nudge. When she didn't move, he gave her the look Amelia had told him was rather daunting. "Your mother would be quite displeased to know you've become lost. She's a stickler for staying on the *correct* path, I hear."

Miss Benson gasped. "You won't tell her?"

"Not if you go immediately."

Miss Benson nodded, shot him a look of extreme longing that made him wish for the hundredth time that he'd never danced with her, and then she turned on her heel and fled.

As he watched to make sure she did indeed depart Amelia came around the corner with her husband—and Nathan's closest, and once wisest, friend—at her side, where the poor fool had stayed since becoming shackled by marriage and dull-witted by love. As they strolled toward Nathan, staring into each other's eyes and oblivious of their surroundings, he first thought about how amazing it was that they did not trip. His second thought was that he felt sorry for Aversley. One day, likely sooner than later, Amelia would crush that heart his friend had so foolishly given her. Nathan had a flash of guilt for helping Amelia win Aversley, but how could he have known the man would turn to putty in her hands? Before Amelia, Aversley had been just as averse to the notion of love as Nathan was.

When it appeared the couple might walk right into him, he cleared his throat, and they glanced toward him in unison. Amelia did not offer her usual lovely smile as greeting. Instead, she scowled at him. "Scarsdale, as the host of the ball, you really should be out amongst your guests and not secluded in the billiard room."

Nathan crossed his arms and leaned against the wall. "I'm not secluded. My cousin and your brother are with me. I made it perfectly clear to you that I would host the ball but not linger amongst the guests."

"Botheration," Amelia grumbled. "All the trouble I went to help you and you refuse to cooperate!"

"Help *me*?" He raised an eyebrow at her, a suspicion forming, fueled by the smirk on Aversley's face. Nathan furrowed his brow. "I was under the impression, given what *you* told me, that I was helping you raise money to fund a shelter for homeless children."

Amelia nibbled on her lip as a blush stole over her cheeks. "You were. I mean, you are. But I confess I had hoped to help you meet a nice lady tonight."

"I know plenty of nice ladies," he taunted.

Amelia pursed her lips. "Not *those* kinds of ladies, who you really cannot call 'ladies' at all. I'm speaking of the kind who want to give you more than their bodies for pay."

"Who says I pay?" Amelia was the only lady he would ever banter with this way. She was his closest friend's wife, yes, but she was different. She was a lady all the way through, but she could joke, laugh, and exchange barbs with razor-sharp wit. And she did it better than most gentlemen could.

"Do be serious," she scolded. "You know perfectly well I'm referring to you meeting a lady with whom you could fall in love."

Before Nathan could respond, Aversley spoke. "I told Amelia it would take more than a ball in your home to bring you out of your cave."

Nathan frowned. "My what?"

"Your refuge, Scarsdale," Amelia said, then scooted around him, dragging her husband with her.

"Where are you going?" Nathan demanded.

"To hold my brother accountable," she retorted, barging into the billiard room.

When he entered the room after her, he motioned between his cousin and Amelia, whom she had not met yet as Ellison had been in Bath for the last year getting treatments on his leg. "May I present my cousin, Mr. Hughbert Ellison. Ellison, this is the Duchess of Aversley, and you already know her lesser half."

"Pleased to meet you, Mr. Ellison," Amelia said before glaring at her brother. "Honestly, Philip. Your only job was to ensure Scarsdale stayed at the ball."

"He *is* at the ball, sister dear."

"Being ensconced in the billiard room does not count as being present at the ball," she complained. "How is he supposed to meet a nice lady in here with you?"

Nathan caught Aversley's gaze and shot him a glare for going along with his wife's ridiculous ploy. Aversley simply splayed his hands as if he'd been helpless to do otherwise. Shaking his head, Nathan strolled over to the sidebar and poured himself three fingers of brandy while Amelia harangued her brother and Harthorne tried to deflect his sister's irritation. Nathan could intervene, but it served Harthorne right for trying to dupe him.

As he was about to put the lid back on the crystal decanter, Harthorne gave him a pleading look. Nathan poured a second glass, then strode toward the arguing siblings and handed the drink to Harthorne before facing Amelia. "When I want to find a lady to marry, I'll simply announce my intention. I assure you plenty of greedy debutantes will trip over one another to marry me for my money and titles, so you can quit worrying that I will die alone."

Amelia arched her eyebrows high as her mouth pressed into a thin line. "I have no doubt you're correct, though it baffles the mind, really, why women would be such nitwits as to marry a man who clearly does not yet understand what it means to love someone."

"I understand perfectly what it means," he corrected. "I simply want no part of it."

"You don't mean that!" Amelia exclaimed.

"I never say things I don't mean, Amelia. Ask your husband."

She turned to Aversley and he nodded. "Sad, but true."

"Setting that little fact aside," she huffed, "I'm not worried you'll die alone, I'm worried you will spend your life lonely."

"I do not get lonely," he replied.

She frowned. "You've been telling yourself that lie for so long now that you have convinced yourself it's the truth."

Nathan took a sip of his drink, contemplated what she

said, and dismissed it at once. She was a woman; therefore, emotions ruled her thoughts. *He* was a logical man. "I hate to disappoint you, but I have no desire to attain someone's love."

"You cannot be serious!" Amelia cried.

"If you had known my mother you would not say that," he said, then flinched as his words registered in his mind. This was exactly why he avoided personal conversations. Once one was knee-deep in them, emotions took over and one tended to reveal too much. He cleared his throat. "I'll eventually marry because I have to in order to carry on my line, but when I do pick a bride, I will do so carefully, after I am certain she meets all my requirements."

Tilting her head, Amelia peered up at him. "Goodness, you sound as if you think picking a wife is like choosing a horse."

"That about sums it up."

She shook her head. "You are worse off than I imagined. You're utterly trapped."

By God, he knew he shouldn't ask but he was intrigued by what she thought was trapping him. "What is it you think has me ensnared?"

"Oh, that's simple. Fear. You are deathly afraid of allowing yourself to want love."

"Wrong," he replied. "I cannot be bothered with love. I fear nothing."

Amelia gazed at him as if she was contemplating what he'd said before she spoke. "That's drivel," she stated. "Of course, I don't know for certain why you fear love. Shall I take a guess?"

Nathan clenched the glass in his hand. He hated talking about personal matters, but he saw no graceful way to exit this discussion without hurting Amelia. Abruptly, he turned to Aversley. "Is your wife always like this?"

"Indeed. It's quite entertaining, I assure you. You should be so lucky as to find a woman like Amelia."

"Thank you, darling." Amelia fairly purred at her husband but her eyes were locked on Nathan, and damn if they didn't hold a knowing look. The way the lady stared, as if disassembling his personal thoughts, was disconcerting. She took her husband's arm while still looking at Nathan. "You have a kind heart."

"Who told you that lie?"

"I've seen it with my own two eyes," Amelia snapped. "You helped Colin and I come together."

"One moment of weakness."

She huffed at him. "You danced with Miss Benson when not a single gentleman would even speak with her."

"One moment of insanity."

"Men!" Amelia growled and scanned the room. Her gaze fastened on Ellison, who blushed deeply, as he always did when a beautiful woman looked at him. Nathan wished there was some way he could give his cousin more confidence, but he was at a loss as to how to do it. His efforts always seemed to make matters worse, not better.

Amelia gestured to Ellison. "I wager your mother would agree that Scarsdale needs a wife."

Ellison shook his head. "That would not be a good wager." His words slurred slightly, betraying his state. Amelia gave him a pitying look that Nathan was sure would set Ellison off again, but his cousin didn't seem to notice and continued speaking. "She doesn't take the usual view that Scarsdale has to marry. She only nags me about that." He poked himself in the chest.

"She doesn't wish Scarsdale to find a wife?" Amelia's voice rang with surprise.

Nathan shook his head. "My aunt encourages me to take my time and remain a bachelor as long as I deem necessary," he offered, not allowing his tone to reveal what he knew to be true. His aunt didn't push him to marry because she was worried she would have to move out of the dowager house if he took a wife. The only reason he allowed his awful aunt to remain there at all was because Ellison wished her with him. And he would grant his cousin whatever he could to make up for convincing him to climb into that carriage that fateful night so many years ago.

"I wish my own mother would be less concerned," Harthorne said.

"Take her concern where you can get it," Nathan automatically responded.

When Harthorne gave him a strange look, Nathan froze. Damn if he hadn't spoken without thought again. He was not himself tonight.

"Speaking of Mother," Ellison said, saving Nathan from having to explain the unexplainable outburst, "I almost forgot that she wants to ask you a favor before we leave for the night." He finished his sentence with a loud hiccup.

Nathan frowned at both Ellison's behavior and the idea of mingling with all the vain and insipid people in his ballroom. "I'm not venturing out there again. Too many unmarried debutantes." He eyed Amelia. "I did not have a hand in creating the guest list."

Amelia narrowed her eyes at his statement, making his lips twitch upward.

When she scowled at him, he chuckled and addressed his cousin. "So, Ellison, what does Aunt Harriet need?"

"She was told of a horse breeder in Newmarket that trains horses for people with…" His words trailed off as he patted his leg. "She's convinced that if the man is legitimate, I will be able to learn to ride again."

Nathan wanted to curse his aunt for continuing to push Ellison when his cousin was so obviously scared to remount a horse. And Nathan wanted to curse himself for crippling his cousin in the first place.

"Excuse us," Nathan said and led his cousin near the window and away from everyone so he wouldn't feel more embarrassment than he probably already did. "Do you want this, Ellison? If you do, I'll be happy to go, but if not, I'll refuse Aunt Harriet's request."

Ellison shrugged. "If it will make Mother happy, even for a brief moment, then I want it."

Nathan cringed. Ellison's words struck a nerve. His aunt

shared more than the blood of a sister with his deceased mother. The women had been the same in personality, too: impossible to make happy and devoid of love.

He stared at Ellison. "But how long will she be happy? An hour if it's a good day, a few minutes if it's bad."

"Scarsdale," Ellison growled.

Nathan shook his head. "No, let me finish. I don't want to see you continue to waste your life trying to make your mother, or any woman, happy. It's an impossible task. You know I understand what that's like." He'd been foolish enough once to think he could make his mother love him.

"She's not like your mother was," Ellison said under his breath.

Nathan leaned closer to his cousin. "You're right. Your mother is still alive while mine is dead. I'm free of her sharp tongue, whereas you allow Aunt Harriet to cut you anew every day."

"Scarsdale, don't." Ellison's liquor-soaked breath swirled in the air between them. "You're wrong about her."

Nathan nodded, stepping back immediately and tugging his hand through his hair. He'd promised himself ages ago that he wouldn't try to talk to his cousin about his controlling mother again, as Ellison always angered when he did so.

A tick started on the right side of Nathan's jaw. It was this damn ball making him cracked. He didn't like feeling trapped, and that was exactly how he was feeling. He clapped Ellison on the shoulder and felt his cousin twitch in surprise. Nathan forced a smile. "I'm leaving, but you may tell Aunt Harriet I'll depart one week from today to meet the horse trainer."

"You're what?" Amelia gasped and rushed toward him. "You cannot leave! This is your ball!"

Nathan resisted the urge to tweak Amelia on the chin for her audacity in claiming such a lie. He was positive that touching the duchess, even in a brotherly fashion, would raise Aversley's temper—his friend was amusingly possessive over his wife—so he quickly added, "My dear, this is *your* ball, and it just so happens to be in my home. Is it not, Aversley?"

Aversley nodded, which elicited an angry huff from his wife, followed by her muttering, "Traitor."

"I'm sorry, darling," Aversley crooned nauseatingly as he moved closer to her and wrapped his arms around her waist. "But I did warn you Scarsdale was apt to leave his own home if you pushed him too far."

The duchess's jaw dropped open, and she stared between the two of them. After a moment, she clamped her mouth shut, crossed her arms, and started tapping her foot. "And just where are you going? And what am I to tell people?"

"I'm going somewhere I cannot speak of in front of a proper lady, and you may tell them whatever you wish." White's followed by a trip to visit his current paramour, Marguerite, seemed like an excellent way to end the night on a high note.

"But—"

"Tell them I've taken ill," he said. "But bid them all to enjoy themselves. As long as they are gone when I return in the morning."

Amelia frowned. "In the morning? But where will you—" Her eyes grew wide as a blush tinged her cheeks. "I think you enjoy shocking people."

"No, I just don't feel the need to pretend to be someone I'm not. And if that shocks or offends, then so be it. Now, if you will all excuse me." He turned on his heel and made his way to the door. His cousin stood there, appearing as if he was waiting to go with him.

That would be a first, and not entirely welcome tonight, given Ellison's current state, but Nathan didn't want to hurt his feelings. "Do you want to come with me?"

"Where are you going?"

"To White's to start."

Ellison shook his head. "I better not. Last time you were in a mood like this was in the country at Whitecliffe. Do you remember? You introduced me to those two young *eager* seamstresses who work for that French woman... What's her name?"

"Madame Lexington," Nathan replied, slightly irritated that Ellison was bringing up a time he knew was the darkest period in Nathan's life. A time he'd acted in ways he was ashamed of.

"Ah, yes," Ellison said. "The only problem with those wenches was they were not eager to be introduced to *me*. They only wanted to entertain the mighty Duke of Scarsdale. I'm still nursing my wounded pride, so I'll pass."

Nathan fought the urge to glare at his cousin, but he knew Ellison likely hadn't considered how Nathan would feel about the subject. So instead, he simply answered, "So be it."

"I'm coming, Scarsdale," Harthorne called and strode across the room.

"Philip!" Amelia moaned. "You cannot be serious."

Harthorne paused by Nathan and faced his sister. "Someone has to keep Scarsdale out of trouble."

"Ha!" Amelia retorted. "It's more likely he'll corrupt you than anything."

"She's right," Nathan added with a chuckle. "Are you sure you don't want to stay here in the warmth and safety of a ballroom filled with ladies looking for husbands?"

"It's become apparent to me that they only want a husband with means, which I currently do not possess. So I might as well go out tonight and have some fun."

"After you," Nathan said, stepping back to allow Harthorne out the door. Behind them, he could hear Amelia bemoaning the night, her brother, but most of all Nathan for not coming to his senses and for leaving her in such an awkward position. He almost relented and stayed, but then he remembered she had tried to play matchmaker. Grinning, he picked up his pace and showed Harthorne to, and through, the hundred-year-old secret passage that had been created…in case there was ever a need to escape unseen.

A couple of hours later, they emerged from White's with

Harthorne leaning heavily on Nathan as he assisted his now-inebriated friend down the steps toward the carriage he'd requested. Outside, the mild temperature had disappeared, replaced by a gusty wind and a chill that caused every exhale to come out in a ring of light-gray smoke.

"I don't feel well," Harthorne said on a hiccup.

"One wonders why," Nathan grumbled.

Harthorne stopped walking and swiveled his head toward Nathan. "I don't think drinking large quantities agrees with me." His face did have a greenish tint to it. "Both times I've ever done so, I've felt briefly unpleasing."

"Unpleasing?"

Harthorne grinned before hiccupping again. "Beg pardon. Unpleasant. My stomach found the liquor unpleasant."

"Ah, I see. And what happened?" Nathan inquired, seeing as if Harthorne lost his accounts it would be all over Nathan. He would do a great deal for his friends, but he'd rather not wear their food if he could avoid it.

"I ruined Aversley's carriage." Harthorne clamped a hand to his mouth and, after a moment, slowly peeled it away. "Do you think we could walk for a minute?"

"By all means," Nathan replied waving to his coachman, Wilson, who had been standing at the ready, to wait.

After strolling for a bit, Harthorne decided he was well enough to ride in the carriage, so they headed back toward White's. As they neared Nathan's carriage, a gust of wind blew his hat off his head and sent it tumbling across the street and into the shadows. Nathan squinted at the ill-lit street where his hat had flown.

"Shall I fetch it for you, Your Grace?" Wilson inquired.

"No, I'll get it. I won't be a minute."

The men nodded, and Wilson helped a staggering Harthorne into the carriage while Nathan crossed the street and located his hat. As he started back, the sound of wheels turning along the road filled the silence. Nathan glanced to his left, surprised to see a carriage whipping around the corner at full speed. For a moment, he froze in his spot, until he realized the carriage was not going to stop. His heart exploded as he jumped back, out of the way of the driver, who had to have been foxed himself to be driving so recklessly. Nathan gaped at the carriage as it disappeared into the dark night.

Wilson and Harthorne reached Nathan at nearly the same moment. Harthorne gawked, open-mouthed in the direction Nathan had been looking. "Made any particular enemies lately?"

Nathan shook his head. "Not lately. Though I've a few men that would probably like to kill me."

Harthorne guffawed. "I'd say. Lord Peabody complains that his mistress always compares his performance to yours when she was your mistress."

Nathan pressed his mouth together in distaste. "I'd rather not know Lord Peabody's failings in the bedchamber."

Harthorne nodded. "Didn't look like Peabody's carriage, anyway."

"No, it didn't."

"Didn't look like any carriage I've ever seen. Who else has you on their kill list?" Harthorne joked.

Nathan shrugged. "I don't waste my time worrying about who thinks I've wronged them. If someone wants to kill me, I dare them to try it."

Harthorne whistled. "Bold words. Especially considering you did just almost meet your maker."

Nathan stared at the spot where the carriage had raced by. "Indeed. One more inch to the right and I would've been the latest on-dit tomorrow."

Harthorne slung his arm over Nathan's shoulder and grinned. "The matchmaking mamas would be bawling over the loss of a marriage prospect such as you."

Nathan snorted.

"Wha's that?" Harthorne squinted with one eye at him. "Don't tell me you plan to never marry."

Nathan couldn't help but chuckle at the incredulous note in his friend's voice. Harthorne needed to relinquish his foolish, romantic notions of marriage. "As I said earlier, I'll marry," Nathan confirmed.

"Superb!" Harthorne crowed with brandy-aided gusto.

"To secure my line."

"What of love?"

Harthorne swayed slightly, and Nathan gripped his friend's arm tighter in case he should fall. "Love is for fools."

Harthorne lurched upright. "Are you calling me a fool?"

Indignation rang in Harthorne's voice, but the grin offset the offended effect of the tone.

Nathan shrugged. "If the cap fits…"

Two

Sophia Vane leaned her elbows against the bar and tried to block out the sounds of the clanking ale tankards and raucous male laughter that surrounded her. She pictured herself floating in the stream just down the road, or lying on the cot that was her bed, or even just sitting among the wildflowers that bloomed in the meadows in the summer. Basically, she pictured herself anywhere but here, just so she would be able to endure another day at the Breeding Tavern without going cracked. Then she pictured the bag of money she'd been saving and the letter her deceased mother had written to her before Sophia had even been born. Both the money and the letter were hidden in the floorboards under her younger half brother, Harry's, bedroll, waiting until it was time to escape.

The letter was her most treasured possession. Sophia had read the letter so many times since her eighth birthday when Frank had given it to her that she knew each word by heart and could clearly picture her mother's lovely flowing handwriting.

Dear sweet boy or girl,

I have a certainty in my heart that I won't live to know you, just as my mother did not live to know me, and I want to impart two things to you: first, how much I love you, and second, a bit of advice that I implore you never to forget. Never lose hope that out there somewhere is a person who will love you and treasure you as you deserve to be loved and treasured. No matter how terrible things get—and I'm sure they will get very bad, indeed, knowing your father as I do—keep this hope in your heart and let it sustain you. I lost faith that I would ever meet someone who would truly love me, and I settled for your father. By the time you read this, you'll likely be old enough and world-weary enough to know how foolish that was of me. Don't repeat my mistake! The best thing about Frank was that he gave me you.

For you, I want passion, laughter, and love. For you, I want the world, which I forgot for a while is full of endless possibilities. Don't you forget it, too!

Your loving mother.

Frank had shoved the letter at her with the odd remark that her mother couldn't haunt him as she'd threatened to do now that he'd fulfilled her dying wish of giving Sophia the letter on her eighth birthday. Thank God her mother had possessed the foresight to prey on Frank's superstitious nature.

The letter had saved Sophia's heart from becoming hard, and the money would save her life. And her brother's. Three more shillings and she would have enough money to get her and Harry away from Frank and this hellhole. Frank may be their father by blood, but love and caring had nothing to do with the sort of father he was. And now that Harry was about to be nine, Sophia had no doubt that Frank would follow through on what he'd been saying since the day Harry's mother had left him on Frank's doorstep. Frank had vowed that he'd sell Harry when he turned nine to Mr. Exington, the town's master chimney sweep, to be used as a climbing boy. The rotten apple had been repeating the vow ever since.

Sophia shuddered at the thought. Being a chimney sweep too often ended in death. She had to get them out of here before that happened. Frank was a known drunk and gambler, and it was common knowledge that he'd produced Harry out of wedlock with a barmaid, yet Sophia and Harry were the ones who paid the price for his reputation. She refused to let

Harry pay with his life.

She'd done her research, quietly inquiring of customers who had come through the tavern from London how much it cost to live there. Two pence a night would buy her and Harry a shared bed in a lodging house. Then Harry could go to school as he deserved, and eventually she'd educate herself as Frank had denied her the opportunity to do. She'd find work and build a real future from there. London held opportunity. Eleanor, her best friend, assured her it was so. Eleanor had gone to London four months ago to visit her spinster aunt and had come back in love. Now she was engaged to be married.

In Sophia's nineteen years, she'd only encountered one man who treated women well and that was Eleanor's father, Reverend Cooper. Of course, Eleanor's fiancé now made two men, but stacked against all the selfish, good-for-nothing men Sophia had known—Frank being at the top of the pile—her chances of meeting someone wonderful were slim. Yet the hope her mother had told her to hold on to had burrowed inside her aching heart and sustained her through many lonely nights.

A mug banged in front of her downcast gaze, and a sun-weathered hand slapped against the dark wood of the bar. Sophia tried not to wrinkle her nose as she peered at the fingernails with black dirt caked under them. Frank, stinking of gin, as usual, leaned toward her. His fat belly brushed her arm and made her skin crawl. She didn't so much as twitch. She knew better than to show her repulsion and risk Frank's ire. Twice—that she could recall—in her nineteen years, she'd displayed her disgust and gotten a cracked lip and a black eye for her disrespect.

Three more shillings, she reminded herself and forced a smile. "What do you need from me, Frank?"

His flinty blue eyes narrowed as his lips thinned.

It only took a second for her to realize her mistake. "Father," Sophia corrected and nervously reached toward her hair to twine a strand around her finger, only to remember Frank had, once again, cut her locks and sold them. Sophia's fingers grazed the jagged edges of the mess Frank had made of her hair. She barely held in her wince. "What do you need from me, *Father?*"

It was blasted hard to call him *Father* when he didn't really deserve the title. Fathers loved and protected their children, or at least the Reverend Cooper did. He was really the only good father Sophia knew, but to be fair, she didn't know if most the men that frequented this tavern were fathers, and if they were maybe they were nicer to their children than they were to her. The desire to snort made her frown. She was turning right cynical. Of course, who wouldn't with Frank as a father?

He was terrible to her, but he was worse to Harry. She suspected Harry's stuttering embarrassed Frank, which then made him angry. The fool only made Harry's stutter worse with his tormenting.

Frank smiled his rotted-toothed grin. "The horse trainers are comin' in for some ale. Get yer arse movin'."

"Yea, get yer arse movin'," Moses, Frank's apprentice and the second-worst man she knew, mimicked. He slapped her on the bottom, letting his hand linger as he'd been inclined to do lately. She smacked his hand away and glared at him. Not that it did any good. He returned her glare with a cheeky smile and a wiggle of his bushy red eyebrows. Her stomach flipped over in disgust.

Frank snorted and stepped between them. "Keep yer hands off Sophia until ye've the money to pay me for her. Once ye get the money we discussed, she's all yers."

Sophia clenched her teeth on the nasty words she wanted to spew. Moses—what a colossally ironic name for the disgusting excuse for a human being—would never be her husband. She'd rather burn to death than let that man touch her. But no need for dramatics. She was going to be gone very soon. Very soon, indeed.

"Get goin', Sophia," Frank snapped and gave her a shove.

Tripping as she walked away from the bar, she smacked into someone coming through the door. They hit hard, causing the breath to swoosh out of her lungs and her balance to shift too far back. Her slipper caught on the raised wood plank that Frank, in all his slothful glory, had yet to fix. Sophia teetered backward and knocked into Moses, who snaked his hand around her torso directly under her breasts. She looked to Frank to help, but he was no longer there.

"Get off me, you beast," she hissed.

"Come on, luv, ye know ye want it."

The racket from the patrons increased around Sophia, right along with her pulse, as she turned her head to glare back at Moses. "I want to gouge your eyes out. *That's* what I want."

Moses's hand slithered upward, and she went rigid, her mind racing to calculate if she could kick back far enough to get him where it would really wound him.

"Release the lady." The man's unfamiliar voice was as cold as the frozen waters of the Tyne River.

Sophia whipped her gaze in the direction of the voice and met blackness. Confusion blanketed her mind for a moment, and then she realized she was staring at a topcoat. A very expensive one by the look of it. It appeared so silky, and the cut molded to the man's broad chest. She trailed her gaze up and over his wide shoulders and to the face that belonged to the commanding voice. He fit his voice perfectly with a strong jaw, angular cheekbones, and dark eyes, at once assessing and calculating.

Those eyes, so dark brown they were almost black, flickered over her, then settled on Moses before narrowing into twin daggers. "Either you're deaf or stupid." The man cocked his head. "I feel certain you can hear so..." A slow, taunting smile stretched his full lips.

Sophia's heart thumped at his audacity and foolishness. Moses was likely to blow any second. She tried to jerk out of Moses's grip to avoid being hit in the crossfire, but he tightened his hold.

"Mind yer own business, ye hear?" he spat at the man.

The man's face grew stony. "I'm afraid I can't do that—honor and all. But you wouldn't know about that."

Sophia's arm pulsed with pain as Moses gripped her harder. "You snobby aristocrats er all the same. Thinkin' you can order everyone around. I'll hold this here wench any way I see fit."

The man's brows arched upward as his gaze landed on Sophia and trailed slowly down her body, then back up to her face. She raised her chin as she met his dark gaze. "I'm no wench."

The corners of the man's mouth lifted into barely a smile. "It's plain to see you're a lady," he said in a deep, smooth voice. "A very lovely one at that."

He was a liar, to be sure, but he was a nice liar. Her cheeks grew warm at the false but smooth compliment, and she couldn't help reaching up and tugging on her short hair.

The gentleman stepped closer to her and Moses, and she got a whiff of a pine-scented soap. Likely expensive rich-person soap. It smelled rather divine. She sniffed one more time, so she'd remember it. Someday, she'd buy Harry a bar of that soap. He deserved it.

"I'm going to give you ten seconds to unhand the lady, and if you don't, you'll find yourself flat on your back with my boot on your chest."

"And jest who do ye think is gonna bring me to my back?" Moses snarled.

The gentleman's lips twisted into a contemptuous smile. "I will, though it pains me to think of touching you." He regarded Moses for a long moment before speaking. "I'm counting."

Sophia tensed. Moses was a brawny man with a bad temper. She eyed the stranger in front of them. He was taller than Moses, and he looked to be rather strong himself, but he was a gentleman. They didn't fight—not like commoners, anyway. Men like Moses used fists and any other means they could, including cheating, to win a fight. Gentlemen pranced around, and—

The flash of a hand in front of her face stole her half-formed thought. Before she could blink, the gentleman was at their backs. Moses cried out, and she flew forward as his hand was snatched from her breast. The air behind her swooshed, and then a loud thump jarred the floorboards beneath her. When she turned to see what was happening, Moses was precisely where the gentleman had said he'd end up—flat on his back with the man's gleaming black tasseled boot firmly planted on Moses's chest.

For a brief moment, the chatter around them stopped, but when it was obvious no more fighting was going to occur, the voices erupted again and the brawl—a rather common occurrence in the Breeding Tavern—appeared to be forgotten.

With a look of supreme boredom, the gentleman glanced down at Moses. "I did warn you," he said in a polite, though aloof, tone.

Sophia barely held in the laughter that bubbled up inside her. She moved to the stranger's side and looked down at Moses, too, savoring this moment rather indecently. Moses had been tormenting her forever, and she lacked the strength to put him in his proper place as this gentleman just had.

She pursed her lips, enjoying watching Moses turn a bit blue as he tried to suck much-needed air into his lungs. "He cannot count past five," she said matter-of-factly.

The stranger regarded her with a hooded gaze. "I'd say that's his problem."

"Let me up," Moses growled and bucked his body.

The gentleman shifted his weight forward, eliciting a wince from Moses, and then spoke. "Talk again and I'll be tempted to crush your windpipe, which will make you rather dead. Understand?"

The hairs on Sophia's arms prickled as Moses nodded while glaring daggers at her. He would seek vengeance against her without a doubt. She'd have to put her dagger in her boot in a little bit.

The stranger followed Moses's pointed stare to her, and his black eyebrows dipped as he gave her a concerned look. "Are you going to be all right?"

The way his gaze bore into her made her heart do a strange flip-flop. "Oh, sure," she managed to finally say. "I'm stronger than I look."

"Most women are, Miss…?"

"Vane," she responded and dipped into an awkward curtsy that Eleanor had tried time and again to show her how to properly execute. "But you can call me Sophia. We don't really put much emphasis on propriety here."

He offered her a brief, strained smile that made her think he didn't smile much. "People cling to propriety to hide secrets."

She shrugged. "I guess we don't have many secrets here. What's your name?" It only seemed right to ask. He had rescued her, after all.

"I'm the Duke of Scarsdale."

"How very proper," she teased, even as her chest heated at her playful words.

A real smile spread across his face this time, and the effect was mesmerizing. His shadowy eyes glistened as if they held a thousand deep secrets, then his thick black lashes lowered to veil those eyes. When he looked up again, those secrets were hidden behind an indifferent visage. "As I said, propriety is a nice mask, and I've many secrets to hide, but you can call me Nathan, nonetheless."

Heat seared her entire body. She was sure her face and chest must be red with her blush. He probably thought her a silly lady who would swoon if he took her in his arms and kissed her. Her gaze inadvertently went to his full lips and then his strong arms, and her legs, much to her dismay, felt a little wobbly. She locked her knees in place. She refused to be the sort of nitwit that swooned. "All right, *Nathan*, what can I do for you?"

"That's rather a dangerous question to ask a gentleman, Sophia."

"Seems a rather normal question to me. You are, after all, standing in my father's tavern. Did you want a drink? A meal? Directions?"

"Touché," he said with a chuckle. "In my defense, I was distracted." He glanced toward Moses. "I'm going to teach

Sophia that clever little boot to the throat trick and a few others she can use to kill you rather easily. I'd behave myself from now on if I were you."

Nathan removed his foot from Moses's chest, and Moses lumbered to his feet. "You'll pay for that," he snarled before stomping off toward the kitchen.

Sophia frowned as he disappeared behind the kitchen doors. "Better be aware on the road today. Or better yet, tell your coachman to keep a look out."

"I left my coachman in London, but I'll be sure to keep my guard up."

She regarded him. "I wasn't aware dukes travelled alone," she teased. She couldn't help it; she was too intrigued.

"I prefer to be alone," he replied.

"Isn't that rather improper?" She didn't usually banter with the men in the tavern, but this was fun. And Nathan was no ordinary man. Besides, it was harmless. He would be gone very soon, and she'd never see him again.

His brown eyes glittered with flecks of light as it held hers. "I'm no proper duke."

His voice had dropped very low and husky, and her heart thumped in response. She swallowed, her throat suddenly dry. "You only pretend to be?"

"That's right. Now you know one of my secrets."

"I'll guard it with my life." She tried to joke, but her voice came out thick and strained sounding, even to her own ears. He must have noticed too because he gave her a strange look before stepping back and putting space between them. "Say, you don't know where Mr. Bantry's horse farm is, do you?"

She did, but if Mr. Bantry owed this man money, she wasn't going to lead him there, no matter if he'd just saved her or not. Mr. Bantry had mouths to feed, and she wasn't going to be the one to make his children go hungry this winter. "Why?" she demanded.

Another tight smile stretched his lips but this one reached his eyes. "I'd like to purchase a horse from the man, so you can lower your hackles."

"Oh," she said, a tad embarrassed, as the tension drained from her shoulders. "I can give you directions, but he trains horses for men who are disabled and I don't see anything incapacitated about you." As she spoke, she found herself following the curve of his massive shoulders down his broad chest toward his tapering waist, and finally to his thighs. He wore tan breeches that fit snugly around his legs so that his muscles strained against the material. Suddenly hot, she swallowed hard. She'd never seen a more perfect example of masculine beauty or power. It made her stomach flutter and her heart speed.

Good God above, she hoped she wasn't a trollop at heart. Her poor dead mother would probably flip in her grave to think the child she'd died giving birth to had turned out not to be worth it.

"*Sophia?*"

Her name rolled off his tongue in three distinct, silky syllables. It made her heart stop and then jolt to a start again when she realized she was staring at him. She whipped her gaze up and found his brilliant dark eyes fixed on her. *Embarrassed* didn't quite cover how she felt. *Mortified* was closer. The wish to have never gotten off her cot this morning and started this day was an even more apt indication of her current state.

"I can give you directions if you wish," she choked out, though her tongue felt thick in her throat.

"That would be very generous of you, and if it sets your mind at ease, the horse is not for me but for my cousin who has a bad leg. I assure you I'm not trying to trick you."

She knew her mouth had parted in surprise because when she sucked in a breath, cold air hit her teeth. She promptly snapped her jaw shut. Tensing, she expected Nathan to make some lurid remark about how she had been ogling him, but instead he offered her a gentle smile, as if being gawked at was something he was used to, which he probably was. Still, gratitude filled her chest. Twice today, this man had shown her kindness and she wanted to return it in kind.

"I can lead you there personally," she said, though there would be the devil to pay with Frank when she returned. "He lives down a road that's hard to find if you don't know just where to look. Let me just get my cape." And her dagger, in case Moses decided to seek retribution for what Nathan had done to him.

Nathan frowned. "You want to show me personally?"

She felt her own brow pull into a frown. "Yes. Is that a problem?"

"Are you bringing a chaperone?"

She struggled not to laugh. Ladies in her social class didn't have chaperones, but he probably didn't know a single commoner besides her. "I don't have a chaperone."

"Won't your father object?"

She glanced over her shoulder and Frank was once again in his usual place behind the bar with a drink at his own lips rather than pouring for the customers. She shook her head and lied through her teeth. "He won't even know I'm gone." She'd ask Mary Ellen to cover her tables for the half hour she'd likely be away. The customers wouldn't suffer at all, though Frank would still complain because that's what Frank did best.

He cocked his head as he surveyed her. "Are you trying to trap me?"

She scrunched up her face, her brow wrinkling. "Trap you?"

"Into marriage?"

This time she did burst out laughing. Then his insult hit her and she clamped her jaw shut and scowled at him before flaying him. "You are a pompous peacock."

"I'm no peacock," he said in a deadpan voice. "Pompous? Perhaps. Careful? Always."

She huffed out a breath at the ridiculousness of this conversation. "You know as well as I do that you could ravish me and everyone would simply look away. No one would expect you to marry me, especially not anyone from your world."

He shrugged. "True, but I wanted to be certain you understood a ravishment claim will not bring me to heel. I find, no matter the class, all women think alike."

She clenched her jaw and counted to ten before she was calm enough to speak. "You don't trust women very much, do you?"

"I don't trust women at all," he said. The warmth that had been in his eyes previously was totally gone, and two hard balls of darkness stared back at her.

"You can rest easy," she snapped. "I've no designs to marry you whatsoever. I don't care if you're the richest man in England." When a telling smile quivered at his lips, she caught her breath. "*Are* you the richest man in England?"

"I do believe I'm a close second. Does that have your scheming wheels turning?"

"My what?"

He tapped her on the head. "Your mind. Are you now reevaluating your desire to trap me into marriage?"

"Certainly," she said cheekily. "What woman wouldn't dream of marrying a man who seems to detest women?"

"I assure you I don't."

She ignored him, her anger bubbling. "I daresay I spend many nights sitting on my bedroll—"

"Your what?" he interrupted.

"My bedroll."

He looked at her questioningly.

"The cot that I sleep on," she tried.

"You mean your bed?"

"Yes, but it's not—" She stopped herself from saying anymore. It would be foreign and unimaginable to a man such as the Duke of Scarsdale to comprehend that she did not have a bed. He would instantly pity her. She was sure of it, and she did not want his pity. "Never mind." She waved a dismissive hand. "Either you can trust me or go on your merry way. Suit yourself. But the house is more than difficult to locate." She eyed him just as she did Harry when he was doing something naughty.

"I do believe I've just been put in my place."

"I believe you have," she agreed, the tension draining from

her. "So?"

"I am at your command," he said in a smooth, gravelly voice. She had a feeling he'd had many women at his command before.

Embarrassed by her own thought, she didn't meet his gaze as she said, "Go wait outside for me. I'll just grab my cape and make sure my tables are tended." She also wanted to tell Harry she was going so he wouldn't be worried.

She found her brother in the kitchen, standing on a stool washing dishes. "Harry," she whispered.

He turned around and grinned at her, making her heart expand. She reached out and wiped some soapsuds off his nose. "I'll be back shortly. I have to show a customer to Mr. Bantry's."

Harry nodded. "I'll b-be here."

She tweaked his chin. "Don't fret. I'll be back soon."

He hugged her and gave her a hard squeeze the way he always did, as if he was afraid she would abandon him as his mother had. She squeezed back with vigor to reassure him otherwise and kissed his head. "We'll make a pie when I come back."

He grinned at that, and she left the kitchen, heading to her bedroom to grab her dagger. She tucked it in her boot and went back down to the tavern. After locating Mary Ellen and asking her to cover her tables, Sophia made her way outside to meet Nathan.

He was sitting atop a magnificent, gleaming, gold curricle with a pair of perfectly matched black steeds. She sucked in a breath, never having seen such a grand sight. Nathan scrambled to the ground and frowned at her.

"You better go back inside and get your pelisse. The temperature is dropping rapidly."

Sophia gathered her threadbare cape tighter and fixed a smile on her face. "I'm warm-blooded."

He squinted at her. "If you don't have a pelisse, retrieve a heavier cape."

She notched her chin up. "This cape will do."

"Is that all you own?" Incredulity tinged his voice.

"I'll be perfectly fine," she replied, refusing to confirm what he likely now understood. To sanction his suspicion would be to welcome his pity. "The drive is short and the sun is only now setting."

Without a word, Nathan stripped off his topcoat and laid it gently over her shoulders. "I admire your astonishing lack of complaint, as well as your backbone, but I insist you wear my coat so you won't take a chill."

His husky voice made her stomach tighten, and her fingers went immediately to the soft luxurious fabric. She could not help but stroke it in awe.

His gaze strayed to her caressing fingers, so she forced her hand down to her side. Something burned in his eyes that she couldn't place, but he spoke, stealing whatever chance she had to place the look.

"I insist you take some money for showing me the way to the trainer's. You could, if you wished, buy a pelisse with the funds since you seem to have misplaced yours."

His kindness and tactfulness in not naming the obvious touched her, but she didn't want his pity or his charity. She shook her head. "That won't be necessary. This is my way of repaying you for helping me with Moses."

He regarded her with a quizzical look. "I've never met a lady that refused a gift."

She grinned. "Now you have. I can take care of myself."

"Yes," he said, amusement lacing his tone. "I saw what a sterling job you were doing."

She scowled at him. "I would have eventually gotten into a good position to wound him where it counts."

He raised his eyebrows, and she could see a smile tugging at his lips. "And where does it count?"

Automatically, her gaze strayed to the juncture between his thighs, and heat singed her cheeks. *Heavens!* Whyever had she glanced there? Reluctant to look back up but left with no other choice, she met his laughing eyes and cleared her throat. "Shall we go?"

"By all means," he drawled and held his gloved hand out to her. She placed her hand in his large one. Even with the soft leather between them, his heat leeched through the gloves and made her fingers curl tightly around his as her breath caught. She forced herself to exhale, and a puff of white came from her mouth.

His fingers suddenly curled more tightly around hers in return. "You're trembling," he murmured. "Are you still cold even with my overcoat?"

She nodded. There was not a chance she was going to admit the cold had nothing to do with why she was trembling. The feelings he was stirring in her were not anything she'd ever experienced before. Confusion blanketed her mind as she settled beside him on the seat of the curricle, situated his coat around her legs, and tucked it under her chin. She started to rub the material again. It was impossible not to. It was the softest thing she'd ever felt in her life, not scratchy at all like the material of her cape.

He turned to her as he took up the reins. "Where to?" he asked, his thigh pressing against hers as his body shifted. She had to clench her teeth to keep from gasping at the tingling sensation shooting from her leg to her head.

The distinct sound of a hiss coming from Nathan tickled her ear. Had she affected him, as well?

She surreptitiously glanced at him from under her lashes, but his face was impassive. If she had affected him, he certainly wasn't showing it. How utterly ridiculous she was being to even think of such things. She was nothing to look at. Her hair had been her best feature, and now it was gone. Her face was too thin from a lack of proper meals, her skin chaffed from hours out in the cold fetching wood for the fire, and she did not posses any curves to make a man look twice. She did have a nice smile, she thought. And her eyes were passably pretty. Her teeth were straight and white, too, thank God. Burying the unfamiliar feelings he had stirred within her, she sat up taller and pointed ahead. "Go straight, and I'll tell you in plenty of time where to turn."

Nathan nodded, clicked his tongue, and set the horses into motion. Within minutes, they were well on their way. The sun was almost below the horizon in the bright orange sky, and the temperature seemed to be dropping rather quickly right along with it, just as Nathan had predicted. She drew his coat up higher over her mouth and peered out ahead, watching for the narrow road that led to Mr. Bantry's house. The road was hard to spot because it was hidden between two massive oak trees.

She would have made polite conversation but she was wary to come out of her cocoon, and it wasn't exactly as if Nathan was attempting to talk to her. He hadn't even glanced her way since they'd started out. She pursed her lips to keep her teeth from chattering, but it was a futile attempt. They clacked together anyway and sounded as loud as a drum in the mostly silent night.

The unmistakable sound of Sophia's teeth chattering from the cold filled the space between them and made Nathan tense. The best way to warm her up would be to get her to slide closer and put his arm around her, but that was a distinctly bad idea. The chit was making him want to do things he never did, and he didn't understand it.

He prided himself on never allowing his emotions to rule him, but he'd reacted without thinking the minute he'd seen her struggling to get out of that man's groping embrace. Anger had fueled his actions, not logic. He could dismiss that incident because any honorable man would have been angry at her predicament, but it was harder to dismiss how she had amused him with her banter and impressed him when she'd stood up to him. It was even harder to ignore the strong sense of pity coursing through him. And pity was a dangerous emotion that could lead to caring.

He stole a sideways glance at her. She was clutching at her tattered skirts with chapped hands. Either her parents were too poor to buy her proper clothing or they were neglectful. And what the devil had she done to her hair? It looked as if she'd carelessly lopped it off with a dull knife. Good God, could she have had fleas? His skin immediately started to itch.

As the chattering of her teeth began to speed up, he could feel his resolve to keep his distance unraveling like a knot being worked at by a knife. Damnation. He eyed her petite, unmemorable form and worked his jaw back and forth. He couldn't very well let her freeze. "If you scoot close to me, we can keep each other warm." He winced at how uncharitable his voice sounded.

She turned her head toward him, and he could see nothing but her pert nose and large, exquisite blue eyes peeking out from under his topcoat. Those cobalt eyes shone bright in the burgeoning moonlight.

A man could forget his worries when looking into those beguiling eyes. They twinkled with wariness at times and laughter at others.

He nearly gasped at the peculiar thought. This wasn't him.

She clutched his coat tighter around her and said, "I'm all right where I am, thank you very much."

He chuckled at the wariness that punctuated every word she spoke. She sounded just as guarded as he felt. "Suit yourself," he said. "But I'm a very hot-blooded man and I guarantee I could warm you up in seconds."

Her brows drew together. "How many women have you said that to?"

"You're the first, I assure you." He'd never wanted, nor needed, to offer anything to a woman he was interested in, except his current mistress. However, he'd only offered her an allowance and home while they were exclusive to ensure she understood the rules of their relationship—no love. He forced his thoughts back to where they needed to be: on the road.

"How much farther?" he asked.

Sophia extracted her arm from his coat and pointed ahead. "See the trees up there? When you get to the third one, take a right and then the house is only about five minutes from that point."

He peered ahead to a long row of towering trees that lined the road on either side, and his suspicions spiked. "If I could have counted to the third tree and turned, you should have just told me that and saved yourself the trouble of coming out in the cold."

She jerked his topcoat away from her face and scowled. "If I had a pound for every person I've given directions to that took the wrong road, I would be rich—perhaps even as rich as you. Why, just two days ago, I instructed a gentleman how to get to Mr. Bantry's, and he hobbled away all high and mighty with his nose in the air without so much as a thank-you. Came back an hour later begging me to show him the way."

Nathan laughed, surprised at the sound. He could not remember the last time he'd let his guard down far enough around a woman to genuinely laugh. Except... He stilled. He'd either been laughing or wanting to since he'd met Sophia. She was not like the typical women with whom he kept company, which must explain why he didn't feel the need to guard himself as much. She was also quite young from the looks of her.

And from what she'd demonstrated so far, she was bold as brass. She didn't try to hide her feelings behind masks. In fact, her eyes were so expressive he wanted to tease her simply to see what her eyes would do. "Did you consider that your directions might be lacking?" he prodded.

Her eyes did not disappoint him. They flared like two burning torches. "They were not!" She leaned forward and jerked her arms out of his coat. "I give perfect directions, you beetle-headed man! You can have your coat. I'd rather freeze!" With that pronouncement, she threw his topcoat at him, just as he had started to make the turn onto the road.

Temporarily blinded but chuckling, he tugged the reins back to bring the horses to a stop. As he did, Sophia gasped beside him. He shoved the garment off his face and turned toward her, expecting to find her glaring at him, but she was staring straight ahead with her lips parted and her mouth in a perfect O. He followed her gaze and froze. Two men stood in the road with hoods over their faces and pistols pointed in his direction. Fury obliterated the chill from the air. He'd been duped, after all, had been bamboozled by a slip of a woman with a shorn hair, tattered clothing, and a forgettable figure. She'd played the innocent and he'd stared into those fathomless blue eyes and believed her.

"How stupid of me, my dear," he mocked, without taking his eyes off the men. "I pride myself in considering all possibilities, but I foolishly never once considered that you would rob me. How very sly of you."

Sophia's small cold hand clutched his thigh and squeezed very hard. "I am not trying to rob you." Her frightened voice sent alarm bells off in his head. She wasn't lying.

He eyed the box on the floorboard that contained his pistol. He was a damn fool not to have been prepared for something like this. Traveling alone was dangerous, and traveling at night even more so. He eased back into his seat and regarded the cloaked figures, one tall and one short but both obviously men based on their stocky builds.

"Gentlemen," he said, instilling a note of nonchalance into his tone, "how can we help you?"

"Ye cannot," the short man said. He had an accent that sounded almost Irish. "We're here ta kill ye, and I'm doubtin' ye want ta help us do that."

"Kill me?" Nathan replied, slapping ruthless control over his body so as not to show the slightest concern. He leaned his elbows on his knees to get closer to the pistol box, but really, he didn't see how he could get it open before they shot him or Sophia.

"Aye. We would've already shot ye, but we were expecting ye ta be alone. We didn't get no instructions ta kill no girl."

"Jest gonna have ta kill her, too," the taller man said. "She's a witness now."

Sophia's nails dug into Nathan's thigh. He wanted to wrap his arms around her and draw her in to the protection of his body, but to move might mean her death. As he searched his mind for a plan, she squeezed his thigh again and then said in husky voice, "I'm no lady, gentlemen."

Nathan turned and gaped at her. What the hell was she doing?

"Lord La-tee-da has paid me for my services, but if you promise to let me go, I'll service both of you for free."

Sophia was mad. And it just might save them both! Nathan clamped his mouth shut.

"Come on down here, and I'll take a sample," the shorter man said with a chuckle.

Nathan clutched Sophia's leg as she started to rise and held her in place. He couldn't just let her go without trying something else. "There's no need to kill me, gentlemen. Whomever I've angered, I'm sure if you'll simply give me his name, we can work it out. And I'll pay you handsomely for doing so."

Nathan never slept with married women or virginal ladies, but still he had managed to anger some gentlemen over the years who'd thought they held some claim to a certain widow or even a demirep. He could think of one particular widow who had tried to make her old lover jealous recently by flaunting her relations with Nathan in front of the man's face. Perhaps it had worked too well.

"The only thing getting worked out here is lust," the tall man crowed. "If ye want the wench ta live send her down."

Nathan hesitated to let Sophia anywhere near those men, but if he didn't do it, they'd likely both die on this road. He turned his head to her and whispered, "Don't be afraid. I'll die before letting them harm you."

"There'll be no need for any more of your heroics," she muttered. "I've a dagger."

"Sophia, don't—"

The towering man snatched her out of the seat before Nathan could finish his sentence. With a yelp, she went tumbling down the steps and slammed into the taller man. Nathan's blood boiled as the man's hands slid indecently over Sophia's thin body and to her face. He was going to pummel that man first, and with extra glee.

"Yer not much ta look at," the man slurred at her.

"The prettiest part of me is under this dress. Want to see?" Sophia cooed in the sweetest voice. Nathan's blood froze in his veins. Was her dagger strapped to her thigh? Did she mean to try to reach it first or just distract the men so Nathan could do something?

Sophia bent over in one fluid motion and never came up. A howl, the likes of which Nathan had never heard, filled the night. "My foot!" the tall man yelled. "Bitch stabbed me in my foot."

In the confusion, Nathan reached down and swept his pistol box up, but before he could open it, a shot rang out. The bullet slammed into his left shoulder and sent him staggering backward onto the seat. The sting of the metal piercing his skin was nothing compared to the sharp, fiery pain that instantly radiated from the site of the wound to his fingers. His left arm went numb, and dark spots danced before his eyes. He blinked, tensed his body, and threw the heavy, wooden pistol case directly at the man who'd shot him.

The wood box thumped the man on the head and he went down in a heap, howling and holding his skull. Nathan scanned the area in front of him. In a sliver of moonlight, Sophia's petite form was illuminated as she struggled with the taller man. Nathan's blood rushed through his veins as he scrambled to make his way down the stairs to help her, but he was losing blood fast and his feet were unsteady. His head became light and the ground beneath him tilted right, then left. Searing heat enveloped him as the nausea rose in his throat.

He missed the first step of the ladder and tumbled to the ground. He landed face-first in the dirt. Beside him, a second shot rang out, and it took all the strength he could muster to turn his head to see who'd been hit. As he did, a body thudded to the ground very near him, and relief snagged in his chest as he stared at the wide, unblinking eyes of the man Sophia had stabbed in the foot. His mouth was parted in the last breath he'd ever taken.

As Nathan struggled to push himself over, pain hit him in

wave after burning wave, from his shoulder out to the rest of his body. Footsteps pounded across the dirt, and he managed to flip over with a guttural cry, in time to see Sophia's concerned face looming over him.

Her gaze skimmed his body, then she looked over her shoulder. "The other devil ran off," she said, facing him once more. "Coward! I'd chase after him—" she smiled grimly as she raised her dagger in one hand and the pistol that had to belong to the dead man in the other "—but you don't appear..." Her words trailed off as her gaze locked on his shoulder.

"You're afraid I might die," he managed to joke, though his vision was becoming increasingly darker.

She bit her lip, and that was answer enough. "We better get you to the physician's house. Can you stand?"

Hell, he didn't think he could breathe much longer but he managed to nod. Somehow, he'd find the strength to get up.

For a petite lady, Sophia surprised him. With minimal staggering, she helped him rise and climb back into the curricle. By the time he fell onto the seat, he was sweating profusely. She grabbed his pistol box, and then she plunked down beside him and took up the reins. He rolled his head toward her, resting against the cushion, and looked at her with the one eye he still had the strength to open. "Have you ever driven a carriage?"

She shook her head. "But don't worry. I'll figure it out. There is no way I'm letting you die on me."

"Of course not," he mumbled. His mouth felt as if someone had stuffed it with cotton. And his head, too, come to think of it. He stared up at the black night, wondering foggily if the stars had disappeared or if he had gone blind. He squeezed his eyes shut and let out a ragged breath. "If I die, you cannot trap me into marriage," he teased.

"Oh, go on and pass out already, you conceited man," she snapped.

The carriage seemed suddenly to be swaying wildly. "Slow down," he hissed, grabbing at the seat.

"I've not even started yet," she retorted and clucked her tongue.

The curricle jolted forward and seemed to tilt downward, and then Sophia's yelp joined the buzzing in Nathan's ears as he blacked out.

Three

Sophia expected all hell to break loose when she returned to the Breeding Tavern with a bleeding, possibly dying duke in tow. After going to the physician's and finding him gone, she'd had no other choice but to come back here. When she did arrive, Frank immediately started yelling at her and demanding to know where she'd been, just as she'd predicted. But she tugged him outside to get his help bringing Nathan into the tavern, anyway, and was shocked speechless when he stopped shouting as she explained who Nathan was. Frank rushed back into the Breeding Tavern and returned within seconds, barking orders at Moses to find the physician. Sophia's heart swelled with the strangest sensation of hope. Maybe Frank was not rotten to the core, after all.

"Frank—" He gave her a sharp look. "Father," she corrected, clearing the lump out of her throat. "You won't regret this."

"Oh, I know I won't, *my dear*."

My dear? Frank had never used a term of endearment to refer to her in all the days of her life. He was certainly up to something, but she didn't have time to figure out what right now. She clambered into the carriage and slipped her arms under Nathan's legs. As Frank hauled himself into the curricle, as well, and grasped Nathan under the arms, Nathan's eyes fluttered open and locked on her.

"Physician," he mumbled.

Sophia nodded. "Dr. Porter is coming." She started to straighten but Nathan grasped her hand. The unnatural clamminess of his skin made her heart stutter, but she tried not to show her fear.

His brows furrowed, as if he was searching for what he wanted to say. "Funny. Not ready to die."

His voice, which had been so deep and confident only hours ago, came out hoarse and weak. Sophia blinked back threatening tears. She didn't really know the man but sadness for him overwhelmed her. She squeezed his hand, even though his eyes were already closing, and said in a soothing voice, "Of course you aren't ready to die, for heaven's sake. You're the Duke of Scarsdale. You have a grand, wonderful life, I'm quite sure."

She could have sworn his mouth thinned before his head flopped sideways and unconsciousness claimed him once again.

She bit down hard on her lip to stifle a cry and struggled to help Frank get Nathan out of the carriage and into the tavern. At this hour, men packed the main room, and all eyes turned to them. She refused to care what they thought; they did not matter. Saving a man's life was more important than her reputation.

Anyway, she was going to London soon, and these men were likely already foxed. She'd be surprised if they recalled seeing her at all, unconscious man in her hands or not. For all they knew, this was one of Frank's drinking cronies being hauled to the spare room to spend the night.

"Make way," Frank shouted, snapping Sophia's attention to him. "Move out of the way for the Duke of Scarsdale. He's wounded and my daughter is taking *special* care of him," Frank said, winking.

Sophia nearly lost her grip on Nathan's legs. Now she knew what Frank was up to, the fool.

"Frank," she hissed. "Your plan will not work!"

Frank didn't acknowledge her. Instead, he glanced around as they moved through the parted crowd and grinned as his eyes settled on Mr. Dalton who was leaning against the stairs and gaping at them. Sophia groaned. Mr. Dalton was married to the town's biggest gossip. Frank's scheming mind was turning rapidly if he'd thought far enough ahead to get him out here to witness whatever lies he intended to set up between her and Nathan.

Frank paused right in front of the man. "Say, Dalton, could ye fetch yer wife to come help Sophia? I'm sure she could use an extra hand."

Sophia clenched her jaw and her fingers tightened around Nathan's legs. "That won't be necessary."

Mr. Dalton looked to Frank, who gave her a glacial look that made her shiver.

"It's necessary because I say it is. Understand, girl?" He fairly snarled the last word.

She refused to agree. Instead, she eyed Dalton to see if it would do any good to plead with him, but he ignored her and ran off to get his wife.

Frank bid a patron to help him carry Nathan up the stairs, and Sophia scrambled away to fetch hot water, clean rags, and brandy. She'd do what she could for Nathan before the physician arrived. By the time she reached the top of the stairs with her arms full of supplies and water sloshing over the sides of the bucket, she was panting and her heart was racing. She ran to the guest room and flew through the door, almost tripping over something on the floor. Glancing down, she grimaced at the sight of her bedroll shoved off to the side, but not far enough to prevent it being in the way of whoever entered the room.

Sophia frowned as she hooked the tip of her shoe under the bedroll and cleared it away from the door. She strode into the room, set the bucket down, and then moved to Nathan's side. He took up the full length of the bed with his long, lean frame. His skin glistened with sweat, and his eyes raced back and forth under his lids.

Without acknowledging Frank, she said, "I know what you're up to. I'll not go along with it."

Frank yanked her around to face him. "You'll participate, girl, or I'll sell that brother ye hold so dear to the chimney master today instead of generously waiting until he's nine. Understand?"

Her gut twisted, and behind her, Nathan moaned. Fear for both Nathan's and her brother's lives danced down her spine. She heaved her arm loose and turned toward Nathan, whose eyes were fluttering open once again. Sinking down next to him, she locked her gaze with his wavering one. "Don't worry. I know what to do."

Frank loomed over her. "How do ye know what to do? Yer a stupid girl."

She was smart enough not to tell Frank she'd been secretly reading books, some of them about medicine. She shrugged and twisted to answer Frank, in the hopes that Nathan would not overhear and become worried. "I'm simply soothing him," she said in a low voice and then faced Nathan again.

His forehead wrinkled and he looked around, as if he was trying to place her and the room, and then his eyes slowly focused on her once again. He licked his cracked lips, spurring her to reach for the liquor and pour him a glass. She slid one hand under his head, her fingers brushing through his thick curls to hold him while she gently lifted his head and pressed the cup to his lips. "Drink," she urged.

He took a long, slow sip and moved back slightly, letting her know to withdraw the cup. As she did, his lips lifted in a half-smile. "Trying to get me foxed to take advantage of me?"

Goodness, the man had audacity. Even wounded he was still worried she was trying to trap him into marriage. Speaking of...

She could feel Frank hovering, and she wished he would either go sit in the corner or actually help. "No, but I need to undress you," she said to Nathan.

"I've heard that before." His tone was an odd mixture of humor laced with pain.

The mental picture she got of him naked made her cheeks flame.

Behind her, Frank coughed. "I'll just go fetch some water."

"I already have water," Sophia muttered through clenched

teeth.

Frank locked his fingers around the bones of her shoulder. She bit her lip to keep from crying out in pain.

"I'll get more," Frank said. "Ye may need it."

She didn't bother responding. Frank was going to do what he wanted no matter what she said.

Once he was gone, she peered at Nathan again. "I'm just going to take off your coat, shirt, and cravat, all right?"

Laughter danced in his rapidly dulling eyes and pain twisted his lips. "That sounds rather boring."

She shoved her embarrassment—and, truth be told, a little bit of curiosity—away. Leaning over him, she slid her arms under his back to get a good grip. When her chest brushed his, she gasped.

He half chuckled, half moaned. "This has to be the strangest seduction I've ever been subjected to."

"I am not trying to seduce you," she spat and yanked him upward. The low hiss that escaped him made her loosen her hold. "Push away from the bed with your good arm."

He pressed with a loud grunt as she tugged with an equally loud one. They careened backward and tilted precariously to the left, but somehow, by the grace of God, did not fall over. They ended up sitting face-to-face on the bed, just as she'd intended. Nathan was no namby-pamby duke. He was solid and very heavy. Thick, corded muscle covered his back and rose under her fingertips as she grasped his arms to hold him in place.

"So it begins," he teased in barely a whisper. His head came to rest on her shoulder and his warm exhalation tickled her neck. Her stomach fluttered as they sat there, pressed so close that you couldn't slide a piece of foolscap between them.

Her heart thudded and the veins in her neck pulsed with each beat. Using the utmost care, she struggled to draw off his coat. The one grunt he made told her it hurt, but other than that, he was silent. Despite the cold room, perspiration trickled down her brow from her effort to hold him up, though that exertion was nothing compared to trying to get his shirt off at the same time.

She spent several minutes attempting to tilt him one way and then the next, but it was futile. Once she got him into a position she thought might do, she realized she needed to untuck his shirt first. She let out a string of Frank's favorite expletives, which elicited a low chuckle from Nathan.

"My ears are burning," he chided.

She snorted. "Somehow I doubt that." Trying to avert her eyes, so as not to see too much, she reached into Nathan's breeches at the tip of the waist and tugged at the fine material of his shirt.

With bashfulness burning her cheeks, she withdrew her hand from his breeches and let out a yelp when his warm hand came to rest over hers.

"I'm sorry."

"Don't fret yourself. It's not often a lady gets to stick her hands down a duke's pants." Heaven above! Had she really just said that? She wasn't sure where the thoughts had come from. Clearing her throat, she added, "Almost done." With care, she quickly removed his cravat, then glanced at his shirt. The slit near his collarbone exposed the top of his glistening chest. A knot formed in her throat. This was certainly not the way she had expected to see a man's naked chest for the first time in her life, but so be it. "Can you raise your arms?"

"The one that doesn't have a gaping hole in it," he grumbled.

"Right, then." She gently laid him back down, reached into her boot where she'd sheathed her dagger, and came up to kneel over him. "I bet you would have never thought to see a lady leaning over you with a dagger in her hands," she joked, trying to relieve some of the tension. Now that Nathan's coat was off and his blood-soaked shirt was visible, her stomach roiled with queasiness and worry.

"You're quite surprising," he managed.

Sliding her dagger from the top of his shirt to the bottom, the material parted to expose his muscular chest marred only by the blood covering his left shoulder. Her nostrils flared, and she inhaled a long, steady breath. Even wounded, she could see why a woman might lose her head over him. He was perfection, at least physically.

Dismissing the thoughts, she reached down and grasped the brandy, then leaned closer to him. "I'm going to cleanse the wound. Are you ready?"

"Hell no," he muttered. "But do it anyway."

Underneath her thighs, the muscle of his legs tensed. *Best to be quick.* Without giving him warning, she tilted the bottle and poured. The amber liquor mingled with blood and ran down his arm onto the bedsheets. As she stared at the mess, she shook her head. It had been silly not to put a towel under him. She glanced at his pale face and clenched jaw, and nibbled on her lip. It was true she had read some medical books, but she was no expert. "Maybe I should do it again?" she questioned herself.

"Not unless you're trying to kill me," he gritted, surprising her with his response.

"Not quite yet. Not until we're properly married and I'm sure I'll get some of your vast fortune," she jested, hoping to turn his thoughts away from the obvious pain. He gripped the sheets in his fists, his dark eyes taking on an alarming, glazed look.

"Funny," he said, but the word was spoken as if with great effort.

Sophia turned toward the door. Where in heaven were the physician and Frank? Blast the devil. Blowing out a frustrated breath, she faced Nathan. "I'm going to get a rag to stop the flow of blood."

His eyes peeled opened, but only to slits. "You're leaving?"

"No." She pressed a hand to his forehead and sucked in a sharp breath at the burning skin that met her touch.

He nodded, closing his eyes once more. Sophia scrambled off the bed, retrieved the rag, and then rushed back to Nathan and gently pressed it over the wound. As she did, the sound of footsteps reached her, followed by several voices all talking at once.

The door creaked behind her, and a woman's high-pitched, nasally voice exclaimed, "He's naked!"

Sophia stiffened. She knew that annoying voice. "He is not naked, Mrs. Dalton. I removed his shirt to care for his wound."

Rotund, crooked-nosed, pock-faced Mrs. Dalton waddled up to Sophia at the same time Frank did. She gave Sophia a sharp glance with her beady gray eyes, then Mrs. Dalton stared at Nathan's scandalously naked chest much longer than was proper. The wretched witch turned her accusing eyes on Sophia once more. "No respectable lady would have removed his shirt. And you alone in the room with him!" Mrs. Dalton shook her head as she clucked her tongue reproachfully. "You'll be ruined when word of this gets out. Not that this isn't expected from the likes of you."

Sophia speared Frank with a glare. He returned her scowl with an ear-to-ear grin. She faced Mrs. Busybody Pain-in-the-Neck Dalton. "I suppose a respectable lady would have left his shirt on and let him die?" she demanded in a seething tone.

Nathan groaned loudly, and Sophia realized immediately she had been pressing harder on his wound in her anger. Blast Mrs. Dalton for riling her temper.

"That's exactly what a respectable lady would have done."

"Then I suppose I am not respectable, as I'm sure you always thought," Sophia clipped and blew at a strand of hair dangling like a brown ribbon in front of her face. Defiance against all the days, months, and years of whispered words and disapproving glances she'd been forced to endure just because she was the daughter of Frank Vane rose up in her. Sophia stood tall and eyed Mrs. Dalton. "I suppose you better take off so your own shiny reputation isn't tarnished."

"I just got here!" Mrs. Dalton exclaimed. "I was dragged out of my house by Mr. Dalton to help *you*, you ingrate."

Sophia eyed Mrs. Dalton for a long moment and could feel the seams of her temper coming undone. "If you don't leave this instant I'm going to give you a punch you'll never forget."

"You don't look like a lady, and you certainly don't act like one!" Mrs. Dalton huffed and stomped out of the room, shoes squeaking as she went.

The door slammed shut behind her. Frank grinned. "Well played, Sophia."

She clenched her fists at her sides with the realization that she'd done exactly what Frank had hoped she would. She'd angered Mrs. Dalton and kicked her out. Now the woman could not even vouch for the fact that nothing untoward had happened, but she *could* certainly tell everyone that Sophia had been in a room with a half-naked man. Sophia hated Frank with a new fervor.

On the bed, Nathan didn't flinch at the noise, which made Sophia's stomach clench. He must be in so much pain he was oblivious to what was happening around him.

Frank threw his arm around her shoulder and brought her to his side, making her lose her grip on the rag she'd been holding against Nathan's shoulder. The cloth fell to the floor and a slow trickle of blood immediately started from the wound.

"Let me go, Frank," she growled.

His fingers curled around her arm as he jostled her a bit. "I always knew keeping ye with me after ye killed yer mum was the right thing to do."

Sophia ground her teeth. "It's true she died after birthing me, but I suspect that's because *you* didn't take good care of her, nor pay for a proper physician to tend to her."

"Watch yer tongue, Sophia, else I'll tug it right out of yer mouth. Wouldn't be so sassy then, would ye?" He cocked his head a bit. "Ye don't know what yer talking about, anyway. Not as if yer mum could tell ye."

"No," she replied, struggling not to rail at him. "But Eleanor's mother said it was so."

Frank made a derisive sound in his throat. "She just hates me cause I picked yer mum over her so many years ago, and she ended up married to a righteous arse. I bet he's as fun in bed as watchin' paint dry."

Sophia barely held in a contemptuous snort. She doubted Mrs. Cooper had spent her years pining over Frank. The lady

had been her mother's best friend, just as her daughter was
Sophia's best friend. Mrs. Cooper hated Frank, that was true
enough, but her loathing had everything to do with what a
terrible husband he had been to Sophia's mother.

Frank gave her a squeeze and said, "I think to make ye a
duchess and me the father of a duchess. No more of this
scraping by day to day, hardly knowing if I'll be able to eat or
drink."

"You cannot make a member of the *ton* marry someone
like me," Sophia said, feeling the shame of being his daughter
from the soles of her feet all the way to the roots of her hair.
She yanked her arm out of his grasp. She knew exactly what
sort of drink Frank was worried about, and it certainly wasn't
tea. The man didn't have a single concern for his children, but
God forbid he not be able to afford his ale.

"He'll marry ye. Men like him have a burdensome code of
honor."

"You are a fool!" she nearly screamed. "He's not going to
feel pity and succumb to marrying me simply because you
orchestrated my ruination."

Frank's face twisted into a scowl. "He will."

She could practically see the creaky, old, good-for-nothing
wheels turning in Frank's head. Her own head started to
pound viciously. "Frank—" she took a long, slow breath and
tried to find a little bit of calm so she could get through his
thick skull "—don't try to make him marry me. You'll end up
with nothing." She prayed that for once he would be
reasonable.

He jutted his unshaved chin out. "He's gonna marry ye.
He's a gentleman, and he'll be honor bound once he sees how
they're gonna treat ye."

She glanced at Nathan—pale, glistening, and bleeding—
and she shoved past Frank, angry she'd gotten caught up
arguing with him when she should have been tending to
Nathan. When Frank grabbed her arm, she wiggled out of his
hold and glared at him. "No one will be marrying His Grace if
he's dead," she snapped, grabbing the rag off the floor and

pressing it against Nathan's shoulder.

The instant she did, his eyes shot open and seemed to look through her. She bent down and brushed a soothing hand through his damp hair. "Shh, Your Grace. The physician will be here very soon and you'll be just like new."

When his eyes fluttered closed again, she stood up, careful to keep the rag in place and her back to Frank.

"Yer an ingrate, just like Mrs. Dalton said. And ye look like a boy."

Fury choked her, which was a blessed thing.

"I'm going," Frank snarled and left, but seconds later the door banged open again and she whirled around to see the physician striding into the room.

He brushed past her with a nod and approached the bed. "By God, it really is the Duke of Scarsdale!"

His voice held an awe that surprised Sophia, mostly because she was not sure how the physician would know Nathan. "How do you know him?" she asked bluntly while peering down at the top of Dr. Porter's silver head. He was already leaning over Nathan.

The physician tapped on her hand. "Move the rag, please." She immediately did as he bid. "Is he going to die?"

"Not on my watch," Dr. Porter said in a grave tone. "This man saved my daughter's virtue when she had her debut in London last year." The physician straightened, opened his bag, and extracted a small bottle before handing it to her. "You can assist me," he said as he unscrewed the cap off the bottle. The sweet stench of laudanum tickled her nose.

Assist him? She couldn't assist him! She needed to take Harry and leave this instant. Her plan to flee to London had to commence today, with or without all the money she needed. She refused to sit idly by and let Frank use her, or worse yet, sell Harry.

"I cannot assist you," she murmured.

The physician gave her a narrow-eyed look as he lifted Nathan's head and leaned down to whisper something in Nathan's ear. After a moment, Nathan slowly shook his head and mouthed the word *no*.

Dr. Porter sighed. "He's refused the laudanum, the stubborn fool. Will you hold his hand when I retrieve the bullet? It may help to ease his fear to know he is not alone."

Had Dr. Porter not heard her? "Dr. Porter, I—"

"Do you want him to die?" the man demanded, cutting her off.

She shook her head.

"Then I need you to stay and help me."

She nibbled on her lip as she weighed her options. If she fled now and Nathan died she would not be able to forgive herself. Heaving a weary sigh, she set the bag on the table where the physician indicated, then moved to Nathan's side. She twined her fingers with his. When he gently squeezed her hand, she blinked in surprise. She returned the gesture and rubbed her thumb in little circles over his skin as the physician started to work.

Nathan grimaced within moments of Dr. Porter beginning, and his eyes opened several times, but he stared blindly past her as before. Eventually, his hand went slack in hers, and she knew he had blessedly passed out. "He's out, Dr. Porter."

The physician nodded. "I hoped it would not take him long. He's lost a good bit of blood so he's weak."

Her stomach clenched. "Weak as in he's in a grave amount of danger?"

"It's too early to tell," he replied without looking up from what he was doing. After a moment, he stood and held out a small, shiny object clasped between the pointy ends of his instrument. He grinned at her. "I go it! If we keep His Grace's wound clean and work to control his fever, he should recover nicely. Do you have something I can put the bullet in?"

Sophia's gaze landed on the small cup she'd given Nathan a drink from earlier. After retrieving it, she handed it to the physician, and he deposited the bullet into it with a *clank*. He cleaned and dressed Nathan's wound, then took out another bottle of laudanum and motioned to Sophia. "Pour this carefully down his throat as I tilt his head back."

"Didn't he decline it?" she asked, not wanting to be difficult but only to honor Nathan's wishes.

"Do you want him writhing in pain as you care for him?"

"Oh, I'll not be caring for him," she blurted. She couldn't stay around *that* long, after all.

He gave her a stern-faced expression. "Gather your courage, Miss Vane. If you don't nurse him, his shoulder will likely become infected and he'll die. He cannot cleanse the wound himself. It is in too awkward of a place, and I cannot play nursemaid. I'm the only physician in this whole town."

Panic shot through her. She couldn't allow herself to get trapped here. Her and Harry's futures were elsewhere. In London, where she could better herself. "Surely, you can send for his family. He's the Duke of Scarsdale, for heaven's sake. I'm sure there are multitudes of loving relatives who will rush to his aid."

Dr. Porter shook his head and tilted Nathan's back. "Pour," he ordered.

Her shaky fingers brushed Nathan's full lips as she pressed the bottle to his open mouth and slowly drained the liquid down him. At first, he sputtered and some of the laudanum dripped out the sides of his mouth, but then he started to swallow until the bottle was empty.

"Very good," the physician murmured as he patted Nathan's uninjured shoulder.

Sophia tensed, half expecting Nathan to sit up and give the doctor a dressing down for daring to disobey his command. Instead, Nathan lay there still as death, though he was still alive. *For now.* The thought chilled her, and her conscience nagged at her to stay, but she pushed forward, determined to go. "As I was saying, Dr. Porter, you can contact his relatives."

The older man's eyes took on a sorrowful downturn. "He has only two relatives that I know of, and I met them both. The aunt seemed like the type to care for no one but herself, and the cousin does not get around easily. It would take him days to get here. Too long. If you don't care for His Grace, who do you think will? Your father?"

Sophia would have laughed if she didn't feel like crying. Or screaming. If she fled, she couldn't be certain Frank would stay sober long enough to help Nathan, or if he would even decide it was worth his bother. Frank had a heart the size of a tick's, and that was being generous. She had always thought people who were well-off had everything, but it sounded like Nathan was missing the exact same thing she was—someone to look out for him. Shoring up her resolve, she decided she would be that someone for Nathan until she was sure he could take care of himself. Then she and Harry would flee.

"I'll nurse him," she said, feeling as if saying the words was sealing her fate irrevocably.

"You have a good heart, Miss Vane. You'll be glad you're doing this. I'm sure you'll be rewarded."

She pressed her lips together. She would not feel right about accepting anything from Nathan just because she had helped him, *but* it would be nice to know she at least had enough money to prevent going hungry for days on end.

"Do you care to know what sort of man you are helping?"

"You mean besides a rich one," she snapped, a trifle irritable.

Dr. Porter smiled with genuine understanding. "This must be very stressful."

"You have no idea," she said, guilt over being touchy causing her to ease her tone.

"The Duke of Scarsdale rescued my daughter from the clutches of a man trying to ravish her," the physician started. "She'd foolishly thought herself in love with a man she met at Almack's, and he turned out to be a fortune hunter. When he realized my daughter had no fortune to offer him, he lured her into the garden and thought to plunder what she did have. His Grace chanced by, rescued my girl, and made sure the villainous gentleman would never mention a word of the incident to anyone."

"How did he ensure that?" Nathan sounded too good to be true, which in her experience meant he most likely was.

"I believe it had something to do with the murderous tone

of His Grace's voice as he threatened to disembowel the gentleman should one unkind word pass his lips in regard to my daughter. At least that's what she told me."

Sophia grinned. Though she barely knew Nathan, she'd seen him deliver a similar threat to Moses, so it wasn't difficult to picture him offering a menacing warning to this other gentleman in a cool, unaffected tone, as if it wouldn't bother him at all to gut a man like a pig, except for the fact that it might soil his expensive clothes. And that last part she instinctually knew was just for show. She highly doubted Nathan would blink an eye at dirtying his clothing if the need arose. Being a popinjay did not fit what she'd glimpsed of his character.

The physician shut his bag with a *snap* that brought her thoughts back to the moment. "You're leaving now?"

"Yes. I'll check in on His Grace tomorrow. Be sure to keep a watchful eye on him tonight."

She nodded and walked Dr. Porter to the door. After he disappeared out of her sight, she turned back toward Nathan. The physician had failed to cover him with the sheet, and as Sophia walked toward him and then clutched the sheet, her breath caught. His beauty struck her with wonder. He was like a dark angel from the tip of his thick black curls, to his long black lashes and dark stubble shadowing his chiseled jaw, to the dark hair that covered a small patch of his very broad, very muscled chest. She swallowed as her body tingled in places she'd not known could tingle.

She followed the trail of his chest hair over the muscular planes, down to his taut abdomen and farther down to the top of his breeches. What would it be like for a man like this to turn his attentions to her? Nathan was more than handsome. Why, he was so exquisite one could almost call him pretty. The thought that he would ever notice her was ludicrous. Her mother had told her to hold *hope* in her heart, not ridiculous fantasies. With a decisive shake of her head, she pulled the sheet up to just under his chin and brushed her fingertips across his forehead. He didn't twitch a muscle at her touch.

Good thing, too, because it tended to get loud and rowdy in the pub at night, and the more he rested, the better.

With a reluctant sigh, she left the room and headed downstairs to check on Harry. She found him in his usual place in the kitchen, washing dirty dishes with a smile on his face. She ruffled his brown hair, while leaning near to whisper in his ear. "Harry, we're going to be leaving a little sooner than I planned. So when the time comes, you must promise to do exactly as I bid."

"I p-p-promise," he said solemnly and turned to look at her with his clear blue eyes.

"And remember, it's our secret," she said in a low voice.

"I re-re-member. I would n-never t-tell Frank a thing. Don't worry."

"When you're done with the dishes, I want you to go up and pack a bag. Store it in our secret place." Harry knew she kept the money in the loose floorboards under his bedroll. "I have to help a man who was hurt, so I may be a little late coming to bed tonight."

"Sophia!" Frank boomed, making her jump. "Get yer arse back upstairs, girl. Ye cannot let yer future husband die."

Sophia pressed a kiss to Harry's forehead and rushed past Frank, but he grabbed her by the arm and stopped her flight. "How's yer patient?"

"The physician says he should be fine with good care."

Frank nodded. "Ye make sure to get him healthy. We wouldn't want him dyin' before he makes ye his duchess."

"Frank," she began in an exasperated tone.

He cut his eyes to Harry. "Remember what I said about yer brother if ye don't obey me."

She gritted her teeth, nodded, and pasted on a fake smile. "Let me go, please. I need to go to the privy before I go back upstairs."

Frank released her at once. "Ye hurry yer arse," Frank said. "Oh, and Sophia, Moses is a mite mad with ye. I'm holdin' him back for now, but cross me and yer all his."

Sophia shuddered at the thought and scrambled through

the kitchen door and into the noisy, crowded tavern, then rushed outside to the privy. After attending to her business, she picked her way through the dark back to the tavern but was delayed by a man too foxed to get into his carriage on his own. When she finished helping him and entered the tavern again, she spotted Frank standing at the bar with a decidedly nefarious grin on his face. He was likely planning what he was going to do with all the money he thought would be his after he attempted to guilt Nathan into marrying her. He pointed to the stairs, and she nodded dutifully, though in her mind she shook her fist at him.

She dashed upstairs and was about to pass by her and Harry's room on the way to the guest room when Harry came flying out into the hall, eyes bugged and face white. He grabbed her by the hand, hauled her into the room, and slammed the door. "I-i-it's g-g-gone," he wailed.

Sophia frowned. Harry's speech was difficult to follow at times, especially when he got upset and his stuttering worsened. "What's gone? And why are you up here already?"

"I f-f-finished quickly, s-so I c-came to do what you s-said."

"All right. Now what's gone?"

He pointed to where his bedroll usually was. It, along with the loose boards, had been moved from its usual spot. Fear started in her gut and gained speed and strength as she fell to her knees by the hole and peered into the darkness. She immediately saw the worn edges of the letter from her mother and let out a sob of relief as she grabbed it and stuffed it in her boot before peering back into the dark hole. Maybe the money had been shoved farther back?

"Hand me a candle," she said.

Harry's footsteps padded behind her as he retrieved the candle and then back toward her. He kneeled down and held the candle in front of them. "It's n-n-no use, Sophia. I already ch-ch-checked. Twice. Your letter was the only thing in there, and I left it 'cause I know how you worry it might get r-ripped." His lower lip started to tremble, and tears welled in his eyes.

Her heart twisted in commiseration. She wanted to cry, too, but she wouldn't. Someone had to be strong for the both of them. Scanning the small, shabby room with its one cracked window and peeling wallpaper, despair wailed in her breast. They'd be stuck here forever. Ruthlessly, she fought against the hopelessness. She grabbed Harry's hand and squeezed it. "We must try to stay calm."

Squeezing her eyes shut against the ravaging panic, she counted slowly in her mind and took a long breath. When she opened her eyes, Harry was staring at her with tears streaming down his smooth, youthful cheeks. "Harry!" she gasped and tugged him to her, enfolding him in her protective embrace. "Don't cry." She ran a soothing hand over his fine, silky hair and kissed him on the top of his head. "It's not your fault."

He tore away from her. "I-it is my f-fault," he groaned. "I l-left the d-door open w-when I was p-p-packing my b-bag and th-then a man stumbled past and I h-helped him d-down the s-stairs."

"Did you pass anyone on the way down?"

Sophia's nerves were a throbbing, balled, jumble of hard knots.

"F-Frank. H-he said h-he had to check on s-someone."

Had Frank taken the money? If he knew she'd been hiding money... Dear God! "Harry did you see Frank again? Did he stop in here?"

Harry let out a shuddering breath and shook his head, but in her gut she knew it had to have been Frank. He was like a snake always slithering around, poised to strike. Sophia rose to her feet, glanced at the loose floorboards, and didn't bother moving them back into place. There was no point. Frank already knew she'd been stashing money, and she could only imagine the hell he'd put her through because of it. Her cowardly side told her to run, but her sensible side reminded her that she had more to think about than herself. There was Harry to consider, and though she may be able to survive on the streets if need be, Harry wouldn't, at least not with the kind-hearted, caring soul she knew and loved intact. She couldn't allow that. She'd have to face whatever came, and she didn't expect whatever that was would take long to arrive.

As if beckoned by her very thoughts, heavy footsteps pounded outside the room, announcing Frank's approach. She raced across the room, grabbed Harry by the arm, slapped a hand over his mouth so he wouldn't protest, and dragged him to her mother's old wardrobe, which for once in Sophia's life she was thankful was practically empty. She shoved Harry in the wardrobe. "Stay in there, no matter what," she hissed and eased the door shut just as the one to their bedroom swung open with a loud *crack* against the wall.

Frank loomed in the doorway, face twisted in rage and hands clutching a birch switch. Dread almost choked her as the skin on the back of her legs and her bottom prickled with the ingrained memory of how precisely a switch could slice into the skin like a thousand tiny knives that left stinging, bloody trails in its wake.

"What's the money for, girl?"

"My dowry," she blurted, grasping at the only thing she could think of that might save her from too many lashes.

Frank sneered at her as he advanced into the room and kicked the door shut with his boot. "Ye don't need no dowry. Yer gonna marry the Duke of Scarsdale, and *he's* gonna pay *me*. Ye never have given me the credit I deserve."

"I don't know what you mean," Sophia mumbled, finding it impossible to take her eyes off the switch that he was tapping against his right thigh. The birch looked thick; it would definitely leave a scar.

"Ye think yerself smarter than me," he said.

Only because you are foxed all the time. She silenced the thought and carefully chose her words. "Certainly, I do not."

"*Certainly, I do not,*" he mimicked, mocking the speech she'd spent so many hours trying to refine. He grasped her arm. "I'm not so dull-witted that I don't see through yer lies. Ye weren't savin' that money for no dowry. Ye don't even like men."

That wasn't true, she thought, startled by the vehemence

that rose inside her. She simply didn't like any of the men she knew.

"Ye was savin' that money to take yerself and yer brother away from me, weren't ye?" Frank thundered.

The fact that Frank's liquor-soaked brain had grasped the truth both shocked and frightened her. She wasn't stupid enough to think she'd hurt him because he loved them. He was spitting mad because he thought she was trying to deprive him of two able-bodied servants and ruin his scheme.

"I don't know what you're talking about, Frank. That money was for my dowry." Even to her own ears, her words sounded pathetically false.

"Filthy rotten liar," he sputtered and spun her around so her back was to him. She struggled to free the arm he still clasped, but the hiss of the birch switch filled the air, freezing her in place. Thin bands of wood cut into the tender skin on the back of her legs and made her knees buckle. Frank hauled her upright, and the air swished around her as he whipped back his arm and lashed her again. And again. And again.

She threw her arm back to stop him from hitting her legs once more, and the switch caught her clean across her upper arm and sliced straight through the sleeve of her thin, cotton gown to dig deep into her flesh. Nausea rose up in her throat as the switch came yet again at her legs. Somewhere in the distance, she thought she heard a high-pitched scream. It was hard to know for sure because her ears were ringing with the sound of rushing blood.

Her vision swam but... Was that the wardrobe door swinging open? Half hanging in Frank's grasp, her head wanted to stay down, but she lifted it enough to watch in growing horror as Harry tumbled out of the wardrobe, gained his feet, and came charging toward them waving his arms wildly, eyes bulging, face twisted, red and glistening wet from the tears streaming down his cheeks.

Frank shoved her away with such force she flew to the ground. The board she'd not bothered to put back caught her smack in the center of the forehead, breaking her fall and jarring her teeth, as well as the rest of her body. Darkness invaded her vision almost immediately, but the last thing she saw was Harry pummeling Frank's legs.

A strange numbness settled over her and the overwhelming fear that she was dying and abandoning Harry choked her, but her tongue seemed as frozen as her limbs. The only things she could do were close her eyes and accept the darkness as reality, and within seconds, as the pain in her legs and arm throbbed and pulsated, she welcomed the darkness.

Four

The lady Sophia was different. Nathan couldn't put his finger on it, but all the teasing, bantering lightness that made her formerly sparkling eyes dazzle like twin sapphires was gone. Now that his body had expelled the last traces of the vile laudanum, his mind was clearer than it had been for the last two days. He shuddered with the knowledge that he had broken his former vow and taken the drug that had once led him down such a dark path. Though, in this case, he'd been unconscious when given it. Sophia sighed and he studied her once again.

She dipped the rag into the sponge basin that she'd used earlier to bathe him. Her head was lowered and her shoulders were slumped. The proud and seemingly fearless lady he remembered had disappeared. Something was definitely amiss.

Water dripped from the rag, leaving a wet trail behind her on the dark wood floor as she walked back toward him. Her narrow hips swayed gently as she walked with her eyes cast down to the rag in her hands, so Nathan didn't bother to pretend he wasn't staring. Her threadbare gown hung more loosely than the previous one she'd worn. She paused beside the bed and lifted her face, yet her eyes did not meet his. A rogue tendril of her rich coffee-colored hair fell forward across her cheekbone, and she raised her left hand to push it behind her ear. Her teeth clenched together as she moved, as if she were in pain.

He started to reach for her, then stopped himself, surprised by his inclination to touch her. "Is your arm hurt?" he asked.

She startled as though she'd not even been aware he was awake. Her jaw tensed visibly. "I see the laudanum has worn off."

He admired the way she avoided his question with a statement. It was a tactic he often used himself. "It has. How could you tell?"

A smile crooked her lips for a moment before she puckered them, as if somehow smiling was wrong. She tilted her head and studied him for a long moment before speaking. "Are you sure you want me to tell you? The answer might embarrass you."

"I don't embarrass."

One side of her mouth broke free of her control and tugged up into a wry smile. "That's quite convenient."

"Indeed. It's suited me greatly, considering some of the choices I've made."

"I can only imagine," she murmured.

"So what did I do or say?"

"Oh, you begged me to kiss you every time I came into your room."

That couldn't be true. His taste ran to a womanlier figure and a decidedly colder personality. Lack of sentimentality was something to be prized in a woman by a man like him, one who didn't believe in love. Sophia seemed to have far too much fire in her not to desire affection. He pulled his gaze to her eyes—intelligent, kind, and peering at him with a look of sad understanding. He felt like an arse. He hoped she hadn't read the utter disbelief on his face at her claim. He didn't want to hurt her. "Did you kiss me?"

She scowled at him. "Certainly not. It wouldn't be proper."

"Waiting on a marriage proposal," he teased.

Her lips pressed together in a thin line.

Where was the lady who had bantered so playfully with him? He wanted to glimpse her again. "Is it too early in the morning for witty rejoinders?" he asked to provoke her into sparring with him.

Her eyes locked on his as she shook her head. Was that fear dancing in the depths of her blue eyes?

"Sophia?" He pushed away from the pillows he was propped against and grasped her, forgetting, until she winced, that he suspected she'd hurt her arm. He immediately released her. "What is it?"

She darted a quick glance over her shoulder, then leaned near. "You have to help me," she whispered urgently.

Wariness flickered to life in him, along with a strange sense of concern. The dueling emotions made him feel more irritable than he already was at the physician's news that he should not travel until the end of the week. Before he could ascertain what had her so obviously upset, a male voice boomed her name from the doorway.

She jumped as if someone had stuck her with a fire poker. Nathan flicked his eyes to the door. The man sauntering into the room filled his mouth with sour distaste. He had flinty blue eyes—shockingly the color of Sophia's—that were locked on Nathan. The closer the man came, the more repugnant the heavy stench of body odor mingled with stale liquor grew, until Nathan felt his brow furrow, which he immediately smoothed. The man's midnight hair hung in long, limp strands to graze his shoulders. He paused beside Sophia and threw his arm over her shoulder.

The slight tremor of her body would likely have gone unnoticed by most people, but Nathan had developed a habit as a young lad to try to read his mother's moods by watching for the slightest movements a person made. They often told something of what one was feeling. Sophia was repulsed by this man, who had to be her father, if their resemblance was any indication. A shaft of pity gripped him, which made him tense. Why was it this woman he barely knew affected him when others didn't?

"It's good to see ye alert, Yer Grace."

"Likewise," Nathan responded, guessing by the smell of this man that he was usually quite inebriated. The man's sun-weathered brow filled with deep creases of confusion while, beside him, Sophia bit down on her lip to keep from smiling. Nathan found that he hoped she'd lose the fight to appear indifferent to his comment and her face would light with that lovely smile, but she darted her gaze to her father and all traces of her amusement vanished, causing a fierce surge of anger in Nathan. Obviously, this man was not good to her.

The man finally smiled, and Nathan barely resisted the urge to tell him to stop. It was hard to believe one mouth could possess so many rotted teeth, but the truth was grinning at him.

"I'm Frank Vane, and this is my tavern yer recoverin' in."

Nathan glanced at Sophia for confirmation that this thing before him was indeed her father. She met his gaze, and her cheeks pinked a bit before she nodded.

"I'm grateful," he said simply, knowing he need say no more. The man had greed shining in his eyes. It wouldn't be long before he asked for money. Nathan fully intended to give him some for the use of the bedroom and for allowing his daughter to care for him when he no doubt would normally have had her working downstairs. Perhaps twenty pounds? That would be a fortune to this man. And Nathan would privately give more to Sophia directly. He suspected she could use it.

"I'm glad to hear yer grateful. The question is how grateful are ye."

"Frank!" The one word uttered from Sophia's lips sounded like a plea.

Frank patted her awkwardly on the shoulder. "Get yerself to town and fetch me some bread at the store. We're out."

"Please, Frank—"

"Go on, girl. If yer lucky maybe ye'll see yer brother if he's in from workin'."

Nathan had seen the faces of many angry women in his life, but Sophia looked as if she wanted to murder her father. Her blue eyes turned to ice and a mask of cold anger hardened her exquisite bones until she looked as if her expression had been carved from a glacier.

"I'll be going, then," she said through clenched teeth as her gaze found Nathan's. "When I return you'll hopefully be awake so I may speak with you, so I can—"

"Girl," Frank warned, "ye better go or else yer gonna miss yer opportunity to see yer beloved brother."

Nathan watched as her jaw tightened and a tick began. Whatever Sophia was she was not a woman without inner strength. He could practically feel her gathering her self-control to keep calm. The question was why? What the devil was occurring here?

Sophia nodded stiffly and started to turn away, but as she did, Nathan grabbed her hand, compelled by a strange need to ease whatever was bothering her. She glanced down at his hand, then over at him.

He released her and offered a slight smile. "I'm not tired at all, so I'm sure I'll be awake." He had many questions he wanted to ask her, not the least of which was how the devil she'd managed to drive his curricle and what had happened to the other man who was trying to kill them. Uncertain how much she had revealed to her father, and not wanting to say anything that may cause her trouble, he instead said, "I wrongly judged you."

She blinked at him, her wary gaze skittering to her father, then back to him. "How so, Your Grace?"

"You saved me, and not a single nefarious trap on my person has been sprung. My apologies and compliments."

A momentary look of discomfort crossed her face that, on any other woman, he would have assumed meant they had just not sprung their intended trap *yet*, but he couldn't summon the desire to be so cynical about her. Maybe it was the brush with death, or perhaps it was the fact that she had saved his life, but whatever it was, he decided she was simply embarrassed by his accolades.

With a nod of her head, she turned on her heel and fled out the door. As the door shut, Vane gave him another rotted-toothed grin. "She's not much of a looker but her mama was the same when her age. She grew to be a beauty. Sophia will, too."

"I assume you are going somewhere with this dialogue," Nathan said, disliking the way the man disparaged his own daughter.

Vane nodded. "My girl saved yer life, Yer Grace. Did ye know that?"

"I suspected," Nathan replied, irritation making his jaw twitch slowly.

"She drove ye here from the woods the night ye was shot, and she insisted in front of me and a packed tavern that she personally care for ye upstairs in this bedroom."

"Did she? Seems a rather unwise thing to say in front of a room full of people. Such a statement could damage a reputation that I imagine already hangs precariously between passable and ruined, considering who you are."

"Jest what are ye sayin'?" Vane demanded, spit flying out of his mouth.

"I'm saying," Nathan replied in slow, punctuated words, "that given your daughter's circumstances, I imagine she has to strive *not* to be labeled as ruined, and she seems far too intelligent not to realize this and do something as stupid as announcing to a tavern of men that she was going to personally care for a man."

Vane nodded his head. "That's exactly what I told her. But she insisted she care for you special, and when Mrs. Dalton came here—"

"Who?" Nathan interrupted. If he was going to momentarily be a participant in this travesty he preferred to know all the details.

"The town's biggest gossip," Vane said.

"Naturally," Nathan replied, the twitch in his jaw increasing in speed. "And the town gossip was here because...?"

"Sophia fetched her," Vane said matter-of-factly.

"Indeed. That makes perfect sense for your daughter to insist the town gossip be fetched to witness her ruination." The man was a liar through and through.

Vane leaned in. "Do ye really think so? I told her I didn't

think it was wise. Especially seein' as how, after Mrs. Dalton got here, she told Sophia no decent lady would have removed yer shirt to care for ye and been standin' in the room alone with ye."

Nathan clenched his teeth together to stop his twitch before he could speak. "How much money do you require to repair your daughter's reputation?"

The man had quite the acting skills. He actually perfected looking offended. Nathan didn't know whether to laugh or commend him.

"I cannot take yer money."

"That's surprising," Nathan said dully.

Vane frowned momentarily before his eyes widened. "What I mean is money cannot repair the silly girl's reputation. I give ye that she should have known better, but she has a huge heart and didn't care enough about herself while ye was hurt. The only thing that will help my girl is yer marryin' her."

"I'm afraid I cannot do that." He allowed the cold fury building inside of him to clip each word.

Vane scowled. "No man with any honor would knowingly allow a lady's reputation to be ruined."

"I'm afraid you've grossly misjudged me, Vane. I may be a duke, but I'm no fool. And if you think to try to force me to marry your daughter with talk of honor, you are mistaken. I'm not that honorable." The words, and the consequences to Sophia if what Vane said about the townsfolk thinking she was ruined was true, pricked at him.

"Ye've got to marry her," Vane demanded, spittle once again flying from his mouth.

Nathan stared at the man until he started to squirm. "Point in fact, Mr. Vane, I do not have to marry your daughter. There is no law that compels me to do so, and I cannot think of a person that would try to force my hand, unless…" He smiled slowly, baring his lip away from his teeth bit by bit. He knew it made him look ferocious and rather evil. Aversley had told him so, and Aversley wasn't one to lie. "If you are trying to tell me you wish to demand retribution on the field of honor, I'll be happy to oblige. I prefer the pistol; it's the weapon I use most frequently, but I am adept with the rapier, too, though something about sliding the metal into flesh makes my teeth grind. Or at least it has on the occasions I've been compelled to do so."

Vane's eyes bulged. "How many duels have ye fought?"

Nathan smiled lazily. "How long do you have to stand here while I list them?"

A bead of sweat trickled down Vane's left temple. The man wiped it away with shaking hands. The tremor was probably a result of too much drink. Nathan pounced on the weakness with glee. A man who thought to unrightfully force another's hand deserved no quarter. "I've been trained by the best marksman in the country, as well as the best swordsman, but I do believe it's the dozens of duels I've been compelled to participate in that have truly honed my skills. Tell me, Vane, what training do you have?"

"None," the man muttered.

Nathan did not hold back the smile that crooked his lips this time. "None?"

Vane shook his head.

Nathan frowned. "How many duels have you fought?"

The man moved his jaw back and forth before answering. "None."

"*Oooh.*" Nathan allowed the word to drag out long and slow. "That's unfortunate." He tapped his fingers against his thigh for a moment. "I'll tell you what, since you were so generous as to allow me to recover in your guest bedchamber and to fetch the physician when I needed him, I will give you a two-second advantage when we duel."

"*When we duel?*" the man practically bellowed. "I never agreed to no duel. This here conversation has got all flum-moxed."

"Has it?" Nathan raised his eyebrows. "It must be my misunderstanding. What is it you said you wanted from me?"

Vane rubbed the back of his neck as he darted his gaze around the room and then let out a disgruntled sigh. "Amends for Sophia's ruined reputation. No decent man will want her now that the town thinks she's soiled by ye."

Not that a decent man would have wanted her in the first place, given her family, Nathan thought. Pity stirred in him again, which was irritating as hell. Pity would be his downfall if he wasn't careful. His instinct was to go depart before he became further embroiled in this ridiculousness, but he couldn't leave without seeing Sophia+, talking to her, and ensuring she would indeed be all right. Her father might be a snake, but it was clear she hadn't condoned his plan.

Why, damn it? Why not just go?

You like her. The thought rankled and shock made him momentarily speechless. He did like her. She was a funny, sharp-witted, bright-eyed slip of a thing, and she deserved better than the life she had. He would find her, make sure she was going to be fine, and then he would give her a monetary reward for helping him.

He glanced around the room, located his breeches, overcoat, and hessians by a chair, and then he eyed Vane, who was staring at him expectantly. "For your daughter's efforts in saving my life I'll give you twenty pounds, but that is all you will get from me." Without waiting for a response, he continued. "You can either graciously accept the money or argue, which will get you nothing. What you will never possess is my name for your daughter. Am I understood?"

The man nodded with a scowl.

"Excellent. I require a shirt and the location of your daughter."

"What for?" Vane demanded with a furrowed brow.

"Because I am departing this deplorable place today and I cannot go about shirtless." Damn the physician's advice that he rest awhile longer. It would be impossible to relax enough to recuperate here.

"I don't have no fancy shirts."

"Any shirt will do," Nathan replied.

"All right," Vane grumbled. "I'll be back shortly."

"Knock before you enter." Nathan intended to be dressed

when the man returned. He didn't care to continue remaining virtually unclothed while speaking with Vane.

After the door shut, Nathan swung his legs over the bed and stood. He'd been out of bed to use the chamber pot several times, so he felt relatively steady, especially since the laudanum was now out of his body, but as he struggled into his clothes, his shoulder started to throb and sweat dampened his brow. By the time he had his breeches and boots on, he was clenching his teeth so hard against the pain that his jaw felt numb. If only his shoulder felt similarly. It ached as if someone had poured liquid fire on it. Driving his curricle was going to be painful and difficult, but he didn't damn well care. At the loud knock on the door, he bade Vane to enter.

"Yer shirt, Yer Grace."

Nathan eyed the darkly stained shirt and assumed it had once been white. He took the garment, as repulsive as it was, and struggled into it, just barely resisting the urge to rip it from his body when he got a whiff of the foul stench of body odor that had seeped into the material. Going without a shirt in public, especially to locate and privately talk to Sophia, was not an option. He refused to contribute in any way to helping Vane's scheme along. If it was as Nathan suspected, the man was greatly exaggerating Sophia's predicament, so there was no need to turn that lie to fact.

"Now, where is your daughter?" Nathan demanded as he pulled the shirt over his head and put himself in some semblance of order. His shoulder seemed to pulsate with every move he made, and it took a great amount of concentration not to groan in agony. Showing weakness was not an option, either. It never was.

"I don't suppose I can say for certain. She's a strong-willed chit."

"Take your best guess," Nathan snapped, his irritation and the pain getting the better of his tongue.

"In town at the Beckford General Store, then likely to the chimney sweep, Mr. Exington's, headquarters."

"Excellent. I'll need directions," Nathan ordered as he

withdrew a full coin purse. "I'll see that the money we agreed upon is here within a fortnight. For now, take this as representative of my word."

"This money extra?" Vane asked as he took the coin purse and juggled it back and forth between his grubby hands.

"It is, but I highly suggest you use some of it to buy your daughter a new cape. One made for the winter."

"'Course I will," Vane replied, not meeting Nathan's eye. The man was lying, which didn't sit well. More disturbing than that, though, was that Vane clearly didn't give a damn about Sophia. It reminded Nathan of his own mother, and he didn't care for the reminder one bit. So much so that after retrieving his pistol and securing his coach, he departed without a backward glance.

Five

Sophia stomped along the road as she walked toward Mr. Exington's, her mother's letter rubbing against the inside of her right ankle. She was afraid to part with it now that Frank had taken the money, even though she didn't plan to go back to Frank's. She'd taken the only thing she could not live without before she was to make her escape with her brother. She still couldn't believe that Frank had sold Harry. When she'd gone downstairs to leave to get the bread, Mary Ellen had told her it had been done.

She sniffed loudly and paused long enough to kick a rock she passed, imagining that it was Frank's head. He was a despicable lout. She had no money, but somehow, someway she would leave Mr. Exington's today with Harry in tow.

As she passed the Beckford General Store, Mrs. Dalton stepped out with a sack clutched in her hands and glared at her. Normally, Sophia would ignore the wretched woman, but this morning she didn't have it in her to be the bigger person. She glared in return, and Mrs. Dalton descended the steps into the street and pointed at Sophia. "Turn your eyes, ladies," she crowed. "Sophia Vane is a fallen woman. She is not pure!"

Sophia's steps faltered as several women standing around Mrs. Dalton gawked at Sophia.

"How do you know?" one of them asked.

Mrs. Dalton puffed up. "I saw her with a naked man with my own eyes. And not a trifle embarrassed was she."

"That's not true!" Sophia seethed. "I was helping him. He was shot."

Mrs. Dalton didn't acknowledge her words. "She demanded I leave, so she could be alone in the bedroom with the man."

"Sinner," an older lady with silver hair hissed.

Sophia curled her fists at her side. "We are all sinners, you old bag."

The plump woman standing by Mrs. Dalton pointed her fat finger at Sophia. "You should hang your head in shame."

Sophia notched her chin higher, though angry tears clogged her throat. "I've nothing to be ashamed of."

Mrs. Dalton reached into the sack she was holding and stepping toward Sophia, threw a handful of flour at her before she could back away. Sophia gasped in outrage as Mrs. Dalton shouted, "You're not welcome in this store."

That was it! She refused to take any more. She strode toward Mrs. Dalton and yanked the sack out of the woman's hands then tipped the entire thing over Mrs. Dalton's head. "I wouldn't visit your store ever again even if you paid me. I'm going to London, where the possibilities are endless!" With that, she turned on her heel and stomped off toward Mr. Exington's.

Sinner indeed, she fumed as she passed the shoe shop, tears blurring her eyes and flour still tickling her nose. She'd never even kissed a man, but the town wouldn't care. Mrs. Dalton had seen to that. They'd condemned her as a whore based on a rumor that Frank had set in motion. Truthfully, they'd condemned her the day she was born.

On top of it all, Frank deserved to be skinned for selling his own flesh and blood. She'd anxiously been watching Nathan, waiting for a sign that his mind was clearing from the laudanum. When it had, she'd been on the verge of begging Nathan for money so she could flee with Harry, but Frank had appeared at the door and now here she was. Stuck again.

Up ahead, she could see Mr. Exington's office. She squared her shoulders, took a deep breath, and charged on.

Nathan muttered to himself as he maneuvered his curricle down the narrow, crowded street and studied the businesses he passed, looking for the chimney sweep's shop. He'd already stopped at the general store and been told in a shrill, hysterical voice by a woman covered in flour that Sophia had been there and had left after pouring a bag of flour on the woman. Nathan could well imagine what had led to Sophia's actions, if the harridan had called Sophia a lightskirt. Grimness settled over him. His conscience over Sophia's clearly destroyed reputation was screaming at him and wouldn't stop.

He clenched his jaw as he continued at a slow, annoying pace down High Street. Why the devil were the streets so busy today? As he drove his curricle, he viewed the buildings, large and small, new and old, crammed together in solid, soldier-like rows on both sides of the street. He drove past the Black Bull Inn, the White Horse Café, a cock yard, and the Crown Inn while sweeping his gaze up and down the street for a glistening, cropped-haired, dark-headed whisper of a woman.

The sounds of bartering, bickering, chattering, and laughing filled the air, along with the solid hum of his curricle wheels against the cobblestone street and the clop of his horses' hooves as they walked. Maneuvering between two carriages in front of him, he had to pull up sharply on the reins when a small boy with a full head of dark hair darted in front of his curricle. The boy glanced up at him with large, frightened, piercing blue eyes that seemed to glow, surrounded as they were by a soot-covered face. He was filthy, rail thin, and looked as if no one cared for him.

Anger recoiled through Nathan at the plight of unwanted and unloved children. The situation was far too familiar for him. If it hadn't been his fortune to be born into wealth, he could well have been a chimney sweep like this boy. He didn't doubt for a second that his mother would have gleefully sold him for the coin he would have brought her, and by the time his father came back around for one of his rare visits, Nathan probably would have been dead.

Nathan reached into his overcoat and took out several

coins, never breaking eye contact with the obviously wary child. He motioned the boy to come closer. The child bent down and picked up the brush he had dropped before shuffling with stooped shoulders and a lowered head to the edge of the curricle.

Ignoring the angry shouts of the men forced to stop their carriages behind him, Nathan bent down and held out the gleaming coins to the child. The big blue eyes moved from Nathan's face to his hand, and back again. Desire and fear swam in the depths of the child's eyes.

"Go on," Nathan said softly. "These are for you to buy a treat and some good food to fill your belly."

The child licked his lips before dashing his hand out and attempting to grasp the coins. Nathan closed his hand around the small one, having been expecting such a maneuver. When the boy cried out and recoiled, Nathan gently increased his hold. "I'm not going to hurt you. I just wanted to say something before you run off with the money. I'll let you go, but you must promise to stand here and listen."

The boy hesitated for only a moment before nodding, and Nathan immediately released him, half expecting the child to dash off, but he stayed put, true to his word. Nathan grinned. "You need to be careful when crossing the street. If I didn't have quicker reflexes, you'd be lying under my horses' hooves right now and *that* would not be a pleasant place to be."

The child swallowed audibly before speaking. "Y-y-yes, milord."

"Your Grace," Nathan corrected gently.

"Yes. Your G-G-Grace."

Pity for the child welled in his breast. He'd been a stutterer as a young lad, too, and it had been made far worse by his mother's constant berating. He hadn't been born such, but living with a mother who was sweet one minute and fearsome the next had made him anxious, until she'd abandoned any pretense of sweetness in the privacy of their home, and he'd set about learning to control his stutter with fierce determination.

"Do you have parents?"

The boy seemed to be contemplating the question. Perhaps he didn't know, or perhaps he knew them but wished he didn't.

He shrugged his slender shoulders. "A f-f-father, but he's no p-p-parent." The last word was spit out in anger.

"I'm sorry," Nathan said softly, shooting a glare over his shoulder at the man muttering curses at him.

The boy shrugged again. "I've a s-s-sister, too," he said with a bright smile.

"Well, lucky you," Nathan responded, sensing the boy's love for his sister. "I bet she would tell you to hold your spine straight and your head proud."

The boy's mouth parted in obvious surprise. "Sh-sh-she would."

Something about the way the boy cocked his head and quirked his mouth stirred familiarity in Nathan. He frowned, and then a bark of laughter erupted from him. "Is your sister's name Sophia Vane, perchance?"

The boy nodded.

"Would you tell me where the chimney sweep shop is?"

He nodded his head, again, and as he did so, a screech of pure rage filled the air and floated above the rest of the racket on the street. Nathan whipped his gaze to his right and just ahead, and for a frozen moment, all he could do was stare in amazed wonder at the sight of Sophia, flung much like a sack of the flour that covered her, over the shoulder of a big, burly man. The second passed with the exhalation of Nathan's breath. Rage filled him, propelling him off his curricle and toward the foray.

Six

" Let me go," Sophia screamed as she beat at Mr. Exington's back. "You cannot keep my brother!"

"I can keep him," the man replied smugly.

Futile tears stung her eyes as she struggled to breathe, crushed as she was under the heavy weight of the man's arm.

Mr. Exington dropped her onto the hard ground and loomed over her. He raised a tattered whip over his head. "If you try to thieve your brother away from me again, I'll use this whip on you *and* him. Do you understand me?"

She stared mutinously at him and sensed the very moment his control snapped by the way he bared his teeth. Her body tensed as he growled and snapped the whip down toward her. Fear caused her to squeeze her eyes shut, as if that would somehow prevent the oncoming blow or somehow lessen the pain.

The hiss of the whip slicing through the air filled her ears but the anticipated stinging pain didn't come. She scrambled backward as she glanced up, astonishment ceasing her backward motion and causing her breath to catch in her chest. Nathan stood behind Mr. Exington, whose arm was extended behind him and over his shoulder in an awkward position.

Not only could she not believe he was out of bed, but he was moving with surprising agility for a man who had almost died and barely had time to recover. And he looked very fine, indeed. Despite the fact that he *had* nearly died. He had on the same breeches, overcoat and boots she had first seen him in, minus the dirt and wrinkles they had acquired in his journey, thanks to her care of them.

His cravat was gone, though, and the shirt that peeked out of the overcoat had suspicious dark stains on the part she could see. That could only mean one thing: it was sloppy Frank's. But even with that dirty old rag on, Nathan managed to appear elegant and… Her eyes travelled inadvertently to his face, and her pulsed skipped a beat. He was foreboding with his shadowy stubble and mysterious narrowed eyes fixed on her.

With one hand, Nathan gripped Mr. Exington's wrist, and with the other, his fingers curled around the strap of the whip. A dark cloud consumed his features, except for his eyes, which seemed lit with fire. He turned his sharp gaze to Mr. Exington. "Do you make it a habit to hit women?" he demanded with a vicious tug on the whip, eliciting a growl from Mr. Exington.

"She hit me on the head with a frying pan and tried to steal my property," the man thundered.

"Hey, you!" a man called to them from the street. "Move your bloomin' carriage out of the way!"

Sophia glanced toward the busy street and Nathan's curricle, which was abandoned in the middle of the lane. Where she saw Harry. *Harry!* Her pulse took off as she realized her brother was standing by the carriage looking very frightened. Forgetting the men for the moment, she raced toward her brother and scooped him into her arms to shower him with hugs and kisses. Her attempt of moments ago to get to Harry had been thwarted by Mr. Exington, and she'd been fearful of what might happen to him before she could figure out how to rescue him.

"Harry," she breathed against his fine hair. When she inhaled, she nearly choked on the soot. Setting her brother down, she rubbed her nose with one hand and took his hand in the other while her eyes darted between the men on the nearby walkway and those in the street behind her. She could dash away now with Harry while Nathan had Mr. Exington distracted. She glanced behind her once more at the busy street. She could get away and never return. Something made her look back, though, and Nathan's gaze locked on her.

"Don't do it, Sophia," he said. "Whatever is happening here, I want to help you."

She bit down on her lip, hard. He sounded so sincere, but how could he really help her now? Harry had been sold, and even if Nathan was willing to buy Harry's freedom, they could not go back to Frank. He'd beat her and simply sell Harry again. "You cannot help me."

"I'm a duke, Sophia. I can move mountains if I wish it. Now, kindly lead my horses to the curb, and let us see what can be done."

When Harry tugged on her hand, she looked down. He gazed up at her with a goofy smile on his dirty, sweet face. "I l-like him. He's g-got honest eyes."

She dashed a glimpse at Nathan and found him staring at her again. Could she trust him? Years of experience with the unfair sex told her no, but her heart told her yes.

"The boy is incredibly astute," Nathan said. "If I am anything, it's honest. You can trust me."

Heat singed her cheeks that he seemed to have read her thoughts. Grabbing the reins, she tugged the horses to the side and secured them to the lamppost. Then she and Harry walked to stand by Nathan, who still had a firm grip on a cursing Mr. Exington. Sophia ignored the bawdy words and looked at Nathan. "I'll trust you...*for now*," she muttered.

Nathan grinned down at her. "Likewise."

She nodded.

With the same startling quickness he'd displayed the day she met him, Nathan maneuvered Mr. Exington to face him so fast that Sophia was not at all certain how he'd accomplished the task.

Mr. Exington opened his mouth to speak, but Nathan thwarted him. "If you can manage to hold your loose tongue and let the lady speak first, I have a strong suspicion it could be worth your while."

"Who are you?" Mr. Exington growled.

Nathan's mouth spread into a thin-lipped smile. "I'm the Duke of Scarsdale."

The fiend pointed a beefy, calloused finger at Sophia. "She tried to steal my property."

"My brother is not your property!" Sophia said firmly.

"I bought him for a fair price from your father."

Sophia was about to show Nathan just how unladylike her vocabulary could be, but before she could utter a word, he was dragging Mr. Exington closer to him as if the man weighed no more than a feather. He gave the man a look that could have caused a frost in hell. "Did you say you *bought* this boy from his father?"

Mr. Exington nodded, which almost made him knock heads with Nathan because of how close they now stood.

Nathan's gaze darted to Sophia, for confirmation she supposed. "Frank threatened to do it if I didn't go along with his plan for you, but he promised he would not unless I made trouble. He's a liar," she spat. Anger at herself for having trusted her father at all filled her.

"How much did you pay for this child?" The low question vibrated with anger.

"Five pounds."

"You think human life worth so little?" Nathan growled and curled his fists tighter around the material of the man's shirt.

"I think that's fair market value for a chimney sweep," Mr. Exington replied in an emotionless tone.

"You're a monster," Sophia raged, trying to swing at Mr. Exington, but Nathan blocked her hand. For one second, his long fingers curled around her wrist as his eyes met hers, and he subtly shook his head. He wanted her to let him handle it, she understood. Though it pained her mightily to trust a man to that extent, she clamped her mouth shut, not seeing any other real choice.

He released Mr. Exington with a slight push that sent the man stumbling backward a bit. When he regained his balance, he stepped forward and raised his fists. Sophia flinched and shuffled away, pulling her brother, who was silently clinging to her leg, with her. Nathan had not even flinched.

He shook his head at Mr. Exington. "I wouldn't pick a fight with me if I were you. The last man who did ended up with his chest underneath my boot. And the man before that, who I count as one of my closest friends, ended up blacking out. I'm not boasting, mind you, these are simply facts. I've had many hours of solitude in my life, and with them, I chose to train in the art of boxing, knife throwing, shooting, and fencing. So you can attempt to hit me or you can take my money."

Mr. Exington blinked, as did Sophia.

"Your money?" the man cautiously asked.

Nathan nodded. "That's right. I wish to purchase the boy from you for...why don't we say double what you paid for him."

"Triple," Mr. Exington threw out.

Sophia ground her teeth at the gall of the fiend but said nothing. Harry circled his arms around her leg. She rested her hand on his shoulder and squeezed in a silent attempt to assure him that everything would be fine. She didn't know how she would ever pay Nathan back for what he was doing, but somehow she would.

Nathan nodded. "Fine. Triple. I'll have my man of business send you the money."

"I'll need a marker until then."

"You've my word," Nathan replied coldly.

"I'm afraid, Your Grace, that don't mean too much to me. I'll keep the lady in exchange for her brother 'til your money reaches me." Mr. Exington leered at Sophia. "I'm sure you know by now she's a lightskirt."

Sophia tried to shake Harry off so she could lunge at Mr. Exington and scratch his eyes out, but he held tight even as she bent down and tugged at his fingers. A crack, sounding much like flesh meeting flesh, resounded above her, and when she jolted upright, Mr. Exington was on the ground on his back with Nathan's polished, expensive boot firmly planted on the wretched man's chest as promised. Mr. Exington's bulbous nose was freely bleeding.

The vein on the right side of Nathan's neck pulsed furiously. "If I hear of you speaking of the lady that way ever again, I'll kill you."

The threat—delivered in a tone of menacing finality—pleased her in a way she was sure was not nice. But blast it all, it felt awfully good to have someone sticking up for her for once. She could quite imagine how a lady might find herself falling for Nathan.

He slid a thick gold ring from his pinky and threw it on Mr. Exington's chest. "When I return to London, I'll send my man of business back with your funds and he will collect my ring from you. Take a care with it. It was a gift from the king, and I'd be highly displeased if you misplaced it."

Mr. Exington grunted and Nathan removed his boot from the man's chest, and before she knew what was happening, Nathan swept her and Harry into the protective, large, and heated circle of his strong arms. He ushered them toward the curricle and then hurried them up onto the bench. The seat was small and Sophia was vividly aware of Nathan's muscular thigh pressed so tightly against her own. Her pulse skittered alarmingly and her stomach fluttered.

He turned them into the street and maneuvered through the traffic while she struggled to control her surprising attraction to this man. He was beautiful, of course, there was that, but her gut told her it was so much more. He'd rescued her twice, and now her brother, too. And in doing this, he now had her trust. It seemed to her this was a good sign that somewhere out there existed a man like Nathan—not him, of course. She wasn't a nitwit. He was a duke and she was a commoner—that would treasure her and love her as she longed to be loved.

They rode in jostling silence until they reached the outskirts of the busy section of town, and without warning, Nathan maneuvered the curricle off the side of the road. He lowered the reins for the horses to relax and turned to face her.

"You are a continuous surprise," he drawled, leaning back against the seat of his curricle and surveying her with an open expression of amusement.

"So are you," she said. "What are you doing out of bed?"

"I was leaving."

Her heart dropped toward the dirt, though she knew she should not be surprised. "Leaving?"

He reached out, ran a finger over the bridge of her nose, and then held up his fingertip covered with flour to her. "Mrs. Dalton?"

She gaped. "How did you know?"

His lips pressed into a hard line. "I had the unfortunate displeasure of meeting her when I was looking for you."

"Why were you looking for me?"

"Ah, because your father tried to force me to marry you. He told me a story I was sure was highly fabricated about your disgraceful downfall due to helping me."

Heat singed her cheeks. "And what do you think now?"

He crooked his lips. "I think we have a problem."

"We?" she squeaked, hardly believing he cared at all.

He nodded slowly. "I'm not sure what to do, to be honest. Your father—"

"Frank beats her," Harry blurted out.

Sophia gasped and scowled at her brother until he squirmed. "Of all the times to speak without stuttering and you chose *now* while you reveal things you have no right to reveal!" she chided Harry. "Frank does not beat me," she lied, giving Harry her fiercest warning look to keep his lips shut tight. She did not want Nathan to pity her.

Harry scowled back. "Sh-she's ashamed. M-make her p-pull up her l-left sleeve. You'll—"

"Be quiet, Harry!" Sophia demanded, but as the command left her lips, strong fingers clasped her left wrist, tugged her arm straight, and pulled up the sleeve of her dress until the ugly, red, puckered cut Frank had given her during his whipping was revealed, along with the yellow-and-purple bruising surrounding it.

Any protest she was about to make was silenced by the dark fury that swept across Nathan's face. With clouded eyes that didn't seem to see what he was doing, he rubbed his thumb very gently near her cut and over her bruises. The tender gesture caused a tremor to race through her body, and his thumb immediately froze as his eyes locked with hers. "I do believe I may be stuck."

The way Sophia's brow creased was so beguiling it made Nathan's chest tighten. Her gaze strayed to his body and back to his face as she clearly tried to work through what the devil he'd meant. He'd gladly give her the time because he needed a moment, too. Was he actually considering marrying this woman?

What sort of life would she have if he didn't? He could give her enough money to live a decent sort of life, but he could not erase the stain on her reputation by simply bestowing money on her. No real gentleman would likely ever marry her because her damaged reputation would follow her as close as her shadow and would make it impossible to have the life she probably dreamed of. And regardless of whether that dream was truly out of her grasp because of her background, helping him had taken away any chance at all of her overcoming who her father was and where she came from. All this because she'd been willing to risk her life and name to try to save him.

He gripped his aching arm as he glanced at her. Sophia was like a fragile bird that he'd inadvertently put in danger by touching. Except he hadn't touched her. The danger came from her helping him and her fool of a father purposely ruining her to try to gain wealth. He could leave her in the nest and she would be destroyed. That free spirit and pride he'd glimpsed would be crushed under the weight of her father's scathing treatment, and she'd have no opportunity to ever have a better life. Or he could marry her and save her from the problem he had inadvertently helped cause.

He studied her as she toyed with her cropped hair. "What

happened to your hair?" he asked, not realizing he was even going to inquire about it until he words had left his mouth.

A fiery blush covered her pale, gaunt cheeks. "Frank cut it off for money." She sniffed and looked down. Her hands gripped the shabby material of her dress. "It was my only good feature," she whispered, her voice throbbing with restrained tears.

Sympathy he hadn't even realized he had the capability to feel with such painful depth pierced his heart, his gut, and his lungs to rob him of breath. It occurred to him clearly, then, what it was he liked so much about her. Despite everything, she seemed to possess hope and an indomitable spirit. He'd be damned if he would let her father kill that and fill her with shame. He knew shame. It dwelled within him like an old cobweb in a high corner that he couldn't quite reach to brush away. It was not an emotion someone should have to live with day after day.

He stared at Sophia's clasped hands, uncertain how to proceed, or maybe simply uncertain what to say. He understood what should be done, and not just for the sake of honor but for the sake of Sophia and her brother. If he took her back to her father and left her there, it would be like leaving a lamb to be slaughtered. She'd run, he was certain of it, but the thought of what she would find as a welcome on the cold, hard streets of London chilled him.

He clenched his fingers in at attempt to stop the throbbing in his injured arm, aware of the child's eyes on him as he did so, so he forced what he hoped was a reassuring smile. The fragile boy reminded him too damn much of himself. After he married Sophia, the first thing he would do was send the boy off to school. He didn't want a constant reminder of the weak child he once was living underfoot.

"Look at me," he commanded. If they were going to be married, it was best she understood from the outset that he had no use for love. He did not need it, nor want it. Weak men longed for love. *Foolish men.* But as her bright-blue eyes bore into him, and he noted the smallest quivering of her bottom lip, he decided there would be plenty of time to make his feelings on the matter clear. It was more important to dispel of her shame right now, which she didn't deserve to bear.

"I want to make sure I have all the facts straight before we proceed. Will you answer a few of my questions?"

"Maybe," she said, raising her chin in defiance.

Nathan chuckled. She may be ashamed but it was only because she had a great amount of pride and fight. He found himself oddly pleased that she did. Scrubbing a hand over his face, he tried to determine what he needed to know. "Do you have any relatives other than your father?"

She shook her head but then cast her gaze to her brother.

Nathan waved a hand. "I mean older relatives that could take you in."

When she frowned, he sighed. "It doesn't matter, anyway. I've already run through that scenario and have concluded it would not help you." She'd not reached her majority; therefore she was under her father's rule.

"I don't understand," she mumbled.

"I'll explain momentarily." He wanted to talk to her, but some of the things that needed to be discussed might hurt the child's feelings. He turned to the boy. "What's your name?"

"Harry."

"Harry, will you please give your sister and me a moment of privacy?"

The boy's eyes rounded, and he gaped.

Nathan glanced to Sophia for guidance. She looked at her brother and tears suddenly glistened in her eyes. "He's not used to a man asking him to do anything. He's used to being ordered, shoved, pushed, and threatened."

Barely checked rage rose in Nathan's throat and made talking difficult for a moment. He swallowed and met Sophia's gaze first and then Harry's. "That's unfortunate. I promise I will never threaten you, shove you, or push you."

Harry smiled. "You left out c-c-command."

Nathan reached around Sophia and ruffled the boy's hair. "So I did," he said carefully, intentionally not promising not to command. Harry was a child, after all. "Will you go sit under that tree for a few minutes?" Nathan asked, indicating the large poplar tree not ten feet away.

Harry nodded and scrambled down and out of the carriage.

Once the boy was five paces away, Nathan spoke. "As I understand things your father—"

"Frank," she corrected with a mutinous look.

He understood all too well her desire not to call the man *father*. "Vane," he conceded. "I'm guessing upon learning who I was he decided he wanted you to be a duchess."

She laughed, not merry but brittle. "It had nothing to do with wanting anything for me. He wanted to get his grubby hands on some of your money, and I suppose he thought your marrying me would entitle him to some of it."

"Vane is not very bright," Nathan replied.

Sophia grinned, and two delightful dimples appeared in her cheeks that he'd previously failed to notice. Was she always going to be such a constant surprise? The notion caused him to tense. His mother had been a constant surprise for years—one minute happy, the next as volatile as a storm, and always dangling the possibility of attaining her love if he could prove he was worthy. He dismissed the useless memory.

"I tried to tell him that you would never marry me and that you weren't the sort to be coerced, but he always has his own ideas." She'd cast her gaze downward again, and she was fiddling with her dress.

Nathan hooked a finger under her chin and nudged her until she looked up. "I believe you have a mistaken notion as to why I would never marry you."

She blinked. "I don't believe so. You don't want a wife, for one."

"I have accepted for some time that I would eventually need to take a wife."

"Oh." Her lips parted for a moment. "But I doubt you had any intentions of picking a guttersnipe."

"You are not a guttersnipe," he growled, enraged that her

father had made her feel so.

"Close enough. I'm no lady."

He cupped her chin, and her beautiful eyes widened. "I've known a lot of so-called ladies in my lifetime, and if you are not one, then I much prefer what you seem to be."

Her mouth had parted again, but after a moment, she spoke. "You're an interesting contradiction."

So was she. She appeared very fragile with her slight build, but she was strong. "In what way?" he asked.

She licked her lips before speaking. "One minute you're hot and the next you're cold. One minute you seem to like me and the next you don't."

Her comments froze his blood. She'd described exactly what he had experienced with his mother before she'd become a permanently cold draft. Was he like his mother?

No. He refused to accept that. The notion was preposterous. But if he was like her... His heart seized beating for a moment. "It seems my mother is having the last laugh on me."

Sophia cocked her head. "What do you mean?"

He considered telling her things he'd never spoken to anyone, but he dismissed the notion as quickly as it had come into his mind. Sophia was going to be his duchess but that didn't mean he would bare his soul to her. "She wasn't the warmest person, and at times could be unpredictable in how she would react." The answer was vague enough to suit him.

Sophia squeezed his arm. "I understand. I'm quick to anger, and I vow I get that from Frank. We all inherit things from our parents, but I firmly believe that, with enough desire and effort, we can control how we react."

Sophia's understanding and acceptance of his flaw touched him deeply. Deeper than he cared for it to touch him. He moved back on the seat so they would no longer be touching and studied her for a few seconds. He liked her—an undeniable truth. In addition, he admired her courage. But he needed to remember that she'd likely destroy the good feelings and obliterate the admiration, just as his mother had done in his father. In fact, he'd do well to expect it. "Tell me what were you planning to do with your life before I came along?"

She looked at him askance. "I am *still* planning to flee my father and take Harry with me."

He'd suspected as much, but he simply nodded for her to continue.

"I've been saving up money to go to London with my brother."

He had a picture of her walking the streets of London toting her brother behind her in search of somewhere to sleep for the night, and his gut hardened with fear. "What had you planned on doing once you were in London?"

She shoved back a strand of hair that the increasing wind was blowing across her face and then she hugged herself, and it occurred to him she was probably cold, dressed as she was in such an ill-suited garment for the weather. Wincing against the pain of his injury, he shrugged out of his coat as she spoke and placed it over her shoulders, giving her a shake of his head when it appeared she would protest.

"I plan to find whatever work I can immediately. But eventually, I'll become a governess, chaperone, or lady's companion."

Her undeniable hope for the future touched him and made him ache for her.

"I'm also going to send Harry to school," she added.

"And you have enough money saved up?"

Her face fell. "I almost did… But Frank stole it, the scab."

"So how do you expect to get to London?" he asked, curious to what it was she had planned.

She eyed him, and as she did, her cheeks turned pink. "I was hoping you might lend me the money. Harry and I cannot go back to Frank. He'll just sell him to Mr. Exington again once you're gone. I hate to tell you that since you just purchased my brother's freedom, which I greatly appreciate, but what you bought was a temporary reprieve."

Nathan had already come to that conclusion himself. "Yes, I suspected, but there was no course but the one I took. I could have taken your brother from Mr. Exington but the man did pay for him."

"Yes, he did," Sophia replied in a cold voice that reminded him of his own when he was angry. He laughed, despite the somber conversation and the pain radiating in his shoulder and arm.

"If you were a man, Sophia, you would be one not to be taken for granted."

"And as a woman?" she demanded, her eyes narrowing and growing dark and stormy.

"Ah, I never take a woman for granted. Doing so can be lethal. I appreciate to the very chambers of my beating black heart how much havoc a woman can create."

She grinned. "I don't think that was a compliment, per se, but I'll take it as such."

"I'm glad," he replied, smiling in return.

"So will you lend me money? I promise to pay you back as soon as possible."

"I'll do better than lend you money to help you escape. I'll take you away myself."

With a frown, she pulled his overcoat up around her chin and gave him a wary look, one that bespoke of years of mistreatment by every man she had ever known. Her pain felt as if it were his own. His blood ran cold, and he had to fight the urge not to run from her. He would not care for her; it was as simple as that.

Sophia nibbled on her lip for a moment before responding. "I don't understand," she said. "Do you mean you will give Harry and me a ride to London?" She looked around them. "Well, the curricle is small, but we don't mind sitting close if you don't."

"I mean I'll marry you, and yes, take you to London, but we will probably go to my country home first."

Her mouth parted, and a look that could only be described as disbelief passed over her features. "You want to marry me?"

"I don't see a choice," he said honestly. "You're ruined. Quite irreparably, it seems. And you cannot stay with your fath—Vane," he corrected awkwardly.

Her cheeks turned a deep shade of red, and she cleared her throat. "You and I both know you cannot be forced to marry me. No one will care that you don't."

Her halting words displayed her hurt. He didn't regret telling her the truth and forgoing flowery lies. He was not one to pretend, whether it would save someone's feelings or not. "I'd care. I'd care what happens to you because you saved my life."

"That's no reason to marry."

"It's reason enough," he clipped, amazed she was arguing with him.

She scowled. "If you will simply lend me money, I'll get my brother and myself to London and the rest will work out."

He clenched and unclenched his jaw before speaking. "I hate to be blunt, but for the sake of preventing either one—or all three of us—from catching our death sitting in the dropping winter temperatures, you force me to be direct. I could lend you all the money in the world but your soiled reputation will remain ruined without my marrying you."

She jutted out her chin. "My reputation here always did hang in a precarious position, thanks to Frank. Besides, no one in London will know about what happened in Newmarket."

"You fool yourself, Sophia. Look at what happened with Mrs. Dalton and Mr. Exington. Do you really think they are the only two people who will be treating you as a lightskirt? It's only a matter of time until some gossipmonger from your town travels to London and takes zealous pleasure in spreading the rumors."

"No one cares about me enough to do that. And no one knows me in London."

"But they know me," he said on a heavy sigh. "And I tell you this without the least bit of pride or pleasure that they care in London far too much about what *I* do. My goings and comings are, unfortunately, like a tantalizing drug to the wickedly bored *ton*. Once they hear a whisper of a scandal with my name attached to it, they'll gobble it up, and you with it unless we are married."

"I don't care. They can talk all they want. I'll go about my business of getting educated and finding work."

"No one will be willing to educate you once they hear the rumors of your dallying with me." He didn't want to hurt her, but she had to understand the reality. "You would never secure a position as any of the things you mentioned because the biggest requirement for those occupations is a sterling reputation, which I'm afraid you no longer come close to having. At best, you could possibly work as a barmaid or seamstress, but you and your brother could not live on either of those jobs' wages, and you'd never be able to scrape enough money together to send your brother away to school. I could pay for you to live somewhere nicer than you could afford on your own, but that would likely have the effect of people speculating that I'm keeping you."

Her brows dipped together in a deep frown. "Keeping me?"

"Yes, for wicked pleasure." They'd never assume he kept her simply as his mistress. As cruel as it made him feel to admit, they wouldn't believe she could hold his interest at all, given how she presently looked.

Her fair skin, already pink from the cold, turned crimson across the high slope of her cheekbones, which was accentuated by her lack of proper flesh. The first thing he would do for her was have his cook feed her lavish meals so she would make a healthy weight.

"There must be another solution besides marriage," she said, shoulders slumping.

As he stared at Sophia, looking so dejected at the idea of marrying him, laughter built in his chest. All the women who had tried to finagle an offer of marriage from him and when he finally proposed to a woman, she didn't seem inclined to accept. "Is it the idea of marriage to me that repels you or is it simply the institute of marriage?" He wasn't sure what provoked him to ask such a question, except maybe his pride.

"It's not you at all," she said quickly and gave him a shy glance that made his chest tighten. "It's clear to me you have a good heart."

"Is it?" His heart squeezed.

She nodded. "If you didn't, you would not have intervened on my behalf...twice."

"Any man would have done what I did," he replied automatically.

"No man I've ever known, except maybe the reverend," she muttered.

"Fine, any *gentleman*," he corrected.

"I do not think it's as simple as that," she said slowly. "I think you did what you did because you are kind and caring, but you don't seem to see yourself as either of those things."

The way Sophia seemed to see him with such naive admiration was both disconcerting and enticing. And the notion that her admiration was enticing to him *at all*, irritated him to no end. "It's getting cold out here," he clipped, retreating behind a wall of indifference "What is it going to be? I've made my offer. Either accept it or don't. The choice is yours. Make it with haste, if you please."

Seven

She didn't know what to do. She was truly torn. Nathan could protect her and Harry. He could provide a life and education for Harry that she never could, even if by some miracle she secured one of the positions she desired. But her gut told her what he said was true. Her soiled reputation would prevent her from ever achieving her dreams. At best, she could hope to slave away in a tavern or as a seamstress for the rest of her life, or she could attract some man's attention and become his mistress. The thought repulsed her.

She only knew one decent man—and she'd been hurt more times than she could count by Frank, who was supposed to be her greatest protector—but she had that little nugget of hope her mother's letter had instilled in her. If she married Nathan would her hope be well-placed or dashed? She glanced sideways at Nathan from underneath her lashes, and her heart tugged.

He was astonishingly handsome with his strong jaw line, patrician nose, full lips, and persuasive eyes. If she was honest, it didn't hurt that he was rich, and therefore, she'd likely never know cold and hunger again. Not that she couldn't handle both those things. She could. But if she had her druthers…

She barely suppressed a nervous giggle. Beyond the superficial, he was honest to a fault, considering his blunt proposal. He was obviously wounded. Physically, he was very strong, but he needed someone to patch him back together emotionally.

Her toes curled when she thought of the way he'd flattened two men for her. He was honorable, despite his protests. And—she sucked in a sharp breath—she was already halfway falling for him, which scared her to death, but she didn't have a clue how to stop it. If she married him, she would be risking her heart. She was certain of it.

She would be good and trapped by marriage if he proved to be selfish and uncaring. Everything in her rebelled at the thought of being under the ruling thumb of a man who didn't love her. It was on the tip of her tongue to decline his offer, but she could not make herself form the words. As she gazed at his profile, she realized that, despite all her fears, the possibility of something wonderful might just outweigh her fears of something horrible.

Suddenly, ahead on the road, Frank's dilapidated carriage swung around the bend. The sound of horses' hooves clopping along filled the silent day. To her right, Harry frantically called her name. She turned in his direction and he was already racing toward her.

"I cannot take you from your father, Sophia," Nathan whispered in her left ear. "You are his property until you reach your majority. But we both know he'll relinquish you, and I vow your brother, too, if we are to be married."

"Then I'll be *your* property," she blurted, watching Frank and Moses draw to a stop. They jumped out toting pistols as they strode toward her, Nathan, and Harry.

"Better my property than your father's," Nathan growled. "I don't wish to see you rewarded for saving my life by becoming a glorified prostitute or worse."

That was hardly a hope-fulfilling sort of proposal. Once again, it was on the tip of her tongue to tell him she would not marry him when Frank marched up and pointed his pistol at Nathan.

"Ye think ye can do anything 'cause yer the Duke of Scarsdale. Well, I've learned I can bring ye up on charges in front of the magistrate in London for what ye did to Sophia. Ye almost fooled me." With an evil grin, Frank rocked back on his heels. "I was gonna settle for the money ye gave me, but now I want more or I'll ruin ye. Do ye hear me? I'll drag yer name through the mud."

Sophia wanted to sink into the ground and disappear. Sophia skid her glance to Nathan and winced at the vicious visage he now wore.

He reached out and used one finger to move Frank's pistol away from his person. Then Nathan gave Moses a look that made goose flesh rise on Sophia's arms. After Moses lowered his pistol, Nathan turned his cold gaze back to Frank. "It is deplorable that you would destroy your daughter's reputation further than you have already done for more money. How much is it you want?"

"Twenty more pounds," Frank crooned.

Nathan's cold eyes ignited with fury. "I'll give you thirty more pounds, but only if Sophia agrees to marry me and you relinquish your son"—Harry had run over to the melee and was hovering by Sophia's side—"to my care."

Frank's mouth gaped open. "Ye want to marry her now?"

Humiliation licked at Sophia's heels.

Nathan inclined his head. "I find we suit. I believe she does, too." His gaze locked on hers.

Without a doubt, he was marrying her to save her. It was the most selfless act anyone had ever performed on her behalf. And it occurred to her that any man who could be so utterly selfless had to be capable of the kind of love she craved.

"Well, Sophia?" Frank demanded. "Do ye find ye suit?" He gave her a narrow-eyed twisted look that said he'd ring her neck if she dared disavow Nathan's words, but Frank need not have bothered trying to frighten her. Her heart pounded a deafening beat in her ears as she nodded her head.

The speed with which the next week passed both amazed and surprised Sophia. What didn't surprise her was the fact that Frank had treated her more kindly than he ever had in her entire life. Nathan had left to secure a special marriage license, see his man of business in London, and speak with his aunt.

He'd also told her in whispered tones that he intended to hire an investigator—someone named Sir Richard—about locating the men who had attacked them in the curricle several nights prior. That had been good to hear. The scab that had escaped deserved justice, and though it didn't seem to make Nathan all that uneasy that someone had hired men to kill him, it definitely weighed on her mind.

She'd been disappointed to find him leaving so soon, but before he had departed, she'd overheard him threaten to crush Frank's bollocks if he harmed one hair on her or Harry's head, and it had lightened her heart immeasurably. Even now, as the carriage that Nathan had procured to bring her and Harry to his country home wound up the long, immaculate tree lined drive, she grinned at how well the threat had worked. She'd not been one bit sad to leave Frank good and well behind her. She'd not even said good-bye.

Beside her, Harry wiggled on the carriage bench, tugged at her sleeve, and then leaned toward her. She hunched down to hear what he had to say.

"I th-thought you s-said His Grace told you this was his smallest country home."

Sophia glanced toward the house that rose majestically in the distance and gulped. A tall tower—it appeared to be a clock tower upon her squinting inspection—loomed high above the massive redbrick home, reaching high into the orange twilight sky. She'd expected a grand home, even if it was, as Nathan had casually mentioned, one of his smallest. He was a duke, after all. She'd been certain even the most inconsequential of his homes would be lovely. But this one stole her breath and made her feel like quite the imposter in her threadbare, ill-fitting blue gown.

She hoped no one had come for the wedding beyond the aunt Nathan had said needed to attend, as it would lend the marriage an air of respectability to Society. He had explained that his aunt held great consequence among the *ton*, though he'd muttered under his breath that only God knew why.

As the carriage rattled down the pebbled drive, past wintry bare-branched trees and alternating massive stone sculptures with ornate urns sitting on rectangular bases, Sophia's stomach flipped. She wished the trip had taken the expected three days and not the two it had turned out taking. They were a day early and she didn't feel ready to face what lay inside this sweeping home. It was silly, she knew, but this was not her world. Granted, her world had not been good, but she'd known it. She understood how to move within it and survive there.

She surveyed the acres of beautifully kept gardens and lawn that surrounded the house. In the sky above them, a dark line of eight birds flew in a V against the backdrop of the soft, deepening blue. She craned her head to follow their flight over the house and beyond, where she glimpsed the dark-blue, lapping edges of a lake in the distance.

This was Nathan's smallest house? A house with a clock tower and a private lake was his *smallest* house? Her stomach twisted into a thousand tight knots, and she started fiddling with her gown. She wished fervently she'd had something better to wear or that she still had her long hair to make her look less…less *pathetic.*

No, this was definitely not her world. Nathan's world was made of grand curricles, fine clothes, mind-boggling mansions, and, she was positive, many beautiful women. He likely would have eventually chosen one among the silk-gowned lot to marry *if* he hadn't had the misfortune to meet her and *if* he hadn't possessed such a good heart.

"Perhaps we should find an inn close-by and send word that we are a day early," she squeaked, her throat suddenly dry. Maybe Nathan had changed his mind. She wanted to leap for love but what if the jump killed her?

Harry squeezed her hand. "It w-will be fine. He's a g-good man."

The words, though coming from her now nine-year-old brother, were comforting. Harry was just as distrusting of men as she was, and if he was willing to trust Nathan, that counted for something in her mind.

Before the carriage came to a complete stop in front of the house, the ornate, dark wooden door of the house, with its eight tiny glass panes set in the middle, swung open. A young man dressed in gold-and-burgundy livery made way for a tall, thin man with peppered hair and a black tie, who marched out to the steps. Sophia moved her ankle to feel the presence of her mother's letter. She didn't know much about the servants in a great household, but she knew enough to assume this was the butler who was greeting them. The man's back was ramrod straight, and his nose was tilted in the air in a haughty angle.

As Sophia and Harry climbed out of the carriage and made their way up the stairs, she counted thirty windows on the main building of the house. Thirty! She'd never seen so much glass in her life. It made her giddy to think how much light the house must get. The tavern had been constantly dark and dreary.

"How can I help you?" The butler's question dripped disdain.

She brought herself to her full height. "I'm Sophia Vane." When the butler gazed at her with a blank stare, her stomach flipped, but she took a breath for courage. "I'm here to marry His Grace."

A look of disbelief crossed the older man's face. "His Grace has no time for such foolishness." The butler waved a hand at them. "Off with you."

"Now see here," she started.

"No, you see here," the servant responded in a cool, un-wavering tone. "If His Grace was to be married I would certainly know about it. There would be many preparations to be made, guests to be seen to, parties to be planned. You, miss, are a liar."

Sophia fought back a wave of humiliation. Nathan hadn't even told his servants he was to be married. Was he embar-rassed by her?

As she fingered her short hair and took in her tattered

gown, she squared her shoulders. "You will announce me right this moment or I will have you dismissed the minute I become duchess."

The man eyed her without moving.

Anger and deep humiliation flared in her chest, but resolve flared stronger. She would get in this door. "If you are wrong about me how forgiving do you think His Grace will be? I wager not very, knowing him as I do."

The butler's eyes widened slightly, and he turned on his heel while motioning them to follow. Harry looked up at her and gave her a wink and a grin.

She winked back and followed the butler into the main entrance hall. She faltered, staring in awe at the luxury of the home. A grand staircase was immediately to the left and rose in an almost processional route to, she imagined, a great chamber on the main floor. She counted eight stairs ascending to a landing and then the staircase curved to another small set of stairs that ascended again and curved yet again.

As she and Harry trailed the butler up the stairs, her pulse seemed to quicken with each step. At the top, the servant led them into a grand room with a parquet floor and a higher ceiling than she had ever imagined existed.

She gaped up at it, unable to help herself. Mythological figures were framed in the panels, and busts sat on brackets all around the room, though she wasn't at all certain whom the busts represented. She made a note to ask someone later. The hall had two majestic marble fireplaces that crackled and gave off a pleasant warmth. The large paneled windows—four on one wall alone—were stacked in twos, separated by an ornate decoration that jutted away from the wall to circle the entire room.

"Follow me," the butler demanded and led them down a wing of the house past a long wall of portraits. Sophia studied each one as she went, counting five men in a row who surely had to be the former Dukes of Scarsdale. They paused outside a door, and the butler turned to them. "Wait here. I'll announce you."

Sophia nodded and hastily grabbed Harry's arm when it appeared he might follow the butler into the room. Voices floated out from the room, and she pressed closer to the door to hear.

"You cannot be serious, Scarsdale."

The woman's cold, brittle tone made Sophia tense. Please God this was not the aunt Nathan had mentioned.

"Have you ever known me to joke?" Nathan's tone matched the woman's, icicle for icicle. "Especially about marriage."

"No. No, I have not, which is why I find it hard to believe you would willingly marry a tavern wench."

"Your Grace," came the butler's voice.

"One moment, Gibson," Nathan snapped.

Footsteps filled the silence as they approached the door but Gibson did not appear. Sophia thought she made out a casted shadow across the floor by the entrance, and she imagined Gibson had retreated to a corner. It gave her perverse pleasure to think the stuffy butler had been chastised. Then she frowned at her cattiness.

"Watch what you say, Aunt Harriet," Nathan warned. "You are speaking of the future Duchess of Scarsdale."

Sophia let out a thankful breath that he had defended her.

"Scarsdale, they will never accept her."

"You will make them, of course, because I have told you to do so."

Sophia gasped. Nathan sounded nothing like the kind man she'd met last week. He sounded aloof and demanding.

"I cannot make the *ton* accept a woman from such a low class."

"I have every faith in you, Aunt Harriet. You are formidable."

"I don't understand you," she practically screeched. "Gentlemen ruin women every day and never blink an eye. If your conscience truly will not let you walk away from this debacle, give the baggage some money. Money fixes everything."

"No," Nathan said in a hard, ruthless tone. "Money does

not fix everything, and you know it as well as I do. If money fixed everything we would both be happy people."

A pronounced silence filled the room. Finally, a long, irritated sigh interrupted the quiet. "I simply cannot stand the thought of you marrying so beneath you."

"What is it you wish for me to do?" Nathan thundered.

"I wish you to be reasonable and forget her. She is not your problem. Besides, Scarsdale, from what you told me, I highly doubt she had much of a reputation from the start."

Sophia curled her hands into fists. Harry moved to her side, slid his arms around her hips, and squeezed her. She managed to unclench her hands and touched a shaking one to the top of Harry's head. Part of her wanted to flee this place and the wretched woman—who would be her relative if she married Nathan. She shuddered at the thought—and part of her wanted to make that harridan eat her words.

"Hear me now, Aunt, for I will never repeat this again."

Sophia frowned at how threatening Nathan sounded.

"I am going to marry the woman."

"I hear you," the aunt snapped. "I still cannot fathom why."

"It's time I take up a charity, and she is it."

It would have hurt less if he'd plunged a knife into her gut. Her heart wrenched. Of course, she had known he likely felt she was pathetic, but to hear him say she was his charity stung as if she had received a ghastly wound. She clutched at her midsection, and Harry squeezed her hand hard.

"She was kind enough to give me directions and offer to lead me to the horse trainer, and in return, she was forced to kill someone to save me. She could have fled and left me there to die on the road, but she once again chose to save my life, regardless of the consequences to her own."

"That is because she knew she would be rewarded," the aunt grumbled.

"She knew no such thing. For all she knew, I would die before she got me to a physician."

"I doubt she had the wherewithal to consider that," the

aunt inserted.

"She's quite intelligent, actually."

"Scarsdale—"

"Enough of your whining," he barked. "She acted selfless-ly. That fact is indisputable. And for her actions, her father purposely ruined what little bit of a pathetic name she likely had, and in the process he ruined her hopes she had for herself."

Nathan's voice rose with each word, and Sophia's pulse sped up. One minute she was certain he only pitied her, and the next she thought she heard admiration in his words.

"I will not repay all she did for me and all she endured for me by knowingly leaving her to the life of a ruined woman. The only way to make it right is to marry her. It is the only thing that will save her reputation."

"Why save it?" the aunt shrieked. "Set her up in a nice house, buy her gowns and jewels, and the gentlemen will flock to her. You know it is true. They will shove one another out of the way to make her their mistress once they think you have had her."

A sound of disgust came from Nathan, and Sophia almost slumped in relief upon hearing it. Truly, he was much more honorable than his aunt.

"She is not meant for that sort of life," he replied. "Even though she has come from the worst sort of circumstance, her eyes burn with hope and she has a certain irrepressible spirit."

A smile tugged at the corner of Sophia's mouth. He did like her! That was an excellent start.

"I will not destroy that hope, nor crush that spirit, and that is all there is to it. She will be here tomorrow. You can either agree to accept her and treat her with the respect she will command as my duchess or you can find somewhere else to live and someone else to fund the lifestyle you love so dearly."

A loud sniff emanated from the room, followed by shuf-fling papers and one of the men clearing his throat.

"What is it, Gibson?" Nathan growled.

"Your Grace, there are two persons here to see you. One

of them claims she is to be your wife."

Sophia cringed at the distaste for her in the butler's tone.

"Only one of them claims she is going to be my wife?" Nathan asked with a chuckle. "How boring."

"Yes, Your Grace."

"Is she a slight woman with dark hair?"

"I believe so, Your Grace."

"*You believe so?*" The mocking tone made Sophia feel bad for Gibson, though he did have a poker stuck up his bum.

"I did not take much notice that she was a woman, Your Grace, except she had on a gown. Her hair is short like a man's."

"Oh dear heaven!" Nathan's aunt cried out.

"Get hold of yourself," Nathan snapped. "Gibson, where did you put my intended and her brother?"

"Outside the door, Your Grace."

"Bring them to me at once."

Sophia scrambled backward so it wouldn't appear she had been listening. She reminded herself that ladies did not hit, but it would be ever so lovely to slap his aunt across the face upon meeting her. But then the woman would know her words had affected Sophia and *that* was out of the question.

The door opened and Mr. Gibson motioned to them. "His Grace will see you now."

Sophia straightened and imitated the butler's stiff walk as she made her way into the room, followed by Harry. A quick glance around at the ornate bookcases containing countless books encased with gleaming covers confirmed she was in a grand library. She inhaled a deep breath and the scent of leather filled her nose.

She had the overwhelming urge to ogle the expensive books, but she didn't want to make herself look like a fool. Instead, she searched the room for Nathan, and her eyes immediately widened and her mouth parted. God, the man was a creation to rival the most exquisite Greek statues.

Nathan wore gleaming top boots over grayish-yellow

fitted buckskins and a simple white linen shirt open at the collar. His dark hair was tousled, as if he had been riding with such speed the wind had blown it hither and tither. Even dressed casually as he was, his bearing was every inch the proud, aristocratic duke. Her heart thumped a greeting.

He held a crop in his hand that, as he stood, he placed on the massive desk he had been negligently leaning against. "You're a day early." An easy smile spread across his face as he came toward her and quickly introduced her and Harry to his aunt, Lady Anthony, who barely acknowledged them. He took Sophia's hand and brought it to his lips.

The contact of his skin to hers caused sparks to shoot from her fingertips straight to her heart, and it was as if she were melting on the inside. A thick lock of his unruly hair fell over his simmering coal eyes as he bent his head. When he came up, he shoved the lock off his forehead and gave her a smile that seemed created especially for her. "I take it your journey was uneventful?"

She couldn't seem to speak. He was like...like the apple in the Garden of Eden. No, she quickly amended, he was likely more similar to the sinful snake. She choked back a nervous giggle.

"Dear God, she's mute," Lady Anthony murmured.

Sophia looked at the woman and frowned. She's expected a fat, wrinkled cow, but Nathan's aunt was lovely—the outside of her, at least. Her ice-blue silk gown showed she clearly possessed the feminine curves Sophia did not. She had pale skin that looked as soft as a baby's and didn't appear to have any rough patches like Sophia's did. Her hair, a rich chestnut color, sat in a high, twined knot atop her head to display a long, pretty neck. Sophia's hand fluttered self-consciously to her short hair and shame filled her, followed quickly by irritation that the woman could cause such an emotion so easily.

His aunt shook her head before speaking. "Scarsdale, you cannot do this! Look at the thing." She waved a hand at

Sophia. "I cannot make anyone accept this...this...*creature*. You will make me a laughingstock."

Sophia nostrils flared and she searched for a clever remark to flay the woman, but before she could speak, Nathan said, "If I were you, I would worry more, dear Aunt Harriet, about being homeless than being a laughingstock. Because if you don't accept Miss Vane, and do everything in your power to help soothe her entrance into Society, I will throw you out of the dowager house, regardless of Ellison's wishes. Are we clear?"

Sophia allowed a great big smile to spread across her face as she gazed at the shrew. She hoped the woman would apologize.

"We are clear," Lady Anthony replied in a glacial tone that contained no hint of remorse. "But hear me now, Scarsdale. You may threaten me all you wish, but I am no magic worker. I cannot turn a weed into a flower. My reach will only go so far. If you take this woman to London in her current state, they will devour her. You'll rue the day you failed to listen to me. I beg you, wait until..." Her frosty, gray gaze swept haughtily over Sophia's body from her slippers to her face. "Wait until you can at least properly clothe her, teach her manners, and do something about her wretched hair before bringing her into the lion's den. I fear there is nothing to be done about the rest of her."

✦✦✦✦✦

Nathan could have cheerfully wrung his aunt's neck for her blistering remarks about Sophia's appearance, especially when he glimpsed how pale Sophia had grown. He had the overwhelming urge to protect Sophia from his aunt. Sophia had not been born into Society. And though her father was a harsh, cruel man, he was a babe at the art of scathing comments compared to the ladies of the haute *ton*.

Nathan studied Sophia for a moment. He sincerely doubted all the training in the world would make her behave as a bored, vain, cruel socialite, which was exactly how she needed to act to fit in with the senseless, malicious ladies of the *ton*. And that fact, among many others, was why he fully intended to leave her in the country. He'd introduce her to Society, as was proper, when she was ready, but her days would be spent at Whitecliffe.

Of course, he'd not really considered just how much it might take to prepare Sophia. As much as he hated to admit it, perhaps his aunt had a solid point. Sophia was going to need a great deal of work to gain the needed polish and requisite aloofness. He briefly thought of Aversley's wife and how well she seemed to have adjusted to life in Town, yet maintained her unique ways, but Nathan dismissed the comparison. Amelia had been born a lady and had both known how to act and had the right family connections.

Sophia lacked the knowledge, connections, and beauty that Amelia had in spades. He glanced down at his soon-to-be bride and found her now scowling openly at his aunt, who had raised her lorgnette to inspect Sophia. He had to bite back a grin at her show of fortitude and restraint in the face of his aunt's obvious disdain. He'd half expected Sophia to fly at his aunt like a wolf attacking its prey.

Sensing all eyes in the room on him, waiting for him to say something, Nathan spoke. "Of course, Sophia will stay here after our marriage until she has time to—" he cast about in his mind for the exact right words to say in order to avoid injuring Sophia's pride or revealing the whole truth of his plans "—order a new wardrobe and feel comfortable in her role as duchess."

There. He smiled, pleased with the way that sounded. Glancing around the room, he first met his aunt's gaze, who nodded approvingly, then Harry's, who shook his head, and finally Sophia's, whose eyes were narrowed quite angrily at him.

The look reminded him of one his mother used to give him and filled him with the sudden need to show Sophia right away that she would never have control over him as his mother had once had over his father. "Aunt Harriet, you will remain here at Whitecliffe with Sophia until she is deemed ready to be introduced to London Society."

"That could take the rest of my life," his aunt muttered.

"Ah," he said without a touch of sympathy, "Then so be it. That will be all for now, Aunt Harriet. Go get some rest." He motioned toward the door, dismissing her.

His aunt's mouth opened and closed as if she might argue, but a single raised eyebrow from him and she clamped her jaw shut and marched out of the room in a swirl of skirts and ire. Once she was gone, silence descended upon the library, though he could have sworn he heard Sophia mentally cursing him. Then Sophia's face turned from angry to hurt, making him uncomfortable. It almost seemed that her lips were trembling.

"Gibson," he barked, desiring the solitude he was used to.

The butler appeared at Nathan's side. "Yes, Your Grace."

"Please show Miss Vane and her brother, Master Harry, to their guest chambers and see that they are provided with immediate baths. The wedding will take place tomorrow afternoon, and I'll be departing the next day for London. Instruct Mr. Dobbs of my plans so he may pack my trunks."

"Yes, Your Grace," the butler intoned, then swept his hand toward the door in his typical snooty fashion. "If you please," he commanded to Sophia and Harry. Nathan frowned. He'd need to remind Gibson later to always be respectful of Sophia, but as Nathan watched Harry and Gibson depart Sophia did not budge and he chuckled inwardly. She had a backbone stiffer than a solid plank of wood. He rather liked that fact, except she could not be allowed to think she could argue with him.

"What is it, Sophia?" he clipped.

"I would like a moment alone with you, Nathan."

He didn't like the demanding tone she had taken. He was not his father to be browbeaten by his wife, or soon-to-be wife.

"Call me Scarsdale unless we are alone," he said, reasserting himself. "Do you understand?"

"All right, *Scarsdale*. I'd like a moment alone with you, if it pleases you, *O Great and Mighty Duke*."

He should have been mad at her insolence, but he found it damned amusing that she had managed to make his name sound like a curse *and* that she had the nerve to reproach him for what she must perceive as high-handed treatment. Clearly, he and his future wife had a few rules to set. He waved Gibson, who was lingering by the door, to leave. "Take the boy."

Harry scowled at Nathan, then appeared to realize what he must be doing and schooled his young features. "Shall I st-stay with you, S-Sophia?"

"I'll be fine," she replied without hesitation.

Deep chagrin that he had made the child worry for his sister's safety filled Nathan. He was not a monster who was cruel to children. To prove it, he strode past Sophia and across the room, and knelt in front of Harry.

"I will never lay a finger on your sister. Do you understand?"

Harry nodded. "Yes, Your G-Grace. But words c-can s-sometimes hurt as much as b-blows."

"Harry!" Sophia admonished.

Careful with his motions so as not to frighten the boy, he nudged his chin with the tip of his knuckle. "Thank you for that much-needed reminder." His mother's words had been like a hammer blow each time they fell, and it appalled him that he'd become cold enough not to realize his words could have the same effect. He would take more care from here on out.

The boy nodded, amusingly enough as if approving what Nathan had said, and walked out the door where Gibson was now waiting.

Nathan stood and braced himself not to lose his temper with Sophia again. He would firmly, but kindly, explain how their relationship would work from this moment forward. He turned to face her, expecting her to be glaring at him, but her eyes shone as if she might cry.

Shocked, he stepped close to her and looked down into her now-upturned face.

Eight

Sophia was hurt and confused. One moment she had been sure Nathan was marrying her as a charity case and that she was making a terrible mistake, and then he had made comments that gave her hope he actually liked and admired things about her. Then he'd squelched that hope, again, by telling the butler to have his bags packed. No man who cared at all about the woman he was marrying would plan to leave her the day after their wedding. Yet, then he'd shown genuine kindness toward Harry, and the look of deep concern in his eyes told her he was truly worried he'd hurt her. But worry was not enough. If he didn't even want to live with her how could she possibly believe that this man could ever love her and treasure her? Her anger drained away and only hurt remained.

She'd not give up hope, she told herself. It was *hers*, and she had precious little she could say that about. She may be a fool for what she was about to do, but she would never receive love from a man who wanted to leave her in the country.

With the decision made, calmness settled over her. "I cannot marry you, Nathan."

His brows drew together, and then his lips pressed into a hard line. "I see. Is this your way of attempting to punish me for hurting you?"

She shook her head. "No. I would never purposely punish you." She wanted to offer explanation without offering the secrets of her heart. She refused to share those with a man who would never love her. "But I did overhear you speaking with your aunt before, and just now you made it clear you plan to return to Town without me. The thought of being left here alone with your aunt made me realize that, no matter what terrible things are to come with a ruined reputation and no husband, being left at the mercy of your aunt would be worse." That explanation would have to suffice.

A dark smile settled on his beautiful face. "You will only be in the country with my aunt a short time."

Sophia's heart began to pound harder as she stared at him. He was so beautiful with his dark looks, broad shoulders, and proud face. How easy it would be to relent to him. She thought she knew why, too. She was already in love with Nathan. Oh botheration. She was a cork-brained fool.

If only there was a chance he would ever truly feel something for her. Then she would stay and marry him.

"And after that?" she whispered. "What will you do with me after I am properly introduced in London?"

He sighed heavily. "You'll come back here and I'll visit you."

Her heart squeezed painfully. "You want to hide me away because you are ashamed of me, and I don't want that."

Weariness registered in his eyes, and he reached out, running the back of his hand down her cheek. "No, Sophia, it's not that. I'm simply not suited to be a doting husband."

"Living with one's wife would hardly qualify you as a doting husband," she muttered. "Clearly, you don't desire me, and I don't want to be married to a man who doesn't even desire me. Frankly, I want much more than that, though it would have been a good start."

⚜

Nathan wanted nothing more than to put an end to this day with a long, soak in the bath and a tumbler full of brandy, and he wanted it to happen in an expedient manner. His mood was foul, not amorous. He liked order, and ever since he'd met Sophia, his life had been marked by *disorder*. Not to mention that someone had tried to kill him—possibly twice—and that fact was ever present in his mind. When he'd gone to London he'd tried to see Sir Richard, the man he wanted to head an investigation, but Sir Richard had been out of town.

Sophia coughed loudly, and purposely by the mutinous look on her face. Nathan focused on her once more. If she needed to feel desired, he would assuage the need and then he'd get some rest, so he could focus with a clear mind on the matter of who wanted him dead. "Close your eyes, Sophia." He dropped his voice low and let it rumble from deep within his chest.

"Whatever for?" she asked, the picture of bright, blue-eyed innocence, which was amazing considering where she had grown up. But that innocence was also the problem at hand.

"Because I'm going to kiss you," he replied, sliding one hand around her narrow waist and inching the other up her back to cup the base of her neck. She stiffened as he curled his fingers around the delicate column of her neck, but given her inexperience, it was no surprise.

He tilted her head back and gently, ever so gently, he brushed his lips across hers. She didn't pull away or stiffen further. She pressed her mouth closer and rose up to her tiptoes, which surprised the hell out of him. Her lips were soft and hot, and damn it all if his lust didn't stir to life. He had intended to only give her a brief, chaste kiss, but those intentions disappeared.

Without hesitation, he deepened the kiss. Her lips molded to his as he massaged them, and he kneaded his fingers through her short, silky hair. She was sweet, like a fine brandy, and melted into his arms, mewling from her throat. Her heart pounded against his as he trailed his mouth down her neck to the beckoning space between her collarbones. He flicked his tongue over her skin and savored the shiver he elicited from her.

His blood hummed in his veins as moved lower to the slight swell of her breasts. He cupped them both with his hands and brushed his fingers over the hard buds straining against the material of her gown. His body responded in kind, hardening immediately with need. *Hell.* This had not been part of the plan. Yet, he found he didn't hate that he wanted her. He didn't love her—and he never would—so there was no danger in the desire she stirred.

Sliding one hand to her waist and the other to her face to tilt her chin up, he glanced down at her. Slowly, her thick black lashes rose to reveal eyes darkened to a stormy shade of blue. She gazed at him with unmistakable wonder. "I love you, Nathan," she said softly.

Bloody hell. "You do not love me," he corrected. "You desire me. There is a difference."

She nodded, frowned, and then shook her head. "No. I mean, yes." She grinned at him, and it was a lovely, beautiful thing that startled him. Hope, which she seemed to want to share with him, filled her smile. "I do desire you, but I also love you. I'm quite sure of it now."

"It will fade," he said, uncomfortable with the adoring way she was looking at him. Adoration could change to disgust in the time it took to exhale.

"Why would you think that?" she prodded.

He shrugged evasively. "Experience."

"I'm going to show you my love won't fade, Nathan. And then you will come to love me, too. I just felt it in here." She placed his palm against her pounding heart.

He stilled. How could she be so hopeful given her past? He admired it and pitied it. "Don't," he said as he moved his hand and pressed a finger to her lips. He wanted to spare her the pain of hope dashed. "I'm not going to explain my entire life thus far to you, Sophia, but you need to know I have no desire for love."

"That can't be so! Everyone wants to have love."

"I don't. Can you accept that?"

She nibbled on her lip for a moment before nodding. "For now."

"Forever," he corrected.

"*Forever* is such a formidable word. I personally have never cared for it. Frank told me I would be forever under his rule, but I knew differently." She gave him a quick peck on the cheek. "I better go to bed if I'm to be married tomorrow. I need to hang my gown and try to get out some of these wrinkles. There's much to do. Good night, Nathan."

Awe for her ability to see the bright side of her situation filled him. He watched as she turned to walk away in her threadbare gown and an idea struck him. He wanted to do something for her, something special. He couldn't give her exactly what she desired, but he could give her many gifts. "Wait one moment, if you please."

She swiveled back toward him. "Yes?"

"You cannot get married in that gown."

She glanced down at her gown, then back to him. "It's the best one I have."

"I thought it might be," he admitted. "If you are to be my duchess, however, you must start dressing the part immediately, and that begins with our wedding." She could have worn a sack for all he cared; it really made no difference since it would only be the two of them, her brother, his aunt, and the clergyman, except he wanted to do something nice for her. "We'll postpone the wedding for a few days. That should be long enough to have a gown made for you."

"Oh, Nathan!" Her face lit up, and before he knew it, she had raced across the room. She threw her arms around him. "I don't care at all about a new gown, but I'm touched." She hugged him with unrestrained fierceness, which had been the exact sort of hug he had longed for from his mother. The thought drove him out of her embrace in an instant.

When a wounded look crossed her face, he felt like a cad. "I'm sorry, Sophia. I'm not used to being embraced."

"Did your parents never hug you?"

"Did yours?" he shot back, employing an avoidance tactic he'd learned long ago when people asked probing questions.

She shook her head. "No. Frank never did, but Harry hugs me so hard I think he may cut off my air. It's wonderful."

"What happened to your mother?" he asked, realizing how

little he really knew about her.

"My mother died at my childbirth, and Harry's mother never was officially with Frank. She left Harry on our doorstep right after she birthed him."

He tried not to react to the news. He hadn't realized they were half siblings. "And then you took up the job of mothering Harry, and that's why you stayed at the tavern, wasn't it?"

She nodded. "I was trying to save up enough money so I could bring Harry with me when I left. I could make it on the streets, I'm sure of it. But I don't think he could."

It suddenly struck him that she was the most selfless person he had ever met, quite unlike his own mother. He was certain she had not ever wanted him. "Do you want children, Sophia?" he wondered aloud. Though, despite whether she did or not, he needed an heir.

"Oh yes," she said on a sigh. "I want to lavish all the love on them that was never given to me. I hope we have at least six."

"Six!" He burst out laughing.

"Too many?" she said, laughing, as well.

He sobered instantly. "I never considered that I would have more than the requisite one to carry on my line."

"It's lucky you met me, then. You have the power to make me a lady, and I have the ability to soften your heart."

With those words, she whispered good night and left the library. He let her go without correcting her erroneous notion that she could ever soften his heart. He'd hardened it long ago in order to survive, and he didn't have any desire to change that.

Nine

Sophia awoke the next morning, sat up, and got her first good look at her bedchamber. When the uppity butler had shown her to the room last night, it had been lit with candles. She had known instantly that it was magnificent by the enormous, breathtaking bed situated in the middle of the room, but the pervading darkness had made it hard to see everything properly. She glanced behind her and to the sides at the four-poster that encased her. The canopy reached all the way to the ceiling. Long velvet panels of rich gold and deep burgundy hung from golden rods at the top of the bed and billowed elegantly to the floor. A gold-and-burgundy wallpaper covered the walls, and to the right of the bed hung an oil painting of a stunning woman whose dark eyes matched Nathan's.

The woman had to be Nathan's mother. In fact, as Sophia looked around the room, she counted three paintings, all of Nathan's mother. It seemed odd to her that there were none of anyone else, and she made a mental note to ask Nathan—or better yet one of the servants—what the duchess had been like. She had a feeling Nathan would not be forthcoming with information regarding his personal life. Not yet.

Thoughts of Nathan brought last night's kiss to the forefront of her mind. That kiss had curled her toes, eased her fears, and changed her mind about going through with the marriage. That kiss had held so much promise.

From his lips, she had tasted his desire. From his chest, she had felt the thundering of his heart. With her ears, she had listened to his ragged breath, and she had known instantly that underneath his cold exterior he was hiding a man in need of love just as much as she was. She'd glimpsed his kindness and honor already. Now all she had to do was help him see that he did want love. He was afraid, she was sure. That had to be it. If she could show him he had nothing to fear from her, he would let down his guard.

A scratch came at the door, startling her.

"Good morning, miss," came a soft feminine voice from the hall.

Sophia took a deep breath and bid the woman to enter. A young, pretty blond girl with curves and luxurious hair opened the door and came in the room. Sophia's jealousy stabbed at her, and she fiddled with her own short hair. She forced her hand away when she realized the woman was staring at her. Sophia didn't take offense, for the woman had kind eyes and a smile played at the corners of her lips.

She dipped into a quick curtsy. "I'm Mary Margaret, your lady's maid. I hope it pleases you." The woman blushed. "I've always wanted to be a lady's maid but thought I'd be stuck in the kitchen the rest of my life, as His Grace didn't seem likely to take a lady, and I couldn't fathom leaving his employment as my family's been with His Grace's family since I was a baby."

Sophia mentally tried to rid herself of the fog of sleep that seemed to be making her brain function sluggishly. She could barely keep up with the woman's rapid speech. Or perhaps it was the glass of wine she'd drank last night. Having never had wine before, she'd been a little tentative to drink it, but when she'd seen the glass on her bedside table she had assumed it was customary to imbibe before bedtime. Why else would it be there? A yearning to fit in to Nathan's world and make him proud had gripped her, so she had decided to embrace its customs.

She pressed her fingertips to her temples. Embracing its customs had left her head a bit achy and her mouth felt dry, too. She made another mental note to discover if everyone partook before bed or if it would be acceptable to pass.

"Miss Vane? Have I lost you? I'm so sorry. My mother says I prattle on entirely too much!"

Sophia blinked, and Mary Margaret gave her a rather odd look, probably because Sophia had been sitting here like a dope, staring off into nothingness and not answering the woman.

"Do you wish me to try to fix your hair?"

Sophia looked at the woman's glossy strands once again, and her fingers crept back up to her shorn, rough edges. "My hair used to be my best feature." The words tumbled from her lips before she could stop them and caused a lump to lodge in her throat.

Mary Margaret nodded. "It's a stunning color. If you'll let me, I'll simply soften the edges and style it for you. Were you ill?"

The question confused Sophia for a moment, as her mind was still trapped in that weird fog, but as she got out of bed, it occurred to her that the maid was referring to her hair. Sophia shook her head as she followed Mary Margaret to a dressing table that stole Sophia's breath. It was made of a dark, gleaming wood and had so many little drawers that it boggled the mind. In the center of the table was a round looking glass.

Mary Margaret smiled at Sophia. "Amazing, isn't it?"

Sophia nodded.

The lady's maid—*her* lady's maid, she reminded herself—bent down and pulled on two tiny brass knobs on either side of the table, and secret doors folded open in an accordion manner. They revealed more drawers and two more cut pieces of looking glass. "This was Her Grace's."

Sophia froze, halfway to the green velvet-cushioned chair. "Nathan was married before?"

Mary Margaret seemed confused. "Do you mean His Grace?"

Sophia nodded.

"I'm sorry. No one ever calls him by his Christian name, so it gave me pause, but goodness no. His Grace has never been married. Truth be told, below stairs we had a running wager whether he ever would get married."

"Oh really?" Sophia said as casually as she could and took her seat. "Why was that? Because he had so very many ladies, I suppose."

Mary Margaret shrugged. "I've already said too much. My mother would be livid if she knew I was gossiping about His Grace, and so would he."

"I'll not tell him or your mother," Sophia promised. "You are to be my lady's maid even after I'm married, I take it?"

Mary Margaret nodded. "If I please you."

Sophia picked up a silver-gilded brush and had to remember not to gape at the expensive thing. She knew so little about Nathan, and perhaps the best way to fill in the missing gaps was to get the information from Mary Margaret. "I've never had a maid, but I would like to think that we will be very good friends." Sophia felt a flash of guilt because gaining a new friend had not really been at the front of her mind, but if she gained Mary Margaret as a friend and learned something about Nathan in the process that would be wonderful.

"Friends?" Mary Margaret's eyebrows had risen with surprise.

"Yes. I realize it's probably not customary, but it's what I wish. And as friends, we will tell each other secrets."

"All right," the woman hedged.

"I'll tell you one now," Sophia offered, praying it would inspire the woman to reveal some information about Nathan's past. "My father is a drunkard."

Mary Margaret's eyes went wide. "My cousin's father is, too."

Sophia let out a relieved breath that Mary Margaret seemed willing to share. "I don't know His Grace very well, but I very much want to, since we are to be married. Would you help me?"

Mary Margaret glanced over her shoulder, then back at Sophia. "May I close the door?"

Sophia nodded, biting back a gleeful smile.

When Mary Margaret returned to the dressing table, she pulled open another drawer and removed a pair of scissors. "My mother is the head housemaid and she's always got her ear out."

"Then it's a good thing you thought to close the door," Sophia said.

Mary Margret grinned. "I've been working in the kitchen with my mother since I was eight and I'm twenty now, so tell me what it is you wish to know. If I didn't personally see it, I'd wager my mother did and has spoken about it. She chides me for all my gabbing, but I get it from her."

"Did your mother ever say what His Grace's childhood was like? Was his mother kind? And his father?"

A dark cloud settled over Mary Margaret's face. "His father was kind enough when he was around, which was scarce little. But his mother..." Mary Margaret pursed her lips. "She was a different story altogether. Wicked mean and unpredictable, that one. The servant children, including myself"—Mary Margaret blushed—"used to hide when we knew she was coming because we feared one of her mood swings or scoldings."

Mary Margaret had been snipping Sophia's hair as she talked, and she paused now. "Look to your lap, please."

Sophia obeyed instantly. "Was she at least kind to Nathan?"

Mary Margaret snorted. "No. She was worse to him than to anyone. Always putting him down and yelling at him. Mother says it got even worse the more her husband stayed away. But goodness, he stayed away because she was such a mean harpy! Terrible predicament, that. Especially for your future husband. A cruel mother and an almost totally absent father." Mary Margaret tsked.

Tears burned Sophia's eyes but she blinked them back. "Nathan must have wanted her love so badly," she whispered.

"No doubt," Mary Margaret agreed. "But that was a useless desire."

Sophia thought about Frank. She understood how painful

124   *Julie Johnstone*

it was to feel unloved. She understood how much the want throbbed in you and ate at you not to have a parent's affection, until you were sure the longing would kill you unless you could just let it go. And she had with Frank. One morning, when she was around twelve or so, she had woken up and had simply stopped hoping Frank would love her. Nathan, it seemed, had taken it a step further than she had. Had he woken up one day and simply stopped hoping to ever be loved at all, or had it not even been a decision he was aware of? She understood now, or she thought she did: he didn't desire love because, in the past, wishing for love had never been successful and it had hurt him deeply.

What she had just learned made her more determined than ever to give Nathan her love and help him see that she would not snatch her love away, nor was it something he had to earn.

"I'm done, Miss Vane. And if I may be so bold, your hair looks lovely, though I do think you should grow it a bit. You never did say if you were sick or not."

Sophia blinked, a trifle irritated that her mind still felt foggy. "I wasn't sick. My father, the toad, cut it for money." Sophia glanced into the looking glass and gasped at her reflection. Mary Margaret had a way with scissors. The choppiness of the crude haircut that Frank had given her, that she herself had tried and failed to make look better, now curled softly around the nape of her neck instead of spiking out in jagged edges. She jumped up and hugged a stunned Mary Margaret. "You are a miracle worker!"

Mary Margaret grinned. "Thank you, Miss Vane."

"Call me Sophia."

"Oh no, I couldn't. You'll be the duchess in a few days, and it wouldn't be proper."

"As you wish," Sophia relented, knowing she had to learn the rules of etiquette and try to follow them. "Rest assured I'm going to let my hair grow, but thank you for making me look decent again."

"I cannot wait to see what Madame Lexington does with

you."

"Who?"

"Madame Lexington. His Grace sent a note into the village for her to be here at noon to fit you for an entire new wardrobe. She used to be the duchess's dressmaker. She was transported straight over from France to please the duchess. She's waiting below to be sent up to you."

"Do you mean to tell me it's noon?" Sophia asked in surprise.

"'Twas noon when I came to wake you. Madame Lexington has been here a half hour already."

"My goodness, really?" Sophia rushed over to one of the windows and drew the heavy silk curtains back to look at the sun in the sky, but down below she could just make out Nathan and Harry standing in the most exquisite garden imaginable, facing each other with what looked like rapiers raised in the air. Such happiness filled Sophia that she felt as if she would burst. She turned back to Mary Margaret, determined to get the business of being fitted for dresses out of the way, so she could go to the garden and thank Nathan, both for his generosity and for giving time to Harry. "Go fetch Madame Lexington, then, please."

Mary Margaret bobbed a curtsy and returned within minutes with the seamstress in tow. Despite Sophia's determination to hurry through the fittings, they took many hours and all she could do was stand there like an obedient dog and get poked, prodded, and tsked at. And all the while, Madame Lexington mumbled under her breath about Sophia's lack of development. The least the woman could have done was mumble in French so Sophia wouldn't have understood her slanders.

When Madame Lexington bustled out of the bedchamber, followed by a housemaid who had just finished cleaning up the lunch repast they'd partaken in, Sophia collapsed into the chair and marveled momentarily that her wedding dress and a few other essential garments would be ready in such a short time, and then an entire wardrobe would follow soon after.

She squeezed her eyes shut and laid her head back to listen to the creaks and groans of the giant house. She tried to picture Nathan here with his mother as a child. How lonely and sad he must have been. For a while, she rubbed her aching neck and back, then finally opened her tired eyes and dragged herself out of the chair to put on the same gown she'd worn the night before. She wanted to find Nathan and she couldn't do so in her chemise. Before she even picked up her gown a knock came at the door.

"Enter," she bade, assuming it was the seamstress who must have forgotten something.

The door opened with a slow creak and Nathan himself, heart-stopping in skintight pantaloons, gleaming black hessians, and another simple open-collared linen shirt, stepped into the room.

✦✦✦✦✦

Nathan had argued with himself all the way up the stairs about whether or not to come see Sophia. But when her brother had told him how she used to take beatings from Frank so Harry would not receive them, all Nathan had wanted to do was see her. He didn't know why exactly. It wasn't proper to be in here, but they were to be married in two days, so what did it really matter at this point if he came into her bedchamber?

As he stepped in the room, though, his gaze fastened on the twin peaks of her hardened nipples straining against the fabric of her chemise, and white-hot lust surged through his veins. It was almost laughable, his sudden desire for this woman who looked more like a girl than a woman. Except she *was* a woman and would soon be *his* wife, and he wanted her with a need that shocked him.

He'd felt plenty of lust in his life, but he couldn't remember ever experiencing such a craving as the one that coursed through him at this moment. It almost made him feel as if he'd go mad if he didn't have her, and he didn't like that one bit. Ever since last night in the library when she'd told him she loved him, he'd been unable to rid her from his thoughts. Getting up before the sun even rose this morning and practicing riding and then swordplay with her brother had not wiped her from the forefront of his mind, especially as her brother relayed stories of how she had endured many of the spankings from their father that had been meant for young Harry.

As he closed the door with the heel of his boot, it struck him that surely she was not as good as she seemed. It was almost a relief to think this. His father had thought his mother good and kind, and been proven more than wrong.

"Come here, Sophia." His voice was more of a growl than anything. She swallowed hard but, to her credit, came across the room and stood directly in front of him. When she glanced up, he blinked at how angelic she looked with her hair curling in soft, dark ringlets around her neck.

He reached out and wrapped a silky strand around his finger. "I see your lady's maid cut your hair."

Sophia nodded. "Do you like it?"

He tensed at the question. His mother used to ask him such trick questions. If he answered yes, she would demand to know exactly why he felt as he did, and then proceed to scream at him that his reasons were not good enough. And if he answered no... Well, it served no good purpose to remember her raging fits on the few occasions he dared to answer in the negative to one of those questions. "It's very becoming," he offered.

She beamed up at him, and his heart did a sort of skip in his chest. With obvious hesitation, she placed her hand on his chest and his muscles jumped to full awareness of the heat of her palms seeping through his shirt. "I'm going to let it grow out again, and I promise I'll look better then."

The eagerness to please him that he saw in her eyes touched him, and softness he hadn't thought himself able to feel any longer slammed into him like a wave. He laced one hand into her soft hair and trailed the other to the feminine curve where her buttocks and back met. *Just one kiss,* he promised himself. One kiss and he would be satisfied. He didn't need more. He didn't need anything from anyone. Slowly, he slid his fingers back and forth over the slight dip and rise of her body until her eyes darkened and her lids lowered to half-mast.

"I shouldn't be in here," he whispered in her ear before he nipped the irresistible thing with his teeth and then flicked his tongue over the sensitive flesh.

She moaned and leaned closer to him, until her lips were near his ear. "If it's not proper, why are you here?"

He paused for a moment, struggling to put words to emotions he barely understood. "To tell you that you are the bravest woman I've ever met," he said, trailing kisses across her neck all the way to her other ear, which he traced slowly with the tip of his tongue. She shivered beneath his touch, and though she clung to his arms, she leaned back and gazed up at him.

"What is that unexpected compliment for?"

"For the beatings you took to protect your brother," he replied. "I admire you. It's as simple as that."

But was it?

Before he could say more, she touched her mouth to his with a sweet, urgent fumbling of a kiss. "Just one kiss," she rasped as she pulled away to press her lips to the pulse of his neck.

"Of course," he agreed huskily, his body responding wildly to the pressure of her lips against his neck.

"Maybe a bit more," she moaned. "I—Well, this feels quite good."

Their one kiss was spiraling out of control fast, but as her hands slid to his shoulders and she tugged on him, he could not have stopped his reaction if he wanted to, and he did not want to.

"Maybe we could kiss on the bed?" she suggested in a throaty voice while he kissed the steady pulse at the juncture between her collarbones.

He nodded and wrapped his arms around her waist, lifted

her, and carried her to the bed. He laid her down gently near the edge, so that her bottom was almost hanging off, and then he kneeled before her and kissed her in long caresses meant to rob her of her senses. But soon he felt as if what he had actually done was rob himself of control.

He needed to feel her. All of her.

He gazed at her eyes as they burned with desire, and her lips, swollen and red from his touch. "Sophia," he began, his tone coming out low and gravelly. He placed his hands on her slender thighs. "I want to touch you. May I?"

She nodded.

Slowly, he pushed up the material covering her legs and her feminine parts, and with the care cultivated from years of experience, he gently spread her legs. When she froze and her legs pushed back against his hands, he paused and locked his gaze with hers. "Do you want to wait until we're married?"

It was reasonable. It was understandable. It was proper. He'd never been proper, but he'd wait for her if it was what she wanted.

"No, but I've never done anything like this," she whispered in a trembling voice filled with unmistakable longing.

Soft, foreign feelings surged through him. "I swear to God I'll go slow, and if you want me to stop, I will."

She nodded and pressed her hand over his for moment before releasing it with a soft sigh.

Swallowing, he slid his hands up the insides of her thighs, curved them over her taut belly, and ran them over her sharp hip bones. He reveled in the quivering answer of her body. Fierce possessiveness gripped him as his fingers brushed her unmentionables, and he drew them down her lithe legs and threw them behind him.

He traced a light path with his palms and fingers over her legs and back to her inner thighs, where he once again parted her legs, never breaking eye contact with her. He watched as her eyes widened and she bit her lip, but she didn't fight him.

"Lay back, Sophia." He wanted to introduce her to pleasure beyond anything she could have ever imagined before he caused her the unavoidable pain of taking her maidenhead.

She slowly lowered her body until all he could see was the gentle slope of her small, proud breasts outlined under the thin gown. His body throbbed with the need to be inside her, but he pushed his need down and moved his fingers into the dark hair that covered her sex, exploring her. He knew the moment he found the spot that would bring her the most pleasure by the bucking of her body and the low, throaty moan that came from her. He rubbed her first in languishing circles, basking in the way she squirmed and how her head thrashed back and forth on the bed. The more pleasure he brought her, the greater his own need grew until it was almost painful, and he combated his own desire with faster strokes against her swollen flesh.

Whimpers came from her and her hands clenched the coverlet of the bed, making it bunch in her tiny fists. "Oh, please," she moaned. "Please, please. I can't take it."

He chuckled as he lowered himself all the way between her legs and kissed one silken thigh and then the other. "This is a prelude, my dear."

"To what?" she asked in a breathless voice.

His answer was to part her folds and draw his tongue slowly down her hot, moist flesh. As she cried out, his blood pounded through his veins. The need to taste her, please her, and possess her overcame him, and he slid his hands under her buttocks and lifted her so he could be closer to her, so he could bring her exquisite pleasure. He answered every cry and whimper with another slow slide of his tongue over her throbbing sex, and when she began to beg him again, he responded by circling his tongue around the spot that he knew would take her to the edge and drop her into perfect, fatigued oblivion.

His heart thundered in his ears as he kissed her, stroked her, and made her his, and when she screamed that she could take no more, he suckled her in long pulls as he moved his hands to her breasts and rubbed the hard peaks of her nipples. Suddenly, her back arched and her hands twined in his hair and drew his face closer to her. Her hips surged upward and her warmth invaded his mouth. She shook for a long moment, and then her body went slack in his hands. Gently, he lowered her to the bed, kneeled, and looked down at her.

In that moment, she was the most beautiful creature he had ever seen—guileless, trusting, and seductively innocent. The trust she had placed in him to do with her body what he pleased obliterated some of the cynicism inside him and made him want to try to trust her as she had just trusted him. Leaning down, he stroked a hand through her short locks, and her eyes came slowly open, heavy with the drug of sexual sedation.

"I want to be inside you, Sophia, but I can wait."

"If having you in me feels anything like the pleasure I just experienced, then *I* can't wait," she said, blushing furiously. "I love you, Nathan, and I want you to give me your love."

Her confession struck a need in him he had buried long ago. And the love shining in her eyes scared the hell out of him. He didn't want to be responsible for making her miserable, but he couldn't turn away from her, either. Looking down at her, he traced his finger over her delicate collarbone before speaking. "Making love will hurt the first time."

"I trust you," she replied softly.

"Christ, Sophia." Her naïve belief that he was good crumbled something in him. He bent down and brushed his lips to hers. The desire to truly earn her trust filled him, yet he felt compelled to make her understand he was not as good as she thought. "Take care with giving me your trust."

Ten

It was on the tip of her tongue to argue with him that his warning proved he could be trusted, but she sensed that he needed her to relent in this. She nodded, and as she did, his mouth slanted over hers in a fierce, hungry kiss. Gone was the tenderness he had shown moments before, and in its place were fierce need and passion. He'd been holding back for her; it was clear when he growled low in his throat and gave her drugging kiss after drugging kiss.

Her senses reeled, and she felt as if she were in a daze. When cool air hit her skin and she realized her chemise had been slipped off her body, she had utterly no idea how it had come to pass. Her instinct was to cross her arms over her breasts, but Nathan stopped her hands and uncrossed her arms. "Never hide yourself from me. Never be ashamed of who you are."

She swallowed the lump in her throat. "That's easy for you to say," she whispered as she glanced at his perfect body.

His hands cupped her breasts and then his thumbs came to her sensitive buds and rubbed over the flesh that peaked to greet him. "It's not," he replied. "The picture you see on the outside may be pretty, but the inside is ugly."

She reached a shaking hand up to his sculpted face. "I doubt that."

His eyes became hooded, and she knew he would not reveal more. She trailed her fingers over his strong jawline. She would reveal some of her fear in hopes that one day he would reveal some of his. "You're so perfect, and I'm so very flawed."

He stood so abruptly she feared he was about to agree with her and then walk out of this room and her life. He looked down at her from his towering stance, reached behind him to tug off his shirt, and revealed a rippling abdomen and muscled chest. She stared in awe and wistfulness; his body—marred only at his shoulder by the bandage covering his healing wound—was every bit as beautiful as his face.

"I have flaws as well, Sophia," he growled as he yanked his boots off, then his pants and undergarments. She gaped at the size and power of his body that could not be denied now that he stood there without a stich of clothing.

"No," she whispered, inwardly cringing at how very unmatched they were.

His gaze grew hard. "Expecting perfection from me will hurt us both. I like that you're not perfect. Do you understand?"

She understood that he'd been hurt deeply and that he was trying to tell her how without saying it explicitly. "I do."

He lowered himself over her, and something fierce glittered in his eyes. "I'll hurt you and I'll fail you, and then you'll see. You won't think me perfect. You won't want to love me then."

"Come to me, Nathan," she replied, knowing arguing was futile. "Show me your imperfections." She wanted to offer him the kind of love neither of them had ever had, and she prayed that in doing so, he would eventually want to give her that same love in return.

Her breasts ached as his fingers once again grazed her flesh. He lowered his head, so that all she could see were his broad, powerful shoulders and his thick, curling dark hair. His tongue flicked her nipple and all thoughts of what she'd planned to do fled, pushed out by need and the desire to meet him in a place she'd never gone. Shivers of delight ravaged her body as he trailed kisses down her belly and back up to claim her mouth in a luxurious kiss.

Then he was parting her legs and her body was so hungry

to know him that she could not have resisted even if she had wanted to. He hovered above her, sweat dampening his brow and the muscles of his arms bulging with the effort to take things slow for her. She was deeply touched that he would make such an obviously painful attempt to hold himself back. She gripped his arms, which was like holding on to steel and tugged at him until he came closer and kissed her once more. His heartbeat pulsed against her chest for one moment before his intense gaze locked with hers.

"Sophia?"

Her name was an aching question and a request for permission from this man who was so powerful, virile, and kind. Tears burned her eyes as she nodded and moved her hands to grip his back as he slid all the way between her thighs and the hard, hot length of him pressed into her folds, making her wince.

Before the hiss fully left her mouth, he covered her lips with his as if to take her pain from her, and then he was inside of her. It was tight at first, pinching. He moved in and out with long, careful strokes that created a friction that made her groin tighten around him. Deep within her belly, an ache blossomed. Each stroke from his tip all the way down his shaft built a pressure inside of her until she thought she would scream with a need she could not name. It wasn't quite the same as before when he'd kissed her down there. This felt more urgent, more sensitive, more pleasurably painful.

"Nathan," she finally whimpered, unable to explain what she wanted him to do.

He answered by plunging deep within her and then withdrawing very slowly, only to do it again. And again. The pressure continued to build, and inside of her everything constricted in an effort to keep her from coming apart. And then she did come apart in wave after pulsating wave that started at her core and washed over her entire body. As she spun out of control, her body contracting around his, he moved faster, withdrawing and plunging until she released a final scream of pleasure he caught with his mouth. Underneath her clinging fingertips, his muscles jumped and coiled as he buried himself to the hilt before shuddering. A flood of warm liquid filled her while his muffled groan caressed her ear.

He lay on top of her, heavy and crushing, as their hearts beat as one, fast and furious. She didn't move and she prayed he wouldn't, either. The moment was perfect, and she didn't want it to end, even though in the recesses of her mind she knew that it must. He rolled off her and pulled her to him so that she was pressed against the full length of his body as he cradled her to his chest. Her head rested against his arm. She stared at his noble profile, wondering when he would speak and what he might say. After a bit, he turned to look at her, a frown creasing his brow. "Did I hurt you?"

"No." His eyes held a world of skepticism, so she decided to try to be as truthful as possible. "It hurt for the briefest of moments, but it was wonderful. You are wonderful. I very much like kissing and all that goes with it."

"We shall see if you still think that after we're married."

"Why would marriage change how I think?"

"It seems to have that effect on women," he said.

"Well, it will not have that effect on me. There is nothing you can ever do that will make me not love you."

Something strange flickered in his gaze. "What if I took a mistress?"

Blast him. She would hate him for that, but... She stared at his face, at once calculating and contemplating, and she barely held in a shocked gasp. She'd stumbled upon his fear quite by accident. She was sure of it.

She licked her lips nervously, aware he was waiting for her to answer. "That would most definitely make me hate you."

He nodded, as if he'd expected her to say her love was not strong and would not be steadfast. She laid her hand on his cheek and felt his muscles twitch under her fingertips. "I would hate you for that. It's true. I would despise you because it would mean you did not love me enough to be faithful to me, to want only me. But I wasn't even considering that you would ever be unfaithful, Nathan. I was speaking of the normal everyday life we will have." She swallowed the large lump of fear lodged in her throat. "Will you be faithful to me?"

"Of course," he said, but he withdrew his arm from underneath her head and then got out of bed. She watched him retrieve his clothes in tense silence, all the while wondering if he would say any more. Sitting up, she clutched the sheet to her breasts as Nathan moved to a chair and paused in pulling on his boots to look at her once again. "I'm sorry if I seem cold."

She plucked at the sheet, wishing she could take the words back and hold them until later, so they could have had a bit more time with his guard down as he held her. "I suppose you think me foolish," she said, trying to imagine how he must picture her.

"I don't think you foolish at all. I think you are full of eternal optimism for life, despite the hand life has dealt you. I wish I could share in that hope."

She scrambled out of bed and gathered the sheet around her as she did. Padding across the floor to Nathan, she knelt in front of him. "You can. Start with me. Hope in me. Give me your heart and I'll fill it up."

"Ah, Sophia." He ran a finger along her jawbone. "I am going to give you my name, my protection, and my fidelity, but you don't really want my heart. It's a black thing."

"Stop saying that," she scolded. "I've seen the good in you."

His hand dropped away from her face, but his gaze bore into her. "You see an illusion. I'm not good. If you knew what I'd done in my life—"

"Tell me," she interrupted. "Tell me your worst." She was going to show him that his past would not make her turn away from him.

"You want to know my worst?" His voice had grown low and harsh, and his face twisted into a sneer. Despite herself, a tremor of fear raced through her. Yet, she nodded.

He leaned very close to her so that their noses almost touched and all she could see was the swirling depths of his eyes. "When I was sixteen I slept with my best friend's mother at his birthday celebration. I knew she was lonely, and I took advantage of her. I took her in her bedchamber while her husband, who worshipped the ground she walked on, was below stairs celebrating their son's birthday with all their guests."

Sophia swallowed hard, fighting back the mental image flooding her mind and the nausea filling her stomach. He wanted her to be shocked and disgusted. She refused to fall into his trap. There had to be more to the story than what he'd just told. "When did your parents die?"

"God, Sophia." A hollow laugh filled the room. "That doesn't matter."

"It does," she insisted. "I'm sure you were lonely, too. Had they died very close to that time?" He probably hadn't been thinking clearly in his grief. Though his mother was unkind and his father absent, Sophia was sure he had grieved them.

"Not long before," he admitted, "but that's no excuse for what I did."

The anguish and remorse he felt for what he'd done was apparent on his twisted face. "I disagree," she said firmly. "Grief doesn't totally excuse your actions, but I imagine when you lose someone you love, grief clouds your judgment."

"I didn't love my mother."

It was said in such a cold, matter-of-fact way that Sophia's breath caught in her throat. He had loved her; he just didn't want to admit it. The bitterness, likely instigated by his unreturned affection, was apparent in his words but more so in how stiff he had become. She swallowed the urge to argue with him. "Well, I'm sure you loved your father and that loss must have hurt."

"The eternally hopeful one," he said instead of answering her. A wry smile played at the corner of his lips, but it did not touch his eyes. "I've some business to attend to before dinner, but I'll see you shortly."

Sophia nodded and watched as he slipped out of the room. Kneeling still, she let her mind recall every detail of earlier when he had held her in his arms and taken her with such tenderness. Now a smile pulled at her lips. He could not hide his gentle, caring side in the moments they came together with nothing more between them than air.

Standing, she strolled to the washbasin while humming a tune she recalled from years ago. She took her time carefully cleaning away the smeared traces of her given innocence on the inside of her thighs, and then she slipped on her gown and hurriedly put herself back in order. She wanted to find Harry and tell him not to divulge any more secrets of their past. She didn't want Nathan's eternal pity. What she wanted was his love.

As she made her way down the ornate staircase, she spotted Harry coming through the terrace door with a grin on his face. "Harry!" she called, then rushed to greet him. "I want to talk to you."

Before she got all the way down the stairs, he met her halfway and flew into her arms to hug her with such force it felt as if her ribs might break. "Guess what?" he asked in a voice brimming with the kind of enthusiasm only children possessed.

"What?"

"His Grace promised to teach me how to ride horseback, and he's already s-started instructing me on how to fence. He says I'll need these skills so I can fit in at school."

"At school?" Sophia asked with surprise.

Harry nodded. "He's g-going to send me to Eton. It's where he went."

Sophia grinned. "Harry, you hardly stuttered just now."

He nodded. "I know! His Grace taught me a secret."

"Did he?" She looped her arm through Harry's and tugged him down the stairs to the first open door she could find. She froze. The room appeared to be a female's sitting room, judging by the color scheme of fuchsia, white, and light green. A beautiful silk material covered several pieces of furniture, and there were no less than three full-sized portraits of the late duchess.

Harry snorted. "His Grace's mama really l-loved herself. Mr. Burk, the stable master, told me there are f-fifteen life-sized portraits in the house of her."

"My, you've been busy," Sophia teased.

"You too," Harry said. "When you didn't come down after your fittings, Lady Anthony sent me back outside. She said you were busy servicing His Grace. Did you shine his boots?"

Sophia's cheeks burned so hot she wanted to fan herself. "No. We had to talk about a few things." How could that horrid woman know what they'd been doing? Or that Nathan had even been in her room? Maybe she had meant something else with her words.

Sophia tried to calm herself. It didn't matter what his aunt thought. In a few days, she would be Nathan's wife. The woman could not harm her.

"Tell me the secret Nathan taught you about your stuttering," she said, changing the subject.

"If I tell you the secret it wouldn't be a secret, but guess what?"

The way Harry grinned at her made Sophia's heart ache with joy. "What?"

"His Grace used to stutter as a child. His mother would make awful fun of him for his problem, so that it g-got to every time he t-talked to her, it would take him an eternity to get the sentence out. She t-took to sitting him in a chair in front of all the s-servants' children and they would throw small rocks at h-him each time he stuttered."

Sophia barely muffled the sob that choked her. If a heart could break in sympathy, hers had just shattered. "Nathan told you all that?"

Harry shook his head. "Just that he stuttered, and then he told me not to feel ashamed 'cause it was just a m-matter of concentrating on the words and the secret."

"Who told you about his mother and what she used to do to him when he stuttered?"

"Oh, Mrs. Prichard, the downstairs kitchen maid. I wandered in there to get a snack and she filled my belly up with

cookies and my ears up with history. I feel very bad for His G-
Grace. That's even w-worse than Frank teasing me."

Sophia nodded. "Yes, it is. I don't think Nathan's mother
was a very nice person." Sophia glanced at the portrait nearest
them. The duchess had been stunning on the outside, but the
inside had been ugly. Suddenly, Sophia didn't mind not being
beautiful if it meant she had a heart.

"Incredible, wasn't she?" a grating voice said from the
doorway.

Sophia's back stiffened at the arrival of Nathan's aunt. She
didn't want to take any chances the woman would say
something wicked about her in front of Harry, so she patted
him on the hand to get him to look at her. "Go wash up before
dinner. You wouldn't want Nathan to see you at the dinner
table with grubby hands."

"Children do not eat with adults," Lady Anthony said in an
acidic voice. "And besides that, you needn't worry about
Scarsdale being offended by the child's grubbiness."

"Why is that?" Sophia asked, giving Harry a shove to send
him on his way.

Harry was barely out the door when the aunt said, "Because, my dear. He won't be back for dinner." She grinned
rather maliciously at Sophia.

The idea of having to sit through dinner with Nathan's
aunt without him there made Sophia wince. "Did he have to
leave to attend to business?"

Lady Anthony smirked. "The business of being a man. You
may have serviced him earlier today, but apparently, you did
not quench his appetite."

Anger surged through Sophia, thankfully allowing no
room for embarrassment. "I don't have any notion what you
mean."

"Come, my dear. We are soon to be related. Let us be
truthful, if nothing else. I saw Scarsdale go into your bedchamber and not come out for quite a long time. Do you mean
to tell me you were simply talking?"

"I don't mean to tell you anything," Sophia said through

clenched teeth.

"Oh dear. I'm sorry. I fear I'm getting us off to a rather bad start."

The lightning-flash change in her demeanor stunned Sophia. Lady Anthony's words were sweet and soft, and a beatific smile lit her face. The woman let out a disgruntled sigh. "I'm angry with Scarsdale and I'm letting my anger seep out onto you. That's not fair. I did my best to raise him to be a good man when my sister died, but so often I fear I failed."

"The late duchess was your sister?"

Lady Anthony nodded. "Yes. Isn't it funny how we married brothers? Everyone used to say so."

"I hadn't realized that was the case. I suppose it is quite ironic," Sophia hedged, not wishing to bring out the other side of Nathan's aunt with the wrong words.

"Oh, yes, my dear departed husband and Scarsdale's father were brothers. Such a small world it is, hmm?" Lady Anthony strolled across the room to stand beside Sophia. She glanced up at the portrait. "People always stared at my sister. Do you know, as far back as I can recall, I cannot think of a time when we were out together that someone did not stop to stare at her or simply tell her how beautiful she was. It was very hard on her when she started to feel as if her beauty was fading."

Sophia remained silent. Lady Anthony was quite pretty herself, but Sophia got the distinct sense that the woman had felt less than lovely in her sister's presence.

Lady Anthony turned to Sophia and gripped her hand in a cold, bony grasp. "From the moment Scarsdale was born he had that same effect on people. They stared at him in awe and wonder, so very enchanted with the perfect duke. I think it quite perturbed my sister," she said with a chuckle.

"Whyever would it bother her that her son was adored?"

"Why, because it was less adoration for her, of course. She got rather testy about it, actually. I didn't have that problem. My son came out fat and slow, and now he's a cripple. No one stares at him, except, of course, in pity."

The woman's vile words made Sophia's stomach turn. It

took her a moment before she was sure her voice would not tremble with disgust. "You mentioned that Nathan would not be at dinner?"

Lady Anthony's eyebrows rose high on her forehead. "Didn't he instruct you to call him Scarsdale unless you were alone with him?"

Sophia couldn't fathom how she would know that. She was sure Nathan nor Harry would have told Lady Anthony. Perhaps the butler had told her? Sophia was not about to ask her, so she nodded. "Where is Scarsdale?"

Lady Anthony's lips turned down at the corners and her eyes narrowed. "At his mistress's home, of course. He summoned her here when he came last week." The words had the precision of a carefully aimed dagger.

"No." Sophia shook her head in denial, even as her stomach plummeted. "He said I'd have his fidelity."

"Oh, my dear." Lady Anthony hugged Sophia to her. "Scarsdale is a rake to the core. He doesn't have a faithful bone in his body. That would mean he loved you, and rakes are above such emotions. But take heart, I'm sure he'll be very discreet. Now my own husband…" She waved a hand in the air. "He was a terrible, cruel brute, but that is a story for another day. Shall we go in to dinner now? It's really time, and I can start your lessons on how to be a proper lady so maybe Scarsdale will concede to bring you into Town once in a while and not keep you hidden in the country." She grinned in a twisted, terrible way.

Sophia couldn't move or talk. Her stomach turned and her head spun. And she was clammy. The room was stifling hot, and she wanted to shove Nathan's aunt away and race out the door into the open air. Or maybe she wanted to go to bed. Was it true? Had Nathan lied to her? Had he said she would have his fidelity, then gone off and left her with his wretched aunt while he bedded another woman hours after bedding her?

Sophia wanted to scream in rage, but she had to keep control of herself. "I think I'll check on Harry and retire for the night. I'm very tired from the trip."

"Quite understandable. I'll see you in the morning, and we can start our lessons."

Sophia nodded and made her way out of the room and up the stairs. She passed her bedchamber and asked a maid where the nursery was, because she knew Harry was there. After seeing that he had a dinner tray and meeting the maid who was acting as a temporary nanny, Sophia made her way to her room, worry and sadness slowing her steps. She didn't want to believe Nathan was with another woman, but her mind raced with terrible images.

When she entered her bedchamber, Mary Margaret was turning down the bed. Sophia's eyes widened in horror. The towel she'd used earlier to wipe away her blood must have been removed by the maid. She blanched instantly, and without meeting the other woman's eyes, she made her way to the bedside table where a full goblet stood, just as it had the previous night. After retrieving it, she tested the liquid and recognized the wine. Tonight, she didn't even hesitate to drink the spirit. She needed something to slow her racing mind and calm her down.

"Miss Vane, do you want me to help you out of your gown?"

"No, that's all right." Sophia picked a string on her gown for a moment, wanting to ask Mary Margaret if she knew where Nathan was, but she was almost afraid to hear the answer. Which was the very reason she squared her shoulders and met the woman's eyes. She had allowed herself to be cowed once by Frank, she'd not allow herself to be intimidated by another man ever again. "Do you have any idea where Scarsdale is?"

A deep crimson tinged the woman's cheeks and she started to shake her head. Sophia clutched Mary Margaret's arm. "Please don't lie to me. His aunt says he's at his mistress's, whom he sent for last week. "Is that true?"

"I don't know, Miss Vane, honestly. Do you want me to try to find out? The stable master may know where His Grace went."

"Could you?"

Mary Margaret smiled. "Of course. And I'll do so discreetly, so none of the busybodies in this household know anything is amiss. I'll be back shortly."

Sophia nodded. Once Mary Margaret quit the room and shut the door, she took off her gown and put on her night rail. Her heart wouldn't stop hammering and her thoughts wouldn't stop racing, so she gulped the remaining contents of the wine goblet down and lay on the bed. Her head immediately began to spin. It seemed she lay there for an eternity, her stomach aching with thoughts of Nathan touching another woman, kissing another woman, and holding another woman as he had just held her.

Angry tears welled in her eyes. Before Nathan had swept into her life, she had only held the smallest hope that she would one day find love. But that tiny, secret hope had given her something to dream about in her darkest hours. *Now*, she was in love, and she feared the devil was going to break her heart. And then what would there be to hope for?

Eleven

Sophia awoke the next morning groggy, with an aching head, and angry that she had fallen asleep before hearing what Mary Margaret had learned. She summoned her lady's maid, anxious to hear what she had discovered.

Mary Margaret appeared within moments and dipped a quick curtsy after entering the room. Sophia found it peculiar to have someone dipping a curtsy to her, but she knew it was proper, given that she was to be a duchess. Maybe. If Nathan was sleeping with his mistress, she couldn't possibly marry him. The fact that not doing so would leave her in dire straights paled at the moment compared to her aching heart. Determined to know the truth, she pushed the thoughts away and focused on Mary Margaret. "What did you learn?"

"Mr. Burk says the coachman did take His Grace to a lady's house last night, but that's all he could tell me."

Sophia's stomach clenched, and her entire body went cold, as if chilled by a winter wind. "Thank you, Mary Margaret," she murmured.

The woman bit her lip. "There's more, Miss Vane."

Of course there was. Bad news always seemed to flow like a stream. "Go ahead."

"His Grace did not come home last night."

The clench in her stomach grew ever tighter, until it felt as if her insides were nothing but knots. "How do you know?"

"I asked the chambermaid. I thought you might want to know."

Sophia nodded, though when she did, the pounding in her

head grew tenfold. "Is His Grace home now?" she asked through gritted teeth. She was not some simpering miss to be trampled on by the man. She was going to find Nathan, tell him what she thought of him, and then she and Harry were leaving. Never mind the fact that she didn't know where they were going. Anywhere was better than here with someone who thought he could bed her one moment, then turn around and bed another the next. That may have been the kind of marriage that was commonplace with the *ton*, but that was not the sort of marriage she wanted.

"I don't think so, Miss Vane. Will there by anything else?"

Sophia shook her head, and as Mary Margaret closed the door, Sophia closed her eyes and let the tears flow down her cheeks. One good cry was all she was going to give that blackhearted devil.

Nathan awoke with a start and stared blankly at the deep-burgundy curtains drawn tight around the bed. His first thought was that he'd been drugged by whoever wanted him dead. But then why the hell wouldn't they have simply killed him?

He squeezed his eyes against the pounding in his head, and when the noise died away, anger erupted and he surged out of bed with a bellow. He knew exactly where he was. He'd gone to see Marguerite the night before to tell her their relationship was over. "Marguerite!" he shouted as he circled the bed-chamber, searching for his missing clothing.

The door swung open, and his former mistress sashayed in the room in a fluttering, pink dressing gown. "You hollered, Your Grace."

Marguerite cocked her head and pushed her lips into a pout he had at one time found sensual. Now, he found it annoying.

"You put something in my drink," he stated, not bothering to ask. It was the only explanation. The last thing he remembered was sitting in the parlor, barely holding on to his patience, explaining to her for the third time this week that she had to go back to London and that his arrangement with her was over, though he would make sure she was well cared for until she found another provider. And the next memory was of waking up moments ago, without his shirt or boots on and with the faint taste of laudanum in his mouth.

Of all the times for Marguerite to decide to take advantage of the house he'd rented for her here, this week had been astonishingly bad timing for her to do so, and she'd not taken it well at all when he had told her he was getting married. He didn't suppose for a moment it was the loss of his attention that bothered her. The loss of his money was undoubtedly her biggest concern.

Marguerite strolled up to him and lifted her arms as if she was going to encircle his neck. Instinctively, he recoiled. It was going to be difficult enough to explain to Sophia why he hadn't been present for dinner last night; he didn't need the scent of another woman lingering on him to make matters worse. Not that he really had to explain himself, but he had just told Sophia she would have his fidelity and he'd meant it.

Marguerite frowned. "You needn't act so testy. You looked like death, and I decided you needed some sleep, not to go back to that girl child who tricked you into marrying her. I gave you just a pinch of laudanum." Her eyes twinkled. "You used to like laudanum, remember?"

She trailed a finger between the valley of her breasts, and a memory of his once licking laudanum off those breasts flashed in his mind and shamed him to the core.

The muscles in his jaw twitched at a violent speed as he stared at Marguerite. He couldn't say why he hadn't ended their arrangement before now, except that she'd made no emotional demands on him and he'd liked that. He'd made it clear to her after he had gotten his life in order once more that he would never dwindle into such depravity again and he hadn't. He'd sought out Harthorne and Aversley once he was thinking clearly and no longer taking laudanum and earned their friendships back, though it had taken some doing. Now, he needed to set Marguerite out of his life once and for all.

It had been foolish to describe Sophia to Marguerite, even if his description had been accurate. It had been thoughtless, and after last night, he saw Sophia more as a forest nymph than an undeveloped woman. He glanced at Marguerite and saw something he had never seen before. He saw his mother. Bile rose in his throat. Marguerite was vain, prideful, and cruel.

"Scarsdale," Marguerite purred and wound her hands around his neck.

He disentangled himself and thought of Sophia. She didn't have an iota of vanity or cruelty. Pride she had plenty of, but it was a pure pride that was different from anything he had known in other women. "She didn't trick me into marrying her," he snapped. "I chose to do so, which I have explained to you repeatedly." He turned away from Marguerite, located his shirt, and tugged it on. He thought to simply walk out the door after delivering an express order for her to leave, or a threat if necessary, but he realized his coachman was likely gone. "What did you tell my coachman last night?"

"That you wanted to stay in my bed," Marguerite said, a wicked grin pulling at her lips. "You will come back to me, you know. Once you bed her and she proves to be a mousy, timid thing that hates the marriage act as all wives do." Marguerite huffed in a breath he suspected was to make her chest rise above her gown and not at all because she was upset. "You will be begging me to be your mistress again. I'm sure I'll have another benefactor by then, Scarsdale, but you are always first in my heart. You know that. I will take you back anytime you wish it."

Nathan glanced down at her, positive he'd never wish it. Even if Sophia turned out to be as cold as his mother had been to his father once they were married, he'd not seek refuge in Marguerite's arms. "I will never be returning to you. My betrothed is neither mousy nor timid or cold."

Marguerite snorted. "Liar. All noblewomen are timid and cold."

Nathan's patience snapped. He snagged a finger under Marguerite's chin and lifted it slightly. "Careful, my dear. You push me too far and you will find no gentleman who wishes to be your benefactor. I want you out of the house by tomorrow. You may use the London townhome for the next month, but I want you out of there after that. Do you understand?"

"Afraid your future wife will find out about me and deny you the marriage bed?"

"I'm afraid of no woman. Nor do I bow to any woman's commands."

With that, he stormed out of the house and started on foot to Whitecliffe only to meet his carriage coming down the road. His coachman rolled the carriage to a stop with a nod and a smile. "Enjoy your night, Your Grace?"

"No," Nathan snapped. "That"—he motioned behind him toward the house, unsure why the devil he was offering an explanation to his coachman—"is not what you think."

Wilson's eyes widened with obvious astonishment. "Of course not. Shall I take you home?"

Nathan nodded, and after climbing into the carriage, he settled into his seat and stared blindly at the passing countryside. Emotion was starting to rule his actions and he couldn't decide if that was a good or bad thing. He'd lost hope in people before he'd met Sophia, and now she was making him feel hope. Whether that would last or not was the real question.

Nathan descended the carriage contemplating exactly what to say to Sophia and whether telling her the truth about where he had been was even wise. Before he could make up his mind, the front door of Whitecliffe swung open and Sophia came marching down the steps dragging Harry and their small, ancient trunk behind her.

He stopped at once, both astonished and amused by the sight of his betrothed, who looked surprisingly fetching in an emerald-green-and-white-striped day gown. Madame

Lexington must have altered something she had on hand and sent it over for Sophia. It was amazing what a properly fitting gown could do for a figure, he thought absently as he stepped sideways to block her flight. Then it became obvious she had no intention of stopping.

She whipped her gaze to his, and he felt momentarily lost in the bright blue eyes made dazzling with obvious anger.

"Please move," she demanded in a low, throbbing tone that made his heart twist as he immediately recognized the hurt in her voice.

"Where are you going?" he prodded with care, stepping closer to her, only to have her lurch away and almost fall backward over her trunk. He caught her at the elbow and steadied her, but when she stiffened, he released her. Harry caught his eye and gave him a dark scowl. Nathan felt almost as bad that he seemed to have hurt the boy, as well as Sophia. "Would you give me a moment to talk to your sister privately before the two of you leave?"

The boy cocked his head to the side and seemed to contemplate Nathan's request for a moment before nodding his head in agreement. Nathan motioned toward the house. "Why don't you make your way to the kitchen and have the cook fix you and your sister a picnic basket for the road," Nathan suggested. Once Sophia reluctantly gave her permission, Harry wandered back into the house, leaving Sophia and Nathan alone on the steps.

"Why are you leaving?" he asked.

Her black lashes lowered against her cheeks to veil her eyes for a moment before rising slowly up again. "Because you lied to me."

He didn't know how she could possibly know where he had been, but it was obvious she did. He was awestruck by the calm and quiet she exuded. There were no tears or threats. She'd simply packed her bag and planned to leave. By God, she was a brave little thing. "I did not lie to you. If you will let me explain…"

She pressed her lips into a grim line. "I don't see how you

can possibly explain going from my bed to another woman's. You promised me your fidelity."

Out of the corner of his eye, Nathan thought he saw his aunt standing at the window watching them, but all he saw now was a fluttering curtain. Still, he didn't want a show for this or any part of his life. "Come with me," he demanded and grasped Sophia by the hand before she could protest.

He quickly led her all the way down the steps and away from the house, toward a path that went to a separate building. They'd have complete privacy in the banqueting house. It hadn't been used in years, not since the time when his mother would have elaborate dinner parties and all the guests would stroll from the main house to this one on warm, starry nights to enjoy confections after dinner.

The door creaked open, but once they stepped inside the main hall, Nathan saw immediately that the staff had maintained the house as if he might request confections be served here at any moment. Candles flickered in the main hall and the two large, ornate fireplaces roared with a crackling fire that further illuminated the room. After calling out to make sure no staff was in here now, he locked the door behind them and drew Sophia into the dining room.

She tugged her hand away as he faced her but kept her proud gaze squarely on him.

Crossing his arms over his chest, he leaned against the table, which put him closer to Sophia's eye level. "What is it you think you know, Sophia?"

"I know you brought your mistress to this town last week and that your coachman took you to her house last night."

"And how do you know that?" He was going to dismiss whoever had such a loose tongue.

"I have my ways," she responded, lifting her chin to a defiant angle. "It's commendable you aren't going to lie about it. Good-bye, Nathan." She swung around to leave and got to the door before he caught up with her, grasped her arm, and swung her around.

"You're going to give up on me that easily?" he demanded,

his pulse picking up speed.

"No. It wasn't easy. I waited all morning for you to reappear so I could ask for the truth from your lips, and when you never returned, it became apparent that you don't care enough to bother with my feelings." She took a deep breath. "But I *do* have feelings. And the one thing I know will make me hate you is unfaithfulness. I told you that, and you lied and promised your fidelity."

"I have not been unfaithful, though I'd like to point out we are not married yet."

She scoffed. "We are to be married *tomorrow*, and if you cared for me at all, which you don't, you would not be sleeping with another woman. I should have known better." She dashed a hand across her cheeks when several tears slipped out of her eyes. "I'm a fool, and clearly a hopeless dreamer, but what are we without hope?" she demanded.

He opened his mouth to answer, but she shook her fist in the air between them. "We are nothing. We are moving through life in misery. I refuse to throw my hope for love away on you."

Moved by her complete honesty, he grasped her by the arms and drew her to him until he could feel her heart pounding within her chest. He gentled his hold and drew his hands to her face, cupping her cheeks. He couldn't give her his love, *yet*, but damn it, he wanted to try. What he could give her in this moment was honesty like that she'd just given him. "I have not been unfaithful to you. Ask me whatever you want to know and I'll tell you the truth."

"Did you bring your mistress here?"

"No, but she is in town. I kept a house here for her that I told her she could use anytime she wished, and she happened to pick this week to come use it. I did ask her to leave."

Sophia quirked her mouth. "And you expect me to believe you couldn't get your mistress to do your bidding?"

She tried to tug away from him, but he slid one hand to the gentle curve of her waist and he placed the other on the back of her delicate neck and held her still. "I don't *expect* you to believe anything, but I find myself in the most unexpected position of hoping you will. I should have been firmer with Marguerite, but I was trying to be kind. I've remedied that and she will be leaving by tomorrow."

Sophia's brows pulled together in a deep frown. "You didn't hurt her, did you?"

He resisted the urge to chuckle at Sophia's sweet contrariness. One moment she was ablaze that his mistress was in town, and the next, she was worried for Marguerite's safety. "Her pride was hurt, to be sure, but she'll survive."

Sophia nibbled on her lip for a moment. "I have to admit I'm inclined to believe your words, except for the fact that you stayed there last night. Why on earth would you stay at your mistress's house?"

He didn't particularly want to share the fact that Marguerite had drugged him, but lying to Sophia was out of the question. "Marguerite slipped laudanum in my drink, and I fell asleep."

Sophia stared at him with a blank look before her eyes narrowed and she pulled away from him.

He reached out and grabbed her once more, afraid she'd dash out the door and never look back. "I swear by God it's the truth. Do you think I'd make myself look like a fool on purpose?"

"No, I don't," she said, squirming in his arms. "Which is exactly why I'm going to find your former mistress and flog her until she knows not to cross me."

He threw his head back and laughed as he crushed Sophia to him and buried his face against her neck. "Life with you certainly is going to be interesting, my dear. But I've dealt with Marguerite and I won't underestimate her conniving ever again. However, I am flattered, amazed, and awed by your willingness to try to protect me."

"Well, what else could I possibly do?" she asked.

He drew his lips to her neck and nuzzled it, reveling in the shivers that he elicited in her. "Marry me," he whispered.

"I'll do more than that," she replied, turning her mouth to

meet his seeking one. "I'll love you forever, Nathan."

He tensed, but not because he had his usual thought that he didn't desire her love. He actually liked hearing her say she loved him and declaring she always would. And that scared him more than any pistol barrel he'd ever stared down. The idea of needing Sophia and desiring her love made his gut clench. He had no idea if he had it in him to break down the wall he'd erected so long ago. Instead of making a false promise that he'd love her in return, he said simply, "Thank you," before claiming her mouth in what was supposed to be a gentle kiss.

But she responded with such fierce passion that he forgot all about gentleness. Within moments, he had her breasts bared, her unmentionables removed, and he stood between her legs with his trousers undone. When her fingers tentatively grazed his hard flesh, he hissed between his teeth and felt his buttocks flex. She wiggled her bottom, which he clasped with his hands as he groaned. This woman beguiled him with her innocence and passion. "You don't mind me taking you here?" he whispered in her ear as she stroked her fingers up and down the length of his staff.

"Mind it?" She looked baffled by his question. "If you tried to walk away from me now and leave me in this state of need I'd chase you down," she said with a wicked grin. Suddenly, her fingers stopped their movement and wrapped around his shaft with a sure grip. "I want you to take me here, Nathan, and anywhere else you wish it. The garden, the conservatory, down by the lake on that lovely grotto would be wonderful."

"Your innocent looks disguise a wicked nature," he teased, leaning down and using his tongue to circle first her right nipple and then her left.

She moaned and moved her hands to his back, clutching him tightly. "I didn't know I was wicked," she rasped, "until I met you."

He lifted her and plunged deep inside her in one fluid motion. She responded by wrapping her legs around him and moving her hips to meet each one of his thrusts. Within moments, the slow movements became rapid, until he was driving into her with a frenzied need that he couldn't control. The need to possess her body and then perhaps her soul drove him. Over the roaring of blood in his ears, he heard her cry out in pleasure and scream his name. Her legs tightened around his waist as her body clenched around his shaft. He plunged into her one final time before a release like nothing he'd ever experienced overcame him. His muscles shook as his body relaxed. He slumped against her, and she wrapped her arms around him and cradled him, whispering her love.

Twelve

Sophia and Nathan's wedding took less time than it did for her to dress for it. Before she could properly take in all the details of the small chapel at Whitecliffe that Nathan had ordered so beautifully decorated, she was being escorted into the sunshine and down the cobblestone path that led through the garden and back to the mansion. As they strolled back to the house, she glanced at the blue sky and saw nothing but the bright possibilities her future with Nathan would bring. A ridiculously elaborate breakfast feast was waiting for their wedding party of five, which included the clergyman who had married them.

After their meal, it hit Sophia that Nathan had never changed his decree that he was leaving her here at Whitecliffe with his aunt while he went off to London. Surely, he would not leave her here after the intimacy they had shared.

Sophia crooked a finger at Nathan and had to fight not to grin when he immediately pushed his chair back from the dining room table to stand. Lady Anthony gave her a cool look, but Sophia refused to let anything ruin her wedding day. She pasted a smile on her face and waited patiently for Nathan, who was leaning over Harry's shoulder and whispering something in his ear.

When Nathan rose and held his hand out to her, she took it, but it was all she could do not to question him about what he'd been saying to Harry. She waited until they walked out of the dining room to his study and he shut the door. "What were you whispering to my brother?"

Nathan gripped her around the waist and drew her firmly against his broad chest. He ran a gentle finger down the slope of her cheek before speaking. "Your skin has softened since being here."

She smiled at him. "Lotions will do that, I suppose. Now quit trying to distract me. What were you saying?"

"To remember what I told him about preventing his stutter. You have to continually practice what I told him to perfect it."

Sophia twined her arms around Nathan's broad back and tipped her face to his until she caught his dark gaze and held it steady. "What exactly did you tell him to help him? It's worked miraculously."

"I told him to picture the person he is talking to as having a body that is part human and part the funniest-looking animal he could think of."

"I don't understand how that helps him to not stutter."

"It puts his concentration on the picture in his head and off the words," Nathan said simply.

"Did you know that would work because you once had a stutter?" Sophia asked, hoping he'd open up to her about his past.

"Harry told you?"

Sophia nodded.

"Yes." He grew very still for a moment before continuing. "As a child I became so nervous that I would say the wrong thing to my mother and spoil her good mood or set her on a tirade. Every time I talked, I worried so much about each word I uttered that I stuttered all the time. Eventually, it became so bad that I did it with everyone, and not just when I was nervous."

"And you recognized that Harry had the same problem?"

"I knew the minute I met your father that he was Harry's problem. So I did what I could to help him."

"Nathan, will you tell me what your mother was like?"

His face, which had been open and smiling, drew immediately closed and dark. "She was beautiful with a black heart.

There is nothing else to say."

It was more than he'd revealed previously, so she accepted the little bit with the hope that he would reveal more and more of himself over time, and heal by doing so. "Are you still planning to leave me here with your aunt?"

Or for good, she thought silently.

"Don't look so worried," he said, tugging on a curl of her short hair. "I *am* going to London, but only for long enough to tie up some loose business ends. I never thought I'd be here this winter—it's not my usual style—so I have some things to attend to there."

She desperately wanted to ask him what his usual style was, but she suspected he was not yet ready to tell her. "How long will you be gone?"

"It shouldn't be much longer than a week. But I wanted to ask you how you felt about me taking Harry with me? I can take him to Eton and show him around so he will be comfortable there."

Sophia frowned. "How do you know they will grant him a spot?"

"Because they want my continued generosity, my dear, and I will cease to be generous if they do not take Harry as a pupil and treat him just like any other boy there."

Sophia kissed Nathan, cutting off his words. "Thank you for helping my bother."

Nathan grinned. "Do you know I rather like the way your eyes sparkle when you're happy? It positively lights your face."

She beamed, feeling happier than one person probably had the right to feel. Suddenly, she was struck with a wonderful idea. "Nathan, I'll come with you to London and to take my brother to school, and I promise not to do a thing to embarrass you. I'll stay inside at the house in London if you wish it, and—"

He pressed a finger to her lips. "I want you to come, but you cannot. The roads are rough in winter, which makes the ride jostling. I wouldn't want you endangering your health."

Sophia frowned. "I'm perfectly healthy. Are you sure you're not simply saying that because you don't want to admit you're embarrassed of me?"

"I'm sure," he said, kissing the tip of her nose and then laying his hand, palm open, over her belly. "You may not have considered that you could be carrying my child, but I have."

A baby! A baby they had made to care for and lavish with love as neither of them had ever been lavished. She smiled as she looked at Nathan. "Do you really think I could be?" She laid her hand over his much larger one and intertwined her fingers with his.

He curled her fingers inward until they grazed his palm. "It's definitely a possibility, and I refuse to put you or the future duke in danger."

"Scarsdale!" His aunt's shrill voice resounding through the room made Sophia jump.

"In here, Aunt," Nathan drawled.

Sophia turned just as Lady Anthony strolled into the room and eyed Sophia with coldness before smiling at Nathan. "There is a rather large group of your tenants here who wish to pay their respects to Miss Vane."

Nathan smiled wryly. "You mean the Duchess of Scarsdale," Nathan said in an unbending tone.

"Yes, of course, how silly of me to forget."

"It was rather silly of you. See that it doesn't happen again." With that, he led Sophia past his gaping aunt and back through the house toward the cacophony of murmuring voices awaiting them.

<hr />

The entire day was spent among Nathan's tenants, who thought him a very generous employer based on all the stories they'd told her, though none of them seemed to really know him. A few of the older women had made references to different scrapes Nathan had gotten into when he was younger and what a precocious and lighthearted child he had been, but all the stories ended much the same. The women would make some statement or another regarding how the late duchess had made Nathan into a cold, withdrawn youth who barely spoke to anyone.

By the time Sophia retired to dress for bed, her heart ached for Nathan. She wanted to wrap her arms around him and make him somehow understand that it was all right to be open with people and not regard everyone as a potential enemy. Mary Margaret was waiting for Sophia in her bedchamber, and she had laid out three night rails—all of which looked nothing like proper night rails—that the seamstress had sent over for Sophia to chose from to wear on her wedding night and the nights that followed.

Sophia slowly approached the bed and picked up the first one. It was made from the finest material, if the feel of it was any indication, and was adorned with pearls and silk ribbons, but the gown was almost sheer. Sophia flushed looking at it, and quickly laid it down and picked up the next one. Each gown had the same problem.

She could feel Mary Margaret watching her expectantly, so she turned to the woman. "This is truly the fashion?"

Mary Margaret smiled while nodding. "They are meant to entice His Grace. This one is my favorite and the one I think you should wear."

"Do you really think Nathan will like it?"

Mary Margaret nodded. "Mama says passion runs hot in the blood of the Dukes of Scarsdale."

With trembling fingers, Sophia took the night rail from Mary Margaret. She'd wear it, but the idea of doing so made her embarrassed and nervous. She didn't know why she should be suddenly shy. It wasn't as if Nathan had not seen her naked. But this was different. In this gown, she felt as if she was putting herself on display, and frankly, she knew she was not much to look at. After Mary Margaret helped her out of wedding gown, Sophia went behind the screen to change. And as she slipped on the skimpy night rail, she called out to Mary Margaret that she could go once the gown was hung up. She certainly did not want her lady's maid to see her in this revealing creation and she didn't see a wrap to go with it.

When she emerged from behind the screen, she noticed that another wine goblet stood on her nightstand, and she rushed over to it and gulped the contents down to calm her nerves. As she set the goblet back on the table, she frowned. She'd had a dull headache ever since coming to Whitecliffe and it suddenly was pounding. Goose flesh covered her arms and legs, so she padded over to the fire and stoked it until it roared in the grate and sent heat wafting through the room.

When her chill persisted and her head started to swim, she pulled back the coverlet from her bed and sat in the center of the bed and wrapped herself in it. As she tried to settle herself, the dizziness didn't decrease but increased instead, and a sharp pain stabbed at her stomach. Suddenly, she felt as if she was going to be ill. She scrambled to the side of the bed and stood to retrieve the chamber pot. The room tilted violently, bright specks of light peppered her vision, and a searing heat overwhelmed her from her scalp to her bare feet.

She bent down, blindly searching for the chamber pot, and lost her balance. She hit the floor with a *thud*, and the air whooshed out of her lungs. The idea of Nathan finding her sprawled on the floor so ungracefully mortified her, but when she tried to push herself up, her limbs trembled violently. She crumbled back down and closed her eyes as another wave of blackness and nausea stole her thoughts and beckoned her into unconsciousness.

⁂

"Sophia?" Nathan called impatiently, tapping on her door for the third time. He hadn't wanted to simply barge in, but when she failed to answer again, he opened the door and stepped into the bedchamber. Shadows and flickering candlelight danced on the walls, and a warm coziness filled the room. He closed the door behind him and glanced toward the dressing screen. "Sophia?"

Irritation rose up in him that she wasn't in here, but he forced it down. Whatever Sophia was doing, he was sure it was important. It wasn't as if she was avoiding him or playing games. *Or was she?* his mind taunted. He shoved the thought away. Looking around the room at all the portraits of his mother, he knew he didn't want to spend the night in here. When Sophia did return they would retire to his bedchamber.

In fact, he would have the chamber adjoining his prepared for her use so they wouldn't have to traipse up and down the halls when he was in residence and they wanted to see each other. *When he was in residence.* The thought smashed around his head. Did he want to stay here at Whitecliffe with her? There was a part of him that did, but there was another part that taunted him, as if staying here meant he was weak and meant he needed her. The idea of needing anyone unsettled him. The decision didn't have to be made tonight.

He was walking toward the dressing screen when a groan reached him. He stopped in his tracks and turned around. "Sophia?"

Another groan came from the opposite side of the bed. Striding across the room and around the bed, he spotted her immediately, crumpled on the floor in a sheer pink negligee. Her eyes were closed but she was clutching her stomach. His pulse exploded as he knelt down beside her and gathered her into his arms. "Sophia," he whispered near her ear.

She turned her head toward him, and her eyes fluttered open for a moment before closing again. "I feel awful," she murmured. "I-I'm going to be sick."

Laying her gently on the bed, he located the chamber pot and watched helplessly as she retched into it repeatedly. When it seemed she wasn't going to stop, he pulled the bell cord to summon her lady's maid. Perhaps she would know what to do.

Within minutes, the woman was there, leaning over Sophia and cooing at her, but Sophia continued to retch until what came out of her stomach was nothing but clear liquid. She lay back suddenly, pale, damp, and shaking. Mary Margaret stood and motioned to him.

"Might I fetch my mother? She knows about different herbs to help calm the stomach."

Nathan nodded. "What shall I do while you're getting her?"

"Perhaps you could hold a wet rag to Her Grace's head?"

He nodded. "Go quickly." As the maid hurried out of the room, he rushed over to the washbasin and dampened a rag, then hurried back to Sophia and pressed it against her head. Her eyes fluttered open again, but the unnatural film that clouded her eyes made Nathan curse inwardly. "Sophia, we're going to get you some herbs to help your stomach."

She nodded, and without opening her eyes said, "Water."

He glanced around, located a water pitcher, and saw a wine goblet on her nightstand. Raising it to his nose, he sniffed it and frowned. Sophia had been drinking? Sourness filled his mouth. His mother had spent more days foxed than sober. He was damned sure he would not tolerate Sophia doing the same. A drink was one thing but so many that she became ill was another.

"Sophia," he snapped. When she didn't respond, he shook her shoulder. After a second, she opened her eyes and this time he attributed the cloudiness to the wine. "How much did you drink?" he demanded.

"Water," she whispered.

He poured a glass of water and thrust it at her. "How much did you drink?" he asked again, not making a move to help her. But when she didn't lift her head or answer, he raised her up and held the goblet to her lips. She took a swallow, sputtered, and immediately rolled over and retched it up.

"Damnation," he swore as Mary Margaret came into the room with her mother, Mrs. Cooke. Before they could utter a word, he motioned to Sophia. "She's foxed. When you've sobered her up, come get me in my bedchamber." He stalked to the door and then paused. He turned and pierced the lady's maid with a scowl. "How much does she drink?"

"What?"

"How much?" he said through clenched teeth.

"Water?"

"Wine, damn it all!" he roared.

Mary Margaret flinched and exchanged a long look with her mother before facing him again. "I have no knowledge of Her Grace drinking any wine," she said in a hushed voice. "If you continue to cover for her you will find yourself out of a position. Do you understand?" The woman nodded, and he turned on his heels and stormed out of the room.

He released the tenuous tether he had on his temper the moment he stepped into his bedchamber. The heavy wood door slammed behind him and rattled in its frame. With a vicious rip, he tore his cravat from his neck, then yanked off his coat and shoes. The shoes hit the wall one by one.

Damn her to hell and back for getting under his skin. He slid a crystal glass across the wood of the dressing table and then tilted the decanter to pour a drink. He stared down at the glass without seeing it. He saw his mother too drunk to stand time and again. Liquid wet his hand and he blinked, hurriedly turning the decanter upright and grimacing at the mess he had made.

He swiped his hand across his trousers and stormed across the room to slump into the chair in front of the large marble fireplace. Staring blindly into the flickering orange flames, he cursed as images of Sophia intertwined with images of his mother. He would have never thought Sophia to be the sort of woman to imbibe in too much spirits.

His heart twisted, and he gripped the glass, feeling the sting of the crystal cutting into his skin but not caring. She was in his head. This was what became of letting down one's guard. One began to feel things, to be hurt by others. He didn't want her in his head. He didn't want her there. *Damn her.* He downed the contents of his drink and made his way across the carpets.

An almost-crazed feeling was taking hold of him. He stared at his bed, the immense expanse of it, and he could see *her* there. In it. With him. Laughing, smiling, her blue eyes sparkling. *Goddamn her.* It had taken a good deal of effort to make himself numb and she'd swept into his life and thawed his heart. Growling, he threw his empty glass on the bed and trod through the door to his study that connected to his room.

Grabbing the first book he came to, he settled in to read. He forced himself to the task, but he realized after a while that he could not recall one damned word he'd read. Yet, he could recall whole conversations he'd had with Sophia. Snarling, he threw the book against the far wall and stalked out of the study, back into the main bedchamber, and over to the large stained glass window that overlooked the acres of parkland on which his home was situated. He placed his hands against the cold glass and heaved a disgruntled sigh. She'd cracked the lock on his heart, and he hadn't even realized it. Hell, he'd even contemplated the notion of love for her.

Before his tirade could really commence a scratch came at the door. "Come in," he bade in a clipped tone.

Mary Margaret entered the room on her mother's heels, and the young lady stayed there, hovering. He raised an eyebrow but didn't make a move to be friendly. So the girl was afraid of him now? Good. She needed to be scared witless after lying to him. "Don't tell me my bride is already sober?" he sneered.

Mary Margaret stepped out from behind her mother. "She's not foxed," the lady's maid said in a rebuking tone. "She's ill."

She glanced at her mother, and Mrs. Cooke, who had been his mother's lady's maid, nodded. "I'd recognize someone in their cups immediately. Her Grace is sick. You need to fetch the doctor at once. I've done all I can, but she's still retching."

Something inside him tingled with fear, but he ruthlessly beat it back. He refused to care. "Mother used to retch up a storm."

Mrs. Cooke shook her head. "Not like this. Your wife cannot stop. She'll die if she goes on in this manner, and if you refuse to send a servant to fetch the physician, I'll send Mr. Cooke and you can let us all go. I'll not have that innocent young woman's death on my hands."

"Let you go?" he asked, surprised, despite the fact that he'd given Mary Margaret that exact ultimatum. "You've worked for my family for as long as I can remember."

Mrs. Cooke nodded. "Exactly. You are wrong about this. Please send for the physician."

"We'll see," he said, sure he was not mistaken. He'd seen his mother in the same state hundreds of times. He strode out of his room and down the hall to Sophia. Outside the door, the sound of her violent sickness filled the halls and set fear in his belly. He shoved through the door and cursed. She lay in a small, pitiful ball in the center of the bed, shaking. Her dark, short hair was slicked back with perspiration, and her eyes were closed but moving violently under her lids. Her skin had an odd ashy tint to it.

Mrs. Cooke was right. This was worse than anything he'd ever seen. This was a great deal more than simply being foxed. Every part of him wanted to go to her, but he sensed there wasn't a minute to waste. "Don't let her die," he commanded and hurried out of the room to the staircase.

He met his aunt halfway down the spiral stairs.

"Scarsdale, where are you going in such a rush?"

"To fetch the physician. Sophia is sick."

"Send a servant, for pity's sake. The staff will think your tragic little wife has you besotted if you go yourself."

"I don't give a goddamn what the servants think," he snapped and turned on his heel to make his way down the rest of the stairs. He was the best equestrian in this house, and he'd reach the physician faster than any of his servants.

Within minutes, his horse was made ready and he dashed off into the night to fetch Dr. Maddox. Each time the horse's hooves made contact with the hard dirt, one thought pounded into Nathan's head. He wasn't good enough for Sophia.

She was an innocent despite her circumstances.

He was jaded beyond repair *because* of his circumstances.

She held hope in her heart.

His heart contained bitterness.

She assumed the best of him always.

He was such a cynical bastard that he was all too willing to assume the worst from her, even though she'd only shown kindness and love.

She trusted him.

He didn't even trust himself.

She claimed to love him and want his love in return.

All he could claim was that he was sure she would snatch back all that she offered the minute he failed her.

But damnation, he didn't want to let her go. And even worse, she had somehow managed to stir an undeniable desire to try to simply feel again. For her.

Thirteen

"Poison?" Nathan repeated with disbelief.

Dr. Maddox nodded. "Seems so. I cannot say for certain, but all her circumstances indicate she was poisoned."

Nathan gripped the bedpost and glanced down at Sophia, who was finally resting peacefully after hours of retching. She looked so small and fragile. A large lump settled in his throat and his blood turned cold. What if he had been the target and she an innocent victim as before on the road when he'd been shot? Someone was trying to kill him, after all. He knew that for a fact.

He cursed under his breath that he had not gotten to see Sir Richard in London. He had wanted to hire the man because he was known and admired for his investigation skills, but just as importantly, he was known for his discretion. *And* Sir Richard had been a personal friend of Nathan's father.

He yanked his hand through his hair. Had he made a grave mistake by waiting to hire an investigator and given whoever wanted him dead another opportunity to try to kill him? Or Sophia? He tugged the bell cord to call a servant, and within seconds, Mary Margaret appeared.

She dipped a curtsy, her gaze darting between him and the physician. "How may I be of service?"

"Summon all the servants to the courtyard," he clipped in a cold, hard tone.

Her eyes widened considerably. "But it's snowing."

"I don't give a damn if it's lightning, thundering, and hailing. Summon every servant to the courtyard from the stable boy to my valet. And tell them that if they do not appear within fifteen minutes, they can consider their employment terminated. I'm going to find out who poisoned Sophia."

Dr. Maddox gripped Nathan's arm. "Scarsdale," he began, pausing when Nathan glanced at the man's hand clutching his arm. Dr. Maddox released his hold before continuing. "I didn't mean to imply someone had *purposely* poisoned your wife. I selected my words without proper thought. I'm sure she simply ate or drank something bad. I cannot tell you how many cases I see every week of people violently ill from consuming tainted meat."

Nathan wasn't convinced it was a simple case of tainted meat, but to avoid having to explain his doubts, he said, "Then I will find out which of my servants was so careless as to serve such meat, and they will be let go." Dr. Maddox didn't need to know that Nathan might also be looking for an accomplice to his attempted murder. "Go summon them, Mary Margaret."

"Yes, Your Grace."

Dr. Maddox made to follow the lady's maid out, but he stopped at the door. "I'll come by tomorrow to check on Her Grace, but I suspect she will sleep soundly. I gave her a fairly strong tonic to help her sleep, and the herbs eventually did the trick in calming her stomach. If she should happen to worsen, then I suggest we bleed her tomorrow to rid her body of the poison. Might I suggest you have her lady's maid sit by her side tonight?"

"I'll sit with her," he replied, his voice gruff. He didn't want to rely on anyone else to do the job. Besides, he'd never sleep wondering if she was still doing all right or if she had taken a turn for the worse.

"Very good, Your Grace," Dr. Maddox agreed and left.

Nathan sat down beside Sophia and steepled his hands in front of him. Who held such a grudge against him that they wanted him dead? It could be Lord Peabody, he realized. Nathan considered the fool and his anger over his mistress comparing their performances in the bedchamber. He supposed men had killed for less, but the idea seemed somewhat absurd. Still, he'd keep Peabody on the list.

Then it hit him. The most likely candidate and the one person he knew for a fact hated him and had the bollocks to try to kill him was Peyton Ravensdale. Nathan didn't like to think back to the time in his life he'd almost destroyed himself, but he cast his mind there now out of necessity.

His spiral into darkness had started after the carriage accident that had killed his parents and had left him with a severely broken right arm. The physician had given him laudanum for the pain, but Nathan had become addicted to the stuff. It had been a nice little way to forget the real pain that was in his heart. His parents' deaths had unleashed memories of the love he'd never felt from his mother and the disappointment he'd felt in his father for forgetting about him, and nothing Nathan had done could quiet the memories.

But the laudanum did, for a time. Eventually, it wasn't enough, so he mixed the laudanum with alcohol. When Nathan became so nasty and difficult to be around, and he destroyed all his other friendships, Ravensdale seemed to be the last friend standing, though up until that time he and Nathan had been more acquaintances than friends. When Ravensdale offered to get Nathan into the Order of the Dark Lords, a club known for its accessibility to all sorts of promising drugs, Nathan had eagerly accepted.

He spent the next several years in a haze, until the morning he awoke in Marguerite's bed with laudanum covering his face. His only memories of the previous night had been shocking ones of things he and Marguerite had done and a vague recollection of Ravensdale, who had been a Bow Street Runner at the time, putting on a hood that matched that of the Hooded Robber, who'd been robbing the *ton* in their carriages at night. And the next night, when Nathan had seen Ravensdale hiding a hood and an emerald necklace, Nathan had confronted him, but Ravensdale had denied it.

Nathan had fallen so far, he was sure he could not climb out of the personal hell he'd created, but that moment had made him realize he'd lost his honor, and he'd slowly and painfully gone about the business of putting the pieces of his life back together. Nathan had even gone to the authorities and told them what he suspected. Of course, he had no proof, and they'd been unable to find any evidence that Ravensdale was the robber. Yet, Nathan was a duke, though a fallen one, and his word still held some weight. Ravensdale lost his position as a Bow Street Runner and a great deal more. Yes, if anyone had a reason to want him dead, it was Ravensdale.

He stared for a long time at Sophia. What would she think of him if she knew how utterly wicked he'd really been? He shoved the useless pondering away, rose, and made his way downstairs. His aunt was turning the corner as he came into the main hall, and her pinched face alerted him to her anger.

"Am I to assume you also want me in the courtyard, Scarsdale?"

Nathan started to shake his head but then paused. "Did you know that Sophia was drinking a glass of wine at night?"

"Yes. I instructed the butler to ensure there was a glass of Madeira by her bedside every night," his aunt replied. "I put myself in her place, coming to a town I do not know, marrying a man I just met, enduring the humiliation of my reputation having been ruined, having no mother to guide me through my days before my wedding, and I thought how nervous I would be, how nervous *she* must be. Was it so wrong?"

Nathan's first instinct was to question his aunt's claim. The woman was rarely nice. But he remembered how he had just unfairly believed the worst in Sophia, and he bit back the acerbic response on the tip of his tongue and shook his head. "That was thoughtful of you, but it seems the wine was poisoned or simply bad."

"Poisoned?" His aunt snorted. "Don't be absurd, Scarsdale. Maybe the little tart simply drank too much. You did say her father owned a *tavern*." She said the word *tavern* with a disdainful tone, as if the place were the breeding ground of sinners.

Clenching and unclenching his teeth, he didn't speak until he knew he could do so without yelling. "I think perhaps it's best if you leave in the morning." One jaded person in this house was far more than Sophia deserved. There was no need for her to have to put up with him *and* his aunt.

"Leave?" An incredulous look passed across her face. "How do you purport to make your new duchess into a lady such as me without my help?"

"I don't mean to make her into a lady anything like you, Aunt."

Her face flushed and she turned on her heel, but he caught her at the elbow. "Who poured the wine and took it to Sophia?"

"The Madeira was poured by the butler," she snapped.

The last thing he saw as he turned on his heel and left his aunt was her gaping jaw.

Nathan located his butler, who had been in his employ for twelve years, and after questioning him, he bade Gibson to show him the Madeira decanter he'd used to prepare Sophia's drinks. Nathan smelled the Madeira and all seemed well, but then he decided to taste it, despite Gibson's protest and offer to taste it himself. Nathan was a large man, more than twice Sophia's size and weight. If the wine had not killed her, it was not about to kill him, and he would not rest easy until he knew, without a doubt, if she had been poisoned. He swigged the glass down and then stormed to the courtyard to speak with the other servants.

From ten to midnight, Nathan personally interrogated each servant. Then, from midnight until the sun started to rise the next day, he oversaw his staff as they checked the entire stock of the kitchens. They uncovered nothing untoward. By the time the sun was fully in the morning sky, he still had not experienced the slightest signs of illness from the Madeira, so he ruled the spirits out as the culprit.

Whatever had made Sophia sick, he could not determine, but he was damn sure going to see Sir Richard as soon as he returned to London and hire him to uncover not only the men who were after him but also whoever did this to Sophia. Until then, he would instruct his staff to be on their guard for any strangers, and he'd instruct a footman to keep a watchful eye on Sophia in his absence. He didn't want her going *anywhere* alone. The idea of her dying made his stomach roil.

As he trudged up the stairs to Sophia's bedchamber, he considered how wrongly he'd judged her. He wanted to make up for it, yet he wasn't sure how to do it. He sat down in the chair he had placed beside the bed last night so he could properly watch her, and he gazed at her innocent, sleeping face.

"Good morning, Your Grace," Harry said. Nathan looked up at the sound of the boy's voice and saw him shuffling into Sophia's bedchamber as he rubbed his eyes with his fists.

Nathan smiled at the fact that Harry had not stuttered once when uttering the greeting and that the boy didn't hesitate to show himself into his sister's room. Though it was absolutely improper, Nathan couldn't bring himself to scold the boy. He rather envied him. It was obvious how comfortable and secure Harry felt with Sophia, who really was the boy's surrogate mother, something with which Nathan was unfamiliar.

He silently motioned to Sophia as she slept. He stood as quietly as possible and waved Harry out the door. The boy had no idea what had occurred last night, and Nathan intended to fill him in and also to explain that they would leave within the week for Eton. Nathan was anxious to get to London to see Sir Richard, but he wanted to ensure Sophia was completely well before departing.

Once in the hall, he knelt down so he could look Harry in the face. "Your sister was very ill last night, but she is going to be perfect when she wakes up."

"Oh. That makes sense. Sophia didn't appear in my room this morning."

Nathan frowned. "Were you expecting her?"

Harry grinned. "I was expecting a gift."

"A gift?"

The boy nodded vigorously. "'Tis the Christmastide season, Your Grace! Sophia always gives me one gift on each of the seven days leading up to Christmas."

"Does she now? Well, what sort of gifts does she give you?" His heart constricted and the desire to please Sophia filled him.

"Well..." Harry scratched his head. "I can't remember everything, but last year I got a new pair of socks. I didn't love those because that don't seem too exciting, but Sophia said since Frank was such a blackguard and didn't care if my feet were warm or not, she had to ensure they were."

"That makes perfect sense," Nathan agreed, wondering what Sophia had sacrificed to get Harry the socks.

"She also gave me a book and made me learn to read it real good."

"A very wise gift and a most judicious endeavor," Nathan said, his heart aching in his chest, much to his surprise.

"On Christmas Day she was going to give me a coat," Harry stated.

"*Was* going to give you?"

"Frank found out she'd been hiding some money for the coat, and h-he gave her a right proper whipping and took it all."

Nathan had the sudden urge to hunt Frank down and give the man a blow for each one he'd ever given Sophia, mental and physical.

"She cried and cried."

"Over the whipping?" Nathan said, his voice suddenly low and throbbing. He tried to clear his throat but something felt lodged in it.

Harry shook his head. "Naw. She took Frank's whippings without so much as a blink. She cried 'cause I didn't have no coat."

Christ. She was good, wonderfully kind, and caring. He swallowed against the hard lump in his throat. "She cried *because* you didn't have *a* coat. If you are going to be an Eton man you must endeavor to speak proper English."

Harry nodded.

Nathan stood and contemplated the thoughts swirling in his head. He'd not celebrated Christmas since he was six when his mother had decreed he didn't deserve to, but this Christmas he wanted to celebrate it for Sophia's and Harry's sakes. He glanced down at the child, who was staring back up at him. "I have an idea. Let's surprise your sister. Shall we decorate the house and make it festive for Christmastide?"

Harry grinned. "Yes! And let's buy her a gift for each day before Christmas!"

"That's an excellent idea," Nathan agreed, feeling his cheeks pull into an answering grin. "I shall go out this afternoon and purchase the first gift."

Harry tugged on Nathan's trouser leg. "May I stay here until Christmas is over?"

"Certainly. We will postpone our trip until then." *But no longer than that.* It made him far too uneasy that someone out there wanted him dead. He didn't fear for himself really. He feared for Sophia and Harry. Sophia had already been put in harm's way because of it—twice. He tensed, waiting for his gut reaction to shove back at the affection that was tugging at his heart, but it didn't come. Letting out a breath, the tension released with it, and he smiled.

Two days after falling ill, Sophia woke up feeling marvelous. As she sat up and stretched, she noticed a large package at the foot of her bed. She pushed the covers back, crawled toward the package, and picked it up. A sheet of foolscap was folded atop it, with her name written on the outside. She opened the paper and smiled when she saw the signature at the bottom was Nathan's.

Don't open this until Mary Margaret has done your hair.

That seemed a strange request, but having never received a present in her life, she was thrilled to do whatever the instructions demanded. Grinning at the carefree feeling in her heart, she jumped out of bed to summon Mary Margaret and struggled for the next half hour to sit patiently as her lady's maid fixed her hair.

Her mind was racing with what might be in the package, but from the looks of it, it certainly appeared to be large enough to hold a gown. And it would make sense for him to request she have her hair done, if that was, in fact, her gift. The rest of the gowns from Madame Lexington should be done by now, and Sophia really did want something lovely to put on to see Nathan for the first time since she'd taken ill. Mary Margaret had told her that Nathan had found her almost unconscious in that scandalous night rail Madame Lexington had created. She also knew that he had sat by her bedside two nights in a row to make sure her condition did not worsen, and she wanted more than anything to be the duchess Nathan deserved. Her love for him was so powerful it felt as if it would burst her heart. She may never be a grand beauty, but she would make sure she was as presentable as possible.

Sophia turned in her chair, regarded her reflection in the looking glass, and smiled. Her dark hair curled softly against her skin, which actually looked more creamy than sallow. Her eyes seemed bright and rather sparkly, and Mary Margaret had crushed some berries and dabbed the juice on her lips to stain them. She puckered her dark-ruby lips and giggled. "Do I look presentable?"

"You look lovely, Your Grace. It's hard to believe you were so sick. You look the picture of health."

Sophia stood and retrieved the package from the bed. "Hopefully, Nathan will not remember how I disgraced myself and how awful I must have looked."

Mary Margaret clicked her tongue and scowled, which she quickly corrected. It only flittered briefly across her face, but Sophia caught her maid's disgruntled look. "What is it?"

"If I may be so bold to speak plainly?" the maid inquired,

which made Sophia want to laugh. Several weeks ago, Mary Margaret would have been considered above Sophia in the social classes, and now the maid was asking permission to speak openly with her.

"You never need to ask permission for such things. Just do so."

The maid shook her head. "I couldn't do that, but I appreciate your saying it. You are a true lady, and it's not you who should worry that you disgraced yourself, but your husband."

Irritation filled her that Mary Margaret would dare criticize Nathan after her maid had told her that he had sat by her side all night and forewent sleep. "Why would you say that?" she demanded, her words clipped, though she tried to make them come out smooth.

"I'm sorry, Your Grace," Mary Margaret rushed out. "I shouldn't have said anything." The woman wrung her hands together.

"Well, you did, so I suppose you better speak your piece."

"It's just when he first found you ill, he accused you of being foxed and he left you in here after depositing you on the bed as though you meant nothing to him. And as good and kind as you are..." She shook her head. "It just made me so mad for you. I'm sorry I mentioned it."

Sophia's stomach twisted. Nathan had thought her deep in her cups? Whyever would he think such a thing? Was it because of Frank's poor habits? Was Nathan worried she would follow in Frank's footsteps? Her first inclination was to feel sadness, but then her temper started to simmer. How dare he assume she would have the same problem! "I'm glad you told me."

When she saw Mr. High and Mighty she was going to tell him a thing or two about what sort of person she was. She ripped open the box, tore the tissue away, and gasped. Lying on a bed of soft white tissue was the most beautiful gown she had ever seen. She ran a gentle finger down the emerald-green velvet, then over the cream ermine collar, and swallowed hard.

"There must be some mistake," she said. "I didn't order any such gown."

Mary Margaret reached into the box and scooped out the gown, then held it up and shook out the folds. The material billowed to the floor in a luxurious wave. "I've never seen anything so exquisite in my life," the maid whispered. "Look here." She pointed at the intricate white lace sewn into the edges of the long sleeves. "I've never seen a day gown with lace sewn into it."

Sophia stared at the creation in wonder. "How do you know it's a day gown?"

"Well, His Grace sent it up with instructions for you to wear it today, so I just assumed."

Sophia nodded. That made perfect sense to her. It was hard to stay too mad at Nathan when he had ordered her such a wonderful gown. The fact that he had thought specifically to do so touched her deeply. She motioned to Mary Margaret. "Help me into it?"

After a few moments of struggling to get Sophia into all the appropriate undergarments, Mary Margaret slipped the bodice and skirts on Sophia. They were actually two separate pieces, attached ingeniously by tapes that suspended over her shoulders. Each piece fastened with mother-of-pearl buttons, and around the bottom of the skirts were two rows of fur. Once she was properly hooked, she turned around and glanced into the looking glass. Her mouth parted.

The dress was exquisite. If only her looks matched. She ran a hand down her waist, which looked quite small cinched in so by the gown. "What do you call this?" Sophia asked, pointing to the intricate creation across her breasts.

"That's an antique stomacher. It's embroidered with robing. His Grace surely paid a fortune to have this gown created in such a short time. He surely knows how to make amends for misjudging you," Mary Margaret said on a dreamy sigh.

He certainly did, but it bothered her just a little that he thought he needed to make amends with an expensive gift. An apology would have done just as nicely. Not that she was going to offer to give the dress back. She grinned and smoothed a hand down the lush velvet. She loved it so much she wanted to sleep in it!

"Fetch my slippers," she instructed, eager to see Nathan and thank him.

Mary Margaret rushed to the wardrobe and came back carrying another package. "Look! This was hidden in your wardrobe!"

Sophia grinned at Mary Margaret, who was grinning back at her. Giggling, she grabbed the package from her maid and ripped into it, gasping at the stunning green half boots. Also inside the box was a pair of the softest doeskin gloves she had ever felt in her life. She immediately put on the gloves with a sigh. She'd never owned a pair. Once Mary Margaret helped her don her boots, Sophia raced out the door and down the stairs to find Nathan.

The sight that greeted her in the main hall stole her breath and filled her heart with joy. Mistletoe, holly, and evergreen boughs decorated the space. Someone had decorated for Christmastide, just as she had always wanted to do, and an entire week before the customary day of Christmas Eve! She squeezed her eyes shut and sent a silent prayer to God for her blessings, and when she opened her eyes, Nathan was coming around the corner from the portrait gallery with a package in his hands and Harry fast on his heels.

He was looking down and fiddling with the package, but when he looked up, he stopped immediately and a smile lit his face. Her heart gave a gigantic lurch at his beauty.

"You look very fetching in your new gown, Sophia." His low, rumbling voice made her blood sing with remembrance of how the hot breath of his words had tickled her ear when he had lavished kisses against her bare skin and then whispered in her ear.

Clearing her throat, she said, "However did Madame Lexington manage to make this so quickly?"

"I do believe my money might have convinced her to borrow some creations she had started for another customer and make them into creations specifically for you."

"You did that for me? To surprise me?" Her voice shook.

His eyebrows arched high and a smile graced his lips. "That is only the beginning of what I will do for you, Sophia."

The statement was so unlike anything he had ever said to her that tears clogged her throat. Was he finally letting down his guard?

Clapping his hands together as if he sensed she was on the verge of crying and wanted to ward if off, he said in a cheerful voice, "You finished dressing quicker than we expected. Hasn't she, Harry?"

Her brother popped out from behind Nathan and ran to her. He squeezed her tightly. "We were going to hide another present for you outside."

Sophia blinked at her brother, who wore a fine shirt and trousers and a very warm-looking overcoat. "Where did you get those clothes?"

Harry hitched his thumb over his shoulder. "His Grace—"

"Nathan," Nathan corrected as he strode up to them.

"Nathan," Harry corrected, "bought them for me. Madame Lexington had made this outfit for another boy my size, but Nathan bought it from her. And more, too. I'll get the rest of my clothes in a few days."

Sophia swallowed the giant lump in her throat. She absolutely refused to cry. Instead, she moved close to Nathan and hugged him, breaking, she was quite sure, a thousand rules of etiquette. Yet, she found it impossible to care. She pressed her lips near Nathan's ear. "Thank you."

He squeezed her waist before pulling back to look at her with his dark, penetrating eyes. "No, thank *you*. I've not celebrated Christmas since I was a boy, and I'd forgotten how much fun it was to decorate and buy gifts for someone."

Sophia blinked at him, feeling a bit dazed. "You decorated? Not the servants?"

Nathan stepped back and tousled Harry's hair. "We decorated the hall together. Didn't we?"

Harry nodded. "I told Nathan how you always gave me

one gift a day before Christmas and how last year you wanted to give me a coat but Frank took the money, and Nathan came up with the idea that we should continue your custom."

"But you gave me three gifts," Sophia remarked.

"Well, we are going ice skating," Nathan replied matter-of-factly, "and I couldn't very well expect you to skate outdoors in a gown that wasn't warm enough. And you had to have gloves to keep your hands warm, and proper shoes to walk down to the lake. And this." Nathan picked up the package he'd set at his feet and handed the box to her.

"What is it?" she asked, feeling quite like an excited child.

"Open it," he and Harry urged at once.

She quickly obeyed, and when she removed the tissue and saw the velvet, fur-lined green-and-gold cape, her eyes immediately flooded with tears. No matter what Nathan said, or didn't say yet—such as I love you—her husband had an enormous heart and a capacity to love that he simply was reluctant to expose to the world, or perhaps most particularly her. She could wait, though. For she knew someday when this man gave her all his love, it would be worth it.

She glanced up to thank him as tears of happiness rolled down her cheeks.

A dark look crossed his face, and abruptly, he turned to Harry. "Would you go to the kitchen and retrieve the picnic from the cook?"

Harry nodded and quickly departed.

Nathan faced her once again, but now his brow was creased. "What's the matter? How did I displease you?"

"What?" Sophia blinked. "You haven't displeased me. Whyever would you think so?"

"You're crying."

Sophia swiped at her eyes. "These are tears of happiness. Haven't you ever seen a woman cry because she was happy?"

"No." He was giving her a dubious look.

She instantly thought of the bits and pieces she'd heard about his mother and of something he had said moments ago. "Nathan, why haven't you celebrated Christmas since you were a young boy?"

"Ah. Well, that would be because Christmas holds nothing but bad memories for me."

"What sort of bad memories?"

"The sort filled with screaming and disappointment. Now, why don't you let me help you into your cape, and then we can find Harry and make our way to the carriage and ride down to the lake. Our plan was to have a picnic on the grotto and then ice skate."

Sophia narrowed her eyes at him. "Do you always avoid personal conversations?"

"Certainly. I find it the best way to guard the secrets I want to keep." He gave her a wink and offered his elbow to her. "Shall we?"

Sophia hesitated. She could continue to allow Nathan to hide his pain from her or she could attempt to draw him out little by little. She suspected it would be hard, indeed, but if she could show him that he could trust her without her withdrawing her love, she was hopeful that he would eventually offer her his love, not simply his elbow, and really accept hers in return. With this in mind, she shook her head at him. "The only way I'll go with you is if you tell me why you didn't take up celebrating Christmas again."

He frowned as he stared down at her. "Because my mother decreed we would not."

Sophia hated his mother, but she'd never reveal it. "And did your father agree?"

Nathan sighed. "What does it matter?"

"It matters to me. We are married, and I wish to really know you."

"Careful what you wish for, Sophia. You might get it and not like what you find."

"I will love all of you, Nathan."

He brushed his hand down her cheek. "You are a dreamer, my dear. You dreamed of a better life when you were trapped in a terrible one, and now you are fantasizing that I am some perfect gentleman. I'm not."

She shook her head. He'd utterly misunderstood her. She'd meant that no matter what she found out about him, she would continue to love him because of who he was on the inside. But before she could speak, he continued.

"I'm a realist, Sophia. London is a bitter, cynical world, and I fit in it perfectly."

"Then I will help you not fit there so perfectly."

"Ah, Sophia. If only it were that simple. Enough of this, though. Harry will be waiting."

"As I am for you to answer one of my questions." She tapped her foot for emphasis.

"Stubborn wench," he said with a chuckle. "My father's specialty was avoiding confrontations with my mother. On the rare Christmases my father was with us, I never asked him if he agreed that we should not celebrate and he never offered an opinion. I did not take up celebrating Christmas again because I am not a liar, and in order for one to celebrate something one must be happy. I simply decided I would not pretend to be happy. Are you satisfied?"

She nodded and bit down hard on her cheek to keep from grinning.

Without him realizing it, Nathan had just revealed that he was happy enough to celebrate Christmas with her. He could lavish her with a thousand new gowns encrusted with diamonds and pearls, but no present would ever match the one he'd just unknowingly given her. He wasn't as cold and cynical as he thought. He was warming and softening, and he was going to love her. She had dozens more questions she wanted to ask him, such as why he was rarely with his father at Christmas, but she suspected it was more of his father avoiding Nathan's mother, as Mary Margaret had mentioned and Nathan had just confirmed.

Getting Nathan to open up needed to be slow and gentle, lest he get scared and hide behind his walls again.

Fourteen

Later that night, after a wonderful day of picnicking marred only by Nathan informing Sophia that she might have been poisoned and urging her to be cautious, he went to her bedchamber door and was about to knock, when her humming reached his ears. The way his heart jerked filled him with dread. He cared for her. More deeply than he was willing to admit yet.

She was like a beacon of light, hope, and warmth. If he held her long enough and tight enough would he eventually feel warmth again? Would he eventually have a use for the emotion that had made him weak and caused him pain? He thought he might, and it scared the hell out of him. Because if he allowed himself to love her and then she snatched it away, he'd never come back from the darkness again. Yet, it was impossible to stand here and imagine that open, honest, guileless woman doing such a thing to him.

Her humming turned into a bawdy ditty about a sailor and his ladylove then, and Sophia sang it with the gusto only she could muster. Suddenly, he wanted to see the world as Sophia did—full of hope, wonder, and the promise of love and there was no better time to start than now.

Forgoing knocking, he opened the door and stepped into her bedchamber. She stood swathed in moonlight, wearing a very sensible white cotton night rail that started just below her chin and went all the way to the tips of her toes.

She had her hands clasped in front of her as she shifted from foot to foot. He closed the door behind him and eyed his nervous bride. Technically, he supposed this was their wedding night since she had been sick the night they had married. "Where is the frothy creation I found you in night before last?"

"I stuffed it in my drawer. I don't have the right figure for that gown."

Nathan raised an eyebrow. Most ladies would never admit they had any flaws, but Sophia was not most ladies. Not that he considered her slight figure flawed. True, she lacked the abundant feminine curves he had previously cared for, but he had grown to appreciate her figure in the last several days. She was slender and graceful, but it was obvious by the night rail she wore, which was more suited for a nun than a duchess, that she did not feel very womanly.

The right words and many well-placed caresses would make Sophia confident in her charms. He quirked his finger and was pleased when she didn't hesitate to come to him. She stopped directly in front of him and wrapped her arms around his waist. "Nathan, I hope I don't disappoint you."

Rather than offer words he didn't think she was ready to believe, he leaned down and traced the soft fullness of her lips with his tongue. She trembled in his arms and crushed her body to his. "Where did you get this night rail?" he asked, trailing his hands down her back and over her firm buttocks.

"I borrowed it from my lady's maid."

He paused a moment, considering what the devil the lady's maid must be thinking, but dismissed the erroneous concern and gathered the material of her gown in his hands until he had enough to slide it over her head. She raised her arms and allowed him to do so without a word of protest, but when the gown was off, she immediately crossed her arms over her breasts.

While holding her gaze, he quickly undressed and then bent to remove her drawers and then gently moved her arms to her sides before trailing his tongue over one pert nipple and then the other. He cupped her breasts in his palms and circled his thumb over the straining bud, reveling in the way her eyes changed from bright blue to the dark, smoky blue of desire. "Don't ever cover yourself to me, remember? *Promise me.*" He tweaked both her nipples very gently while waiting for her response.

"I promise," she said in a hoarse voice.

He brushed his lips to hers as he trailed his hands to the juncture between her thighs and slipped his fingers inside the silky hair to find the spot that made her moan. She hissed as he grazed the engorged flesh and stroked her slowly, then faster. Her eyes closed and her fingers curled into his back.

He moved one arm to the small of her back when she began to sway, and her eyes briefly flickered open. "You make me feel so wondrous, Nathan."

The surge of need he felt for her was more than he could contain. With searing desire, he grasped her under the buttocks and lifted her to his hips. In two strides, they were at the bed, and he set her down and motioned for her to turn over. He had a primal urge to plant himself as deep as he could, and the best way to do that was to take her from behind. Her eyes rounded, but she obeyed.

He slipped an arm under her belly and drew her up until she was on her knees, then found that sweet spot between her thighs again and worked his fingers with a frenzy that made him tremble and her scream. When she was slick and panting, he thrust himself inside her, grasping her under her ribs and pumping his life into her until he couldn't hold back anymore. He rode the tide that took him until he felt his seed spill into her, and she arched backward with a loud cry of pleasure.

It was as if all his cynicism had been purged from him. Gently, he lifted his weight and lay down on the bed beside her. He pulled her to him and smiled as she nuzzled her head against his chest.

For a moment, they lay there in silence while he trailed his fingers over her silken backside. When she lifted up to look at him, her bright and brilliant eyes shone with pure love. He tensed as she confirmed what he saw. "I love you, Nathan."

Before he could fight against his fear and see if he could

offer her the words he knew she wanted to hear, a knock came at the bedchamber door.

"Sophia, I had a nightmare," Harry called.

Sophia bounded out of the bed and donned her white night rail. She disappeared from his view, then reappeared just as quickly. "Harry is used to sleeping with me. He's scared."

Nathan saw the unspoken plea in her eyes. Hell, he could not believe what he was about to say. "Let him come in. I'll make myself a pallet on the floor, and he can sleep in the bed with you."

Sophia raced back to Nathan and kissed him. "There's no need for a pallet!" she exclaimed. "We can all fit nicely on my bed."

Hours later, as Nathan lay there listening to the even breathing of Sophia and Harry in sleep, he rolled over to get more comfortable and almost fell off the bed. Growling, he flipped onto his back. Tomorrow he would have a man-to-boy talk with Harry. He listened to their breathing awhile more and he realized with a start that he was smiling yet again. Sophia made him happy, and he fought back against the feeling he knew was not bound to last.

⚜

Sophia awoke the next morning alone with a smile on her face. Any man who would allow his wife's brother to sleep in bed with them had to care. She rolled to her side to get out of bed, and as she did, she saw a folded note with her name on it on the pillow Nathan had slept on. Her first love letter, perhaps? Grinning, she snatched the note up and unfolded it.

Dear Sophia,

I received an urgent missive from my cousin, Ellison, my Aunt Harriet's son. When I'm absent from London, Ellison reads all correspondence I receive in regard to my recently purchased shipping line, Zephyrus Shipping. It seems one of my ships was caught in a terrible storm. It sustained great damage, and we lost several of the crew.

Sophia's breath caught in her throat as she read. *How awful!*

I cannot, in good conscience, leave it to Ellison to inform their families, as I am the owner.

Sophia looked up at the ceiling with a sigh. She was supremely glad Nathan was the sort of man who felt compelled to notify the unfortunate relatives personally, even if it did mean it had taken him from her side.

Rest assured, I will be back within the week. And as I think I know you a bit by now, you can quit worrying. I did not wake you to say good-bye because it would have been that much harder for me to leave, and time was of the essence.

A grin quirked Sophia's lips. He *did* know her mind. She had wondered, and now he had just set her at ease and given her hope. Not only had he been concerned about her feelings but he had admitted that leaving her would be difficult. She pressed the letter to her chest for a moment before lowering it and continuing to read.

I've informed Mr. Dobbs and Gibson that you are completely and utterly in charge in my absence. If you need anything at all, simply ask them. Now, there is a surprise in the stables waiting for you. Go there and find Mr. Burk the stable master.

Your husband (that feels odd to write),
Nathan

She lay there for a moment and pondered his last words. *That feels odd to write.* Was it bad that he'd written that or was she reading too much into it? After all, it felt strange to her that she was now a duchess. He could have just signed the note

Scarsdale and not *Your husband*. But he was, indeed, her husband.

Forever.

The small nugget of hope that her mother had told her to keep in her heart was now a large boulder. Humming, she got out of bed and struggled valiantly into one of her new morning gowns, which was made of a delicate, rose-colored muslin. Of course, the proper thing to do would have been to allow Mary Margaret to dress her, but honestly, it seemed a tad ridiculous to constantly be dressed by someone else. She had been putting on her own clothes her entire life, and whether that made her less of a lady or not, she intended, for the most part, to keep taking care of herself.

After donning another pair of new slippers—it felt very indulgent but lovely to own two pairs of shoes—she took a quick glance in the looking glass and went downstairs in search of Harry. She found him in the dining room, cheeks puffed with a mouthful of food. She told him she was headed to the stables and he could meet her there, and then she made her way out the door.

As she did so, she noticed a footman slip out behind her, and when she inquired as to why, he informed her that he was to accompany her wherever she went. She smiled at the thought that Nathan was concerned about her safety, even if it did seem a tad overcautious. She didn't see how a stranger could possibly slip past all the staff here.

Sophia strolled onto the terrace where the steps led to the garden, the footman walking a respectful distance behind. She made her way through the topiary garden with its formal plots lining both sides of a gravel path she knew led to a tunnel-like arbor. Inside the tunnel, she took a deep breath and filled her lungs with the crisp scent of the fresh, chilled air.

As she ventured closer to the stables, her jaw dropped open. The building was so grand it could be a house all on its own. It was a quadrangle, and at the main entrance, benches sat along each side of a covered space.

Male voices drifted from the interior of the stables, and

then four men came ambling outside. As they saw her, the laughter and talking stopped, and they all stared at her. She suddenly felt very self-conscious, but she straightened her spine and raised her shoulders, determined to make Nathan proud.

"Are one of you perchance Mr. Burk?" she asked.

The tallest of the men—a barrel-chested, red-haired, red-bearded man—raised a hand. "Aye, that'd be me. Can I help ye?" His words held the ring of a Scot.

She nodded. "I'm Sophia."

"*Criminy!*" Mr. Burk pulled off his hat and sketched a jerky bow. "I'm sorry, Your Grace."

The three other men quickly removed their hats and bowed, as well, each mumbling their apologies.

Sophia laughed. "Heavens! There's no need to apologize. My husband said to find you, Mr. Burk, that you had a surprise for me."

"It's a grand one," he said with a twinkle in his sky-blue eyes. "Go on with the three of ye." He waved his hand at the other men. "Ye too," he commanded the footman who had been following her.

"But I'm to stay with her when she's out," the young man replied.

"I'll watch her, ta be sure, and deliver her back ta the house myself."

The footman nodded, and all the men departed with backward glances and whispers. Sophia self-consciously straightened her gown and toyed with her short hair. Out of the corner of her eye, she caught Mr. Burk staring at her. "I suppose I'm not the sort of duchess everyone would have expected Nathan to marry." She was sure they wondered why he had not chosen a great beauty.

Mr. Burk smiled as he motioned her ahead of him and through the door. "No, Yer Grace, ye are not, but that's a good thing, not a bad. Yer husband has a great deal of good in him and a keen mind, but until ye, he never seemed ta use his mind when choosing his female company."

She felt her eyes widen in surprise at the man's honest words, and his face turned so red it nearly matched his beard.

"I'm sorry I overspoke," he mumbled.

"You didn't. You just surprised me with your candor."

He laughed. "My mother always said the good Lord gave me too much of it."

"I think you have the perfect amount," Sophia said. "Have you worked for Nathan long?"

"Oh, aye. I've been stable master here longer than His Grace has been alive. I was here when he was born, helped him grow into one of the finest equestrians around, and then watched him get into a heap of mischief. If ye ever want ta hear some stories, just say the word."

With that, Mr. Burk strode ahead into the stables, which were two-stories high and resounded with male voices, yapping dogs, and neighing horses. He passed three stalls and stopped at the fourth, where a glorious white horse stood majestic and silent.

"That is the most beautiful horse I've ever seen," Sophia whispered in awe.

"That's good, Yer Grace, because Scarsdale purchased her for ye."

"But I don't even know how to ride!" Sophia exclaimed.

Mr. Burk chuckled. "I know. Scarsdale told me. He intends to teach you himself, but I'm ta get you started. He jest did not say it was ta be today."

A wonderful thought occurred to Sophia. "Mr. Burk, how long would you say it would take to learn to ride a horse like this?"

"Well, it depends on the person doing the teaching and the person being taught."

She locked gazes with the man. "Well, Nathan will be the teacher and I'll be the pupil."

Mr. Burk tilted his head. "I'd say a good month for ye ta feel steady."

Joy spread like fire through her veins, rapid and consuming. Nathan wanted to spend time with her. And she was going to use every moment of it to show him that he loved her, too.

Fifteen

Nathan went straight to White's when he arrived in London late at night three days later. He wanted to speak to Ellison and learn what he knew about the accident with the ship. Ellison always spent Saturday night at White's. He made his way inside, and after handing off his overcoat, gloves, and hat, he wound through the crowded room searching for his cousin, nodding to acquaintances as he went.

Near the front of the establishment, at the table occupying the space in front of the bow window, Ellison, Aversley, and Harthorne sat engaged in conversation. Nathan strode toward the table, and as he did, he caught Ellison's eye. His cousin waved a hand in greeting and then said something to the men. Aversley, never one to show emotion, glanced at Nathan and raised his drink as if he was toasting.

Nathan frowned. He had a suspicion Ellison had told them Nathan had married, and when he neared the table and Harthorne turned and grinned at him, he knew it had to be so. Wariness caused him to slow his progress toward the table. He'd not told Harthorne or Aversley about his impending marriage when he'd come to London to get his aunt because he'd known they'd ask questions, and frankly, he'd not known exactly what to say. He raked a hand through his hair as he reached the table and realized he still didn't know what to say.

He'd married Sophia out of pity and guilt. Now something more was there, but he was not ready to speak of it. He didn't even understand it yet.

"You old devil!" Harthorne exclaimed as he shoved his

chair back, clapped Nathan on the shoulder, and thrust a drink into his hand. "I would have bet my entire fortune—not that there's much of it—that you wouldn't succumb to marriage for at least another ten years! Thank God, I didn't make that bet. I cannot believe you're married. A toast!"

Nathan glanced around the room. This was one of those times when Harthorne's perpetual optimism was annoying. Luckily, the other gentlemen in the club appeared too preoccupied with their own conversations to pay attention to Harthorne.

Harthorne elbowed him in the ribs. "Raise your glass, Scarsdale. Don't you want to toast your marriage?"

Nathan raised his glass to his lips, downed the liquor, and savored the instant warmth the brandy created from his throat all the way to his belly. He pulled out a chair and sat beside Aversley as Harthorne returned to his seat.

Aversley stared across the table at Nathan with assessing eyes. "I noticed you didn't answer Harthorne when he asked you if you wanted to toast your marriage."

Nathan ground his teeth. He should have known Aversley would not miss a thing. "I toasted it, didn't I?"

Aversley drummed his fingers on the rim of his untouched glass. "Not really. You gulped down your drink, which is not the same. Why didn't you tell us you were getting married?"

"How did you know I was married?" Nathan shot back.

Aversley glanced at Ellison, who shrugged. "Sorry, but how the devil was I supposed to know you didn't want anyone to know?" Ellison defended. "I'd say that's going to be a pretty hard secret to keep unless you plan to never bring your wife to London and introduce her to Society."

Nathan stared down at the glass in his hand and swirled around the few drops of liquor that remained. Ellison's innocent suggestion held a certain appeal, but only because Nathan didn't want the *ton* to change Sophia, or worse yet, hurt her with cruelty.

"Good God, Scarsdale, your cousin isn't right, is he?" Harthorne demanded, his face turning red with, knowing

Harthorne, indignation. "Even if you've been trapped into marriage, you cannot keep your wife a secret. That's callous, even for you."

"It's nice to know you think my callousness has its limits," Nathan said.

"You know what I mean," Harthorne replied.

The problem was Nathan *did* know what he meant. He was callous to most people because he believed it better to be unfeeling than wounded. But Sophia had made him question himself. "I was not trapped into marriage," he said, choosing his words with care.

Harthorne grinned. "I knew it! You married for love!"

Nathan stiffened. He'd not yet decided if he could relent to love and he certainly wasn't going to discuss it here and now.

Harthorne leaned forward and motioned to Scarsdale and then Ellison. "Pay up. I win."

"You bet on why I married?" Nathan said, irritated that his marriage had been the topic of a wager.

"Stop glaring, Scarsdale," Aversley replied. "We included no one in the wager but the three of us. It's not as if we announced your marriage to everyone here."

"At least one of you comprehends when to be discreet," Nathan snapped, spearing his cousin with a look, which Ellison carefully avoided meeting.

"So," Aversley began, "as much as I know it pains you, you must confirm or deny if you married for love so I will know whether to pay my greedy brother-in-law the large sum I wagered."

"How much did you wager?" Nathan asked.

"One hundred pounds. Did you or did you not marry for love?"

"I did not," Nathan said, wishing his conscience would let him lie, but it simply wouldn't.

Aversley grinned triumphantly at Harthorne and Ellison. "You both owe me one hundred pounds."

Harthorne groaned as Ellison cleared his throat. "Not so fast, Aversley. We do not yet know why my cousin married. I may be the winner, after all. You said it was because he was trapped and he's already told us that was not the case. So, cousin, I wagered that you married for pity. After Mother described what your new duchess looks like, I knew it had to be pity. And no one knows better than I that you have an abundance of that *one* particular emotion. Tell us, did you marry the wench out of pity?"

Nathan's pulse pounded in his ears as he searched for a thread of control. Normally he would have felt remorse that he'd unknowingly made Ellison feel pitied, but the anger surging through his veins washed away any regret. He placed his palms flat on the table and leaned in. "You have crossed a line, Ellison. I suggest you retreat or the consequences will be dire."

Ellison didn't respond, but Nathan noted his cousin's flared nostrils and sweat-dampened brow. "*Never* refer to my wife as a wench. That will get you an appointment with my pistol. Are we clear?"

"Yes." Ellison swallowed audibly. "I'm sorry."

He would have accepted an apology from his cousin for almost any slight he could think of, but not one against Sophia. She didn't deserve it, and he wanted to make the point unforgettable. "Never ask me again why I married." He made sure his gaze included Aversley and Harthorne. "It's none of your damned business. I value each of your friendships, but I will cut all ties and never look back if you ever say another word that could hurt my wife."

"Agreed," Ellison said weakly.

"For the record," Harthorne replied, "I never uttered a disparaging remark against the duchess. I'll be pleased to meet her and count her as a friend."

"I appreciate that."

Nathan turned to Aversley, who shrugged. "Your secrets are yours to keep. Who am I to pry? And another point for the record, I don't give a damned four Sundays to the next why you married. I simply like to win and felt I would. Amelia and I will do everything in our power to help ease your wife into

Society. If you think she needs help, that is."

The tension vibrating through Nathan trickled out of him. He leaned back in his chair and raised his glass to signal he needed a refill. As the waiter appeared and whisked their tumblers away, he thought about what Aversley had offered. "To be blunt, I've not yet decided whether Sophia will live most of her days in the country or stay in Town with me when I'm here. But I do plan to introduce her to Society as is proper. I hadn't considered it until now, but if there is a chance Amelia would lend her expertise in helping Sophia prepare for that eventuality, I would appreciate it. I could have you both out for an extended stay, or just Amelia, if you could spare her."

"I make it a habit never to let Amelia out of my sight," Aversley said. "I'll come, as well. When and where?"

"To Whitecliffe. Two weeks should be sufficient time."

"What brings you to Town now?" Aversley inquired as the waiter reappeared and handed them each a fresh glass of brandy.

"One of my ships was caught in a storm, and I lost several of my crew. I've come to let the families know, assess the damage, and determine how much it's going to cost me."

"I told you it was ludicrous to buy a shipping line," Ellison said. "Trade is for the lower classes."

Nathan trained his gaze on Ellison. "And I've told you a man's worth is not measured in pounds but in hard work and honor."

Ellison snorted. "You hold a minority opinion."

"I don't much care if I have company in my beliefs or not," Nathan replied, struggling to keep his tone civil.

"Actually," Aversley said, "I agree with Scarsdale."

"As do I," Harthorne added.

Nathan leveled Ellison with a look. "Taking my beliefs out of the equation, steamships are the future, and I will be part of changing the world."

"I agree," Aversley said. "If you've need of a partner, I'd be eager to come down to the docks and hear more about your company."

"I'd be eager to come and listen, as well," Harthorne inserted. "Though I cannot currently invest."

Nathan grinned. "I'll take you both up on that. Why don't we say on Wednesday? Three days should give me plenty of time to inform the crew's relatives of their losses and set my affairs to order."

"I'd like to help, too," Ellison said quietly. "I can inform the relatives so you can use your time to go over the records and meet with Aversley and Harthorne."

"I appreciate it," Nathan replied, glad to see his cousin was willing to be more open-minded, especially since Nathan had been paying him a small fortune to run the shipping office for him. "Though, I need to be the one to see the families. I'm the owner of the shipping company, and those men were my responsibility. But I appreciate you offering, Ellison. Can you tell me anything of what happened?"

"Not much. But we are to get a detailed report from the captain late tomorrow afternoon, and I'll make sure it's on your desk for you when you come in the next day."

"I'll come by the office tomorrow night to read the report after I see the families."

"It'll be dark by then!" Ellison exclaimed.

"I'm not afraid of the dark," Nathan drawled, irritation flaring. He had known Ellison hadn't particularly wanted to work in the shipping company, but he also knew his cousin could use the extra money. "I don't expect you to be there. Just have the report on my desk."

"It's not safe at the docks at night. You're not thinking, man," Ellison said.

"I am thinking perfectly," Nathan clipped. "I'll be at the office in the morning to get the list of men who perished and take a look at the ship. We can talk more then." Travel weariness had caught up with Nathan, and he found himself eager to leave. He pushed back his chair and stood. "Gentlemen, if you'll excuse me, I need to retire for the night."

Aversley rose, as well. "I better go, too. Amelia worries when I'm out late. I'll walk out with you."

After they said their good-byes, Nathan and Aversley made their way to the door, retrieved their coats, hats, and gloves, and stepped out into the cold night. They stood in companionable silence as they waited for their carriages—or in Nathan's case, his curricle—to be brought around.

"Do you want any marriage advice?" Aversley said with a chuckle.

Nathan laughed. "Not yet."

Aversley cleared his throat and spoke again. "What shall I tell Amelia to expect?"

Nathan glanced up at the twinkling, burning stars and thought of Sophia. What could he say about her? "Tell Amelia to expect the unexpected," he replied, not wanting to voice his thoughts that Sophia was not a beauty on the outside, but on the inside, she might just possibly be an Incomparable. That she was rough, yet gentle. Fragile, yet fierce. Smart, yet uneducated. Worldly, yet naive. And that he felt as if he had only peeled back the first amazing layer of his complicated wife.

"Forthcoming, as always," Aversley said, his voice light but his face full of tension.

Nathan grunted. "Had you expected marriage to change me?"

"Yes," Aversley clipped, as his carriage rumbled to a halt in front of him. "Yes, I had." With that, Nathan's closest friend departed, and he was left standing alone in the cold with the disconcerting knowledge that marriage was, indeed, changing him.

※

Nathan was at the docks first thing in the morning as he'd promised. As he made his way down to his office through a blanket of thick fog, he passed scores of lightermen carrying heavy loads between ships. He paused to watch a bevy of porters balancing wood and seeming to effortlessly get aboard the ships with mind-boggling acrobatic moves. Farther down the dock, he stopped to admire a large schooner and watched as several men scaled one of the masts to begin repairs on a torn sail.

As he stood there observing the men, a tall, black-haired man with a matching patch of dark hair on the tip of his chin strode across the deck with a cocky gait. He slowed as he seemed to catch sight of Nathan.

Ravensdale.

Nathan fingered the pistol holstered at his waist. He always wore it to the docks, usually at his ankle but tonight he'd worn it at his waist. He didn't know if seeing Ravensdale here after all these years was a coincidence or not, but he damned sure wasn't taking any chances. Ravensdale made his way off the ship and halted in front of Nathan. His green gaze fastened on to Nathan's right hand where it rested on his pistol.

A slow, contemptuous smile spread across Ravensdale's face. "Is that any way to greet a friend?"

"We're not friends."

"You wound me, Scarsdale." He paused and made a show of unsheathing a dagger without looking away from Nathan. He held the dagger up and ran his finger down the shiny blade. "I once considered you a friend during our days of midnight-to-dawn debauchery at the Order of the Dark Lords. I hear you no longer go there."

Nathan flicked his gaze from the dagger to Ravensdale's eyes. "That's correct. I've no use to go to a club where most the men lack scruples and honor. Have you been checking on me?"

Something menacing flickered across Ravensdale's face. "But of course. Did you think I'd not seek revenge for your ruining my life?"

"I hadn't given it much thought," Nathan replied.

Until lately.

Immediately after he'd told the Bow Street Runners what he'd seen, he became determined to fix the mess he'd made of his life and seek forgiveness from his true friends. Ravensdale had been the furthest thing from his mind.

The vile man brought the tip of his dagger to his finger and pressed until blood appeared and dripped down his hand. "I waited every night for weeks at the club after you betrayed me. To ambush and kill you, of course."

"Did you?" Nathan gently placed his finger on the trigger of the pistol.

Ravensdale nodded. "I did. Outside, that is. The hypocrites wouldn't let me in the door since I'd been accused of being the Hooded Robber."

Nathan clenched his teeth. "You somehow escaped being found guilty, though. You and I both know you were the Hooded Robber."

Ravensdale's fingers became white on the hilt of the dagger, and Nathan could see his jaw ticking furiously. "I lost my fiancée, my family, and my position as a Bow Street Runner. It didn't matter to anyone that I wasn't found guilty, because they could find no evidence. They believed your accusations. Neither my mother nor my sisters speak to me anymore." He laughed bitterly. "Everything I did was for them, to give them a better life. The kind *you* have. The kind you always took for granted and complained about." He stared at Nathan accusingly.

Nathan flinched at the last remark. To someone who didn't really know him, his life would have seemed ideal. He had far more material possessions than most, but that was all he'd had, and to a boy, that had not been enough. He was supremely glad he no longer cared. "You should have done it honestly. For Christ's sake, Ravensdale, you used your position to rob people."

"Oh please," Ravensdale scoffed. "We both know a poor viscount's son like me can never honestly make the sort of money that was handed to a nobleman like you." He waved his dagger in the air between them. "You pretend to be so goddamned virtuous. You ratted me out when the last I saw you, you were lapping up laudanum and drinking liquor as if it were in danger of ceasing to exist. What makes those vices less evil?"

"Nothing," Nathan said, washed in shame. "But I am no longer that crazed man, no thanks to you."

"I'm not your keeper," Ravensdale snarled.

"No, you're not. I don't blame you for my choices. They were my own, but you had no qualms encouraging me to drink more, take more laudanum, and allow my honor to disappear." Damnation, but he'd not meant to say so much. He truly did not blame Ravensdale. Nor did he blame the physician that had first insisted he needed laudanum to alleviate the pain in his injured arm.

Neither Ravensdale nor the physician had the power to make decisions for him. He alone had been a fool. But not blaming Ravensdale for his own folly was a very different beast then knowing the man was the thief responsible for robbing carriages when he was supposed to be protecting them. Nathan narrowed his eyes. "What do you want, Ravensdale? Are you going to try to take this opportunity to kill me now that we're face-to-face? It might be a little hard to cover up in broad daylight on the docks."

"I don't intend to kill you." A strange smile twisted Ravensdale's lips. "I decided some time ago that death was too good for you. I have other plans for you, Scarsdale. I've been biding my time because I was certain it would come."

Just then, a group of seamen who worked for Nathan strolled by and one of the men, Stephens, stopped. "Everything all right, Your Grace?"

Nathan stepped around Ravensdale. "Perfectly fine. Just on my way to the office." He walked away from Ravensdale without looking back. As he walked toward his office, Stephens asked him questions about the damaged ship and lost crew, but Nathan's mind was on Ravensdale. He was sure the man was trying to kill him, despite what he said. *Someone* was, and the man's motive was sound. But Nathan didn't see how Ravensdale could have possibly snuck into Whitecliffe and poisoned Sophia. It didn't seem possible, but he intended to get answers.

With his temper simmering, he slammed his office door.

Ellison startled in his seat and the paper that he'd been holding fluttered to the ground. Shooting a glare at Nathan, he bent down and snatched it up. "I see your mood has not improved from last night."

"Sorry," Nathan grumbled. "Ellison, have you heard anything about Ravensdale?"

Ellison paused with his quill in midair. "Why? You haven't had a run-in with him again, have you?"

Before Nathan could respond, Ellison continued, his tone defensive. "I haven't seen him since the night you had him out to Whitecliffe. What was that, two years ago?"

"A bit more," Nathan replied. "I didn't think you had seen him," he clarified. "I asked if you'd heard anything about him."

"I've heard he makes his money as a renegade privateer, but I don't think anyone has any proof. Why?"

"I just ran into the man. Before I leave Town, I'm going to hire Sir Richard to look into the matter."

"Why do you care so much about him?" Ellison asked while standing and handing Nathan a piece of foolscap.

Nathan took the paper and glanced down at the list of four names of the men who died in the storm. "Because I suspect he is trying to kill me."

Ellison's mouth went slack. "Did he say as much to you?"

Nathan noticed his cousin's quill tremble. "Don't worry, cousin. I'm not. Not for me. I do want to make sure Sophia is safe, though. It's good to know your enemies, wouldn't you agree?"

"Of course," Ellison replied.

Nathan nodded. "I'll be back after I see some of the crew's families. What time will the report be here?"

"By four."

"Good. I will come back later, then, and I'll see you first thing in the morning, so we can overlook the ship's damage together."

Ellison nodded. "I still don't think you should come here so late by yourself."

Nathan patted his right hip. "I won't be unarmed, don't

worry," he said and headed out of the office to perform the gruesome task of notifying families they had lost loved ones.

It had taken the entire day to inform the relatives of the four men. Exhaustion hung heavy on Nathan, and he briefly considered waiting to come to the docks until tomorrow morning, but that would undoubtedly set him back a day in returning to Whitecliffe. Surprisingly—*or maybe not*, he thought with a grin—he was eager to see Sophia. The sooner he could leave London the better.

As he walked by the pubs, gas lamps flickered in the darkness and rambunctious singing spilled out from underneath the doors. But once he moved past the pubs, the walkway from those buildings to the quiet offices reminded Nathan what it must be like to walk the cold, black corridor into hell. The kind of darkness that pervaded many areas of the docks at night made the hairs on the back on Nathan's neck stand on end. He shook off the anxiety and hurried toward his office with his pistol firmly gripped in his hand, his finger on the trigger.

As he rounded a sharp corner, something flashed out of the darkness and hit his hand with such force that the pistol flew out of his vibrating fingers. He lunged for it but stopped short as the moon broke out from the clouds. He stared into the barrel of a pistol and the tip of a large, gleaming dagger pointed at his face.

Standing all the way up, he met Ravensdale's gaze, then glanced at the tall, bucktoothed man beside him. It took a moment for Nathan to remember the man, but when he spoke, Nathan tensed.

"Hullo, Lord Scarsdale."

"That'd be 'Your Grace' to you," Nathan snarled.

Ravensdale laughed. "Pompous as ever, I see."

"And you're still a liar, I see."

Ravensdale pressed the point of his dagger into Nathan's chest at his heart. "Watch your tongue or I'll cut it out."

"I thought you said death was too good for me," Nathan said dryly, refusing to show any fear. He could not die tonight. He had to take care of Sophia and Harry.

"It is. Which is why, upon my considering the matter after the first attempt on your life was botched, I reconsidered the plan."

Nathan flinched at the confirmation that Ravensdale was behind the attempts on his life. "What now, then, if not my death?" he asked, trying to buy some time to figure a way out of this. As it stood at the moment, he'd be shot dead by one or both of them before he could retrieve his pistol. And shouting for help was pointless. There was no one around to hear him.

"I'm glad you asked," Ravensdale said. Eerie enthusiasm rang in his voice. "You know, I'm embarrassed to say it took me awhile, but I've figured out that by not killing you, I can achieve revenge *and* become rich."

"How industrious of you," Nathan snapped. "Do you care to share your plan?"

"Certainly. I'm going to use you as a slave to pay off a debt I owe to a Barbary corsair. They don't know you, nor give a damn that you are the Duke of Scarsdale. To them you are no more than fresh slave meat. When the year of debt is paid off, I'm going to sell you to another foreigner. I have a rich Barbary lord who has a penchant for strapping Englishmen. He likes to use them for pleasure, if you know what I mean."

Nathan would rather be dead than submit to that fate. He lunged forward, knocked Ravensdale's dagger out of his hand, and swung toward the taller man, but as he did, a shot rang out and he staggered back as a bullet pierced his leg. The man leaped forward and smacked him across the right cheekbone with the butt of his still-smoking pistol. But Nathan was in a rage. He barreled into the man and knocked him to the ground. Then he swung around to take care of Ravensdale, and as he turned, Ravensdale's dagger gleamed in front of him, then was plunged straight down into his other leg. Nathan's knees buckled and he dropped to them, blood pouring from the gash in one leg and the bullet wound in the other. His burning legs throbbed in time with each other. Above him, he could feel the men hovering. He tilted his head up, and the world sloped with the movement.

Ravensdale stood there grinning. "You always were one to make things fun, Scarsdale." He kicked out, his foot connecting with Nathan's chest with the force of a log. Nathan fell backward and hit his head against the dock. The ringing in his ear was instantly deafening, and as he rolled over to gain his feet, something hard struck him on the left side of his face. Warm blood poured down that side to match the blood trickling down the right. He collapsed back to the ground and stared into nothingness. Darkness consumed the night, speckled by a few stars, which Ravensdale's leering face blocked within seconds.

Nathan swiped the blood out of his eyes to glare at Ravensdale. "Changed your mind about killing me?" he taunted, in too much pain to care.

"Certainly not. As I said, you will make me rich and I'll be fulfilling my word."

Nathan calculated his odds of escape. Grim, at best. Ravensdale now had two loaded pistols and one he could reload. Nathan's best hope of survival was to bide his time.

Ravensdale shoved one of the pistols against Nathan's temple. "I see your mind plotting, Scarsdale, and you can forget getting away. You're going to be chained to a wooden seat where you will eat, defecate, urinate, and sleep for a year as you row a pirate ship in payment of my debt. If you survive, which truly I hope you do, I'll sell you across the ocean in Algiers, where you will be beaten daily until you willingly submit to your master." Ravensdale brought his face inches from Nathan's. "I told you I would get my revenge, and I told you a quick death was too good for you. Get used to your new life, Scarsdale. Now you will be the one to know humiliation. Now you will be the one to lose everything with no hope of ever getting it back."

"We'll see," Nathan replied, as his stomach clenched violently. Fear clogged his throat, keeping him from saying anything else, yet it was not fear for himself. Sophia and Harry consumed his mind. What would she do? What would she think when he simply disappeared? Before he could answer his own questions, the pistol flashed above him again and hit him straight across the forehead with a force that rattled his teeth and stole his consciousness.

Sixteen

As the Duke of Aversley stared at the passing countryside three day's later, he took his wife's hand in his, interlaced their fingers, and brought her smaller hand to his chest. "I don't think I'll be able to find the right words to tell Scarsdale's wife that he's missing."

Amelia laid her cheek on his shoulder and offered the comfort only she could. "You will. He'd find the words to tell me."

"But he knows you. I don't even know this woman. We've never met her, and I told you—"

Amelia pressed a finger to his lips as she raised her head and looked at him. "He married this woman out of pity. Yes, I know what you said. Yet, I still find it hard to believe. Darling, whyever he married her, she is his wife, and therefore, we will be her friends. You told me yourself that he wanted me to help her."

Colin sighed. He wished to the devil that he'd not gone home the night he saw Scarsdale at White's and told Amelia that he had requested her aid. That conversation was the reason they were riding behind Ellison and Lady Anthony on the road to Lincolnshire. He'd thought it proper that the aunt or cousin inform Scarsdale's wife that her husband was missing, but Amelia had insisted she must go, too, and so must he.

Disagreeing with his wife made him unhappy, so he made it a habit to avoid it whenever possible. Besides that, Amelia had made a very good point. Though Scarsdale's cousin was a good enough chap, Scarsdale's aunt was a harridan. Colin wouldn't put it past her to bully, belittle, and otherwise make the new duchess's life hell as she waited for news of whether Scarsdale was alive or not. And if he wasn't… Colin refused to acknowledge the possibility.

So here they were. It was going to be bloody awkward not knowing the chit, but they would aid Scarsdale's wife, bloody awkward or not.

"Darling, when do you think the Bow Street Runners will have news?"

Colin shook his head. "I don't know. But I hired a private investigator, Sir Richard, as well. Do you know, the odd thing is, when I spoke to him he told me he had several messages from Nathan requesting an appointment to see him, but he had only just arrived back in London the day I went to see him."

"That is odd," Amelia murmured, her brow puckering. "And Scarsdale never mentioned anything?"

Colin shook his head. "You know how private Scarsdale is. I didn't even know he was married until Ellison told me, and Ellison only knew because Scarsdale asked his aunt to be a witness. At first I couldn't see why he'd ask her over me or Harthorne"—Colin grinned, ruefully—"but then it occurred to me he likely thought it would be the perfect way to keep tongues from wagging that his family was not supportive of his marriage."

Amelia tilted her head in obvious thought. "Why did you hire a private investigator when Ellison already spoke with Bow Street?"

"Because I don't think the runners will be sufficient to ferret out the truth. My gut tells me time is of the essence. Press gangs roam those docks, and if Scarsdale got pressed into service accidentally—" Colin clenched and unclenched his fingers around his wife's before raising her hand to his lips and kissing her knuckles "—it could be very bad. Many of those men never make it out alive."

"He will," Amelia insisted, displaying one of the characteristics he loved most about her. She had unshakable faith in those she cared about, and though it sometimes made Colin ridiculously jealous, Scarsdale had earned Amelia's faith when he had helped her try to win Colin's love. The memory of what an ass Colin been to Amelia made him tense.

Amelia frowned, as if sensing his discomfort. "What is it? You don't agree?"

Colin thought about her insistence that Scarsdale would come out alive. "If Scarsdale loved his wife the way I love you, I'd say I agree. I would cross oceans and endure hell to make my way back to you. But for a man who doesn't have anyone to fight for…" Colin let his words trail off. It suddenly hit him hard that he may never see Scarsdale again. His chest tightened. "No one seems to know anything. So many of the ships that were there that day have already shipped out, so if anyone saw anything, he is likely gone."

"We are here," Amelia whispered.

Colin blinked. He'd been staring out the window, but he'd not even noticed that the carriage had turned onto the long, winding drive of Scarsdale's favorite country home, White-cliffe. "Do you think she'll create a scene when she learns Scarsdale is missing?"

"I certainly hope so," Amelia replied.

"You do?" He didn't bother to try to disguise his surprise. Amelia knew him too well.

"Certainly." She pulled on her gloves before elaborating. "Then I'll know whether she loves him or not. If she doesn't have much of a reaction, then I doubt she loves him."

As the carriage slowed to a stop, Colin put his hat on his head. "I, for one, hope she doesn't create a scene."

"Whyever not?"

"Because he doesn't love her. And whether he comes back or not, it will be better for her if she doesn't love him."

"Men!" Amelia exclaimed, drew off her glove, and smacked him on the head with it. "You told me he became rather vicious with his cousin when the man called her a wench."

"What does that matter?" Colin demanded as the carriage dipped with the loss of the coachman's weight. Within seconds, the door was opened and the steps let down. Colin held out his hand to his wife. "Shall we?"

Amelia answered with a mutinous glare. "It matters," she hissed under her breath.

"I don't see how," he grumbled back.

"Because." She leaned close to him and said under her breath, "It means he cares about her."

Colin snorted. "It means he doesn't want his wife disparaged because it makes him appear the fool. That is all it means. You don't know Scarsdale as well as I do. His mother belittled him at every turn. He'd never stand for someone doing that to another."

"I suppose you might be correct," Amelia said on a sigh. "It's much nicer to think they may be in love, though."

"I know it is, darling." Some things were not worth the fight disagreeing might cause.

Once everyone was inside, the butler informed them that Scarsdale's wife was out having her riding lesson.

"What do you mean she's having a riding lesson?" Lady Anthony demanded.

"I believe the man means the duchess is sitting on a horse learning how to ride it," Colin replied, unable to resist prickling Scarsdale's irksome aunt. Out of the corner of his eye, he saw Amelia scowl at him and Ellison fighting a smile.

Lady Anthony pinched her lips together, and for a brief moment, he thought she may stay blessedly silent, but then she said in a shrewish voice, "That woman should not be on a horse."

Amelia stiffened beside Colin. It took a lot to anger his wife, but woe to the man or woman who did. Colin barely held in an amused chuckle as Amelia stepped around him and faced Lady Ellison. "That woman, as you so ineloquently put it, is your nephew's wife and the Duchess of Scarsdale. And why should she not be on a horse?"

"Well, what if she's with child? She could be carrying a

boy, and obviously, he would be the next duke."

Colin frowned. "You talk as if Scarsdale is dead. He is missing. *Not dead.*"

Lady Anthony's mouth gaped open. Ellison took her by the elbow and waved a hand in the air. "Mother is overly distraught. Forgive her. She, um, that is, *we* both believe Scarsdale will be found alive. We pray for it. Don't we, Mother?"

"Yes. Of course we do."

Colin stared at her. The woman said the right words but she sounded like a wooden puppet. He forced a smile he didn't feel. The alternative was shaking the woman to see if she would crack, and that seemed extreme for now. "I'm sure the duchess will take every precaution if she is with child."

"Of course, you're right," Lady Anthony murmured as she turned toward the butler, but even with her back to Colin, he caught a snatch of her grumblings, which had to do with the mockery that would befall them all if that common woman bore a son who was to be the next duke.

He curled his hands into fists and opened his mouth to flay her, but Amelia came to his side and shook her head. She was right. Arguing with Lady Anthony would not help. "Where might we find the duchess?" he asked the butler.

"She's riding in the east fields with the stable master, Mr. Burk."

"Very good." Colin held his elbow out for his wife. "Shall we?"

The wind whipped Sophia's hair across her cheekbones as she hovered over her horse as Mr. Burk had taught her. They raced side by side to the finish line near the trees. At the very last moment, she whispered in Aphrodite's ear and the horse sped up. The cold hitting her face caused tears to leak from her eyes, but she still crossed the line two strides in front of Mr. Burk. She slowed her horse to a stop and threw up her arms in an unladylike victory celebration.

Mr. Burk, grinning from ear to ear, guided his horse beside hers, and the two beasts panted in unison.

"I bested you!" she exclaimed.

"That ye did. His Grace is going ta be shocked when he sees ye."

"Do you think I could best him?"

Mr. Burk chuckled again. "Not yet, Yer Grace. Yer husband is the best rider I've ever seen. Everyone used ta say so, except his mother."

"What did she say?"

Mr. Burk made a scornful sound. "'Twas plain that she dinnot like the fact that he could outride her."

"Oh my." Sophia swallowed the lump that had lodged in her throat. "Did he know how she felt?"

"Hard not to. She took ta pointing out everything she thought he did wrong. He was a good boy with a hard life. Ta look at all the grandeur at his wee fingertips some would disagree, but what's all the money in the world nary love?"

Sophia sniffed back tears, and she sensed his discomfort when Mr. Burk looked away. But she was grateful for every bit of knowledge she had garnered about Nathan. Every day she'd learned something new that convinced her that Nathan was simply afraid to love because of how his mother had treated him. She sniffed again at the thought as she glanced across the wide, open expanse of land. In the distance, a coach, and what appeared to be a curricle, came to a halt near a row of trees. It was hard to tell from her position if it was Nathan's curricle, but all the same, her heart leaped. "Nathan's back, I think! And by the looks of it, he's with company!"

"Do ye care ta show him what ye've learned?"

"I cannot think of a better way for him to find out than my besting you in another race," she challenged.

He nodded, and together they counted and took off when they hit *three*. They flew neck and neck across the land. The wind once again whipped Sophia's hair and stung her face, while exhilaration and anticipation filled her body. She couldn't wait to see Nathan's face!

She crossed the finish line a half-stride ahead of Mr. Burk. Whooping out a victory cheer, she pulled up on her reins and turned her horse toward the tree by which the two coaches were parked. Disappointment filled her that it wasn't Nathan's curricle. As everyone descended from the carriages, her heart squeezed. Nathan wasn't among the group, but his aunt was, and three people Sophia had never met. Lady Anthony stared at her agape.

Gritting her teeth, Sophia dismounted her horse and led her toward the group. As she neared them and took in the faces of the handsome man with dark-blond hair and observant hazel eyes and the woman holding his elbow, who had mounds of gold-spun hair that hung in luxurious waves down her back, acute self-consciousness attacked Sophia. She immediately raised her hand to her short hair and frowned at the wild disarray it seemed to be in. Beside the woman stood Lady Anthony and a man leaning on a cane.

"Hello, Lady Anthony," she said. "We weren't expecting you. Nathan isn't here. Did you not see him in London?"

The woman pursed her lips and stared for a long moment before answering. "He did not deign to visit me."

"Now, Mother," the chubby man beside her said in a scolding tone. This had to be Nathan's cousin. She was about to introduce herself when he spoke again. "He was there on business and only in town one night before..." His words trailed off, and he glanced quickly at Sophia and then to the golden-haired man who stood scowling beside him. The woman—who appeared to be the epitome of grace and loveliness, of course—paled to a whiteness that matched the clouds as she looked at Sophia. Something deep within her gut clenched and her heart constricted.

Something was wrong. She couldn't say why she thought so, but she knew it to be true. She fisted her hands at her sides and stared at each of these strangers in turn—because really, Nathan's aunt was unknown to her, as well. She drew herself to her full height, which was diminutive compared to everyone in this group. "Before we get on with why you're here, perhaps Lady Anthony could introduce us."

She speared the older woman with a prompting look, and Lady Anthony let out a long sigh, as if she'd just been tasked with the most tedious chore of her life. She stepped forward and swept a hand at the man at her side. He gave an awkward bow that showed he favored his right leg. When he came up, he shoved back a thick lock of blond hair that had fallen over his brown eyes. He smiled and two dimples appeared in his plump cheeks. "I'm Hughbert Ellison, Scarsdale's cousin."

Sophia stared at him for a long moment. He looked vaguely familiar. "Have we met?"

His eyes widened. "Yes," he mumbled. "Yes, we have. I wasn't going to mention it unless you did, because I wasn't sure..." He shifted his weight awkwardly from his good leg to his cane. His knuckles curled tightly around the top of the cane and turned white. Sophia dragged her gaze back to his face, ashamed she had been staring. Around her, the group was silent.

Then the memory of when she'd met Mr. Ellison hit her, and she gasped. "You were lost and I gave you directions!"

"That's right," he nodded.

Sophia recalled it all now. "How funny! I told Nathan about you when *he* was lost. He said if I'd just directed him where to turn to find Mr. Bantry's he could have. He was so pompous about it." She laughed at the memory. "And I recalled you and told him how—" She caught sight of the deep flush that had crept up Mr. Ellison's cheeks, and she halted her words. How unthinking of her to retell a story that painted the man as a fool. No one here need know what had happened. She took a deep breath. "I told him he likely would have found it, since you had, and was sorry I'd insisted on taking him to Mr. Bantry's myself because I'd delayed him. Maybe then he wouldn't have been shot."

"Shot?" the beautiful woman exclaimed. "When was Scarsdale shot?"

Sophia wished she had kept her mouth shut. She was

going to have to explain it all now. Maybe Nathan didn't want everyone to know. Before she could speak, Mr. Ellison stepped near her and gave her a reassuring smile. "Scarsdale was shot on the road between the duchess's father's pub and the horse trainer he was searching for. Likely it was thieves after some jewels."

Sophia shook her head. "No. They were trying to—"

"Enough!" Lady Anthony snapped. "Neither the Duchess of Aversley nor her husband has time to stand around and listen to fanciful tales. We've come to tell you that Scarsdale is missing."

"What?" Surely, she could not have heard correctly.

"He is missing," the woman snapped.

"Oh, do be quiet!" the Duchess of Aversley snapped herself. "Can you not see you've given her a shock?"

Was she shocked? Sophia knitted her brows, trying to make her mind answer the question. The ground did seem to be swaying. She reached out to grab something to steady herself and Mr. Burk was there suddenly, like a solid, immovable tree. He gripped her elbow. "Are ye all right, Yer Grace?"

She nodded, studying the four faces around her. Three held lines of concern, and one, Nathan's aunt, held annoyance. Sophia wet her lips and forced her throat to work, despite the fact that she was sure it wouldn't since her heart had lodged itself there. "How long?" Was she whispering? She cleared her throat and tried again. "Where was he last seen? Is anything known?"

Lady Anthony rattled out another long, annoyed sigh. "Let us have this conversation back at the house. It's entirely too cold to stand around outside explaining it all." She turned on her heel and the word *No* shattered the brief silence.

Sophia couldn't say how long she stood there, not realizing she'd been the one to screech, but after the blood that was roaring in her ears abated, coherent thought returned. Her heart still slammed unmercifully against her ribs, but she looked around the group and acknowledged mixed expressions of horror and shock leveled at her. She had screamed. She should be embarrassed, but in this moment, she didn't care. A league of horses could not drag her back inside until she had all the information they did about what had happened to Nathan.

His aunt sucked in a deep breath that made Sophia stiffen. "How dare you—"

"Cease talking," Sophia ground out, not caring that she was being rude and unladylike. "Which one of you can tell me what happened?"

The handsome man, who she could only assume to be the Duke of Aversley, stepped forward, bringing his wife with him. She came to Sophia's side and took her hand. "No one knows for sure."

"The Bow Street Runners are on the case," Mr. Ellison added.

"I've hired a private investigator, as well," the duke supplied.

"When did he disappear?" Sophia's voice was gravelly, and the ground was doing that funny tilting thing again.

"The night after he came back to London," the duke said. "His curricle was at the docks, so we know he'd been there." The duke stopped talking and glanced to his wife, who nodded. He swiped a hand across his face. "It seems he never left, however."

She hadn't known she'd grown to love Nathan so much until this moment. Sophia's heart splintered as sure as if it were made of china and someone had bashed it with an enormous piece of wood. She sucked in a sharp breath and squeezed her eyes shut on a wave of piercing, nauseating pain. A hand came to her elbow again, and Sophia forced herself to open her eyes. The Duke of Aversley gripped her. "Are you all right, Duchess?"

"Sophia," she interrupted. "Call me Sophia."

He inclined his head. "As you wish it."

She smiled weakly and glanced at his wife. "You must call me Sophia, too."

The woman nodded, reached into her reticule, and held

out a handkerchief to Sophia. "You must call me Amelia. My dear, you are crying."

Sophia glanced at the handkerchief still in Amelia's grasp, then swiped a hand across her cheek and blinked in surprise. Amelia was right. She was crying. Her world was spinning out of control. She took the handkerchief and dabbed first her cheeks and then her eyes. "I'm sorry. I'm sure Nathan would be mortified at my display."

Amelia smiled and then hugged Sophia. "And I'm sure he'd be pleased to know you care so much."

Sophia was so grateful to have Amelia and her husband here to buffer Nathan's aunt. And she was glad, she supposed, his cousin was here, too. He seemed nice enough, though he did keep casting wary glances between her and his mother. She took a long, steadying breath. "What can I do to help find him?"

"He'd want you to stay here where it's safe," the duke replied, and Amelia nodded her agreement.

Amelia squeezed Sophia's hand. "I'm sure they will locate him in a few days. In the meantime, we will stay here with you, if you would like."

"All of you?" Sophia couldn't help but hope Lady Anthony was leaving.

Mr. Ellison nodded. "Yes. We should be together at a time like this. We are family."

She thought she saw a grim smile pull at Lady Anthony's lips. *Family.* Her heart, which she'd been sure could not splinter further proved her wrong and opened like a yawning, cavernous hole. The sound of the crack echoed in her ears. Nathan and her brother were her family. Certainly not his aunt. And she didn't know his cousin well enough to judge yet.

She grasped Amelia's hand, very glad she had offered to stay. She felt more at ease with her and the duke than Nathan's relatives, and that realization sent a pang of sadness through her for Nathan. She struggled to fight the tears that threatened to come again.

Seventeen

Ravensdale's men held both Nathan's arms as the man's fist connected with his face time and again. The ship he'd woken up on dipped underneath his feet in the rough, stormy waters, but the movement didn't stop Ravensdale's onslaught. The sound of bone crunching filled Nathan's ears, and darkness overtook him.

He awoke in blackness to a boot kicking him in the side. It connected with his ribs and he coughed until he thought he might die. Several pairs of hands gripped him and jerked him to his feet. His head lolled as he was dragged out of the darkness and into the bright day. Immediately, he was blinded, unaccustomed now to the light. And the sounds—the lapping of waves, calls of the birds overhead, men moving about the ship and talking, and the hum of the water parting as the ship glided across it—were deafening, threatening to drive him mad.

A hand gripped the back of his still-lolling head and yanked up his face. He forced himself to open his eyes, though the fever ravaging his body made even that slight task seem almost impossible. Ravensdale stood before him with a smirk on his face. "Ready to address me as captain yet?"

Nathan didn't bother to answer. He simply spat at Ravensdale's boots.

His reward was a hard jab to the gut that sent him slump-

ing forward almost to the ground, except he was snatched back
up at the last moment. Ravensdale stepped so close to Nathan
he could smell the liquor seeping out of the fiend's pores. "I'll
tell you what, Scarsdale. Since you refuse to call me *Captain*,
I'm going to make a special trip back to Whitecliffe after I
leave you with the pirates, and I'm going to find your new
duchess and bed her every way you can imagine."

Rage exploded in Nathan's head and through his veins in
painful shots. He roared and wrenched his arms out of the grip
of the man who held him and locked his hands around
Ravensdale's neck with only one thought in mind. He was
going to kill him. He was going to cut off his air and watch
him die.

Ravensdale's face turned red and white as he clawed at
Nathan's hands. The thugs grabbed him, trying to tear him
away from Ravensdale. He thought he heard shouting, but his
blood roared in his ears as he pictured Ravensdale touching
Sophia. Someone punched him in the side, but he didn't move,
didn't flinch. He squeezed harder and harder, determination
making him feel invincible. Something hit him in the head
with such force his legs buckled instantly and blackness
consumed him once more.

⚜

His legs were on fire! Nathan's eyes popped open, and he tried
to surge upward to bat at his legs but he was tied down. He
squinted against the light, and when his eyes finally adjusted,
he opened them slowly, again to the face of Ravensdale.
Nathan's gaze immediately went to the man's black-and-blue
neck. Ravensdale's eyes narrowed on him. "You surprised me
with your determination to kill me, Scarsdale. I didn't think
you had murder in you."

Nathan swallowed, his throat incredibly dry. "For you I
have it in me." His voice was cracked and creaky, not having
been used much in the days since he'd been taken.

"You'll not get another chance," Ravensdale said and

motioned behind him. A young boy stepped forward holding a bucket that sloshed. "Again," Ravensdale commanded as he stepped back and the boy stepped forward, then tilted his bucket over Nathan's legs. Instant heat seared the gash and the bullet wound in his legs, and he had to fight blacking out again. *Salt water.* The sting of the salt against the raw open wounds felt akin to being set on fire. Nathan gritted his teeth against the pain, which ebbed slightly, and perspiration dampened his brow.

Ravensdale motioned the boy away and moved back toward Nathan. "The physician will be here shortly to examine you."

"Afraid to untie me?" Nathan croaked.

"Not afraid. Just smart. You're going to stay locked below for the next two days until we reach Saint-Malo. I'll be stopping there to pick up a Barbary corsair I'm hiring and to hand you over to be a slave on his brother's ship—payment for the corsair's services in helping me capture some white slaves, you see. I must thank you, really. Your betrayal has made me quite rich."

"Glad I could be of service," Nathan snarled as the door banged open and a pirate came in with an older man leaning heavily against him while singing a lusty tune. The pirate looked at Ravensdale. "Dr. Rowley's been at the spirits again."

The man lifted his gray head. "I've only had four drinks."

Ravensdale growled under his breath. "Damn it, man. I told you I need you to sew him up"—he motioned at Nathan—"and retrieve the bullet. I need him alive."

"I can do it," Rowley said on a hiccup. "Bring me my thread and needle."

Nathan's blood turned icy and his muscles jumped. A bad physician was worse than no physician, but he wasn't in a position to put up a fight.

Within moments, the man was sitting beside him and leaned over his leg. "Do you want him to have laudanum for the pain?" he asked Ravensdale, who stood directly behind him.

Ravensdale's gaze locked with Nathan's and he smirked. "I know how you love laudanum, but I find I want to see you squirm."

Nathan was careful not to show his relief. He didn't welcome the pain, but he didn't want to take the drug he'd felt unable to live without before. "I won't be very entertaining."

"We shall see," Ravensdale commented and motioned to the physician to begin.

Each jab of the needle made bile rise in Nathan's throat, causing it to burn and his eyes to water. He didn't cry out during the stitching of his gashed leg but he did shake, and he hated himself for showing weakness.

When the physician was finished, he sat up and mopped his sweating brow as Ravensdale peered over the man's shoulder at Nathan's throbbing leg. "You've made a mess of it, Rowley. You're too foxed to retrieve the bullet today with those trembling hands. You'd kill him, and I've plans for him. Get yourself sober, or *I'll* kill *you*," Ravensdale snarled. The physician backed out of the room with mumbled apologies and Nathan was left alone with Ravensdale, who walked over to a counter and came back holding a bottle.

He shook the glass bottle at Nathan. "I've changed my mind about the laudanum," Ravensdale said. He leaned over Nathan, and after much struggling, pried his jaw open and poured the contents of the bottle down Nathan's throat. The familiar sweet liquid made Nathan want to gag. He tried to spit it back up, but Ravensdale clamped both hands over his mouth and leaned against his chest. "If you don't swallow, you may choke, and I'm in the mind to let you do it. Then I'll go visit your wife and comfort her."

Black fury blanketed Nathan as he swallowed and watched helplessly as Ravensdale turned and left him alone. Images of Sophia being ravaged by Ravensdale tormented him. He turned his mind toward escape. Ravensdale's cockiness made him careless, and Nathan was to be sold to a pirate in two days. If he had any chance of getting away he had to do it the day they were docked. He'd never make it off a ship run by pirates alive. His mind began to feel groggy, but he fought the pull of sleep and concentrated on his plan. Ambush from his cell seemed the most likely, but he would need to be unchained. How to get unchained? As he struggled to figure out the details, sleep claimed him.

The ground underneath Nathan swayed as he awoke. Or at least he thought it was the ground. He tried to open his eyes, but when he did, pain so great he almost cried out vibrated up his right leg. His left leg had a dull throbbing pain. Grunting, he tried again and got his lids open enough to see more blackness.

Moaning and creaking filled the heavy, damp air around him.

He was in hell.

Where you deserve to be.

He squeezed his eyes shut and struggled to sift through the thick fog blanketing his mind. At first, nothing came, and then awareness hit him in nauseating pangs. He was on Ravensdale's ship, and Ravensdale intended to find Sophia and harm her.

Nathan's gut clenched, and he rolled to his side, dry heaving repeatedly until he was left panting. Intense agony radiated from his right leg, onto which he'd rolled. He struggled to his back and lay there trying not to retch again. It felt as if sand filled his mouth.

Christ.

He needed… "Water." The sound of his raw voice shocked him. How long had he been out since being sewn up?

"There's no water to be had, Your Grace."

Your Grace? Whoever was in here with him knew him. Nathan tried to recall who that might be, but his memory wouldn't cooperate. Unwilling to reveal the weakness, he kept quiet and forced his eyes open as much as possible. He held his hand in front of his face. He couldn't see his arm, but he knew it was there because he touched his nose with his fingertips. His nose felt wrong. Crooked and caked with something crusty. He ran a finger down the bridge. The unfamiliar sharp veer of his nose to the left told him Ravensdale had broken it.

"You all right?" came the deep voice again from the dark.

Nathan ignored the voice and the other sounds, which were muffled and came from somewhere above, for the moment. Whether the man knew him or not, *he* didn't know if a friend or enemy was near. Though he thought he heard concern in the tone, he didn't trust himself enough in his current state to decide anything too quickly. Wincing, he reached up and fingered the bridge of his nose again. When he inhaled, the high-pitched sound of air trying to enter his nasal passages pierced his ears.

He'd once seen a boxer at Gentleman Jackson's straighten his own broken nose. Nathan clutched his nose with one hand and the floor with the other. Wet, slick slime met his fingertips, and a shudder coursed through him. With grim determination, he inhaled a sharp breath and jerked his nose back to the right.

Nausea gripped him, but when he inhaled, air came through his nose this time. Water leaked a steady stream out of his eyes. He wiped the moisture away, the gesture reminding him of wiping Sophia's tears from her soft cheek. His chest hurt at the memory of her, and a throbbing regret consumed him.

Regret would have to wait. The time for survival was at hand.

"Where am I?" he demanded of the unknown man.

"We're locked in a cell in the far corner of the cargo hold. You were passed out when they dragged you in here," he explained. "The captain delivered you personally with one of his crew."

"Captain, is it?" Nathan sneered.

The man made a derisive noise from his throat. "He's a renegade privateer who works with the Barbary corsairs to capture white slaves. He's a bit of a legend on the sea."

"You're a seaman?"

"Your Grace, I work for *you*. It's Stephens."

"Stephens?" Instantly, Nathan had a mental picture of a scrawny, redheaded young man who could not be more then nineteen. Nathan felt his lower jaw part open. The simple movement caused pain to radiate once more. "How the hell did you end up in here?"

"I saw Ravensdale and his man carrying you onto their ship and I tried to rescue you."

"Oh Christ, Stephens. I'm sorry."

"You would have done the same for me, Your Grace. They stuck me in this cell after dragging me on board, and I've been here ever since."

Nathan swatted at something crawling up his arm while he forced himself to sit up. Light danced in his vision, but it was only speckles from his efforts. He swayed where he sat until he collapsed backward once again.

With the hesitancy of one fearing to find a limb gone, he searched his throbbing leg until his fingers came to the bullet wound. Around the wound, the skin felt soft. Too soft. Like mushed porridge. When he inhaled, the foul stench of rotting flesh filled his nose. The wound was festering. He moved his leg, suddenly afraid he no longer could. And then realization struck: he was unchained.

"Have we docked in Saint-Malo yet?" he demanded, fighting the fear that he'd missed his only opportunity to escape.

"No, Your Grace. We'll be there tomorrow, according to the conversations I've managed to overhear."

Relief made Nathan fall back against the deck with a thud. He lay there and struggled to concentrate. Sweat dripped down his forehead and hot flashes consumed him. He didn't need to be a physician to know a fever was ravaging him. Trying to sort out the details in his mind of what he needed to do was like walking through the thick mud of the riverbank near his home after a long storm. Impossibly slow-going.

He shoved himself up and turned in the darkness to Stephens. He still couldn't see the man, but he could smell the sticky stench of unwashed skin. He owed this man a debt for trying to stop Ravensdale and his men from dragging him aboard this ship while he was unconscious. "I have to get this bullet out before tomorrow. I'll be of no use to you if I don't."

"Because you'll be too weak?"

"Because I'll likely be dead."

"I'll call for the guard," Stephens said hastily. "Ravensdale said to call for a guard if you looked like you were taking a turn for the worse."

"Wait one moment. We need a plan. Last time Ravensdale poured laudanum down my throat. If I'm asleep when you feel the ship being docked at port, awaken me. You'll call the guard and say I'm dead, and when he comes, we'll overtake him." The guard carried a cutlass and a pistol, and Nathan planned to take both. He'd find the strength. Somewhere. Somehow.

"And then we'll fight our way out of here?"

"Hopefully, we will sneak out of here. But if we're spotted we'll fight until the death."

"Hopefully not ours," Stephens said.

"I should hope not, as well. My wife would not like that at all," he said, trying for levity, but it felt as if a hand gripped his heart and was squeezing it like a vise. "Go ahead and call for the guard."

The shuffling of feet sounded in the small cell, and then Stephens started yelling for the guard. Within moments, the groan of the hatch opening filled the room, and in the distance, a lantern light seemed to bob in the dark as if suspended from nothing. Footsteps clapping toward them filled the air, followed by the clank of jingling keys. Now Nathan could make out a tall man with a covered head and a beard holding the keys in one hand and a pistol in the other. The cell door creaked.

"What?" the guard snarled.

"His Grace is dying," Stephens supplied.

"His Grace is dyin'," the man mimicked while lowering the lantern to shine it in Nathan's eyes.

Nathan immediately had to shield his eyes from the bright light.

The guard smirked at him. "Can His Grace get his arse up?"

"I'll manage," Nathan replied and slowly started the process of shoving to his feet. Once he was standing, he took a step toward the guard and Stephens, but his weakness caused him to stumble and he ended up crashing into both men.

The guard shoved him hard in the chest. "Get off me."

Nathan eased toward Stephens, grateful for the man's hand as it clasped his arm and held him steady.

"You," the guard barked at Stephens, "you make sure he don't fall on his face on the way to the captain's cabin. If the captain wants you to live so bloody much, I don't see why he hasn't ordered the bullet taken out of your leg," the guard grumbled.

"That would be because he desires me to suffer as much as possible," Nathan replied as he leaned against Stephens. They followed the guard out the cell, across the cargo hold, and up the creaking ladder into a dim passageway. The trek from the cell to the captain's cabin left Nathan panting, sweating, and on the verge of passing out. It also left him with a gnawing sense of how difficult escaping would be tomorrow.

"Your Grace?" Stephens nudged him in the side, and Nathan blinked, realizing he'd been caught in a haze of his own thoughts.

Ravensdale stood in a small room that Nathan thought he must use as his office. Bolted to the center of the room was a table that had maps and charts spread across it. The only other pieces of furniture in the room were a chair and a table, which were both bolted to the floor, as well. Ravensdale grinned maliciously, displaying his rotted, yellow teeth.

Much like his personality, Nathan thought.

"I'm told you're about to die, Scarsdale." Ravensdale nodded to the guard and the man reached toward Nathan, but Nathan lurched back out of his grasp.

"Lucky for you, Rowley is sober now. I'd hate for you to

die and ruin my special plans." Ravensdale motioned to the guard. "Fetch Rowley and tell him I have a patient in need of his skills."

The guard snickered but nodded.

Not ten minutes later, Nathan was tied to a table in the surgeon's quarters. The guard, Ravensdale, and the physician all stood over him. Stephens had been taken back to the cell because Ravensdale cheerfully pointed out that he might try to interfere when his employer was thrashing in agony. Nathan vowed to himself that no matter how bad the pain, he'd not give Ravensdale the satisfaction of moving a muscle or making a sound.

The physician's cracked, leathery face loomed over Nathan, and the smell of strong liquor washed over him from the man. The physician narrowed his eyes, causing his bushy, silver eyebrows to come together. "This is going to hurt. Would've hurt anyway, but especially now since the captain says you get nothing to dull the pain."

Nathan nodded and prayed Ravensdale would hold that train of thought and not force laudanum down his throat once more.

With a rattling sigh, the physician leaned over Nathan again, but this time he held a sharp knife in his hand that he lowered to Nathan's leg. The hard tip touched his skin, and it was as if someone had shoved a fire poker into his body. His instinct was to buck and scream. Instead, he gritted his teeth until pain hummed in his ears a steady noise that refused to relent. Dr. Rowley turned his head slightly toward Ravensdale. "You can cleanse the wound now."

Nathan tensed as Ravensdale held up a jug. "I cannot tell you how much pleasure this gives me. We call this here"— Ravensdale patted the jug—"Mercy of the Sea. You can drink it to dull the pain, but it can also be used to cleanse a wound. I've only ever had it poured on a wound when I was too foxed to protest, but I'll tell you what, I wanted to rip my leg from my body when they poured it over the cut." With those cheerfully spoken words, he tilted the jug and whistled as he poured.

For a moment, the liquor cooled Nathan's skin and offered relief against the heat that had been building there. But the moment was fleeting. Cool turned to warmth that morphed into a hot, licking flame. The fire singed Nathan from the inside out and raced toward his head. He was certain the liquid was eating him and his flesh alive. The ringing in his ears increased until he was certain he would scream. But pain battered his head and made sound impossible to come by. Blackness invaded the color of the room and wiped away everything. Then mercifully—*mercifully*—the sound died in his ears and a chill enveloped him, burrowing into his bones and mind. With a ragged breath, he welcomed the nothingness.

"Wake up," a voice whispered in his ear. Nathan batted a hand near the right side of his face, but the voice came again, this time more urgent. "Your Grace, please, wake up! We're here."

Nathan struggled to open his eyes, which felt as if someone had stuck them together with muck. Once they were open, he stared into the almost-darkness. He blinked and a lantern appeared, along with Stephens's worry-drawn face.

Nathan licked his lips and tasted blood. He spat and then swallowed before speaking. "They left us a lantern?"

Stephens nodded.

"How long have we been in Saint-Malo?"

"Not long. Maybe ten minutes. I've been trying to wake you for about that long."

Nathan pushed up to a seated position, biting back the pain the movement caused in his leg. "Are you ready?"

"I don't suppose there's any choice but to be ready."

"I don't suppose there is," Nathan agreed. "If we do nothing, I'll be chained to a ship for a year, and I couldn't say what Ravensdale has planned for you, but I doubt you would like it."

"I'll be chained beside you," Stephens replied. "The captain said so, and you're right. Nothing against you, Your

Grace, but I prefer not to sleep where I eat, nor eat where I defecate and urinate. Do you know what I mean?"

"I believe I do," Nathan said with a cynical chuckle that hurt his belly. "Now listen to me. When you call the guard and he comes in, lead him directly in front of me so that he has to bend down and is face-to-face with me. Can you do that?"

Stephens nodded. "But why? What are you going to do? You've no weapon?"

Nathan tapped his head. "This is my weapon. It's hard as a rock and I know just how to hit another man with it. I would have done it earlier, but it would have been pointless out at sea with nowhere to flee and a crew of twenty against two. He's got a pistol, and it's your job to make sure he doesn't shoot me. I'm counting on you."

"I won't fail you."

"Call him," Nathan said and lay back to play dead.

Shuffling feet resounded for a moment, then the rattling of the cage and Stephens shouting for the guard. "He's dead," he hollered. "His Grace is dead. Come quick!"

Footsteps pounded above, and then the hatch door banged open in the distance and booted-feet hurried through the cargo hold vibrating the air. The ship creaked ominously to join the jangle of the keys, and then the screech of the door being opened joined the chorus of noise.

"Wha' do you mean he's dead? The captain is gonna be furious."

"I meant to say I think he's dead," Stephens said in a high-pitched voice that rang with false fear. "He doesn't appear to be breathing."

"Ya ratty fool. Did ya feel where his heart beats?"

"Did I what?"

A derisive snort filled the air. "Never mind. I can see God didn't give ya much brains."

Nathan tensed his shoulders as the footsteps thumped toward him. The air swished above him as the guard bent down. The moment his stench invaded Nathan's nose and his hand landed on Nathan's chest, Nathan cracked open his eyes, judged the angle to be perfect, and threw his body up and forward until his head connected with the guard's nose with a *crack*. Before the man could make a sound, Nathan punched him in the mouth and Stephens secured the pistol that had fallen out of the man's hand. The guard fell backward and Nathan scrambled to his feet, ignoring the protesting pain from his legs. His body fought every movement, but his mind rebelled against captivity with greater intensity. He lunged forward and punched the man again, this time hard enough to knock him out.

Stephens stood beside Nathan, panting and holding the pistol. "Should we kill him?"

Nathan bent down and retrieved the man's cutlass and the keys that had fallen when he fell. "I'd rather not take a life if I don't have to. We'll lock him in here and shut the latch. We should be long gone by the time he wakes up, and if we're not, well, then I doubt we will be escaping, anyway."

It took a few precious seconds to lock the cell and make their way out of the cargo hold and toward the stairs to the quarterdeck. They picked their way up the ladder in tense silence. Each rung up took them closer to the hum of noise above. On the main deck, a flood of voices, salty air, and sunlight greeted them, but there was a quietness to their movements. They ducked behind a set of twin barrels so they could figure out the route to freedom.

Nathan located the gangway and calculated the distance from them to it. Then he found himself searching, brow furrowed, for the crew. He followed the sound of catcalls and bawdy curses and spotted a group of men circled around the mizzenmast. He couldn't see what the men were doing, but by the snippets of jeers he caught, someone had angered Ravensdale and was being punished.

The huddle parted for a moment and Nathan got a clear side view of the devil as he raised a whip then sliced it through the air. The circle closed again before Nathan could see who was being punished, and the cheers from the crew drowned any sound the victim may have made. Frankly, Nathan didn't give a damn if Ravensdale was punishing a member of his crew. For all he knew, it could have been one of the men who had held him down that first day on the ship while Ravensdale beat him.

He nudged Stephens in the side and pointed toward their escape route. "There's not going to be a better time to go than now."

Stephens nodded, and they crouched low and scurried toward the gangplank. Whatever aches would plague Nathan later were currently subdued by the excitement of freedom within his reach. He paused with one foot on the gangplank and turned for one brief second, ensnared by a burning desire to kill Ravensdale. It would be utter foolishness. Eventually, he would pay Ravensdale back, he vowed, as he followed Stephens off the ship.

A high-pitched scream cut through the calls of the seamen. Nathan froze and looked over his shoulder at the circle of men, which had parted once again. In the center of the melee, tied naked to the mizzenmast was a petite, short-haired, dark-headed woman. Coldness slammed into his core. *Sophia? Could it be?*

Stephens tugged on his elbow, but Nathan just stared at the woman, willing her to look up. Her head hung limp and her shoulders shook. Had Ravensdale had Sophia all this time? It made no sense. It was impossible. Yet, he could not turn away as Ravensdale's taunts played through his head.

"Your Grace," Stephens hissed in his ear.

"My wife," he mumbled, swaying suddenly with fatigue.

Stephens yanked Nathan's arm. "We must go."

But even if it wasn't Sophia, how could Nathan leave a helpless woman to Ravensdale's treatment? Before he could answer the question in his head, Ravensdale's gaze locked on him. His brow furrowed, but even in his confusion, the man raised his arm and threw something.

Silence fell and then so did Nathan as Ravensdale's dagger hit him in his worst leg. The deck took the air from him but not so much that he didn't shout to Stephens. "Save yourself, man."

Stephens gaped at him for a moment, raised the pistol he held, and shot the closest pirate charging them, but a sea of men swarmed behind the downed man coming at Nathan and Stephens like a powerful wave. "Go now!" Nathan commanded, knowing Stephens could do nothing but try to escape. Stephen glanced down, regret and sorrow etched on his young face, and then he turned and fled as the pirates reached Nathan.

Eighteen

*E*arly in the morning, a scratch came at Sophia's door, followed by her lady's maid pleading with her to let her enter and help her dress. Without coming out from under her coverlet, Sophia told Mary Margaret to go away. Today marked three weeks that Nathan had been missing.

Three weeks! The realization made her shudder. She had gotten up every day, dressed, and forced herself to go through her routine, though when she retired at night and lay in her bed she could not recall a thing she had done from day to day. What she could recall was that Ellison, as he'd bid her call him, spoke Nathan's name in the hushed tones one used to speak of the dead. Because of that, she could hardly countenance talking with him and had gone out of her way to avoid him, even as he had tried to be nice.

Amelia and her husband were wonderful people and had taken to entertaining Harry, thank heaven. Sophia couldn't muster the energy to smile, let alone keep Harry occupied. Despite liking Nathan's friends, whenever she spied them in unguarded moments, the perpetual smiles they wore when vowing to her that Nathan would be located in perfect health slipped away to the frowns of concern. Fierce anger at them would surge through her when that happened. Thus, she had taken to avoiding them in the last few days, as well. She felt awful for it, but she couldn't stomach knowing they didn't really believe he would be found alive.

And Nathan's aunt... Sophia shuddered. That woman was a wretched witch. She had told Sophia that if Nathan had never met her, he would not be missing now. Thankfully, Lady Anthony preferred to ignore Sophia for the most part, but the few times she did speak to her it was with icy disdain.

Sophia had teetered for weeks on the brink of hysteria. She felt helpless, useless, and unwanted in the house that was supposed to be her home. Sadness pressed against her chest like a thousand quilts and worry was like a boulder on her shoulders. Suddenly, her cocoon under the blankets stifled her, and she struggled for a proper breath. She threw the covers off, scrambled out of bed, and rushed over to her window. With trembling fingers, she parted the heavy curtains and opened the window. Cold air blasted her in the face, along with several snowflakes. Wind whistled around her and tickled her nose. Was the wind tickling Nathan's nose? Was he looking at the snow now, too?

Oh, Nathan! She didn't want to live without him. He'd appeared in her life and rescued her in every way possible, and she had fallen hopelessly in love with him.

Below her, laugher floated up from the gardens. She glared down at Amelia, her husband, and Harry until her head hurt and shame burrowed in her chest. She should not begrudge Harry a bit of time outdoors and some laughter, as well. He had been almost as downtrodden as she was since she'd told him Nathan was missing. The first thing he'd asked was if Nathan had left them like his momma had. The question had stolen Sophia's breath and haunted her, even though her heart told her Nathan would never do such a thing.

A carriage rolled into view as she stared out the window, and her heart leaped when a man dressed in a dark coat and trousers got out. The Duke of Aversley had described the detective he'd hired to search for Nathan, and this had to be the man! He was tall with a shock of white hair and a thick, neatly trimmed white beard. She raced across her bedchamber, flung open her door, and was halfway to the stairs when she realized she was only wearing her dressing gown. Crying out, she whirled around and scrambled back to her room to don a dress.

This was the one time she wished for Mary Margaret's help getting into her day gown. Sophia's hands shook so badly, it took her an impossibly long time to get the buttons secured. When she was finished, her heart pounded and her brow was damp from her efforts. She took the stairs at an unladylike two-at-a-time, and as she bounded down the last steps and into the main foyer, she saw the man who had arrived not more than twenty minutes ago, already departing.

"Stop!" she shouted, not giving a fig about how she must appear.

The man turned, and his bushy white eyebrows shot upward. "I beg your pardon?"

She rushed to him and gripped his arm. "Are you Sir Richard?"

"I am," the man replied in a deep, gruff voice.

"Please," she said, her voice cracking. "Did you bring news of my husband?"

The man's eyes widened, and as his gaze swept over her, disbelief registered on his face. "*You* are the Duchess of Scarsdale?"

She nodded with impatience.

"Wouldn't you care to have your family with you while we discuss such matters?"

The misery etching each of his words ripped at Sophia. She clenched her fists at her sides as a low ringing started in her ears. "*What?*"

"Your family," he stated again. The timber of his voice dropped, and his eyes took on a regretful gleam.

Suddenly, the room seemed to be swaying, and someone's hand gripped her elbow.

"Sophia, come sit down," Amelia urged.

Half stumbling and half walking, Sophia followed Amelia to one of two mahogany, red velvet armchairs that lined the marble wall. She remembered how lovely she had thought they were when she first saw them. Now the red color only served to make her think of death. She caught a glimpse of herself in the gilded mirror that hung above the marble commode. Her blue eyes stood in stark contrast to her snowy skin, and her hair was in wild disarray. Turning away, she lowered herself into the seat and gripped the armrests as if they were lifelines.

She glanced up, surprised to see the Duke of Aversley and Ellison standing there. Where had they come from? She moved a questioning gaze to Amelia, whose red eyes and nose caused Sophia's heart to falter. Whatever information Sir Richard had found, it could not be good. *No...* She didn't want to know anymore. She shoved toward the wall, determined to get away, but there was nowhere to go. No escaping the horror.

Nathan would expect her to be brave. And calm. And regal. She took a shuddering breath and locked her gaze on Sir Richard. "Tell me," she commanded, albeit hoarsely.

He glanced to the Duke of Aversley for confirmation, and she watched, through an invisible fog, as Nathan's friend nodded. Sir Richard placed the other chair so it was facing her, and indicated to Amelia, who shook her head and instead kneeled beside Sophia to grasp her hand. Sir Richard sat and swiped a hand across his face. The prickling sound of beard growth rubbing against his palm tickled her sensitive ears.

"As you likely know, the Duke of Aversley hired me to find your husband."

She forced herself to nod.

"I was working in conjunction with the Bow Street Runners."

Another nod, though it was harder this time.

"Three days ago, a seaman called Mr. Stephens arrived at the London Docks, conveyed there by an English privateer by the name of Lord Worthington, who as it happened, went to university with your husband and the Duke of Aversley."

Sophia glanced at the duke, and he nodded.

Sir Richard let out a long breath before continuing. "Worthington was in Saint-Malo last week, hired by the king to track down and capture Ravensdale, a renegade privateer accused of kidnapping some nobility traveling at sea and selling them on the slave market. It seems Worthington had a lead that Ravensdale would be going to Saint-Malo, so he took his ship and hid in a cove to ambush Ravensdale's ship."

Sophia digested the information slowly, finding that concentrating was terribly difficult. "Where is Saint-Malo?" she asked in a whisper.

"In France," Sir Richard supplied. "Shall I continue?"

Must you? her mind screamed, yet she inclined her head for him to do so.

"Mr. Stephens, who worked for your husband on board his ship *Woodwind*, was kidnapped at the London Docks, along with your husband, the night the duke was last seen. Ravensdale intended to sell your husband on the slave market in Algiers, and Mr. Stephens tried to save your husband and was taken for his efforts."

Tried to save your husband. The words and their implication made Sophia slump into her chair. With effort she choked out, "Go on."

"Mr. Stephens and your husband had been attempting to escape together and were seconds from making it off the ship when your husband turned back to save a woman who was being abused by Ravensdale in plain sight."

Sophia swallowed. "Yes, he would do that."

Sir Richard gave her an understanding look. "Mr. Stephens informed me that the duke was hit in the leg with a dagger standing right there on the gangway, and when he went down, and surely knew there was no way for him to move fast enough to flee, he told Mr. Stephens to go without him. And he did."

Fury boiled her blood. Nathan would have never left anyone whether it meant he sealed his own death or not.

Sir Richard's eyebrows drew together. "Your Grace, Mr. Stephens is a good man. He feels terrible about leaving the duke behind, but he knew, as your husband did, that they would both be killed if he stayed. Mr. Stephens had to make a quick decision, and he thought, understandably so, that if he could manage to escape and find someone friendly to his cause to bring him back to England, then he would have enough knowledge to lead us in the direction of your husband."

Shame curled in her belly that she had judged Mr. Stephens so readily, but a sliver of hope rose as well. "My husband could be alive! Mr. Stephens did not see him killed," she added, her words rushing out of her now. "You know the name of the ship and you know where this pirate is going!" Tears of relief streaked warm tracks down her face. "Do you see?" she demanded to the blank faces around her. "He could still be alive. I'll search for him with you!" She dashed a hand at her tears as she looked at Sir Richard.

His face turned ashy, and he inhaled a quick, audible breath.

"*Oh, Sophia!*" Amelia sobbed and hugged her.

"What is it?" Sophia struggled to disentangle herself from the weeping Amelia.

Sir Richard cleared his throat and tugged a hand through his hair. "The *Commoner's Revenge* was sunk near Saint-Malo while trying to escape capture by Worthington. I am so sorry, but there were no survivors. Your husband is dead."

The ringing that had been a dull hum became a deafening roar. Sophia pressed her palms to her ears for a moment before speaking. When she peeled her palms away, she said only one word, loudly and with a force that made Amelia jerk beside her. "*No.*"

Sir Richard gaped, and she had the sudden urge to slap him. He nodded. "I'm afraid so. Ravensdale fired on Worthington, and he returned fire to avoid being killed."

"No!" Standing, she glared at Sir Richard. He was a stupid man. A fool! How had she not seen it?

The Duke of Aversley startled her when he grasped her elbow. She tried to pull away, but he swiveled her to face him, and his viselike grip was inescapable. His eyes held a depth of sorrow that made her chest feel as it had been ripped open and crows were pecking unmercifully at her heart.

"Yes," he said with a finality that made her sway in his grip. He took her other arm, as well. "Stephens would not lie, nor would Worthington. When Worthington docked in Saint-Malo for emergency repairs, Stephens made his way to Worthington's ship and told him that Scarsdale had been on board *Commoner's Revenge*. Worthington searched the waters for any signs of life. He even had locals help him search. Scarsdale is gone."

"No!" She tried to break free of the duke's hold once more. If she just kept repeating that Nathan was not dead, then it would be so. "No! No! No!" she screamed until she was sobbing and sagging against the duke's chest. Her world spun so quickly she was sure she would faint. She longed to faint. She wanted to slide into oblivion and never return.

❦

"Your Grace,"

Sophia struggled to open her eyes to no avail. Her lids wouldn't budge.

"Your Grace," the voice came again, insistent and annoying.

Sophia tried to lift her arm to bat the person away, but her arm was heavy as the barrels Frank had made her roll from the kitchen to the bar.

"Your Grace, the Duke of Scarsdale says I must get you out of bed and dressed. It has been two days."

Sophia's eyes flew open at those words and rage hit her. Reaching up, she gripped a startled Mary Margaret. "There will ever only be one man worthy of that title," she growled, tears instantly leaking out of her eyes.

Mary Margaret pressed a hand to her mouth, a soft cry escaping her clamped lips, but she nodded. After a pause, she cleared her throat. "Yes, Your Grace, but the Duke of Scarsdale did say—"

"Help me stand," Sophia snapped, livid that Ellison was so eager to take Nathan's place.

Instantly, hands came under both of Sophia's arms. "Your Grace, perhaps you should sit for a minute until the laudanum wears off completely."

Sophia searched her foggy memory for who had given her laudanum, and she dug out a picture of the physician, Amelia, the Duke of Aversley, and Ellison standing over her with worried looks, but it had been Ellison who had ordered she be given laudanum.

A burning flame spread from her head to her stomach, and whatever small control she had on her emotions broke under the weight of her grief and newfound rage.

Ellison.

"He cannot call himself that!" she screamed, knowing even as her wail vibrated the room that he could. Fury boiled up from her belly to nearly choke her. She shoved past Mary Margaret and flung open her door with a bang. Behind her, Mary Margaret called frantically, and as Sophia bounded down the stairs, her lady's maid caught up with her and grasped her arm.

"Your Grace, you are in your bedclothes."

"What do I care?" she demanded, breathless with rage. "How foolish it would be to cling to etiquette when my heart has been ripped from my chest!"

Wordlessly, Mary Margaret draped a wrapper around Sophia's shoulders. "He would not want you to go about like this. He would want you to clothe yourself in dignity."

He! A whispered word, not even her husband's name. Not even in normal tones. "*Say. His. Name.*"

"The Duke of Scarsdale."

Sophia could not quell the rage. "*Nathan.* Say it. His name was Nathan."

"Nathan," Mary Margaret said in a trembling voice.

She might as well have slapped Sophia in the face. *His* name, from her maid's quivering lips, had the stinging effect of a well placed hit. Sophia stood there opening and closing her mouth, tears pouring down her face. Her maid was right. This display would not have made Nathan happy. He would have wanted her to act with grace, even in the pits of despair. Yet, when Ellison appeared at the bottom of the stairs and glanced up at her, all reason fled and despair took its hold once more.

"*You.*" She spat the word. "You should not be the duke. Nathan was the duke. *Nathan!*" She crumpled to the floor, drew her knees to her chest, and laid her forehead against her knees. "Nathan should be duke," she repeated again and again until it sounded almost like a tune swirling around her.

Ellison's footsteps grew louder as he drew near, and he kneeled beside her. She tensed and refused to look up and acknowledge him. After a moment, he cleared his throat. "You're right. I should not be the duke. I'm nothing compared to the man Nathan was, and I know it as well as you do."

Her heart twisted at his tortured words and his apology to her. *He'd* apologized to *her!* She was being utterly wretched and cruel, and he'd humbled himself to her. Suddenly, all her anger drained away, and only deep sorrow remained. She glanced up and locked gazes with him.

"I'm sorry," she whimpered. "I'm sure you will make a fine duke. Forgive my outburst."

He held out his hands, and she took them and allowed him to help her stand. "You are part of our family now, Sophia. There's no need to worry that you will have to go back to the life you had."

She stared at him blankly for a second, and then his insinuation registered. She clenched her teeth in irritation. Perhaps she was being touchy. Still… "I've not given a single thought to what might become of me." Except for the thousands of moments she had thought about how Nathan would never caress her again. Never make her laugh again. Never exchange barbs with her again. He'd never decorate his home for her at Christmastide again. A large, immovable lump formed in her throat. She swallowed and spoke. "I do not care what becomes of me."

Ellison gave her a doubtful look. "Well, Scarsdale cared. And his solicitor is downstairs now in my study waiting to speak with you."

His study! Her nostrils flared that he so easily took over Nathan's home, but then, it was no longer Nathan's. She drew the wrapper tightly around her. "I'll be there in a moment. Let me dress for the day."

With Mary Margaret's help, it didn't take long to don a gown, and as she put on the light-blue morning gown, it struck her that she would need to have black gowns to wear for mourning. She worried her lip, unsure whether she should ask Ellison's permission to purchase black gowns or not. When she had a moment alone with Amelia, she would inquire as to what she should do.

When she entered Nathan's—*no, Ellison's*—study, Amelia, the duke, and Lady Anthony were all seated there.

Lady Anthony glared at her with reproachful eyes. "We've been waiting half an hour for you."

Before Sophia could decide whether to apologize or not, Ellison spoke. "Mother," he clipped, "if you cannot be civil, then I suggest you leave the room."

Lady Anthony stared at him as if she didn't know who he was. Sophia barely knew Ellison, but from what Mr. Burk had told her, Ellison had succumbed to his mother's dictates his entire life. Good for him for not doing so any longer! At least the tiniest sliver of something good was coming out of Nathan's death.

Ellison quickly introduced Sophia to Nathan's solicitor, Mr. Nilbury, and once she was seated, he cleared his throat and sat behind Nathan's desk. In her heart, everything here would always be Nathan's, whether he was gone or not. Mr. Nilbury spoke at length of different legal matters that didn't seem to concern her, and her mind drifted to Nathan. She outlined the curve of his jawbone, his broad shoulders, his wide chest, and the length of his long, powerful legs. She trembled, recalling his drugging kisses and featherlight touches.

"Sophia!"

Amelia's voice snapped her out of her remembrances. She blinked and glanced at Amelia. "Yes?"

"Have you any questions about what Scarsdale left you?"

Heat flooded Sophia's face as she looked around the room

and found all gazes on her. She hurried past Lady Anthony's hostile glare and latched on to Mr. Nilbury's friendlier visage. "I'm sorry," she mumbled. "Could you please explain it to me again?" She refused to admit that she'd been daydreaming.

"Certainly," he replied. "The former Duke of Scarsdale left you two unentailed properties: a townhome in London on Mayfair and a country home in St. Ives."

Amelia put a gentle hand on Sophia's arm. "That's where our country home is. Scarsdale redid the property last year, as no one had visited it since his parents' deaths."

Sophia nodded. "Thank you, Mr. Nilbury."

He furrowed his brow. "But, Your Grace, that's not all. You also have been left an income of two thousand pounds a year."

She could not have heard correctly. "I beg your pardon?"

"You heard him, you insufferable piece of rubbish!" Lady Anthony hissed.

Sophia's jaw dropped as much from the news of the money as Lady Anthony's words. "That cannot be correct."

"Your Grace, I assure you I am never mistaken in matters of money. Your husband was one of the richest men in England. True, he inherited a great deal, but he was the most astute businessman for whom I have ever had the honor of working."

"I cannot take so much money."

Mr. Nilbury appeared flummoxed for a moment, but then he gave his head a decisive shake. "Oh, but you must. It was your husband's greatest wish that you never need worry about money again. He came to see me the morning he disappeared. He said that he wanted to make sure you and your brother were taken care for the rest of your lives should anything ever happen to him. He wanted to leave an amount that would ensure you'd be more than comfortable with or without a husband. I do believe he assumed you'd never remarry."

Desperate not to cry in front of everyone, she bit her lip until it throbbed in time with the pulse in her neck. He must have loved her, too, if he'd not wanted her to remarry.

Anguish wrapped around her like a cocoon. "I will never remarry. The memory of him is all I will ever need."

"What a fine actress you are," Lady Anthony said, her voice cold and bitter. "You must be some sort of temptress for the fool to have left you that much of my son's inheritance."

"Mother!" Ellison snapped and rose from his chair. "That was Scarsdale's money to do with as he wished, and he rightly wished to ensure his widow was taken care of. Please cease the nonsense."

"Nonsense?" she fairly shrieked. "Nonsense!"

"Good Lord, Lady Anthony," the Duke of Aversley thundered. "You act as if your son has been left destitute. That money Scarsdale left to his wife will not be missed in the sea of vast and deep fortune in which your son now floats. Try to contain yourself. Your behavior is vulgar."

Her face twisted into an ugly visage, wiping everything pretty away. "I'm vulgar?" Lady Anthony pointed at Sophia. "She's a common wench who grew up in a tavern with a drunkard for a father and a half brother whose mother abandoned him, but I'm vulgar!"

Hurt pricked Sophia that Nathan had shared so much of her private affairs with his aunt, but rage shoved the hurt to the background. Sophia rose up and stood ramrod straight. "You are vulgar," she said in a quiet, firm voice. She was determined to make Nathan proud and be a worthy widow. That meant not descending to his aunt's level. But her pride—God help her there was a good deal of it—would not allow her to quit the room without saying anything. "You know, you are pretty until one gets to know you. But once the cruelty flows from your mouth, you are quite the ugliest creature I've ever seen."

She marched to the door but paused there and turned back to face everyone. "Your Grace, I'd ask a carriage be sent round to collect me. I wish to depart immediately for my new home."

Ellison opened his mouth to speak but Sophia cut him off, not wanting him to give her the option of staying. He was a kind, good man but if she had to live under the same roof with his mother one of them would surely kill the other. "Amelia, if you would not mind giving me a private moment, I have a request of you," she said.

"It would be my pleasure," Amelia replied as she stood. When she passed Lady Anthony, she frowned at her fiercely, and Sophia's insides warmed at the new friend she had gained. She'd only ever had one friend in her life, so a second was very welcome, indeed.

Once she and Amelia were in the privacy of her bedchamber, she turned to her new friend. "I need to learn to be a true lady. The kind Nathan would have been proud to call his duchess. Will you help me?"

Amelia worried her lip for a moment. "I will, but dearest, you didn't mean what you said about never remarrying, did you?"

"Of course I meant it," Sophia replied. "You cannot know this, but he never told me he loved me."

"I'm sorry," Amelia said, her voice hitching.

"Don't be sorry." Sophia hugged herself and, for one brief second, recalled his lips running across her collarbone. "When I learned he was dead so many thoughts kept streaming through my mind, and one of them was that I would never know for certain if he loved me. But now I know, Amelia. Don't you see?"

Amelia shook her head. "I'm afraid I don't."

"He took the time to make sure I was going to be well provided for the rest of my life. He even thought of my brother. And the solicitor said he was sure Nathan didn't think I would ever remarry. He loved me. He did not want me ever to marry another man, and I will abide by his wishes. It is the least I can do after everything he did for me."

"But Sophia," Amelia cried, "you are so very young! I vow he would not have expected you to be alone the rest of your life." She gripped Sophia's hand. "You're distraught right now, but you'll change your mind. You'll see."

"No." Sophia tugged her hand free. "No, I won't. Would

you remarry if your husband died?"

Amelia gaped for a moment, and then she slowly answered, "No, I would not, but that is different."

"How?" She was getting rather perturbed with her new friend.

Amelia worried her lip once more. "Well," she hedged, "it's different because we married for love. We are in love."

"I love Nathan. And he loved me. Now, either you will help me become a lady or you will not."

"I'll help you become a lady," Amelia muttered. "But I most certainly will not help you live as a perpetual widow who refuses to allow herself to be happy. If I'm going to help you, I have one condition."

Exhaustion overcame Sophia in a wave. Whatever Amelia's condition, she was too tired to argue. "All right," Sophia mumbled and stifled a yawn, though it was still fairly early in the day. "I accept your condition," she said, not even caring at this moment what it might be.

"You do? But I haven't even told you what it is yet."

Amelia had such a look of astonishment on her face that Sophia almost thought she could have smiled. *Almost.* Her sadness refused to allow her lips to make the expression.

"At the end of your mourning, you must promise to come to London and let Colin and me present you to Society as I know Scarsdale wanted." Tears shone in her eyes.

She fought back her own tears at the sight of Amelia, who she knew had been trying to be strong, breaking down. "All right," Sophia agreed. "If that's all, I need to pack now. I plan to leave today."

"We're going to leave, as well," Amelia said with a sniff. "I insist you stay with us until we have your house staffed once again and you hire a companion. And if you are at our home, I can more easily help you do all that. Your brother is welcome, too, though have you thought about his education?"

Tears welled in her eyes again. She dashed them away but not quickly enough that Amelia didn't see. Her friend clutched her in an embrace. "That was silly of me." Her voice hitched.

"Of course you want him with you."

"No, that's not it. I'd be happy for him to be with me, but he was supposed to go to Eton. Nathan was going to take him weeks ago."

Amelia's face went pale, but she gave her head a firm shake and squeezed Sophia reassuringly. "Then Colin shall do it in Nathan's place," she said with forced gaiety.

The offer touched Sophia but also made her heart throb with pain at the potent reminder that Nathan was never coming back. He would no longer be around to help her brother become a better man. She desperately wanted to be alone. "Do you mind," she choked out, trying and failing to keep her voice steady, "if I start packing? I'll meet you both downstairs in two hours."

"Of course not. Do you want me to send your lady's maid to you?"

Sophia turned her back on Amelia as tears leaked from her eyes and tracked down her cheeks. "No, thank you. I'll call her up in a bit."

Amelia squeezed Sophia's shoulder. "It's going to be all right." Her strained voice hinted at her sadness. "You'll see."

Sophia nodded, because she knew that was what Amelia wanted, but in her heart she did not see how she would ever be happy again.

Nineteen

$\mathcal{F}$or the second time in the week that Sophia had been staying with Amelia and Aversley, she rode in their carriage seated opposite them and trained her gaze out the window trying desperately to hold her tears at bay. It seemed surreal that her first trip to London had been to attend Nathan's memorial service. After a moment, the spasms in her throat died away and her nose quit tingling. She glanced dispassionately at Amelia and Aversley's massive stone home that sat amid rolling hills. Twin lakes banked the house on both sides, and a forest rose up in the distance.

A month ago, she would have been awed at the grandeur of this home, but now she couldn't muster up enough energy to feel anything but sadness. Well, that wasn't quite true. She'd rallied enough energy at Nathan's memorial service to briefly feel scared when she'd walked in the church and a sea of inquisitive faces had turned to gawk at her, but Amelia and Aversley had flanked her as she stood quietly in the church and her fear had given way once again to sadness. When the service was over, she had begged to depart quickly, keenly aware that she did not look the part of Nathan's duchess, nor did she yet know how to act enough like a lady that she wouldn't make him wince in his grave. Even when she'd been stopped at the door by Ellison and his mother, Sophia had felt only sadness. Her anger at Ellison was gone. He was a kind man who told her, again, that she was part of their family, even as Lady Anthony glared at her.

She was jolted out of her thoughts as the carriage came to

a stop, and in a haze, she descended the carriage steps and forewent the offer for refreshments, instead choosing to head to her room. Halfway up the stairs, she remembered that she'd not had a chance to ask Aversley how it had gone taking Harry to Eton, but a familiar ache in her throat made it impossible to form words, anyway.

Even Harry was lost to her! He'd told her he was not a baby and preferred to be taken to Eton without her. He was likely sick of all her tears. When she felt better she would go visit him. Once she was in her room, she pulled the cord to summon Mary Margaret, who had agreed to accompany her to her new home, and she stood in silence as her lady's maid undressed her and then helped her to bed. On Sophia's request, Mary Margaret slid the heavy velvet curtains shut. Sophia wanted to block out the sun. Darkness seemed more appropriate to her mood.

"Should I be looking in here?" Colin asked his wife.

A dark glare was his answer, followed by Amelia crooking her finger at him. Once they moved out of the doorway of Sophia's bedchamber and moved into the hall, Amelia shut the door with a soft click and set her hands to her hips. Damnation. Hands on the hips and a no-nonsense look from Amelia meant he'd made her mad.

"Do you see what I mean now?" she demanded.

It was on the tip of his tongue to tell her he was bleary-eyed from his quick trip to London and could barely see her lovely face, let alone decipher what she meant, but he knew better. Nor did he want her to question him about what he had gone to London for. He'd gone to see Sir Richard and asked the man to keep working on tracking down any information he could on the men who had worked for Ravensdale. If there anyone left to pay for the deeds against Scarsdale, Colin was personally going to make sure they met their justice. So instead of saying what he felt, he rubbed the back of his knotted neck and thought carefully about exactly what to say. Questions were always good. They seemed to get him in less trouble than statements that could be misinterpreted. "You say she's been in bed all week since I left?"

Amelia nodded.

"And the physician has been to see her?"

"She is not physically ill, Colin." Amelia spoke in clipped words, which was very unlike her. "Her heart is broken."

He forced himself not to react. "What does Dr. Jameson recommend?"

"Laudanum in high doses." Amelia's taut tone displayed her disapproval, not surprising given her mother's former laudanum addiction.

"Jameson is dicked in the nob," he said, confident that statement would be met with approval and not misinterpretation.

Amelia beamed before coming to her tiptoes and placing a quick kiss on his lips. "I'm glad you agree, darling! I knew you would. What shall we do? I've tried everything. Each day she slips further away. It's as if she has lost the desire to live."

His wife's voice wobbled, and tears pooled in her eyes. He was done for, now. He wanted nothing more than to take to his bed and enjoy his wife's body, but that would never happen while she was so distraught. "I'll speak to her."

"Will you?" Amelia asked happily and kissed him again. This one held the promise of a long, sweet night to come. "I was hoping you would say that. Give me a bit of time to rouse her and I'll send her to your study."

This night was becoming longer by the second. "I thought you said she would not get out of bed."

"I'll make something up."

He didn't doubt it. His wife had the heart of a saint but the scheming mind of a sinner. Instead of arguing, he simply nodded.

Colin had never met a woman truer to her word than his wife. Which was why it didn't surprise him in the least when, precisely twenty minutes later, a knock came at his study door, followed by Sophia's weak voice asking if she could enter. Colin bid her to come in, and as she did, he experienced a moment of stunned shock at her ghostlike appearance, followed quickly by a burning, seething anger. Damn Scarsdale. He'd married this woman out of pity, she had fallen hopelessly in love with him, and then he'd gone and gotten himself killed.

Now the pity must have been transferred to Colin because he felt as if a hand was squeezing his heart. He motioned for her to sit down and took the opportunity to study her. Not that she would have noticed if he were openly gaping. She moved as if in a deep dream. Dark hair curled at her neck and around her face, which enhanced the stark whiteness of her skin. Too-sharp cheekbones defined her face, along with hollows where flesh should be. She was obviously not eating. Blue eyes that should have sparkled with youth stared dully at him, unblinking and unseeing.

He'd say just about anything to snap her out of her trance, but he hadn't a clue what would work. He didn't even know the entirety of her story or the details of how she had met Scarsdale and come to love a man who'd had no qualms letting anyone know that he'd sooner give his trust to a poisonous snake than a woman. Colin leaned back in his chair and drummed his hands against his thigh. In order to help, he needed to know all the facts.

"Tell me the entire story of how you came to meet and marry Scarsdale." He'd purposely made his words sound like a command in hopes that she would simply obey.

For one second her shoulders visibly stiffened, and then she sagged into the chair. "Amelia said you wanted to speak to me about my brother."

"Ah, yes. He loved Eton, and said to tell you he will write often." The lie didn't even bother Colin. The boy had been giddy at the sight of Eton, and Colin had practically had to box his ears to extract a promise that he would write his sister. The promise, given with much wiggling, grunting, and mumbling, was typical of a boy, Colin thought. But Harry had also said his sister was no longer herself. Colin promptly told the boy to get used to women's moods, which changed more often than the wind.

"That's nice to hear," she responded in a small voice. "May I go now? I'm so tired."

"I'd like to know how you met Scarsdale first."

Her words came out hesitantly for a bit, but then picked up pace and began to flow. When she finished, Colin realized he had been gaping as she'd told her story. He snapped his jaw shut and tried to picture Scarsdale decorating his home for Christmastide and buying gifts for a woman he simply pitied. Suddenly, Colin had a gut suspicion that his friend may have married Sophia out of pity and a sense of honor to save her, but she had awoken, if not captured, his heart. The thought produced the conclusion that the best way to rouse Sophia from her melancholy was to fabricate a bit. He despised the word *lie*, and what he was about to say may have very well been the truth, or could have one day been so, at least.

"It is time you got out of bed. This show of weakness would have embarrassed Scarsdale. Why, when I saw him in London the night before he died, he could talk of nothing but you. How brave you were. How strong you were. How you would never crumble in the face of adversity. He would be astonished at how you are not picking yourself up and carrying on."

He made his tone chiding at first, and then almost harsh. She didn't need to be nudged gently; she needed a mental slap. He stood up and moved around his desk to grip her by the elbow, then forcibly helped her to stand. "And what of your brother? It's scandalous to squander away the opportunity for him to have a good future. His acceptance into the *ton* will be difficult at best, but it will be near impossible if you do not become the lady you said you were going to become. A duchess does not overindulge in laudanum."

Technically, he had only known ladies of lesser titles who indulged in laudanum, so he wasn't lying. His mother's vice had been spirits. "A duchess does not go about with unkempt hair and bedraggled clothes. A duchess is daunting. Indomitable." Had he forgotten anything? Good God, he was tired. "And flawless." That should give her something to strive to achieve. "Can you become those things?"

Her eyes, suddenly sparkling with fierce determination, locked with his. "I can. Thank you, Aversley. Thank you very much."

"Think nothing of it," he replied. Amelia was going to be so pleased she'd likely do all sorts of sinful things to him. He struggled to keep a grin off his face as Sophia made her way to the door. She paused there and turned back to him.

"I'd like to visit his country house tomorrow so I can see for myself what sort of staff I will need to hire."

"That's an excellent idea." He was brilliant! His talk had worked miraculous wonders! "I'm sure Amelia will be happy to accompany you and help you make decisions."

"Will you come, as well?"

"I'd be happy to." Instead of waiting for her to leave, he escorted her out of his study and up the stairs, and then they parted ways.

Candlelight flickered in his bedchamber, and Amelia lay draped across the bed in his favorite creation—nothing but her bare body. Desire throbbed to life as his wife rose to her elbows and gazed at him with slumberous eyes.

"Well?" Her husky voice made him hard. "Did you convince her to rejoin life?"

He nodded while stripping off his clothing in a manner of efficiency that indicated his need for his wife. Once he hovered over Amelia, she encircled his neck with her arms. "Tell me how you did it."

"I convinced her that Scarsdale had loved her dearly and would be embarrassed by her lack of will. I gave her a speech about duchesses being indomitable and flawless," he said with a grin.

Amelia puckered her brow. "But you lied."

He brushed his lips against one of her taut nipples and then the other. She moaned and her eyes fluttered shut. Satisfaction coursed through him. "I stretched the truth. But darling—" he paused a moment and suckled her breast until she was squirming and making mewling sounds "—please can we finish this talk tomorrow? I vow I will tell you every word we said."

"Tomorrow will be perfect," she said breathlessly as he took her nipple in his mouth once more.

Twenty

The next day Sophia stood in the portrait gallery of the home Nathan had left her and gazed up at the wall of family pictures. Aversley and Amelia stood silently beside her. A heaviness centered in her chest as she moved her gaze from one portrait to the next. The wall contained twenty portraits by her quick count—seventeen of Nathan's mother, unsurprisingly. In them, she was lounging on a chaise with her hand clasping her hair, or pressed against the voluptuous bosom displayed, or grasping a dazzling necklace around her neck. One particular portrait depicted her dressed in a blazing-red riding habit with a tall black hat on her head and a hand planted firmly on her hip. Her face held a haughty expression. In another, she held a small, repugnant-looking dog in her lap, which she gazed down at adoringly.

There wasn't a single portrait of Nathan and his mother together. Certainly, there wasn't any loving family portrait. There was a portrait of Nathan's father, a dark-haired, handsome man with a friendly smile. He leaned negligently against a pianoforte with one hand on his hip and the other splayed on top of the gleaming wood. One leg was crossed over the other and his sparkling coal eyes matched Nathan's in color.

Sophia's gaze went to the next portrait, which was of Nathan sitting on his father's knee. Father and son looked at each other, the love between them so very apparent. Nathan, with his chubby cheeks and legs, was obviously much younger in this portrait than the one next to it. He wore a smile, and his eyes glowed with unrestrained happiness. In the other portrait, he had shed all visible signs of baby fat. His smile was now sardonic, as if he would rather be anywhere else than standing for a portrait. Finally, she tore her gaze away and glanced at Amelia. "You said Nathan had recently had this house redecorated?"

Amelia nodded. "He mentioned the project and I asked him about it. That's when he told me he had not spent a night in this house since the day his mother and father had died. He'd been called here to tend to some business with a tenant, and while here, he decided it was time to update the interior."

Her throat constricted with sadness. *Oh God!* Why had Nathan put back up portraits that so obviously showed his mother held no love for him? Was he trying to punish himself? Remind himself? She'd never know. She'd never be able to help him heal his tattered heart as she had hoped to do. She fought the tears that threatened to come. The time for being melancholy was over. She was going to become the duchess Nathan would have wanted her to be.

"I'd like to speak to the butler," she said.

She'd met him a bit ago at the door. He was an ancient man with a hunched back, thin lips, and no visible hair save his silver eyebrows, but she would keep him on for all those reasons and more. He had a kind smile, and his eyes had grown very sad when he had offered her his condolences. She could tell he had cared for Nathan, and maybe he could reveal things about her husband she would not learn otherwise.

Aversley pulled the bell cord to summon the butler, but when he didn't appear after a bit, Aversley pulled it again. After a while, it became apparent that the servant was not going to come. Aversley snorted. "The first thing you need to do is hire a new butler. The man is deaf. I can't imagine why Scarsdale kept him on."

"I can," Sophia said, and Amelia nodded her understanding.

"Scarsdale liked to pretend he cared for no one, but he cared for his servants' welfares," Amelia said.

Sophia gasped. "Maybe he thought of them as family!"

"They probably treated him better," Aversley added as Sophia swiveled on her heel and dashed out of the gallery.

She had an idea.

She found the butler in the dining room with a table of silver spread out before him. He didn't turn when she walked into the room, probably because he hadn't heard her. She stood and watched him for a moment, struck by the urge to giggle at his judicious counting of the silver, as if any might have disappeared. She moved to stand beside him, and when he didn't look up, she cleared her throat. He dropped the fork he'd been holding and gawked at her.

"I beg your pardon, Your Grace. I did not hear you. Do you need me?" asked Mr. Lewis.

"Yes. I'd like to ask you a question about the portrait gallery."

He nodded.

"Did my husband personally oversee the placement of those portraits when the house was redecorated or did he have someone else do it?"

"He did it. He was very particular. The portraits had to be hung just as his mother had ordered them the year she died. I thought he might be changing the order, since he had me give him the keys to the attic and he spent days up there looking at the other portraits, but he ended up hanging the same pictures in the exact same places."

Sophia's heart pounded so hard she felt breathless. "Are the other portraits still in the attic?"

"Of course, Your Grace. I vow I've not touched a thing."

"No, of course not," she hurriedly supplied to assuage his concern. "May I have the keys?"

"To be sure, you may have anything you want, but I'm not the keeper of the keys. My wife is responsible for that."

"Your wife? You're married?"

He smiled. "It surprised me that she'd have me, too. Took me nearly forty years to get over the shock of it. She's the cook. Shall I get the keys from her?"

"Yes, please. I'll come with you to meet her."

After meeting his wife, who was in the middle of preparing for lunch, Sophia made her way to the attic with Mr. Lewis, while Amelia and Aversley went to look around the gardens at her suggestion. She felt that if there were any secrets about Nathan's past to be revealed, he would not have wanted them revealed to others. It didn't take long to locate the large portraits. They stood against a far wall with enormous, white sheets hung over them.

After assuring Mr. Lewis that she was not too fragile to help him remove the sheets, she started tugging them off one by one. In total, there were five long rows of portraits with ten paintings stacked in each row. She started at the first row.

Nathan could not have been more than five in the first piece she uncovered. He had the characteristic chubby legs, cheeks, and arms that he had in the portrait downstairs. And— she narrowed her eyes and furrowed her brow—he seemed to be wearing the same brown trousers, cream jacket with gold buttons, and gray-and-cream hat, tilted the exact same way. Maybe this portrait had a mistake, so the painter had done another.

She stared at it, but when she could find nothing amiss, she simply moved on to the next one. Her breath caught at the sight of Nathan in the exact same clothes. He appeared as if it was, in fact, the very same day. She studied the green trees behind him and counted them. Then she took note of the placement of his hands and the number of creases in his trousers. She then flipped back to the second and third portraits and compared them. They were identical.

She pressed her lips into a hard line. Something wasn't right. She flipped through all ten portraits of Nathan and they were identical in every way except one. From the first to the last painting of Nathan, the expression on his face went from cheerful to miserable. In the final portrait, the painter had made it obvious that Nathan had been crying.

She let the portraits fall back into place, dust swirling like tiny specks in the air, and swiveled toward Mr. Lewis, who had been standing quietly behind her as she had looked at the first row. "What are those portraits about?" she demanded, her voice high and her pulse increasing.

He sighed. "Her Grace took it in her head that the young master was purposely making his face look odd, so she made the painter redo the portrait."

"But there are ten portraits here!"

"Yes, Your Grace." The butler's voice had taken on a hard edge of disapproval. "The young master was made to put on the same clothes every day and stand in the same place and position for two months. It was the entire length of their visit. *Poor lad.* My wife wept for him. Secretly, of course, so as not to anger Her Grace."

A bitter tasted filled Sophia's mouth, and her stomach twisted violently. "He stood all summer? But why did no one stop her?"

"The only one who could stop her was His Grace, and he did, when he finally learned what she was doing."

Agitated, she waved her hand at the row of portraits she had just gone through. "Why did it take him all summer?" Her question came out as a high-pitched shrill.

"He was rarely around. One could say, if one was inclined to gossip, he avoided her and, therefore, ignored his son, as a result. And it took much longer than the summer for him to figure out what went on here every summer for five years."

"*Five years?*" The very thought made her ill.

He nodded and then motioned to the rows of portraits she had not had a chance to look at yet. "The row you just went through was the first year. The young master was five then. In the next row, he was six. With each row, his age increases a year until his father found out what was going on during a rare occasion they were all together at Whitecliffe. The young master didn't want to leave Whitecliffe to come back here with his mother, and we heard, through gossip, mind you, that he pitched the most gruesome outbursts in front of some twenty-odd dinner guests when he learned they were to come back here, which culminated with the young master running away from Whitecliffe in the dark."

Mr. Lewis shook his head. "When his father found him, he discovered what had caused the outburst. His Grace, in an unusual show of defiance against his wife's control, came here in a rage, toting Her Grace and his son along. He ordered every painting removed. She'd put every one of them up in the portrait gallery; there were so many you could hardly see the walls. He threatened to ship her to America and never allow her to return should she ever make their son pose for another portrait again."

Sophia trembled with rage. Nathan's mother had been as bad as Frank, but in her own nasty way. She glanced back at the remaining portraits. She almost feared looking through the rest and seeing the pain etched on Nathan's face. No wonder he'd had no use for love. He'd equated love with pain. "I'd like to look at the rest alone, if you don't mind."

"Of course, Your Grace."

After Mr. Lewis left the attic, she moved to the second row of portraits, then the third, the fourth, and finally the last. They were, as Mr. Lewis had said, placed in order of years. With each new row, Nathan had gotten one year older, his eyes a bit duller, and his expression vastly more cynical. By the last row, she bit her lip on a sob at the angry, contemptuous set of his face.

Oh, Nathan! She ran her hand over his young face and wept for him.

She slid to her bottom and cried for what seemed an eternity for the years, the love, the children, and the laughter they would never have. He had given her such joy, and he had risked his heart and his pride, she was sure, to take a chance on loving her. She dried her eyes and stood. She was going to do everything in her power to be worthy of the gifts he had given her. She would love only him forever and honor him by becoming an Incomparable.

The captain's whip hissed through the air and sliced into Nathan's back, still raw from the beatings he'd received every day since being held on board the Barbary ship as a slave. They were somewhere in the Mediterranean Sea, now.

Warm blood oozed down his back, and every time the whip struck anew to cut deeper into his mangled flesh, he flinched but did not cry out. He'd quit trying to get out of the ropes that bound his wrists to the whipping pole after the first week. It was futile, and he'd learned quickly that the captain only whipped harder, and would turn Nathan around and whip his chest, for what he considered cowardly behavior.

All the new slaves were beat morning, noon, and night like clockwork. Nathan glanced up at the darkening sky. He couldn't say how long the whipping lasted because he'd slipped in and out of consciousness, but he came fully to himself when they shoved him back in his regular rowing spot and chained him there.

Pain snaked through every inch of his body, but he grabbed hold of his oars and rowed in time with the rest of the crew. To not row meant death and he had to survive for Sophia. *Sophia.* He cast his mind to her with a yearning that made all the cravings he'd ever had for laudanum or opium pale in comparison. She was his drug of choice.

He saw her in the tavern in Moses's arms with her eyes blazing in defiance. He saw her kicking and screaming in Mr. Exington's arms, determined to rescue her brother. He saw her naked before him, professing her love for him. And then slowly, like a man savoring his dying breath, he recalled every second he'd ever touched her, tasted her, heard her, and every feeling that had been elicited. His fingers tingled with the memory of her silky skin. His ears rang with her laughter. His mouth watered to taste the sweetness only she possessed.

The hours passed as he relived each moment in his mind, and near dawn, when his arms rebelled against rowing any more, he invented new places he would bed her. Under the stars would be his first choice. He longed to see her eyes twinkling in the moonlight. In lush green grass would be another place, with the sun beaming down on her creamy, pert breasts. In his memory he could smell her hair. And as the sun rose in the sky, he thanked Sophia in his head for, once again, helping him live to see another day.

Twenty-One

After that fateful day in the attic, Sophia stayed true to her vow with a zealous determination. With the help of Amelia, she hired a staff of twelve, including Mr. Burk, who had written to her wondering if she might be looking for a stable master. It seemed he could not tolerate Lady Anthony, which Sophia understood all too well. Once the staff was in place and she was settled into her home, she cloistered herself from everyone in the outside world except Amelia, who visited three days a week to give Sophia lessons on how to become an Incomparable.

As the winter months drifted into spring, Sophia pored over Debrett's and spent hours learning the correct forms of address for anyone and everyone she might encounter. She learned how to sit, walk, talk, dance, and sing. She studied French and history, and took lessons on playing the pianoforte. She rode Aphrodite every day and became an expert jumper and foxhunter, with Mr. Burk's aid.

In her free time, she would go to Nathan's library and write letters to Harry or read one of the books that she thought Nathan might have read, snuggling under a blanket that smelled of pine, as he had. By the time spring had turned to summer, she had read "The Wanderer," *Principles of Political Economy*, every single poem by Wordsworth and Shelley, and so many other books she lost count. Sometimes she would call Mr. Burk into the study at night and they would sit while she read poetry to him. In turn, he would tell her stories about Nathan.

It was on the third or fourth story about Nathan rescuing an injured animal that tears suddenly filled her eyes with a realization.

"Wha' is it, lassie?" Mr. Burk asked, stopping his tale.

She dabbed at her eyes with a handkerchief. "I think Nathan saved animals because deep down he wished someone would have saved him."

Mr. Burk nodded. "Ta be sure. Especially that mangy, three-legged dog he loved so much—Duke."

Sophia's brow furrowed. "I never saw a three-legged dog at Whitecliffe."

"Ye would'na have. He kept the dog with him always. When ye were in residence at Whitecliffe, the dog was in London because, if ye remember, His Grace's trip to Newmarket was supposed ta be brief."

"Where is Duke now?"

"I dinnot know, Your Grace."

It took Sophia several weeks to locate Duke and have him fetched to live with her, and then it took several more weeks to get Duke to quit growling at her, but by the time August rolled around, Duke was her best friend, constant companion, and guard. Everywhere she went, so did Duke. And for a three-legged dog, he got around rather impressively. The only thing the large black-and-white, long-haired dog ever did that she didn't care for was to bring "gifts" to the house. She liked gifts just fine, as long as they were alive, but Duke especially loved to bring her dead gifts. She eventually got used to it and overlooked this one flaw. In her heart, she understood that Nathan had viewed himself like that dog, the one no one had wanted, and so for her, Duke could do no wrong.

On a snowy day in January that marked the end of her mourning period—which she was only aware of because Amelia had been reminding her that she had to keep her promise to formally enter Society—Amelia surprised Sophia by appearing at her home earlier than was socially acceptable. And the duchess was not alone. Trailing behind her was Madame Lexington, who Amelia had asked to come. And trailing behind Madame Lexington were two girls, both of whom appeared to be twenty-one, the same age as Sophia now.

She'd quite forgotten she had turned twenty-one until Amelia had asked her several visits ago when her birthday was. Only then had she realized the day had come and gone.

"What's all this?" Sophia asked as Amelia, Madame Lexington, and her assistants entered Sophia's bedchambers.

Madame Lexington paused and appraised Sophia. Her lips parted and her eyes grew wide. *"Mon Dieu!* Nature has given you a great gift to make up for your great sorrow."

Sophia was on the verge of asking Madame Lexington what she meant, but Amelia grasped Sophia by the arm and hugged her. "This is your birthday present! I've planned a dinner for your birthday tonight, and it will also be a test to see if you are ready for the house party."

Sophia furrowed her brow. "What house party?"

"Oh my," Amelia replied. "Did I forget to mention I have planned a house party in your honor?"

Amelia's face was such a comical display of her trying to look innocent and failing that Sophia giggled. "You did forget to tell me that most important fact. When is this house party?"

"At the end of this week, so the dinner was of the utmost importance to allow us to see if there is anything else on which we need to work. I'll expect you to stay at our house for the duration of the party, too. It's a week long."

"But I only live down the road from you."

Amelia narrowed her eyes and plopped her hands on her hips. Sophia laughed and threw up her hands. One thing she'd learned this year was that Amelia had a stubborn streak in her as long at the Thames. And Sophia *had* promised she'd enter Society once her mourning period ended. Plus, she was getting a bit restless, and though she was nervous, she would like to make new friends and see new places.

Madame Lexington cleared her throat. "Your Grace—"

Sophia and Amelia both answered yes at the same time and then promptly burst into a fit of laughter. Sophia was the first to gain control. "Madam Lexington, call me Sophia."

The woman gave a definite shake of her head. "No. I could not. It's not proper."

Sophia bit her lip. If Madame Lexington knew where Sophia had come from, she'd be happy to call her plain old Sophia.

"Call her Duchess, then," Amelia inserted.

Madame Lexington looked as if she was about to object but then simply nodded before giving two sharp claps and saying, "Show her the gowns."

There was a moment of flurry, and then both of Madame Lexington's helpers scurried forward to present gowns to her. Sophia's jaw dropped at the sight of a crimson gown that was cut so low she would be in danger of spilling out if she wore it. And she now had plenty to spill out. In her year in mourning, two things had grown: her hair, which hung midway down her back, and her breasts, which had gone from entirely too small to shockingly voluptuous. With an apologetic smile to Amelia and Madame Lexington she pointed at the crimson silk and shook her head. "I would never be so bold as to wear a gown like that."

Madame Lexington eyed her askance. "You *should* be so bold," the woman said blandly. "You have a figure that puts the very best I've ever dressed to shame, and my dear, I have clothed many Incomparable ladies."

She gaped at the seamstress. She knew her figure had filled out, but when she studied herself in the looking glass, she saw the same old mousy-appearing lady. Just now with breasts and hips. "That is kind, but certainly too kind."

"*Non,*" Madam Lexington replied, slipping momentarily into French. "French women are never too kind. Too nasty, yes. Too kind, never! And I tell you honestly that you will beguile in the blue gown, but in the red one the eligible bachelors will chase you like bloodthirsty hounds after a fox."

"Then the blue gown, with a fichu placed at the chest, will be perfect for me, as I do not want any eligible bachelors chasing me."

Madame Lexington puckered her forehead and with a long-suffering sigh, turned a quizzical gaze to Amelia. "But I don't understand! You specifically said—"

"Never mind about any of that," Amelia interrupted. She tugged the sapphire gown out of the unsuspecting lady's hands and shoved it at Sophia. "Go slip this on so we can see that it fits properly."

Sophia took the gown and offered Madame Lexington an apologetic smile. "Despite whatever the Duchess of Aversley told you, Madame Lexington, I am most definitely not searching for a gentleman to marry. In fact, I plan never to remarry. No one could replace my husband."

Madame Lexington's assistant, completely silent until now, burst into giggles as they glanced at each other.

Madame Lexington turned scarlet as she looked from Sophia to her assistants. "Shh," she hissed. "Get hold of yourselves."

Sophia furrowed her brow. Whyever were they giggling like silly fools? "Is something wrong?" she asked them directly. She caught the sharp, dark look Madame Lexington gave them.

"No, Your Grace," they hurriedly replied as one and with downcast gazes.

Sophia's gut twisted. They were hiding something. "What is it?" she demanded.

Madame Lexington waved them away and faced Sophia. "They, like most women, thought your husband extremely handsome. They probably had silly hopes that one day he might notice them."

Sophia thought of her mother's letter that was tucked away for safekeeping in her dresser. "Hope is never silly," she said. A lump formed in her throat. Her hope had given her Nathan, and she would never regret that, no matter how short their time together had been.

The fitting of the gown did not take long, but it took the better part of the rest of the day to be bathed and lathered in lotion, and to have her hair dressed and her face painted to perfection. Madame Lexington, it seemed, was not only a renowned seamstress but she was known for her abilities with cosmetics, as well.

She hovered over Sophia with something dark that she insisted Sophia simply had to wear on her eyes. Sophia studied what Madame Lexington was holding. "What is that?"

"Kohl. It will give your eyes a mysterious, alluring look."

"None of that, then."

"But—"

"No." Sophia gave a firm shake of her head. "I want to appear respectable, not alluring."

Amelia sighed. "Sophia, you are a widow. And not just any widow. Scarsdale was one of the most powerful and wealthiest men in England. You will be granted a wide berth to do as you wish. If you want to appear alluring, I assure you no ballroom doors will be slammed in your face. They will be scampering over themselves to admit you because the women will want to know what you possess that they did not that enabled you to capture Scarsdale's hand, and the men will simply want to possess you. All you need to do is ensure they understand you desire marriage and not a romp."

"Unless you do desire a liaison," Madame Lexington said rather boldly.

"Do hush, Madame Lexington," Amelia scolded. "Sophia is not the sort of widow to wish for a liaison. She is the loyal sort and wishes for love."

Sophia's throat suddenly constricted, but she somehow swallowed. "I don't wish for either. I will remain loyal to the memory of Nathan as I know he would have wanted and expected me to."

Madame Lexington and Amelia exchanged a long, not-so-subtle look that Sophia decided to ignore. They simply didn't care for her decision, and that was all right. "I am entering Society as I promised you, Amelia, and truly I want to do so.

But it is so I can make friends and get out in the world. Just because I do not want to replace Nathan doesn't mean I want to be lonely; therefore, I desire friends, something I previously did not have in spades." There was no need to announce the fact she had only had one friend before meeting Nathan. Amelia now made two.

"Oh, Sophia," Amelia muttered but said nothing more.

Madame Lexington tsked several times but also said nothing to her. The dressmaker told her assistants to gather her things, and the ladies scurried to do her bidding. As they were carrying out the seamstress's supplies, Sophia finally took a look at herself. She stared for a moment in wonderment at what she saw. And then she grinned.

"Madame Lexington, you are a genius and a miracle worker. I actually look passable." The blue gown hugged her curves in all the right places, but fairly respectably so. Her hair had been drawn high on the crown of her head, and the look actually accentuated her cheekbones quite nicely. Several tendrils had been left loose and were curling about her neck, the contrast of her dark hair to her light skin striking.

There was not a chance she would be able to repeat how lovely Madame Lexington had made her look, but she was eternally grateful that she would look her best tonight.

Madame Lexington surprised her with a hug. "You are like a breath of fresh spring air," the seamstress said. "Anytime you need a new gown, come to me and I will put you above all others."

⚜

An hour later, the first guest knocked at Amelia and Aversley's door. Sophia looked nervously at Amelia, who sat beside her on the lush blue velvet couch in the parlor, and Amelia smiled back, then worried her lip for a moment. "I have to tell you something."

Sophia nodded her encouragement.

"This is more than a dinner party."

"It is?"

Amelia nodded. "I've planned a surprise birthday celebration for you, and I invited some guests to stay here for the weekend. I hope you don't mind."

Sophia was touched that Amelia would go to the effort for her. "Who did you invite to celebrate my birthday?"

Amelia offered a rueful smile. "I would have invited your family, but there is only your brother and your father, and your brother could not leave school for this and your father..." Her words died away.

Sophia understood why Amelia would hesitate to invite him. She'd confided to Amelia about her life with Frank, and she was glad her friend had not invited him. He'd never been a true father, and he'd proven he never would be. Once he'd gotten money from Nathan, he had not bothered to write her once or try to see her and make sure she was faring decently. She wanted to surround herself by people who truly cared for her, and he was not one of those people.

"Thank you. So what strangers are here to celebrate my birthday?" she asked with a grin.

Amelia grinned back. "Ellison is coming. I thought you would like that. You are family, after all."

Sophia was ever so grateful Amelia had referred to Nathan's cousin as Ellison and not by his new title. She didn't think she could handle hearing that tonight. "I like Ellison, but please tell me—"

Amelia snorted. "Of course I did not invite his wretched mother! I don't care if it was a snub or not. That woman is vile."

Sophia felt the tension drain out of her. "Who else?"

"My brother."

"I have a vague memory of meeting Lord Harthorne at Nathan's service." Remembering that awful day tinged her with sadness.

Amelia patted her hand. "Philip has a heart of gold. He will make you a good friend. I also invited Miss Jemma Adair and her twin sister, two minutes younger, as Jemma loves to say, Miss Anne Adair. They are from America but moved here over a year ago when their parents died and they learned they are the granddaughters of the Duke of Rowan. That's an interesting story there, but a long one. I'll tell you all, I promise, but—"

She stopped talking and a beatific smile spread across her face as she jumped from her seat and rushed to Aversley, who had strolled into the room. "You almost missed the party!" She smacked him on the arm, then pecked him on the cheek. "No more hunting before dinner parties for you!"

He answered her command with a chuckle, and then he craned his neck around her and his gaze locked on Sophia. She tensed. She'd not seen Aversley in almost a year. She had insisted that she see no one but Amelia until her mourning was over, but really, it was to give herself time to feel confident and hopefully hold herself with grace.

His eyes widened, and a slow, appreciative smile graced his lips. She could clearly see why Amelia was smitten. With one smile, he had set her utterly at ease. He strode to her and bowed low, then took her hand and raised it to his lips where he pressed a kiss to her gloved fingers. "Sophia, my dear, you take my breath. But please don't tell my wife."

He winked at her as Amelia chuckled behind him and then clapped her hands together like an excited child. Before they could exchange any more words, a cacophony erupted outside the parlor door, and two women and a man spilled into the room. The butler came charging after them, looking as if he could cheerfully strangle someone.

"Your Grace," he said in stiff tone. "I wanted to announce your guests, but—"

"But I told him I could announce myself," the petite red-headed woman said as she stepped forward, her curls bouncing. "I'm sorry, Amelia. I'm still having so much trouble getting used to all the formality you English people live by."

"That's quite understandable and perfectly all right," Amelia answered, giving her butler a look of warning when he opened his mouth as if to protest.

Amelia quickly introduced Sophia to the Adair sisters, who both instructed her to call them by their first names, so she asked them to call her by her first name, as well. She instantly liked them. Jemma, with her head full of luxurious red hair, clearly was not used to English rules, as she had put it. Her hair was down and flowing about her shoulders in a million lovely ringlets for the dinner hour, while her sister, Anne, had her blond hair swept up in a perfectly proper chignon.

Sophia next greeted Amelia's brother, who she realized, now that she was not in a daze of mourning, was a very handsome man. He was tall, though not as tall as Aversley was or Nathan had been. He had lovely russet hair, worn slightly longer than fashionable, and the friendliest brown eyes that fit perfectly with his warm, welcoming smile. He asked her about Duke, which told Sophia that Amelia had been talking to her brother about her, but she didn't really mind. Knowing Amelia, she probably had it in her head to make a match of them, though Sophia had made it clear she wanted no match.

Everyone took a seat to wait on Ellison, who had yet to arrive, and Sophia ended up on the couch between Lord Harthorne and Jemma. Lord Harthorne turned his back to Jemma, which struck Sophia as odd. Suddenly, Jemma poked her head around Lord Harthorne's shoulder. "I should warn you, Sophia, that Lord Harthorne is intolerably rude."

"I am only rude to you," he grumbled.

Sophia wasn't sure she wanted to know what that was about, nor did she get the chance to ask because Lord Harthorne surprised her by saying, "You are not at all what I was expecting."

"I'm not. What were you expecting?"

A flush crept up his neck and spread across his face. "I don't know," he replied. "I, er, could not really see your face in church that day, shrouded as it was behind the black veil."

He sounded genuine enough, but the sudden tick in his cheek bespoke of a lie. Had Nathan described to his friends how she had looked before? She winced at what an awful description that must have been. "Well, people do change," she mumbled, unsure what to say.

"Scarsdale would have been astonished," Lord Harthorne said, then reddened further. "I'm terribly sorry. Please forgive me."

Jemma leaned around Lord Harthorne once more. "I told you he was rude."

"I am not rude," he snapped. His gaze turned to Sophia, beseeching her. "Nor am I usually blunt, but your beauty is making me witless." He said the flirtatious words to Sophia, but his gaze had trailed to Jemma before settling back on her. She wondered briefly if he liked the woman.

"Do you know Byron?" he asked Sophia.

She nodded, thrilled that she actually now did know of Byron. "I've read him in Nathan's library. I adore his work."

Lord Harthorne smiled. "So do I. When I saw you, I thought of the poem 'She Walks In Beauty.'" He paused and then began reciting the piece. "'She walks in beauty, like the night / Of cloudless climes and starry skies; / And all that's best of dark and bright / Meet in her aspect and her eyes; / Thus mellowed to that tender light / Which heaven to gaudy day denies...'" His words trailed off, and he shrugged. "Pardon my foolishness. I'm working on becoming less of a romantic and more of a rake."

Impulsively, she pressed a hand to his arm. "I should hope not. I daresay there are plenty of rakes and not near enough romantics. I'm honored that you would think of such a lovely poem when you saw me."

"What poem do you think of when you see me?" Jemma demanded of Lord Harthorne.

He flashed a smirk at her. "That's easy. I don't think of a poem at all but of *The Taming of the Shrew*."

Whatever retort Jemma made was lost on Sophia as the butler came to the door and announced Ellison.

"It cannot be," Ellison said when Amelia led him over to say hello to Sophia. He took her hand and pressed a kiss to it, just as Aversley had done. When Ellison's gaze met hers, he studied her for a long moment. "You were quite the caterpillar and none of us knew it, especially Scarsdale or he would not have spoken about you the way he did."

She flinched at the statement, but the dinner bell rang then, so she let it go and allowed herself to be led to the dining room. But the remark bothered her all through the meal and made the food—she was sure it was scrumptious, as everyone around her ate heartily—taste like ashes. She passed much of the dinner speaking with Lord Harthorne, and despite the fact that he was terribly clever, witty, and handsome, she struggled to focus on him and their conversation. Ellison's comment, in combination with Lord Harthorne's surprise at her appearance could only mean Nathan truly had spoken poorly of her to his friends, and it occupied her every thought.

Relief washed through her when dinner was adjourned and they went to the parlor. Anne was to play the pianoforte and sing for the ladies, while the men shared a glass of port. Sophia tried to put her worries out of her mind, and she even succeeded for a bit as she, Amelia, and Jemma joined Anne in singing some of the songs. Yet, when the men entered the parlor, her mind returned immediately to what Ellison and Lord Harthorne had each said.

She wanted desperately to ask Ellison, in particular, what he had meant but thought perhaps it would be best to discuss it in private. But as the night wore on, there didn't seem to be a chance to get him alone.

After a game of charades, Lord Harthorne read a poem by William Wordsworth, "A Slumber Did My Spirit Seal," and as he was reading it, Sophia could picture the poetry book that contained that poem, *Lyrical Ballads*, in Nathan's library. The page had been dog-eared and obviously read many times by the wear of the paper. She'd run her fingers over the words many nights, as she was sure he must have done. Her fingers would tingle as she traced from line to line, her heart aching with every word. Sophia didn't feel as if she understood the entire meaning behind the poem, but it did not seem a happy one.

Lost in her thoughts, it took her a moment to realize Lord

Harthorne had stopped reading and was staring at her with a frown. "What's the matter?" he asked.

She tried for a smile, but her cheeks would not cooperate. "Nathan had that book in his library. I think he must have loved that poem. It appeared to have been read many times."

Beside her, Ellison set his port glass down with a *clunk*. He turned to her with an incredulous expression. "Scarsdale? Read poetry? Clearly you did not know your husband."

"Be quiet," Aversley snapped from across the room. "You've imbibed too much."

Sophia stiffened her spine. "I knew him." She did not like Ellison's condescending tone or the way he seemed to be trying to belittle the man Nathan had been. "He was the kindest man I ever met. And the bravest. And he had more honor than you. He would never sit here and smear your name, especially if you were not here to defend yourself. *He* was loyal."

Ellison's face twisted into an ugly sneer. "What sort of poppycock have you been fed about my cousin?"

Sophia gasped, and Lord Harthorne rose to his feet and advanced toward Ellison. "I think you better retire for the night. You're saying things you do not mean."

"I'm the only one in this room speaking the truth about Scarsdale!" His eyes scanned the parlor in a wild manner, but no one said a word. He stood, swaying on his feet and almost falling back to the couch until Lord Harthorne grabbed him by the arm and steadied him. Ellison wrenched away and swiveled toward Sophia. "If they won't tell you, then I will. Because if someone doesn't tell you now, by my honor I swear you will become a laughingstock if you go into Society speaking of how virtuous and honorable Scarsdale was. Do you want to know or do you want to remain oblivious, as everyone here seems pleased to have you?"

Sophia was about to demand he leave when Amelia cried out, "That's not it at all! We did not want her oblivious. We wanted her happy, and we wanted to be kind."

Sophia's heart dropped. For a moment, she struggled to breathe. Disbelief poured through her, but as she sought out Amelia's gaze and locked her own on it, the sorrow in Amelia's eyes sent a painful shaft of betrayal through Sophia, shattering her core. Her entire body trembled, but she made herself face Ellison. "I'd have the truth, if you please." How regal she sounded. How duchess-like. Nathan would have been proud, if it still even mattered.

"He was so honorable that he sat at a table at White's the night before he died and told me, Harthorne, and Aversley that he had not married you out of love."

It stung like a thousand wasp bites, and the humiliation burned her skin like a scorching flame. She'd known Nathan had not loved her when he married her, but she had been sure that by the time he'd left for London that he had grown to feel something for her. No, *more* than *something*. The cusp of love. Was she an utter fool?

She sought out Aversley to ask him if what Ellison said was true, but she did not have to say the words. He gave her a curt nod, his mouth drawn into a tight line of rage. She raised her chin and turned back to Ellison, refusing to believe Nathan had not loved her or had not been very near to it.

"Well, we did not marry for love, but that does not mean he didn't grow to love me. You heard his solicitor. Nathan planned so well for me because he expected me never to remarry. He had grown to love me." It had to be so.

"Grown to love you?" Incredulity mingled with cruelty and laced Ellison's words. "Nathan loved no one, Sophia. As much as he hated his mother, he was just like her. Self-absorbed and self-indulgent. He didn't think you would ever marry again because he thought you a pathetic-looking girl child. He told me so word-for-word when he came to ask Mother to witness your wedding."

"That is enough!" Lord Harthorne and Aversley thundered at Ellison simultaneously.

"*No,*" Sophia didn't recognize her own cold voice. "I will

hear every word."

"Scarsdale's grand plan for you was to leave you at White-cliffe and visit you once, maybe twice, a year. He would live his life in London as he always had. And as for loyal, if you consider a man who instructed his mistress to go back to the London townhouse he kept her ensconced in for his visits, then perhaps we simply differ on what loyalty in marriage means."

Sophia grasped her throat, feeling as if someone had a hand around it and was squeezing until her air was cut off. "I can't breathe!" she gasped.

Amelia was at her side in a moment, begging her to come away and let them talk. Shaking and clammy, Sophia shook her off. "When?" She hated the hoarse, desperate sound of her voice. "When did he tell his mistress to stay in the London townhome?"

"He rendezvoused with her the night before you were to marry and assured her their arrangement would not be changing. I only know because when I went to visit all the property on the list from the solicitor, she was still there, bold as brass. She claimed Nathan would want her to stay, and then she told me of their liaison the night before he wed you."

Sophia's stomach twisted and turned. She slapped a palm over her mouth and ran blindly from the room. Behind her, voices called her name and clattering footsteps rose around her. Aversley caught up with her in the main hall and swiveled her toward him.

Amelia rushed up behind him, tears spilling from her blue eyes. "Sophia, I'm sorry. We didn't mean to lie. We weren't even sure of what the truth was. And we thought perhaps he might have grown to care for you. And..."

Sophia clutched her stomach because it felt as if her body was caving in on itself. "I understand why you did it," Sophia choked out. "Please, I want to go home." *Home.* Where she had built a future on a lie. Where the man she had thought kind and perfect turned out to be the cruelest man she had met by far. No amount of physical pain she had ever endured compared to the dizzying pain she was experiencing now. She'd never loved anyone the way she had loved Nathan, and she prayed to God she never would again.

Twenty-Two

With his legs and arms chained, Nathan had no other way to try to rouse the American prisoner in the oarsmen row ahead of him but to spit at him, which he did repeatedly to no avail. Warren had stopped rowing some time ago, and any minute, the corsair guard, Murad, whose duty it was to walk the manned rows of the galley and make sure none of the slaves were slacking, would be coming by their section.

In the past year of captivity on the ship, he had survived by doing three things: planning his escape, which meant knowing the exact times the guards came around to do their checks; reliving every second he had spent with Sophia; and imagining every second he had yet to spend with her. The last had delivered him from the edge of insanity and given him the strength to survive.

Nathan counted down the seconds in his head until the guard would appear. *Five. Four. Three. Two. One.*

The guard stopped at the row in front of him and kicked Warren. The man's head lolled farther to the right, but bound as he was by the chains, he did not fall over. The guard kicked him again, this time directly in the head with a sickening *thud.* Warren still didn't move. Murad muttered the word for *death* in Arabic, and Nathan turned away and looked out to sea. He would not feel sadness for the man. Not now. He could not afford sadness for anyone.

He forced himself to keep rowing, still staring at the lapping waves in the distance. Sometimes he imagined how peaceful it must be under the water. No pain. No sound. But no Sophia, either. He squeezed his eyes shut and exhaled a long breath. Damn sorrow was trying to creep in.

He refocused his mind by concentrating on what the guard was saying. Arabic was a bloody complicated language, but he'd managed to learn a few words that were repeated often on the ship. *Death, beating, starvation, fight,* and the most pleasant one of all—the one he was waiting for—*attack.* Because when and if this ship ever came under attack by the privateers he knew to be out there somewhere hunting down the slavers, Nathan would escape. It was his only hope, unless they ever took him off the ship to work in the quarries or be sold in Tripoli or Algiers. He would try to escape at that time, as well, if it came, but success was even less likely then.

The major flaw in his plan to escape when under attack was ensuring he was unchained. And the only time he was ever unchained was to fight. The captain was a predictable bloodthirsty man who liked to see a good fight every day, and Nathan had realized quickly that if he volunteered to fight, he would be unchained, which would keep him fit. The downside was he could very well be killed. Those who didn't fight slept, defecated, urinated, and if they were very good, received a sip of dirty water or a scrap of food when they were not rowing. Those skeletal men died quickly or went out of their minds. In his year on the ship, twenty had died and at least that many had gone mad. But a man could still row while mad. The thought chilled him to the bone, despite the relentless sun that was beating down.

The clanking of Warren's chains being undone reached Nathan's ear, but he did not take his gaze from the sea. Watching a dead man being dragged from his place sent Nathan to a dark place that hard to overcome. After a few moments, he heard a faint splash over the steady creak from the rowing. Dark thoughts of the relief death would bring beckoned to him like a siren song. He replaced the sweet whispers with memories of Sophia's laughter.

"Five minutes," Jean Luc whispered beside Nathan as he rowed.

Nathan offered the Frenchman a quick nod to acknowledge he'd heard him. He calculated how many times he had pulled the oars today and concluded Jean Luc was correct. They had five minutes until the call for fighting volunteers would ring out over the slapping of the ocean against the wood and the groans of the enslaved men.

They had been sitting beside each other for an entire year, and Jean Luc was one of six men, other than Nathan, who volunteered to fight regularly. They didn't ever have to fight each other because the captain, smug bastard that he was, always matched one of the corsairs against a prisoner. That was very lucky because one thing Nathan understood about himself was that he had lost whatever morals he had once possessed. He was now just as barbaric as his captors, and he wasn't certain, if faced with the choice between his own death or Jean Luc's, that he would not kill the Frenchman.

The thought made his skin crawl, as if trying to get away from his mind. Killing had become a necessary part of living. Sometimes the captain would say the fight was to the death and sometimes until first blood. Six times it had been to the death when Nathan had fought. He had killed six men. As he rowed, his fingers tingled with the memory, making knots form in his gut.

Would he ever be able to confess to Sophia what he had done? Her image appeared in his mind in perfect detail. She smiled her radiant smile and her cerulean eyes, which matched the color of the sky above him on many days, twinkled. She worried her lip for a moment before tugging on her short, dark hair with her slender fingers.

He wanted to tell her that he loved her. She'd offered him her unconditional love, and he'd been too goddamn afraid to accept it. He'd feared that the moment he took what she offered, she would snatch it away or show herself to be someone other than who she'd portrayed. He'd been a fool. The only thing he truly missed other than freedom was *her*.

If he ever had the chance to see her again, he was going to take everything she wanted to offer him. He was going to drink her in. Breathe her. Cling to her. Cherish her. And lavish her.

He wanted to start his life over with her and see all the possibilities for happiness in the world, and all the promise of love between them, just as she saw it. She was stronger than he'd ever been.

"It's time," Jean Luc rasped.

Nathan blinked, clearing his thoughts as the call for a fighter rang out. He raised his hand, along with Jean Luc and four others, and they waited in tense silence to see who would be chosen. Nathan had not had a turn in four days and he desperately needed to stand up, but he gritted his teeth in an effort not to show his desperation. The guard stopped in front of him, then moved on to Jean Luc before turning back and smiling while saying the Arabic word for *Killer*.

He tensed at the moniker the guards had given him. They meant it as a compliment, yet it destroyed another piece of his humanity every time they said it. Within moments, he was released and standing away from the galleys, holding a chain for a weapon and facing his opponent. He stepped from foot to foot, awakening his body. The time the captain was giving him to get used to standing was close to gone. The captain never gave more than four minutes.

Nathan stared at his opponent, a bald-headed, hulking giant. He didn't know the man's name, but that suited him just fine, especially since the captain had called for a fight to the death. During these fights was the only time the slaves were allowed to talk, and like a faint hum that came from somewhere far off but increased as it neared, the chants from the galley grew until they seemed to vibrate the salty air and the slick deck. The thundering cry to kill burrowed through his flesh and into his bones. His heartbeat sped as his muscles tensed and rage thicker than blood flowed through his veins.

The captain called out to begin, and Nathan surged to attack. Waiting was futile and showed weakness. His opponent was surprisingly agile for his size and managed to almost avoid Nathan's first swing of his chain, but the clattering metal caught the giant at the last second and wrapped around his right ankle in one full circle. Nathan barred his teeth as he yanked the chain with enough force that his biceps strained painfully and burned as if torched from within. But he did not relent. He welcomed the pain because it meant he was still alive.

With pull after grunting pull, he dragged the corsair to him as the man growled and struggled to get free. But the guard's bulk hampered his flexibility and made twisting to reach his ankle impossible. Nathan took full advantage of his downed opponent, stepped toward him, and stomped down on his head with all his burning, searing rage. The brittle sound of something snapping pierced through his rage. He'd broken the man's neck. Bile immediately rose in Nathan's throat, but he forced it down as he always did. He could not afford a conscience when it came to the corsairs. They would be happy to kill him or sell him to a lord who wanted to use him in ways that he refused to contemplate.

He stepped back from his dead opponent, expecting to be rewarded with the usual cup of ale, but urgent shouts came at him from all directions. Nathan looked around, not understanding what they were saying. The corsairs scrambled across the deck toward their guns, and the word _attack_ rang in his ears. For a moment, he thought he was hallucinating, but when he glanced across the shining, shimmering sea, a ship waving the British flag came into view. And in seconds, Nathan was darting toward the edge of the slave ship, ready to jump into the water as the British fired upon them.

❧

Sophia spent days alternating between huddling under her coverlet and pacing the floor of her bedchamber. The thing both situations had in common was that crying, wailing, and bemoaning herself for her stupidity accompanied them both. She continuously replayed the last year in her mind, how she had thrown herself, heart and soul, into becoming a duchess worthy of Nathan.

"Saint Nathan!" she muttered. She'd made him faultless in her mind. He was so perfect he could not imagine loving a woman like her. Bitterness clawed at her.

He'd pitied her. He'd not wanted to be around her. He'd planned to leave her at Whitecliffe while he carried on with his mistress in London. He'd lied to her face about bedding the woman, and she'd drunk in the lie as if it were a delicious cup of steaming chocolate. He'd been cuckolding her before they were even married.

She pounded the walls, the bed, and the floor with her fists until they throbbed with pain. *Good!* Pain in her fists meant less pain to travel to her heart.

He was a...he was a...pre-cuckolder! Yes, that's what he was. She didn't give a damn that there was no such word. He truly was a blackhearted devil. No, that was too good. He had no heart!

He saved you, her hated inner voice shot back.

She screamed until the voice faded. She screamed so long that Mary Margaret rushed to her bedchamber and begged her to take laudanum. She refused and sent her lady's maid away.

She wore a path in her carpet and thought of the millions of ways Nathan had likely been laughing at her.

I love you, she had said like a supreme fool.

You do not love me, he had replied. *You desire me. There is a difference.*

She didn't stop there. *No.* She had persisted like a naive country girl who'd never encountered a sophisticated, acerbic libertine. Because she'd foolishly hoped for love.

He's not a libertine, that dreaded voice whispered.

She began to hum to tune it out. She would hate Nathaniel Ellison, Marquess of Deering, the fifth Duke of Scarsdale until the day she died. She would hate him because he had made her love him. And then his death had nearly destroyed her. And now he had humiliated her more from the grave than any of Frank's beatings, verbal attacks, and withheld love ever had. She'd never expected more from

Frank, but Nathan… Sobs wracked her body. She'd dared to hope as her mother had encouraged her. More the fool, she was.

Sophia stormed across her bedchamber, ripped open her dresser drawer, and yanked out her mother's letter. She tore it into tiny pieces and watched them flutter to the ground in a mess at her feet. The bits of foolscap blurred as she stared and remembered.

I do desire you, but I love you, she had said.

She didn't want to remember how he had answered but there was no way to hold it back.

It will fade, he had replied.

She raked her hands through her hair until her scalp stung, and she forced herself to stop. She could not even properly hate him because he had warned her. There was no denying it. Her blasted memory would not let her forget what he had said: *You need to know I have no desire for love.*

He had not lied about that. He had been very clear, and she had refused to listen.

She cried until there were no more tears, and then she sat and stared out the window, unsure what to do with herself and the rest of her life, now that she no longer had a mission to be the perfect duchess.

On the seventh day of her self-imposed isolation, among the dozens of notes from Amelia, Aversley, Lord Harthorne, and even Jemma, begging her please to allow them to see her, she received a letter from Harry:

Dear Sophia,

I hope you are cheerier now. I think of you often and of Scarsdale. I miss him still, as I'm sure you do. Guess what? I have been invited to be part of a prestigious club here, and I was told that Scarsdale used to be the head of it. I have to confess, I get special treatment because you are his widow. I don't even feel guilty because of all the years of terrible treatment we had. I decided this just evens things out a bit. Do you think that's wrong? I am looking forward to seeing

*you soon. I'd like to invite a school friend to come home
with me, if that's all right. He says his mother will not care,
as you are a duchess.*

Your loving brother,
Harry

Something about the letter did what her week of carrying
on had not. She read it, and she knew what she had to do. She
had to get up and go on with life for Harry's sake, and for her
sake, as well. She had been given the chance to provide Harry
with a grand future, and she would not ruin it by having
people whisper that she was the mad duchess or by neglecting
to make the social connections that would help him.

She picked herself up and smoothed her hair. She would
attend the house party Amelia had planned and she would
make friends. But she would never, ever again, allow herself to
fall in love with a man. Love was a wretched thing, and she
wanted no part of it. If Nathan could train himself not to feel
love, then so could she. She didn't need love to be happy.

In fact, the sooner she took a lover the better. She wanted
to wipe the memory of Nathan's body from her mind, and
what better way than to replace it with the memory of another
man's? Her cheeks heated at her thoughts, but she simply
fanned herself. She knew widows of the *ton* took lovers
without being ostracized. It was practically fashionable.

She marched across the room and yanked the bell cord to
summon Mary Margaret. She *would* become an Incomparable.
She *would* be happy. No man would ever look at her again and
think her pathetic or unworthy of his love. She was going to
amaze the *ton*. And when she was finished bedazzling the most
eligible gentlemen, she would pick the coldest-hearted rake as
her lover, for he would not desire that which she no longer
cared to give—*her heart.*

Twenty-Three

$\mathcal{N}$athan stood on the open deck of *Queen's Splendor* with his face toward the oncoming wind. The simple joy of being free to move his arms and legs made him smile. He took a deep breath and turned to Jean Luc, who stood silently beside him, clasping his friend on the shoulder. Nathan had almost died trying to break the Frenchman free of his chains when the slave ship had been under attack, and while he may have saved Jean Luc, the act of doing so had saved him. He had not been sure he had enough humanity left in him to care about anyone but himself, but he had. Nothing had ever felt as good to learn.

Jean Luc raised an eyebrow at him, and Nathan chuckled, realizing he'd been staring at the man. "I smell England."

Jean Luc shook his head and pointed ahead. "That's France, my friend. I'm almost home. Do you know what I'm going to do when I get there?"

Since Jean Luc was not married but had a woman whom he loved deeply, Nathan had a fairly good idea. "I imagine you will be asking Isabella to marry you."

Jean Luc grinned, and then his smile faded. "What if she has married another? It's been fourteen months. I'm sure she thinks I'm dead. Aren't you worried your wife has found someone else?"

The thought had crossed his mind, but he had dismissed it with a single memory of the way she had looked when she had told him she loved him. He saw her shining, love-filled eyes every night when he went to sleep. She had loved him. She would have mourned him. He was sure of it. And he would wager his life that she would not seek out the company of another man so quickly.

"No," he finally said, his voice thick with emotion.

A deep voice came from behind him. "It must be nice to have such faith in a woman."

Nathan turned and smiled at Worthington. "It's a feeling I never believed possible for me."

Worthington moved to the railing. He popped the cork off a jug, took a long swig, and handed it to Nathan. "I've been saving this. It's my father's finest whiskey. I took it when I left because he told me he'd drink it when looking down at my grave. He was sure I'd end up there for my foolishness in becoming a privateer."

Nathan took the jug and drank. The whiskey warmed his throat as it went down, then swirled into his belly with a satisfying burn. "What were you sure of?"

"I was sure that if I kept on the course I was, I would no longer be able to live with myself. I'd lost my honor. Becoming a privateer who captains a ship that hunts down slavers gave me my honor back. I like to have a drink of my father's whiskey every time I return home."

Nathan passed the jug to Jean Luc and then looked out to the sea, thinking on how things change. He'd never been as shocked to see anyone as he had been when Worthington had boarded the slave ship and overtook it. And Worthington had further shocked him when he'd confessed to thinking he had killed Nathan, since it was Worthington's ship that had sunk Ravensdale's ship. He was supremely glad Worthington had become a privateer. He'd likely not be standing here now, if he had not.

Jean Luc passed the jug back to Nathan, and when he did, his friend nudged him in the arm and winked. "I wager I know the first thing you will do when you return to Whitecliffe."

"I'd wager you're incorrect."

"Don't try to tell me you don't plan to take your wife to bed."

Oh, he did. Most definitely. But first he was going to tell her he loved her. And then he was going to tell her again. And again. And again. And then he was going to beg her to forgive him for being so foolish as to have stayed silent the very first time she had told him.

It had taken Sophia precisely one week of careful observation to come to the conclusion that most people in the *ton* were vain, caustic aristocrats who were desperately bored and hungering for something different than what they knew. So she gave it to them.

When most of the ladies would agree with whatever one of the yapping, pompous gentleman of the *ton* was saying, Sophia would disagree. When other ladies spoke of the weather, or embroidery, or the pianoforte, she spoke of politics, poetry, and the future of England. Coming from a lower class, she had a burning desire to one day see those class differences obliterated. She was careful to temper those opinions when she spoke, of course, but not so careful that those around her didn't understand that she thought simply having a title and money did not make one person better than another.

Her behavior, which might have gotten someone else ostracized or cut directly, drew ladies to her because they were in awe of her boldness, and drew men to her because they were in awe of her beauty, or so they said. She knew better. They perceived her as unattainable; therefore, she was a prize to be won.

She was slyly propositioned many times a night but always answered with a kind smile and a little shake of her head. Eventually, she became the most whispered-about person in the *ton* and wagers started to fly on who would win the hand of Scarsdale's widow.

Only Amelia and Madame Lexington knew that Sophia did not want a husband. And *no one* knew that she desired a lover to obliterate the memory of Nathan's hands on her body. She fervently prayed her plan would work, because while she could control her thoughts of Nathan in her waking hours, when she slept he filled every second of her dreams. And what was sweet in dreams tormented her when she awoke.

"Might Ah join ye?"

Sophia blinked out of her daze and scooted over in the circle of people she stood among to allow the tall, handsome redheaded man to saddle up to her. She knew of him, but they had not been properly introduced. But as his light-blue eyes drank her in, she was suddenly supremely glad that Jemma, who was less concerned with English rules than even Sophia was, had invited the self-made railroad tycoon—who the *ton* gossiped was ruthless in business and unparalleled as a lover—to her grandfather's home for her ball. Sophia also had the annoying thought that Nathan's eyes had been more compelling in all their simmering darkness, but she shoved that thought away and concentrated on the feeling of intrigue that was stirring.

Lord Barnes tried to step between them, but Mr. Frazier cut him off with the grace of a fox outmaneuvering a pack of hounds.

"I think Lord Barnes might have been trying to speak to me," she said in a low voice, not wanting the odious man to hear her. She was only trying to ferret out if Mr. Frazier was interested, not bring Lord Barnes back to her side. Frankly, she was glad he no longer stood beside her. Earlier, the gentleman had not understood why it mattered if poor children were used as chimney sweeps. She may want a coldhearted lover but not a stupid one.

Mr. Frazier leaned toward her, and his scent—a pleasant enough one of leather and soap—surrounded her, but also stirred a memory of Nathan's scent of pine. She shoved that blasted memory to the ground, too, and then mentally stomped on it.

"Dae ye really caur?"

It took her a moment mentally to translate his thick Scottish brogue, but when she did, she said, "No. I found him to be tedious."

"Ah fin' ye ta be fascinatin'."

She waited for her pulse to speed up as it had the first time Nathan had fastened his dark, brooding gaze on her, but her heart beat the same steady rhythm. Perhaps it was best that her heartbeat did not increase. She didn't want a man to affect her as Nathan had. If what they said about Mr. Frazier was true, then he would be perfect for her. And he was extremely attractive in a way that was quite opposite Nathan's suave, aristocratic looks, which suited her, as well. Whereas Nathan had possessed dark beauty, Mr. Frazier had light eyes, ginger-colored hair, and a fair complexion. And his brogue certainly would never remind her of Nathan's cultured speech.

"You do not even know me," she replied, fully turning toward him so others would not hear their conversation. "So I'm curious exactly what it is about me you find fascinating."

He grinned, a lopsided smile that made a dimple appear on his chin, and would have made him seem harmless if his razor-sharp eyes hadn't held hers so. He leaned close to her ear. "We need privacy fur me ta teel ye that."

She'd been in the Duke of Rowan's home several times as she and Jemma had become friends, and it was not far from her own. She glanced toward where she knew the study was, considering what to do.

Don't do it, said that despised inner voice, the one that had been quiet for the past week. She was going to kill that inner voice if it was the last thing she did.

"Meet me in the library in ten minutes," she whispered. "And be discreet."

He gave a barely perceptible nod and then departed to the other side of the ballroom where she watched as he asked Lady Spencer to dance. He led her to the floor to swirl her around in graceful effortlessness.

"I'm glad that odious man is gone," Lord Barnes said. "Did you see how rudely he shoved me out of the way to stand beside you? What was he saying to you, anyway? I hadn't realized you even knew him."

Everyone was now looking at her, which made her want to stomp her heel on Lord Barnes's foot. Preferably when his foot was bare and she had on boots. Jemma hurried over and linked her arm through Sophia's. "I introduced them. He is a personal friend of my grandfather's."

That was a dangerous lie that could get Jemma in all sorts of trouble, but Sophia was eternally grateful. Jemma smiled brightly at her, which she took as her cue to elaborate the rest of the story. "I was considering investing in the railroad and he wanted to make an appointment to speak with me about it."

Everyone nodded in understanding except Lord Barnes. "Why would you bother your pretty head with things of that nature? You have a man of business, I'm sure. Let him take care of such things."

"I bother because my 'pretty little head' is not an empty little head. Now, if you will excuse me," she said sweetly over the subtle, and not so subtle, laughter coming from the other gentlemen in the group.

She got ten steps away when someone grabbed her arm from behind. She turned to find Amelia, whose brow was drawn together. "Where are you going?"

She refused to lie, though she knew Amelia would not approve. "To the library to meet Mr. Frazier."

"Why?"

Sophia's cheeks heated instantly.

"Oh, Sophia!" Amelia bit her lip and lowered her voice as people moved around them. "You cannot mean to take a lover?"

Sophia refused to be embarrassed. "I mean to do exactly that," she said in hushed tones.

"Please don't do this! Give yourself more time. Your wounds are raw and your hurt great. Doing this will not erase your memories of Scarsdale. Whether you like it or not, you loved him, and taking a lover will not change that."

Sophia's heart pounded so loudly that it drowned out the music. She took a long, deep breath. "I need a new memory to layer over the ones of him or I will go mad. Can you not understand that?"

Amelia bit her lip again but finally nodded. "I do. I wish I could say I didn't, but I do. And if you decide he is the one, what then?"

"Then I will invite him to come to my home."

"*Tonight!* Can you not wait and give yourself time to sit with the decision?"

"Of course not tonight." The very idea suddenly made her tense. "Tomorrow night."

That was better. If she decided he was the one and did not act upon it quickly she might back out. And besides, she was going to go stark raving mad if she could not rid herself of the memory of Nathan caressing her body and bringing her to ecstasy. This had to be the answer.

Twenty-Four

Upon stepping foot on the London docks, Worthington offered Nathan his coach, since Nathan, of course, would not have one waiting, as his family and servants thought him dead. He'd wanted to personally tell each of them, so he had asked Worthington to keep the news to himself until Nathan had the opportunity to do so. Which was why, when he did take his first step onto English soil in fourteen months, he strode straight for his old office to see if his cousin was there and could direct him to Sophia.

As he passed the docked ships, he was reminded of the night Ravensdale had kidnapped him. Worthington had vowed Ravensdale had drowned, but they had also believed Nathan to be dead. Ravensdale could be alive. The man was certainly cunning enough. After reuniting with Sophia, Nathan would hire an investigator to ensure Ravensdale was, indeed, deceased. And he would have the man track down anyone who might have worked for Ravensdale. He was going to personally see to it that they ended up at Newgate for what they had done to him.

As he walked toward the office, he considered where Sophia might be. He had left her very wealthy, so he knew she and Harry were provided for, and he had left her the townhouse in Mayfair as well as the country home in St. Ives. Knowing his little minx, she was probably living in St. Ives, as he could not see her among the brittle set of the *ton* by choice. Yet, he hoped she had found a reason to come to London anyway because that meant she was very close.

When he strolled through the door of his office, he almost collided with Stephens, who was looking down at some papers. Nathan was so happy to see the man alive that he hugged him straight away.

Stephens looked up, and shock registered on his face. "Your Grace! My God!" The man turned white. "You're alive!"

Nathan grinned. "Believe me, I'm as surprised as you sound!"

Stephens's brow furrowed as he gaped at Nathan. "I told everyone you were dead."

Nathan clapped a hand on his back. "Understandably so."

"I watched the ship go down." His voice had dropped to an awed whisper. "And they searched for hours for your body. Captain Worthington was relentless in the search."

Nathan nodded. "I know. It was actually Captain Worthington who ended up rescuing me in the end, but that's a story for another day. I was fished out of the water in Saint-Malo by a corsair who had claimed to be helping in the search. Really, he was gathering anyone he found alive and not too wounded, to enslave on his ships."

"Good God," Stephens whispered. "I *left* you." He paled even more.

Nathan squeezed the man's shoulder. "I told you to leave me. It was the only thing that could be done. So forget it. I did the minute you stepped off the ship."

Stephens let out a sigh. "Thank you."

"No, thank you, for trying to save me in the first place. Now, is Ellison here?"

Stephens shook his head. "His Grace, I mean, Mr. Ellison has gone to St. Ives to get your widow, er, your wife, to sign some papers."

Nathan grinned. "So Sophia is living in St. Ives?"

"I do believe so, Your Grace. I just returned from sea myself, and I only saw your cousin briefly. He left not an hour ago. Will you go there now, I suppose?"

Nathan scrubbed a hand over his beard and then through his long hair. "I think I may scare my wife if I show up looking like this. I've not had a proper bath, shave, or trim since the day I was taken. I'll go by my townhome first."

He actually had three townhomes in London. The largest one he was sure Ellison would be occupying, and although he knew Ellison was not there right now, his aunt might be, and she was the last person Nathan wanted to see. The second largest townhome, he'd left to Sophia, and he now knew she was not there. And the third townhome had been the one he bought for Marguerite, but she would not be in residence. He was sure if Marguerite had decided to linger there upon learning he was presumed dead, Ellison would have undoubtedly sent her packing when he learned of the townhome from Mr. Nilbury.

That home, if he had any luck, would still be stocked with some of his clothes, or maybe they would be packed up and stored in the house. Best of all, there shouldn't be anyone around but his servants, so stopping in wouldn't require a reunion with friends and family. Not that he didn't appreciate his servants, he did. But he highly doubted they would have been too saddened over his loss. He intended to remedy how he had kept others at a distance, as well as many other things.

A short time later, he was in Worthington's carriage and headed to his townhome. As the carriage rolled along, he considered how Ellison would feel about having the title and lands taken from him now that Nathan had returned. He was sure his cousin would be thrilled he was alive and glad to return to Nathan what was rightfully his, but he regretted that his aunt would likely be irritated. Knowing her, she had probably been happy to become the mother of a duke.

When Worthington's driver arrived at Nathan's townhome, he bid the man to wait. He planned to be here just long enough to clean up and change into fresh clothes. He knocked and had to chuckle when Moreland, the normally unflappable butler, answered the door and his jaw dropped opened.

Nathan stepped through the threshold and patted the older man on the arm. "I'm glad to see Ellison retained you. Did he retain all the servants that were employed here?"

Moreland opened and closed his mouth but no words came out. He stared at Nathan, his eyes wide.

"He did," came a familiar feminine purr from the top of the staircase. Nathan glanced up, and for a moment felt as if he was not seeing correctly. But a quick blink revealed that Marguerite was indeed standing in a pale-yellow gown on his staircase.

Nathan stared up at his former mistress, and his hands balled at his sides as he fought the urge to march up the stairs, drag her down, and throw her out on the street. He didn't know how the devil Marguerite was still living here, but he had a suspicion. "I need a moment alone with Miss Mason," he said through clenched teeth.

"Certainly, Your Grace," Moreland replied, back to his unflappable self. "Shall I go upstairs to draw you a bath and prepare for a shave and cut?"

Nathan allowed a brief smile. "You always could read my mind, Moreland."

As the butler ascended the stairs, Marguerite descended them, until she stood on the last step. Nathan stood on the black-and-white marble tile, and she tilted her head back and caught his gaze, a seductive smile pulling at her lips.

The difference between the sorts of people she and Sophia were was clearer in this moment than it had ever been. Sophia would be crying with joy to see him, running to throw her arms around him and profess her undying love. She would be trembling and showering him with kisses. Marguerite was already scheming to seduce him so she'd not be thrown out of his home. She'd never really given a damn about him as a man; she'd only cared about what he could do and provide for her.

She slowly licked her lips. "I would say I cannot believe you are alive, but who would know better than I that if anyone could conquer death, you could." She wound her arms around his neck. "Welcome home, *lover*."

Her touch repelled him. He wanted no touch but Sophia's. "What the hell are you doing here?" he demanded as he removed Marguerite's arms from him and took a step away. He could only think of one possible reason she could still be here, and she confirmed it with her slow smirk before she ever said a word.

"I suppose you might say your cousin found he wanted to inherit more than just your money, title, and lands." She traced a finger across the top of her plump breasts, which were revealed by her low-cut gown.

Of all the available paramours in England, Ellison had to have Marguerite? The idea didn't sit well, but as he glanced at Marguerite's voluptuous figure, flashing green eyes, and fiery red hair, he knew damned well his naive cousin had been seduced. This is what came of not bedding a woman before you were in your thirties.

"You must leave. As you can clearly see, I'm not dead, and my wife will not be pleased if I allow my former mistress to stay in my home. I will give Ellison the funds to buy you a home where he can visit you."

She pursed her lips in a pout. "I don't want to keep Ellison as a lover. He's an oaf, unskilled and quite boring. I want to be your lover again."

Before he realized what she was going to do, she threw herself into his arms and locked her lips on his. He shoved her away and swiped his hand over his mouth in an effort to remove the taste of the laudanum she must have drunk earlier. "I don't want or need a lover. I have a wife and I love her." He wasn't ashamed to say it. He was going to say it to everyone to whom he spoke. Hell, he'd proclaim it from the tallest building in London if Sophia requested.

Marguerite narrowed her eyes. "I've heard about your wife, though I've yet to have the privilege to meet her. Seems she's not quite as mousy as when you left."

"I was kidnapped. I did not *leave*."

"Yes, yes." Marguerite waved her hand. "And while the cat was away the little mouse did play."

"If you have something to say, Marguerite, simply do so. I've neither the time nor inclination to stand here listening to you spout twisted proverbs."

"I'd have sworn it wasn't possible, but with your beard, tanned skin, long hair, and slightly nasty edge, you excite me even more than you did before."

"Marguerite," he said, barely controlling his temper, "I'm one second from throwing you on the street without your belongings or any money to get even a hack and a room."

"Oh, all right," she purred. "You're not fun at all when it comes to your wife. It seems she's been having a grand time in your absence. Ellison says she is the toast of the *ton* everywhere she goes. I hear—through gossip, of course—that she's quite the coldhearted flirt."

A vein pulsed in his neck, and his stomach twisted. "You are mistaken. My wife is neither a flirt nor coldhearted."

"That's not what Ellison says. He says two young bucks in Yorkshire fought a duel over her, and she turned both their offers of marriage down flat."

Could that be true? He refused to believe Sophia would act the trollop. Besides, *he* thought her beautiful, but she was not a classic beauty who would lead a man to act a fool.

She has your heart, his inner voice said. But that was different.

"I'm certain Ellison is mistaken."

"Then he is not the only one. One of my, er, other *admirers* relayed a story about your duchess in which she was at the Duke and Duchess of Aversley's house party and had one man sing to her, one man write a poem for her, and another act out a play he had written about her. All in the effort to win the chance to partner with her in a scavenger hunt. And then she turned around and picked a different gentleman as her partner!"

"I am sure," he drawled, "it was because she thought those three gentlemen utter fools." And when he found out who had been trying to win his wife's affection, he was going to make sure they damned well understood it was time to quit.

Marguerite cocked her head to the side. "I do not think that was it at all. I think your wife has developed a penchant for naughty rakes. I daresay she developed it when she was married to *you*. She chose Lord Roxbury as her scavenger hunt partner, and Ellison said they disappeared for quite some time, even *after* everyone else had returned to the house. I wonder what could have possibly taken them so long..."

Nathan gripped Marguerite by the arm. "Moreland!" he shouted, losing his hold on his control.

His butler and a footman appeared immediately. Nathan stared at Marguerite as he spoke. "The lady is leaving *now*. Prepare the carriage to drive her anywhere but here."

"You're a devil!" Marguerite screeched.

"I was," he retorted, handing over Marguerite to the footman, who helped her out the door, against her will, as gently as he possibly could. When the door shut, what was left of Nathan's control snapped. The first thing he broke was a vase his mother had loved. Then another one she had hated but had bought because it was expensive. Then he threw a chair and sent his fist into the wall, splitting open his knuckles. He glanced at the blood oozing from the gash and he froze.

What the hell was the matter with him? Sophia would not do those things. Sophia was not his mother. She had loved him. She would mourn him. She would never turn into the sort of lady who disappeared at house party scavenger hunts with a man known to be on a quest to bed as many women as possible.

He glanced at the chaos he had created and groaned. He had to restrain himself. The barbarian he had become aboard the slave ship was not who he was truly. He simply needed to see Sophia and then everything would be all right. With that in mind, he hurriedly bathed, sat for a shave and a cut, then dressed quickly, and set off at full speed toward St. Ives.

Twenty-Five

Sophia was so nervous she had goose flesh. Which was ridiculous. She had invited Mr. Frazier to her home tonight to bed him. Or was he bedding her? Perhaps they were bedding each other? Yes, that was it! That *was* how it worked. She fidgeted with the flimsy night rail she wore and sent a silent prayer to heaven that she would not toss up her dinner on Mr. Frazier.

The moment he stood from stoking the fire and turned to face her, her stomach churned queasily. She wasn't ready for this. She clenched her teeth. *You are ready*, she commanded herself.

He strode to her with an easy smile and predatory eyes. The look did not surprise her. He'd told her last night exactly why she intrigued him, and it had everything to do with what they were about to do. He hauled her into his arms, then ran his hands up and down her bare flesh. "You're still braw."

"I'm what?"

He chuckled. "Culd."

She nodded, though she knew by the perspiration on his brow that the room must have been blazing hot. When she was very nervous, she always became cold.

"Ah ken a surefire way ta warm ye up."

She swallowed hard and nodded. Her nerves made it impossible to talk. As he took her hand and led her to the bed, she started talking to herself in her head. *You can do this. You will do this. You want this.* She kept the chant going as he leaned her back and his hands, hot like coals, touched her skin. She bit her lip on a cry and squeezed her eyes shut. Any minute she was sure to want him.

Nathan held the key up in the moonlight and kissed it. At the last moment, before he'd left his townhouse, he gone to his study and fetched the key to his country home that he'd left in one of his drawers. He'd worried he might reach St. Ives very late, and he was right. It was near midnight when he got there and the house was dark, except for some candles burning in the window of the master bedchamber.

Sophia.

His heart sighed her name. He crept into the house and then slowly made his way toward Sophia. His wife. His love.

It wasn't that Mr. Frazier's hands were not nice hands, or gentle hands, and likely they were skilled hands, but the moment they grazed her bare thighs and landed on her breasts, she knew she could not do this. Not yet. His hands were not *Nathan's* hands. Tears leaked from her closed eyes, and she rose onto her elbows to tell him to stop. But as she opened her eyes, an apparition of Nathan appeared.

She blinked, but he was still there.

Oh God! She was finally going mad.

She squinted at the mirage. He looked so real that her heart lurched. The odd thing was that he was gaping at her, and she couldn't fathom why she would conjure an image of her unflappable husband looking at her that way.

Her heart tripled its speed as she stared at his mouth. It *was* hanging open. Then it snapped shut and twisted wryly, then twisted again and set into a threat.

Dear sweet heaven above! Her gaze flew to his eyes, and the raging anger simmering in the dark depths made her scream.

Nathan flew across the room, bellowing an animal sound like she had never heard. Her heart, which was beating so fast now that she thought it might explode, stopped and started again with a jerk that made her grab her chest. And then she was grabbing at the apparition, except her fingers clutched hard, hot flesh and bone. A wave of hysteria threatened to make her swoon, but she shoved it down.

He was real. He was here. And he was going to kill Mr. Frazier.

The huge Scot flew backward in Nathan's grip, and the men fell to the ground in a heap that shook the furniture and surely woke the staff. Sophia scrambled off the bed, determined to pull them apart, but then she was simply trying to pull Nathan off Mr. Frazier. She wrapped her hand around Nathan's bulging arm as he drew it back and then hit Mr. Frazier in the nose. It was as if she had no grip on him at all. He towed her entire body along with him every time he drew his arm back and struck again.

The *thump* of his fists meeting flesh vibrated in her ears.

"Nathan, stop it!" she screamed.

Thump. Thump. Thump.

"You will kill him," she yelled in his ear.

Mr. Frazier's crunching bones made bile rise in her throat.

She released Nathan's arm and yanked back on his hair, intent on making him listen, but her actions allowed Mr. Frazier to get free, and when he did, he came at Nathan with a wild look that caused her to scream again. This time Mr. Frazier's fist connected with Nathan's chin.

Nathan flew backward, taking her with him, and crushed her to the ground. The air left her lungs with a sharp hiss of pain. Nathan rolled off her immediately, and when it appeared he would continue the fight, she screamed, "Stop! I invited him here!"

At that moment, her bedchamber door flew open again and a footman rushed in.

"Get out," Nathan ordered in a voice that made her shake.

The footman, eyes bulging, backed out the way he had

come and quietly shut the door.

Nathan stood and looked down at his wife barely dressed in a translucent, white night rail that he swore to God was one that had been created for their wedding night. His mind careened for a moment at how she had physically changed. She was temptation incarnate with her dark, gleaming hair tumbling in waves down her back. That hair alone would drive a man wild, but a man would be driven to his knees to beg if he thought he could caress her lush curves, her perfect, heart-shaped face, and her generous lips. But her eyes were what had changed the most. He saw no warmth there. Those cold eyes would send a man to the brink grasping for the futile hope of her love.

This was the woman he had made a saint? This was the woman he had survived for? This was the woman he had allowed himself to love? Rage and disgust flowed through him. She had never loved him. She had dangled her love to make him want it, but she had never planned to give it. Thank Christ, she didn't know he'd wanted to take it from her.

He combed back his disheveled hair with his fingers and then spared a glance for the man he'd just almost pummeled to death.

"You're alive!" Sophia exclaimed in a trembling voice that, if he were a fool, which he was not, he'd almost believe sounded happy.

He didn't acknowledge her comment or her but kept his gaze trained on the man who had been groping *his* wife's breasts. "I'm afraid, Lord…?"

"Mr. Frazier," the man offered.

"Ah, but of course. I'm afraid, Mr. Frazier, that I've re-turned from the dead, and though I have absolutely no desire to ever touch my wife again, I must admit I also have no desire to let you or any other man do it for me. And I find that I'll be happy to kill you or anyone who dares to try. Are we clear?"

Mr. Frazer obviously had large bollocks because he stared hard at Nathan for a long moment, as if he would dare protest, but then he slowly nodded. "Aye, we er clear."

"Excellent. I'll see you out." He turned without sparing Sophia a backward glance and then saw the Scot out in stony silence. His staff, some old and some new, were lined up in their nightclothes to bid him welcome. He greeted each of them with a quick nod, and then he strode to what had been his study but now had decidedly feminine touches. But the sidebar was still there.

Perhaps that was left for Sophia's lovers, his mind taunted.

He poured three fingers of brandy and drank it in one gulp. Then he drank two more glasses before walking to the sofa and falling backward onto it. The soft cushions felt odd and foreign. He allowed himself to see her in his mind as she was now, and his heart swelled with pride at the beautiful creature she had become. He grimaced at his own reaction.

Damn her. She didn't deserve his admiration, and he needed to remember that.

He refused to contemplate seeing her again tonight. First, he needed to rid her from his soul. With the precision of a physician lancing a wound, he spent the rest of the night recalling every detail of seeing her with another man's hands on her breasts. Love was for the foolish and the weak. How the hell had he allowed himself to forget that?

Hatred and fury overwhelmed all other emotion. From here on out, it would be as if Sophia, the Duchess of Scarsdale, meant nothing to him. She did not exist. Except, goddamn it, she did.

But he had a plan for that particular problem.

For hours after Nathan had left her bedchamber, Sophia sat on the floor afraid to move for fear he would come back and do God only knew what. And then, when dawn broke and he had not come back, anger surged through her so fiercely she had to bury her head under a mound of pillows and bellow her rage. Then astonishment set in.

Nathan was alive! She could picture, in excruciating detail, how he had looked when he'd barged into her bedchamber. Tanned skin, hair longer than she had remembered, and a close shave that highlighted his taut jaw. He was more ruggedly virile now than ever. The dark, tight-fitting breeches had barely seemed able to contain his muscled thighs, and the crisp white shirt he had worn open casually at the collar without a cravat had kindled every vivid memory of her hands on his skin.

Her body burned with the memory of touching him, and she hated herself for still being attracted to him. And he...*he* had stood here on his return and humiliated her, yet again, by telling her almost-lover that he had no desire to ever touch her. Could it be that he still found her lacking? She forced the doubt from her mind. That could not be it! Why would he fly into such a rage over finding her with another man if he didn't even want her for himself?

She stilled, all the breath leaving her. Had he really been kidnapped or had he simply left her? No. She shook her head at the foolish thought. He had been kidnapped. Sir Richard had investigated it, and Nathan's employee, along with others who had no ties to him, had confirmed it. She rubbed at her temples. Why had he been furious if he had never truly wanted her?

Because, silly fool, her inner voice taunted, *he does not share what is his even if he does not want it. He is like a spoiled, greedy child in a man's body.*

Well, he was a child who was about to get a lesson. If he was not going to have the courtesy to come speak with her, she would go to him and demand to be heard. They would live separate lives as they pleased, whether he liked it or not, or she would make him rue the day he refused her. She wasn't certain how, but she didn't care about that particular detail at the moment. She was livid! She knew he would take a lover, so she should be able to as well, though her first attempt had made her feel wretched and not gone well. She simply needed more practice with that sort of behavior.

Without bothering to ring for Mary Margaret, Sophia dressed herself in one of the most alluring day gowns she owned. It had a daring neckline, especially for the day, and its blue color matched her eyes. She shouldn't care if he found her attractive now or not, but her pride wanted him to regret losing her. She spent extra time brushing her long hair and allowed it to hang over her shoulders in loose waves. When she decided she looked as seductive as she possibly could, she took a deep breath, straightened her shoulders, and made her way downstairs, determined to see him.

It didn't take long to ascertain that he was in his study, because she could hear male voices coming from within. She considered barging in, but after his display of temper last night, she hated to admit it, but she was afraid to anger him. So, she sat in one of the chairs outside the door. And then, when she recognized Aversley's voice coming from inside the study with Nathan, curiosity got the better of her, and she crept closer to the door and pressed her ear to it.

"The galleys you say?" Aversley asked.

"Yes. Once I was fished from the water after Ravensdale's ship sank, I was put on board the slaver and chained to my spot in the galleys, same as all the other slaves." Her ears drank in the deep voice she had committed to memory, then struggled to forget. *He was alive.* It was so very hard to believe, yet it was true. He was alive, yet nothing would ever be the same. The hope she had once had for love was still gone.

She trembled as he spoke again. "The only way to ever stand up was to volunteer to fight."

"My God, Scarsdale. Don't harbor regret over that. You did what you had to do to survive. If that had happened to me, I would have done the same damn thing."

What had he done? What had happened to him? He'd been on a slave ship? At least she knew for certain he hadn't abandoned her. She fisted her hands at the unwanted thought. It did not matter! She'd not allow it to matter.

"Have you told Sophia what you just told me?"

She exhaled with annoyance when she realized she was holding her breath waiting to hear what he would say.

"I don't want to talk about her."

"Scarsdale—"

"No." The word resounded with force and finality. "She means nothing to me; therefore I feel no need to share what I went through with her."

Sophia's heart wrenched at his confirmation of how he truly felt about her, which infuriated her. She had to control her emotions when it came to him.

"Scarsdale, she loves you."

A loud *clunk*, as if glass had been slammed against wood, made her jerk.

"Women don't love. They beguile, seduce, and destroy if a man is foolish enough to allow them to. I'm no fool. And that is the last time I will ever discuss that woman with you or anyone else, so tell Amelia not to bother trying."

That woman! She was *that* woman! She couldn't take it any longer. She's spent over a year mourning him, loving him, missing him, only to be devastated by him. And now he was here and he was alive, and all the hurt she felt that he'd stolen her hope and crushed her heart erupted. Fear and reason fled. She flung open the door and marched into his office. Her heart slammed painfully as she took in her husband, here and alive and so very, very cruel and cold.

She would not play the foolish woman ever again. She turned her narrowed gaze on her husband, and her breath hitched. He was dressed casually in another open-collared shirt and leather breeches. A longing to touch him tried to well within her, but she shoved it down.

She hated him! And she especially hated the way heat pooled in her belly at the blasted sight of him. Striding to his desk, where he sat leaning negligently back in a chair, she slapped her palms down and loomed over him, irate when his manly smell, the one she'd dreamed about so many lonely nights, filled her nose and her heart fluttered. She willed her heart to still.

"*You* will not have any need to discuss me with anyone ever again, you foul beast! Believe me, I want away from you just as much as you want away from me. I demand to live separate lives!" she said, hurrying her next words, as his gaze narrowed dangerously. "And I generously offer you carte blanche to take lovers, but hear me now, I demand the same freedom!" Her body shook as she sucked in a breath.

It took Nathan a moment to get over the shock that Sophia had barged into his study and demanded carte blanche to take lovers, and then it took another second to get his lust under control. Whether he liked his wife or not, he wanted her. That was abundantly clear from his hard cock and heated blood. All he could think about was peeling her blue gown off and exploring the new lushness of her body.

Pretending she did not exist had been a rash decision. There was no reason he should not enjoy his beautiful, heartless wife's body. In fact, there was every reason he should. He still needed an heir, she was exquisite, and he was in no danger of losing his heart to her a second time. He drew his gaze over her round hips and tiny waist, pausing when he got to her delectable breasts. After a blush covered her chest, he suppressed a cynical chuckle that she should act so uncomfortable being desired. He inched his way to her face and met her fiery gaze.

Without blinking, he leaned forward. "No."

Her brow furrowed. "*No?*"

He raised his eyebrows in what he knew to be a mocking gesture. "Is my pronunciation too proper for you?"

Her face turned a deep crimson, and a momentary pang of regret for his nasty referral to where she had come from seized him until the image of her lying on her bed with her hair fanned out and Frazier's hands on her breasts filled his head. Nathan curled his hands into fists under his desk. He should have damn well killed that man.

She stood, looking every inch the haughty, heartbreaking duchess. "No you don't want to live separate lives or is it no you will not give me carte blanche to take lovers as I know you will," she bit out.

"No, you may not take lovers *any longer*," he said through clenched teeth, his temples pounding.

Aversley bounded out of his chair and almost tripped over it as he beat a path to the door. "Scarsdale, if you don't call on me tomorrow, I will be calling on you to check on Sophia."

Nathan drew his lips back in a menacing smile, more for Sophia's sake than anything. Aversley knew Nathan wouldn't harm a hair on Sophia's head. Didn't he? After all, his friend didn't even know that Nathan had found Sophia with another man last night, so why the devil would he be concerned about her welfare? "I will call on you on my way to London."

Aversley nodded, and after sketching a quick bow to a gaping Sophia, he left. As the door clicked closed, Nathan moved from behind his desk and stalked toward her. He'd dreamed of touching her every night for the last fourteen months. His fingertips burned with the need to trace them over her skin and plant himself deep within her body. He refused to allow any other emotion, but that one—*pure, unadulterated lust*—to enter his mind.

As he stepped toward her, her eyes rounded, and she stepped sideways away from the desk and then back. "I don't desire your touch."

"You will have to force yourself to somehow stand it then, for mine is the only touch you will ever have again," he replied, continuing his advance.

It was almost amusing the way she took another step back, except the thought that this was not at all how he had dreamed of being reunited with her suddenly broke through his haze of anger. He slammed another mental wall up and concentrated on the way her chest rose with each breath. He could swear her rosy nipples were near the edge of the material.

"You're like a child who wants to possess a toy!" she flung

out, her voice pitched high and desperate. "You never truly wanted *me*."

"But I now truly *desire* you," he returned, hearing his cold tone. "And as my wife, I have every right to take you and let no other do the same." He took a large step toward her, and she retreated farther until her back smacked against the wall. Her eyes widened, and she pressed her hands against the wall, so that her creamy skin struck a contrast against the dark wallpaper. Nathan stepped directly in front of her and raised his arms to either side of her shoulders before splaying his own hands against the wall. Now she was caged by him, as he had been by her. His gut wrenched at the weak thought. He had to do better. Her scent—a sweet, spicy concoction that was very different from how she had once smelled—surrounded him. She licked her lips and his groin hardened to an almost unbearable state. He forced himself not to shake as he reached out and caressed her cheek. The touch of his skin to hers sent a bolt of need through him so strong he fought not to wince. "*You* were supposedly in love with me. *Remember?* If that had been true, it seems you would now welcome my touch."

"Supposedly?"

Her voice throbbed with almost-believable emotion. It was a good thing he now knew what a superb actress she was. He nodded. "Come, we both know you never loved me."

She inhaled a sharp breath before speaking. "I did love you! Right up until I found out you were a liar. Right up until I learned you told your aunt I was pathetic and that you had every intention of leaving me to waste away in the country after you wed me while you went back to London."

He winced at that because he had said those things, but that had been before he'd spent much time with her. But he damn sure wasn't going to explain himself to her. "You loved me so much that you mourned for me by bringing your lover into the home I left you. You have a very interesting way of mourning, my dear. The usual custom is to wear black and at least pretend you miss the person who has died. How many men did you bed in my home, *Sophia?*" He turned all his rage at himself for falling in love with her outward and let the burning, biting fury he felt flow from him.

Sophia had been telling herself she would not lose her temper again, but the nasty look he gave her, his awful accusation, and the way her mind kept chanting in disbelief that he was alive made her snap. After all the heartbreak he'd caused her, her blasted heart still wrenched for him, longed for him, and wanted only him. She hated herself for it, and it made her want to hurt him as much as he had hurt her.

"Hundreds!" she spat. "A new lover every day! Why, I could hardly wait for my mourning period to be over, so I could invite the men in and spread my legs!" The last words made bile rise in her throat, but she would die before ever taking them back.

There was no mistaking the hatred that blazed in his eyes. His lips pressed into a cold, hard line, and he leaned in until his mouth almost touched hers. "Well, my dear, then I shall have to sample what skills you have acquired as a lover, because when last we were together, you had much to learn."

The threat and insult blew over her like a freezing winter wind, but the unmistakable tingle of desire to feel his hands on her again swirled in her belly and tightened her loins. She gritted her teeth at the way her treacherous body still responded to him. Anger at herself for loving him so desperately for so long, and at him for rising from the dead and upending her life once more, settled in her gut and burrowed into her bones. She could practically feel the rage rolling off him in hot waves, and it made her all the more angry that he would dare be mad at her! After all the love she'd given him that he'd thrown back in her face and he stood there so sure that she'd allow him to bed her once again.

"I will never succumb to your touch again, so you can forget sampling my skills. You will have to amuse yourself with fantasies of me because I vow I do not want your hands on my body."

An amused smile came to his lips, and he raised his eye-brows in a disbelieving manner that infuriated her. "We shall see about that."

The fact that he'd dropped his voice to a low, silky tone was not lost on her. He thought to seduce her! He thought she was that gullible and weak. She lifted her chin in defiance. "Don't you dare put your hands on me."

A wolfish smile crossed his face, and then suddenly he leaned forward and his mouth claimed hers. His kiss seared her body and her mind. She weakly thought to protest, but as his lips massaged hers with a silent command to open her mouth and let him in, her thoughts of protest seemed impossible to retain. She parted her lips and his tongue slid inside her mouth to tease her, torment her, and tantalize her. He tasted of whiskey, and by heaven, he tasted salty, as if the sea had become part of him. Before she knew it, she was clinging to him, grasping him, and he, blast him, had yet to touch her with his hands. His mouth blazed a fiery trail across her neck and between the valley of her breasts displayed by her daring gown. He licked her and lavished her, and she groaned in desperate need. The sound of her yielding moans froze her, as if she'd plunged into the frozen river water by her childhood home.

She whipped her eyes open, foggily wondering when she'd closed them, and looked down at the top of his head of thick black hair. His mouth was on her chest but his hands were still pressed against the wall on either side of her. How weak she was! She barely held in her sob.

"Stop," she choked out.

He stilled immediately and raised his gaze to hers. The desire burning in his dark eyes whispered to her soul.

"If you truly want me to stop, I will. I will move back, allow you to leave this room, and never touch you again."

Her heart rebelled at the thought, but her mind told her it was the wisest course of action. Yet the need to feel his hands on her pounded through her. He was her husband, she thought ruthlessly. Why shouldn't she enjoy his body? She'd use him as men had been using women for centuries. She could allow him to bed her without allowing love to be part of it ever again.

"I no longer love you." The words felt terribly wrong but she'd get used to saying them. She had to.

He swept his gaze down the length of her body, lingering quite obviously on her breasts, and then slowly his eyes came back to her face. "I did not say this was about love. This is desire."

"Yes," she said, unable to make her voice less throaty. She ached painfully with need. "Desire. *Only* desire."

Before she knew what was happening, he swooped an arm under her legs and she found herself pressed against his hard, unrelenting chest as he strode toward his study door, reared back, and kicked it open. The doorframe rattled behind them as Nathan stomped through it, and she clung to him, her hands flat against his beating, very-much-alive heart. The moment was a dream come true, yet it would not have a happy ending.

As his footsteps pounded through the corridor toward the stairs, they passed the butler, whose eyes bugged at their approach before he immediately turned and headed the other way.

She knew she should feel ashamed that she'd relented to desire, but it was hard to feel anything beyond the swirling heat inside her body. Nathan took the steps two at a time and, to her horror, took her to the bedchamber he'd discovered her in last night. He glanced between her and the bed where she'd been lying half-naked last night, and his face took on the look of granite as he stared at the bed.

"Try not to judge my performance today too harshly. Remember, I've been chained to one spot on a slave ship for fourteen months where I ate, drank, slept, defecated, urinated, and rowed unless I volunteered to fight, and then I would sometimes kill a man or simply beat him before he tried to do the same to me."

Tears filled her eyes at the horror of what he was telling

her, even though she already overheard it, and at the emotionless way he was revealing it. The compassionate man she had glimpsed, the one who'd saved her from Moses and her father, and rescued her brother from near death was gone. Or maybe she had made him up in her head. But she didn't make up the gifts he had bought her. Or the way he had decorated his home for her. Or the tenderness with which he had made love to her. She struggled to get her confusing emotions in order as he carried her across the room and laid her on the bed.

As he stared down at her, his eyes narrowed. "Is this where you took all your lovers, Sophia? Right here, in this bed?"

"Yes," she lied, her pride refusing to let her admit to him that she had not even kissed another man but him. *Ever*. The closest she had come to being intimate with another man was when Mr. Frazier had put his hands on her breasts and that had made her feel ill.

"How many?" he demanded.

She jutted her chin out. "I told you. Hundreds."

"I want an exact number."

She despised the way he thought to command her. "One hundred and one." The very idea was ridiculous. Surely he knew that.

"Then I will be one hundred and two," he growled, reached his hands up and behind his back, and yanked off his shirt.

Her gaze riveted to the scars zigzagging across his rippling abdomen. Her mind recoiled, and her heart cried out at the evidence of the pain he had endured. And suddenly the anger burning in her chest was gone. No wonder he was so cold now. Becoming this emotionless, hate-filled person had been the only way to survive. It did not obliterate the past, but it changed how she felt now. She didn't want to hate him anymore. Tears spilled down her face as he threw off his pants and the bed dipped with his weight.

"What's this?" he mocked. "Do you want me to believe

you're crying tears for me?"

She bit her lip to keep from responding and saying anything more that would fuel the anger between them. Whatever else had happened, whatever ways he had hurt her and betrayed her, he had given her and her brother a new chance in life and every advantage money could offer, and in this moment, she wanted to offer him the tenderness she thought he needed.

"Your scars," she whispered, reaching a shaking hand out to trace a finger over one that looked as if a whip had cut him from shoulder to hip.

He smiled without humor. "Ah, yes. Ravensdale and the other men who held me captive did so love to beat me. They wanted obedience and submission, you see."

So much emotion clogged her throat she could barely talk, but she forced words out. "And did you give it to them?"

His eyes, so dark, glassy, and unforgiving they could have been chiseled from obsidian, locked on her. "I do not give pieces of myself to anyone. Surely you know that."

She nodded, because she did know it and the pain was excruciating. She had foolishly thought she had captured his heart, but she now knew it had never been so. And her own heart stung with the knowledge and throbbed with the loss of hope.

He reached out and clasped a hand around the back of her neck to tug her close. His mouth came down over hers in a devastating kiss that stole her breath and her thoughts. Even if she had wanted to deny him, which she knew she did not, she could not have done so. Her body responded to his touch, whether her heart and mind wanted her to or not. Soon, she was ravaging his mouth with as much fervor and intensity as he was hers.

His kiss punished her lips in a way that sent sparks of aching need to her core. She moaned, and his lips softened while his tongue darted out to lick her and trace the seams of her mouth. She twined her hands through his thick hair and ran her nails across his scalp, feeling his muscles jump at her touch. She reveled in the fact that she could make him react to her. She may not have his heart, but in this moment, he desired her, and the bulging hardness of his shaft showed her he did not think her an object to be pitied anymore. Yet, she needed to hear him say it.

She pulled her mouth from his and leaned back so she could see his eyes. "What do you think of me? I know you must see I have changed?" She didn't give a whit that she was practically begging for a compliment.

He smiled like a wolf about to pounce on prey. He tugged the bodice of her dress, along with her undergarments, down until both her breasts spilled out. "I think you are the most exquisite creature I have ever beheld. You are making me mad with desire. I want to do this." He licked her right nipple and she hissed, which caused him to grin. "And I want to do this." He took her left nipple in his mouth and suckled until she screamed, which he silenced with a long, drugging kiss. When he finally broke the contact, she felt boneless and barely able to move. She *was drugged* with need and desire.

He seemed to know her predicament because he pulled her up, scooped her off the bed, and made waste of her gown within moments. Then he turned her until her back was to his chest, and he moved them forward until she was inches from the wall. "Put your hands against the wall," he commanded.

She didn't hesitate to comply.

He slid one hand down between her legs and parted the secret folds of her body while his other hand found her nipple and circled it, pinched it, and teased it, making her moan from the dual pleasure he brought her. His fingers increased the pressure between her legs until she demanded he take her.

And he did. In one motion, both his hands disappeared and landed on her hips, and she was tugged backward as he thrust into her and filled her with his hot staff. He rode her hard and fast and with abandon, in a way he never had before, but she loved it and screamed her pleasure repeatedly, until a wave of ecstasy seized her and robbed her of the ability to scream. As she tensed and her body pulsed and sucked him in deeper, his mouth came to her neck and his arm across her chest to hold her in place as warmth poured into her and his fierce cry of release joined hers.

When her climax subsided and she was left with the aftershocks, she sagged in his arms. He caught her and carried her to the bed where he gently laid her down. She opened her eyes and blinked, surprised to find him staring at her and shocked at what she could have sworn was love shining back at her. But before she had the chance to study him, an impenetrable mask descended and he turned without a word and went around the room gathering his clothes.

She studied him as he dressed, crying on the inside for the scars on his back that matched those on his front. She couldn't care less about the marks, but the pain he must have suffered made her ache for him. When he walked to the door and turned the handle to leave, she bit the inside of her cheek to stop herself from begging him to stay. He turned back and swept his gaze over her body, his eyes seeming to freeze on her hips and chest. She furrowed her brow as a dark look swept over his face and then disappeared.

"I'm sorry," he clipped. "I fear I'm far more barbarian now than gentleman. I hope I did not pale too much in comparison to the lovers you have known in my absence." With those spiked words, he quit the room.

She was left, once again, alone in her large bed and too-quiet bedchamber, where she had spent so many nights crying tears of loss, and more recently anger, over him. She crawled under the coverlet and recounted the seconds since he had returned. And then she spent what seemed like forever staring up at the ceiling in utter disbelief that he was alive. She replayed every word they had exchanged, every look he had given her, every reaction he had shown, and then she considered the things he had not revealed and the obvious torment he had borne.

And then she thought of what she'd learned from Ellison about Nathan betraying her. What if he hadn't? Why had she not considered the possibility before? What if Marguerite had lied? Sophia groaned. She had been so hurt when Ellison had told her, and her life before Nathan had been filled with Frank failing her that she'd all too willingly believed that Nathan had failed her, as well.

His mistress had nothing to gain with lies, of course, except she could just be a wretched person. Sophia had encountered plenty of purely evil people to know they existed. What if it wasn't true and he had actually started to care for her? Nathan would never be the sort of man to admit that to his friends. Her stomach twisted. *Dear heaven!*

How would she feel if their roles were reversed and she had been held captive for fourteen months, suffered unspeakable torture, and survived it all only to return and find him in bed with another woman? And then what if he had told her he had been bedding hundreds of women instead of mourning her? She cried out at the thought.

His words were cold and cruel but his touch was tender and loving. Her breath caught in her throat, and her mind raced with the horror of how she might have pushed him away, especially because she knew, without a doubt, that if he had not betrayed her, she could forgive him anything. She loved him and she was quite certain she had never managed to stop.

She lay in bed, her mind whirring and whirring. When dawn broke, she could take it no more and she hurriedly dressed and raced out of her room to her husband's bedchamber. She didn't bother to knock for fear he would deny her entrance. But when she flew through the door, she was surprised to find a maid in there, bent over a blanket and pillow that had been tossed on the floor.

The maid popped up and curtsied. Sophia eyed the spot by the fire where the blanket and pillow had been. "Did Nathan sleep on the floor?" Sophia demanded.

The maid bit her lip but nodded. "I believe so, Your Grace. He murmured something this morning on his way out the door about not being used to soft beds anymore."

Sophia frowned. "Out the door?" Surely he had not left her

without them talking.

The maid nodded. "He had the whole staff up at three, and he was gone by three thirty."

"He's gone?" She clutched at her chest, feeling as though her heart would explode any moment.

Oblivious to her mistress's rising hysteria, the maid nodded. "Yes, Your Grace. To London. He said he'd not be back for some time, and I overheard him tell Mr. Burk you were not to go anywhere unaccompanied by Mr. Burk himself. Not even to see the Duchess of Aversley, 'cause Mr. Burk inquired about her particularly."

A hysterical bark of laughter escaped Sophia. The noise must have alerted Duke, who was half-deaf with age, to her presence in his master's chamber. She stared openmouthed at the dog, shocked to see that Nathan had left Duke behind. Mr. Burk had said Nathan loved that dog and had always kept him with him.

"He left his dog," she murmured, more to herself than the maid.

The maid nodded. "Yes, Your Grace. He told Mr. Burk the dog had become a nuisance and to get rid of him."

Her stomach tensed, then flipped. What was Nathan doing? She clenched her teeth. He was cutting out everything from his life for which he had ever allowed himself to care. She was almost sick until she realized that if he was cutting her out, too, it had to mean he cared for her. She had to learn the truth somehow.

"Is Mr. Burk at the stables?" She had to demand he take her to London.

"Yes, Your Grace."

Sophia murmured her thanks and raced down the steps. She had to find out if Marguerite had lied to Ellison, though she had no idea how to go about even finding Marguerite. She didn't even know what the woman looked like. Somehow, she would find a way. And then she would have an honest talk with Nathan, even if it meant she had to admit he truly didn't care for her.

She strode out the door and toward the stables, but she got no more than a few feet when Mr. Burk came walking toward her. He had a troubled, reluctant look on his face as he held an envelope to her. "His Grace ordered me ta give ye this."

Dread seized her. Her hands trembled as she broke Nathan's wax seal.

Mr. Burk cleared his throat. "Shall I leave ye to it alone?"

"Please stay," she choked out while glancing down at the note.

Sophia,

I regret my actions last night and taking you so brutally.

A blush singed her cheeks, and she held the note a little closer to ensure Mr. Burk did not see it. Nathan had given her nothing but pleasure, but apparently, he did not think so. She brought her fingertips to her pounding temple and started to read again.

> *Please send a note through Mr. Burk when you know if you are with child or not. Never fear, I will not visit your bed ever again if you are with child, and if not, I will only visit until I have my required heir. I hope for your sake and mine that my seed has planted in your womb and my duty is done. In my absence, the following are rules I command you to follow. Do not test me, Sophia. You will consider your father's punishments mild to what I will distribute if you break one of my rules.*
>
> *Do not even think of going on a scavenger hunt with a gentleman as your partner ever again.*

She gaped at the paper. How had he known she had gone on a scavenger hunt? And what was harmful about a scavenger hunt? Lord Roxbury had been a perfect gentleman, except he had gotten them lost by refusing to listen to her directions. She huffed and continued reading.

I forbid you from speaking with any gentleman other than the staff here, or Aversley or Harthorne—Harthorne's name had been scratched through then rewritten again—*unless you are accompanied by Amelia until my aunt arrives to chaperone you. I will be sending her to live with you since I cannot trust you.*

Sophia had to stop reading for a moment because she was shaking with anger and horror at the thought of his aunt coming to live here.

When I do summon you to London, dress as a duchess should. And do so everywhere else, as well. In other words, throw out the gowns you had made in my absence. You look like a cheap doxy.

She dug her nails into her palms to keep from spouting foul curses.

Wear your hair up unless you are in your bedchamber about to go to bed. Your hair is the sort that tempts gentlemen to do bad things.

That edict, though annoying, made her smile with satisfaction. There was at least one thing about her he found alluring.

If you find yourself at the same party, dinner, ball, any occasion at all with Mr. Frazier—except his funeral, of course—leave immediately. I vow if ever you allow him touch you again, I will kill him without regret.

That statement made her shiver. Nathan was not a murderer, but she knew he had been forced to kill in order to survive. Clearly, the law of the sea still ruled in his mind.

I suggest you shelve the flirting skills you acquired when you should have been mourning me. If word reaches me that another sonnet, poem, or play has been written for you by some lovesick fool, I will be forced to defend your

*honor, which we both know you don't possess, in a duel. I'd
rather not accidentally kill some poor fop who had the
misfortune of thinking he loved you.*

"The misfortune of thinking he loved me!" she sputtered.
Anger danced up her spine and made her head pound harder.
She took a shuddering breath before continuing to read.

> *I forbid you from coming to London unless I give you
> express permission.*
> *Lastly, never question my authority over you. You are
> my wife. You are my property. You may not take a lover
> now or ever. You are stuck as my duchess and under my
> commands. Follow my rules and we will rub along without
> strife.*

She crumpled the paper in her hand. *Rub along without
strife! Ha!* If she followed his rules they would see each other
only if she wasn't pregnant and he had to visit her bed again,
and if she was with child, what then? Would he swoop in and
take the child from her because of his treatment from his own
mother?

These rules would not do. They would not do at all. Slowly, she opened the balled paper only to rip it to tiny pieces that
fluttered from her hand to the ground. She was going to
London to confront Nathan, and that's all there was to it. She
didn't care what sort of punishment he delivered. Living as he
suggested would be the worst sort of punishment imaginable.
She could not simply sit here and not know the truth of
whether had had been unfaithful or if he truly did not care for
her at all.

She looked up at Mr. Burk, who was still standing there
silently and watching her. "Mr. Burk, I need you to ready a
carriage. I'm going to London."

"We are going ta London," Mr. Burk amended. "His Grace
told me ye were ta go nowhere without me."

"Oh, yes, I see." She worried her lip. Mr. Burk hadn't read
the "rules" Nathan had left her, so he had no way of knowing

she was not to go to London without Nathan's permission. But in good conscience, she could not allow the man to accompany her without knowing the anger he may face from Nathan. She cleared her throat. "Er, Mr. Burk, I should tell you that—"

"Yer not ta go ta London without His Grace's consent?" he interrupted.

She nodded, heat making her cheeks burn. "He told you?"

"Aye. He read his rules ta me, lassie, with orders ta keep my eye on ye for any infractions. But he's a fool. I ken ye love him, even if neither of ye do. And if ye don't go ta him now and make him realize he loves ye back, I fear he will become so hard even ye can't soften him."

She sniffed back tears. "I want to try, but I need answers."

"Then let's go get them," he said with a grin.

By midafternoon, Sophia was headed to London with Mary Margaret across from her and Amelia beside her, because her friend had insisted she come as moral support. Amelia had also reasoned that she'd intended to leave for London tomorrow to meet up with Aversley, anyway. It seemed Aversley had departed for London this morning on business, and they were to attend Mr. Frazier's ball, one of the first of the Season. Sophia had quite forgotten her invitation to Mr. Frazier's ball. After a moment's thought, she decided if Nathan somehow avoided talking to her, she may have to break a few of his rules to force him to the task. So she had Mr. Burk go back home before leaving St. Ives, and Mary Margaret quickly packed Sophia's most daring gown, though she had not yet garnered the nerve to wear it.

The trip to London, which was already dreadfully long, was made longer each day by Sophia's increasing nervousness about confronting Nathan. She spent the first day of the trip barely talking to Amelia, who was more than understanding, but by the third day, she thought she would go mad. When Mary Margaret began snoring, Sophia broke down and confessed to Amelia how Nathan had found her in a very compromising position with Mr. Frazier the night he had come back. She could not bring herself to say she had been almost completely undressed, but Amelia gave her a knowing look and lowered the novel she had been reading before Sophia had broken the silence.

"Did Scarsdale happen to find you in this compromising position in your bedchamber?" Amelia whispered.

Sophia blushed but nodded.

Amelia nibbled her lip for a moment, and then a thoughtful look came over her. "How did he react?"

Sophia told her of how he had almost killed Mr. Frazier and then about the rules Nathan had written out for her.

"This is very good," Amelia said in hushed tones, nodding her head slowly and smiling. Sophia had her own hopeful theory that he had reacted so violently because he did care for her, but she held her tongue as she did not want to sway Amelia's initial inclination.

"Why do you think it is good?" Sophia whispered.

"I have never seen Scarsdale react to anyone, even someone purposely trying to bait him, except my husband."

The hope Sophia had once felt bubbling inside her sparked to life once more.

Amelia continued talking, unaware how her words were affecting Sophia. "Usually, he is unflappable and characteristically blasé. Yet, when he wanted to mend his friendship with Colin, and Colin wouldn't listen, Scarsdale lost his temper. And I tell you, it is because Colin is one of the few people Scarsdale allows himself to care about. The other is my brother, and you would make the third."

Sophia's heart felt as if it were expanding.

"You know," Amelia said, "come to think of it, after Ellison told you all those things that night of your birthday celebration, Colin later informed me that Ellison had not portrayed that night at White's exactly as it had occurred. I had thought to tell you of it, but then you refused to see me, and when I did see you again, you were determined to forget Scarsdale and refused to speak of him."

Sophia gaped at Amelia. "How did Aversley say Ellison misrepresented the night at White's?"

Amelia cocked her head as if she was searching her memory for her husband's exact words. "Well, for one, he said Scarsdale became very angry with Ellison when he called you a wench and said Scarsdale must have surely married you out of pity based on his description of you."

"Maybe he simply felt it made him look the fool," Sophia replied, disliking the fact that Ellison had called her a wench. And to think she had once thought him nice!

"Scarsdale has never given a whit what people think of him, Sophia. It's as if he trained himself not to care about other's opinions."

Sophia thought about all those paintings of him stashed in the attic in St. Ives, and her breath caught in her throat. As a child, he had, no doubt, cared deeply what his mother thought about him, and she taught him with torturous cruelty that to desire approval was to welcome pain. Sophia hugged herself on a shiver.

"What is it?" Amelia asked.

"He *has* trained himself not to care if others like him or not. You are absolutely right."

Amelia flashed a grin. "I do so love when people say that! Though, that is so very sad. It does, of course, prove my point: he would never become angry over his cousin or friends thinking he looked foolish for marrying you. But he became livid when Ellison besmirched you because, whether he realizes it or not, I do believe he loved you and loves you still. What are you going to do?"

Sophia swallowed. That was exactly what she had to figure out.

Twenty-Six

After Sophia dropped off Amelia, she directed Mr. Burk to Nathan's largest townhome, assuming he would be there, but the staff had not seen him since he'd been there two days ago to give them the news that he was still alive. As she made her way to his next townhome—luckily, Mr. Burk knew where it was, as Nathan surely hadn't told Sophia anything of it—the hour was growing late, and by the time she arrived, the moon was shining brightly in the sky.

She took a deep breath as she got out of the carriage, knowing full well that she could come across his horrid mistress at any moment. But when she questioned his servants, there was no one home. Once again Nathan had come to let them know he was alive, but he had not returned.

She made her way back to the carriage, but as Mr. Burk took her hand to help her in, a hackney pulled in front of the house. A woman, adorned in a gaudy gown of green-and-yellow silk, stepped out of the hackney, took one look at Sophia and her eyes widened as her mouth thinned. "Well, look what we have here. The infamous Duchess of Scarsdale."

Sophia narrowed her eyes, her heart racing and stomach knotting. She tilted her chin up. "Marguerite, I presume."

The woman laughed. "I recognize you as well. Ellison provided a detailed description."

Sophia turned to Mr. Burk. "Will you give me a moment?"

He nodded and walked a few feet away, but she could see him with his eyes on her, guarding her like he'd been told. And she could see Mary Margaret peering out the window of the carriage, but when their gazes locked Mary Margaret's face disappeared. Sophia faced the woman once more and stepped toward her, wishing only to get information without being overheard by Mr. Burk. Then she could get out of there as quickly as possible.

Marguerite lurched backward. "Don't you dare try to keep me out of this house! Scarsdale cannot just kick me out without my wardrobe! La-tee-da, he loves you. I understand. I heard him loud and clear. But I want my clothing. I need it to survive. What the devil does he think? I'm a paramour! I cannot go around looking wretched and wearing borrowed gowns that don't fit properly. And I cannot acquire new gowns instantaneously."

Sophia's mind whirled with everything Marguerite had just said. "When did you see my husband?"

The woman gave her an irritated look. "Don't fret yourself. I know when I'm beaten. I should have known it the night I saw him in Lincolnshire before he married you. He was already not himself then. Demanding I not touch him. Demanding I get out of this townhome, the one he had purchased *for me.*"

Sophia sucked in a sharp breath at the confirmation that what Nathan had told her so long ago was true. Marguerite truly *had* misled Ellison. "You are a wretched liar," she spat.

Marguerite gave her a haughty look. "We are all wretched liars, my dear."

Fury exploded in Sophia's chest, and she whipped her hand out and slapped Marguerite. The smack resounded in the silence, and her hand instantly tingled from the force of the hit. Marguerite's head snapped to the right, but when she focused once again on Sophia, she curled her lips back and raised her hand as if to strike back.

"Don't even think about it," Sophia warned. "I will lay you flat if you dare. And I learned a rather smart trick from my husband about how to cut off a person's air by putting my boot just there." She pointed to Marguerite's throat.

Marguerite's face paled, and she lowered her hand. "I only

want my clothing."

"When did you see my husband?" Sophia repeated her earlier question.

Marguerite's jaw thrust out in mutiny, but she spoke. "When he came back from the dead, of course. He came here looking for Ellison but he found me."

Sophia felt her jaw drop open. "You mean you and Ellison…?"

Marguerite smiled. "Don't look so shocked. He's a man with needs, like all men. And I'm the best at what I do."

"I will have the butler send you your gowns," Sophia said through stiff lips. That Ellison would sleep with this woman sickened her, though she knew she shouldn't be all that surprised. She'd seen plenty of men who were driven by lust and nothing else. "Don't ever come back here again. Are we clear?"

Marguerite nodded. "Perfectly." The woman held out a card. "Send my clothing here, if you please."

Sophia snagged the card without looking at it and watched Marguerite walk to the hackney. Within moments, the hackney disappeared.

Shaking with anger at Marguerite, relief that Nathan had not been unfaithful, and fear that she might have driven a permanent wall between them, she allowed a silent Mr. Burk to help her into the carriage. Mary Margaret gave her an understanding look but wisely said nothing.

"Where to now, Your Grace?" Mr. Burk inquired.

Frustration gripped her. "I don't know."

"Perhaps His Grace went to your townhome."

She frowned. She couldn't fathom why Nathan would be there, but with no other place to look for him, she nodded, and they set out to the house on Mayfair.

The place was small, compared to his main home but large compared to the one in the Garden District. She'd never been here, even though it had been over a year since it had become hers, but as she walked up the four steps to the bright-red front door of the dark brick home, she instantly liked it. It had four large windows that faced the street, so she knew the rooms must get a great deal of sunlight. There was something cozy about it, despite its location in Town.

She knocked on the door. The footman answered it and then showed her inside where the butler, Mr. Tims, immediately greeted her. It took only a moment to learn that Nathan was, indeed, in residence here and then took less time than that to learn he was out for the night at a ball. Sophia frowned. Knowing what she did of Nathan, she couldn't believe he'd willingly attend a ball, and when she inquired as to what ball he was attending, she nearly had a heart palpitation. It was Mr. Frazier's ball!

The only reason she could think of to explain his attendance was that he intended to finish what he had started with the Scot. In a frenzy of worry, she raced up the stairs to his bedchamber as she issued commands for her trunks to be carried up. She paused in the center of his bedchamber and took in the lacy coverlet and feminine dressing table. She stilled in wonderment. This was *her* bedchamber! He was sleeping in the room he had ordered to be hers. Nathan had come to London to forget her, to put so many miles between them, yet he had chosen to stay in the house he bought for her and in the bedchamber that had been decorated for her.

And he had not been unfaithful to her! He had been true!

Heat radiated in her chest. She had to see him immediately and learn once and for all whether he loved her or not. She called for Mary Margaret, and together, they quickly got her ready for the ball. She rushed her lady's maid through putting her hair up because she wanted to hurry, but after everything that had happened since Nathan's return, she feared if she showed up at the ball with her hair down, she would be pushing Nathan too far. Once Mary Margaret was finished, Sophia raced downstairs to where Mr. Burk was waiting to take her to the ball.

On the way to Mr. Frazier's home, she concentrated on one thought—she would vow they had been happy those few days at Whitecliffe and that she wanted that again and would do just about anything to have it back.

With tension cramping his shoulders and his anger barely caged, Nathan entered Frazier's home, stalked past the gaping footman, and bypassed the line that led to the host. One by one Frazier's guests, most of whom Nathan knew, started to whisper and gawk, and a few braver souls thought to greet him with exclamations of delight that he was alive. He ignored every single person and trained his gaze to his target: the tall, redheaded Scot who'd dared to invite Sophia to this ball and when Nathan had specifically told the man to stay away from his wife.

He didn't give a damn that Harthorne had said the invitations had come weeks ago. He didn't give a damn that Sophia had accepted the invitation before she had known he was alive and before he had expressly told her to stay away from Frazier and to not to dare come to London without asking Nathan's permission first. What he did give a damn about was ensuring his wife was not actually going to defy him and show up here. Because if she did he would drag her out of here and ship her to America if that's what it took to keep her away from Frazier. He would demand she not desire that man. The fact that his thoughts sounded mad in his own head didn't concern him in the least.

Harthorne nudged Nathan in the side as he stalked toward Frazier. "Your rise from the dead is causing quite a stir."

Nathan flicked his gaze at the blur of people he was passing, and he locked eyes with Lady Hornsby. She gawked at him and then poked one of the matron's beside her, who immediately ceased talking, and after angling her ear toward her friend, she turned to stare at him. Her jaw went slack, and then she started tugging on another woman beside her, who listened to her friend's quick but loud whispering that the Duke of Scarsdale was alive and here at the ball, and then she too gaped at him.

It was almost funny to watch the shock on their faces. If he'd had a sense of humor left it would have been a riot, but he had no room for any emotion save anger. When he nearly reached Frazier someone grabbed Nathan's elbow. With a scowl he turned on his heel and stared into Ellison's pale face.

His cousin reached out with a visibly trembling hand and touched Nathan on the chest. "My God."

Nathan smiled. "That seems to be a reoccurring reaction upon first seeing me."

"My God," Ellison said again, his voice cracking. "You *are* alive. It *is* true."

"You don't sound happy," Nathan joked, wishing to lighten the moment as he heard the furious whispers from the line and noted a multitude of gazes fixed upon them.

Ellison shook his head. "I'm shocked. Not unhappy. *Shocked.* My God, I cannot believe it."

"And yet, here I am," Nathan said. "I went to see you, but Aunt Harriet said you were still in Lincolnshire. Did Aunt Harriet tell you I had returned?"

Ellison shook his head. "Marguerite. She was waiting at my townhome, er, your old primary one, when I returned."

Nathan stared at his cousin. He was acting odd, but it was likely the shock and embarrassment, maybe, of Nathan knowing about Marguerite. Nathan drew closer to Ellison and turned his back on the line of gapers. Harthorne discretely stepped away, and Nathan caught Ellison's darting gaze. "I will not lecture you on Marguerite, nor ask you why of all the paramours, you chose to bed her. I know why. She's beautiful and beguiling, but she's also cruel. All I will say to you is to be careful. She is not to be trusted."

Ellison gave Nathan a hard stare. "I'm not a child in need of protection, Scarsdale."

"All right," Nathan said, his right temple beginning to tick. He flicked his gaze toward Frazier. There was a great deal more he and Ellison needed to discuss, but it was going to have to wait. The line of people waiting to speak with Frazier was dwindling, and Nathan didn't want the man to become lost in the crowd of people at his own ball before Nathan dealt with him. "Ellison, I need to have a word with Frazier, if you'll excuse me. I'll come see you tomorrow so we can talk, all right?"

Ellison nodded roughly. "How soon do you want me out of your townhome?"

The halting question surprised Nathan. "Stay in it. You may keep it. I've two more and already have settled into the one on Mayfair."

"How very kind of you."

Nathan sighed wearily at his cousin's petulant behavior. He was in no mood to appease him tonight. "As I said, we can talk tomorrow." With that, he left Ellison standing there alone and headed toward Frazier.

Harthorne immediately fell into step beside him. "How did it go with Ellison?"

Nathan shrugged. "About as well as I expected, seeing as his life was upended with my death and has now been upended again with my resurrection."

Harthorne clapped Nathan on the shoulder. "Take heart. He'll get over it."

Nathan paused and looked at Harthorne. "Frankly, at this moment, I don't give a damn whether he gets over it or not."

"Understandable," Harthorne said with a nod. "I think I'll wander into the ball and see if I can find Amelia and Aversley. I suspect you'd like a moment to speak with Frazier privately."

"Thank you," Nathan said.

After Harthorne walked away, Nathan closed the distance between him and Frazier. He offered Lady Chatworth, who was speaking with the Scot, a smile and joking assurances that, indeed, he was not a ghost, and she excused herself, likely sensing Nathan's anger.

Frazier must have sensed it, too. He motioned for to Nathan to follow him, and the two men strode through the crowd, which parted with stares of wonderment and a flurry of prattling and exclamations. Nathan nodded to people as they greeted him, but he didn't stop and neither did Frazier. When they came to the man's study, he gestured Nathan inside and then shut the door behind him and turned to face Nathan.

Frazier crossed his arms over his chest. "Ah dinnot remember inviting ye ta th' baw."

"You invited my wife; therefore, you invited me," Nathan clipped.

"Ah see. 'Twas weeks ago, ye ken."

"I don't give a damn when you invited her. You should have rescinded the invitation if you valued your life."

"Ah value mah life. Neither o' us thought ye alive. Given that, kin ye blame me fur desiring yer wife?"

Hell no, Nathan couldn't blame Frazier for desiring the temptress, but that didn't make Nathan want to kill the man any less. Instead, he flexed his fingers and clamped control on his anger. "Well, now you know I'm alive. So there will be no more forgiveness on my part. Do you *ken* me?"

"Aye," the man said with a courteous, slightly cocky smile. "Now, 'f ye'll excuse me, Ah need ta attend ta mah guests."

"As long as you're not attending to *my wife*, I can excuse you forever," Nathan replied and walked away without a backward glance. When he entered the crowded ball he paused, even more distasteful now than he had previously been of such affairs. Where the hell was Sophia? Was she here? Would she dare? He glanced over the guests and forced a false smile to his lips as people waved at him.

Frazier's question rang in Nathan's mind. Could he blame him for desiring his wife? Nathan clenched his teeth. He knew personally how hard she was to resist, because when he'd touched her for the first time in fourteen months, he'd lost every bit of civilized self-control he had ever maintained. A need to possess her that he could no more stop than the act of breathing had driven him to take her like a savage. He'd held nothing back, and she had taken it all and even made a good show of enjoying it. He'd been deeply sated when finished, but on the heels of that satisfaction came shame and dread—shame that he could not control himself and dread that she would gain power over him every time he touched her until he became like the child he once was, longing for love that she would never give.

I don't love you anymore, she'd said.

It had reminded him so much of something his mother had said to him so long ago. He'd tried to flee the hurt he could not deny by fleeing her, but he could not put thoughts of her out of his mind. And the hurt was still there like an open wound. She haunted his every moment, awake and asleep, and it was driving him mad.

"Scarsdale!"

Nathan turned to the right to see who had called to him. Aversley was walking toward him with Amelia at his side. He raised his hand in greeting, even as he scanned the crowded ballroom once more for Sophia. In the distance, at the top of the stairs on the far side of the room, a flash of crimson caught his attention, and his body grew rigid as he caught sight of his treacherous wife descending the staircase in a dress that would tempt the angels themselves to sin. And on top of that, hovering around her, were two soon to be sorry gentlemen who appeared to be vying for her attention.

"Excuse me," he bit out and sidestepped Aversley and Amelia just as they reached him. As the thin thread of self-control he had left broke, he cared about nothing in the moment but reaching Sophia. He pushed through the crowd, glaring at every person who tried to stop him, but just as he was passing the refreshment table, he was grabbed from behind. He swung around and met Aversley's knowing stare.

"Judging by the look on your face, you have seen your wife."

"Indeed. Now unhand me."

Aversley increased his grip. "I think you should get your temper under control before you talk to her. I don't know what she has done—"

"No, you don't," Nathan snapped.

"Well, I do!" Amelia chimed in, huffing out a breath as she came to Aversley's side. "And it is not as you think! But even if it were exactly as you thought, you deserved that and much more. She gave you her love and you...you...*you* sent your mistress back to London to the townhome you bought for her."

Of course he had. But how the devil did Amelia know that? "What else would you have had me do?"

Her eyes narrowed, and she set her hands on her hips. "I would have had you been faithful to Sophia."

"What?" The woman babbled nonsense.

"Don't pretend you don't understand," Amelia snapped. "She worshiped you. You made her fall in love with you. Heaven knows how! And she almost died mourning you. She refused to eat, to drink, to live. We had to lie to her to get her out of bed. And then she spent an entire year trying to make herself into a duchess you would be proud of. You are a fool!" Amelia whispered harshly under her breath.

What Amelia said was impossible. Wasn't it? His stomach clenched with doubt. He scanned the faces and found Sophia across the room with her head pressed close to Frazier's, the stupid bastard. Nathan jerked his arm out of Aversley's hold. "Then how do you explain what I came home to? How do you explain me finding her in her bedchamber with Frazier?"

Amelia's shoulders sagged. "It's for her to explain, Scarsdale, not me. I urge you to go to her. Give her a chance. Give yourself a chance."

"She's had plenty of chances," he growled, determined not to let his guard down again. "I'm going to go to her certainly. I'm going to drag my coldhearted wife out of this ball, whether she likes it or not." And before either of his gaping friends could protest, he stormed away, fairly shoving Lord Peregrine, who was grinning at him, out of his way.

"Please go away!" Sophia begged, discreetly pushing at Mr. Frazier. Of all her ill luck, he had been one of the first people she had seen, and she had only stopped when he'd asked her to so she could tell him she simply could not speak with him anymore. The minute she had pressed her head near his to whisper the private words, she'd felt, rather than seen, Nathan. When she had looked up and swept her gaze over the buzzing crowd, she nearly swooned at the sight of him plowing through the ballroom like a man bent on revenge.

"Go now!" she hissed again and abandoned propriety to shove Mr. Frazier in the arm.

Mr. Frazier was looking in the same direction she was and his jaw had hardened into a line of stubborn determination. "I'll nae leave ye alone. He looks angrier than th' devil himself. Ah em nae a coward."

She fisted her hands at her side. "You're a fool! He will kill you, and I don't think he will pause to hear explanations. Not that he'd believe them, anyway."

She glanced back up and gasped. Five more breaths and he'd be on them. She swiveled toward Mr. Frazier. "I love my husband. I've only ever loved him. It was a terrible, foolish mistake to think I could forget him, and I'm sorry I almost used you. Now, please, go."

"I suggest you do as my wife says," Nathan said in a tone so cold Sophia shivered.

"Nathan," she rasped, turning toward him and losing all thought for a moment at his nearness. His raw power overwhelmed her senses. She pressed her fingertips to her temples and inhaled a shaky breath. "Please. It's not what you think. It never was. If you will just give me the chance to explain."

His dark, gleaming gaze slid from her face to Mr. Frazier's, who still stood there like the daft man he obviously must be. Nathan moved his arm in front of her and slid her behind him, as if she were a mere chess piece he moved on a board. The contact of his hot skin to her abdomen almost made her moan. All that effort to forget him had been for naught. She would never forget her love for him, no matter what happened tonight.

He stepped toward Mr. Frazier and said something she could not hear, and Mr. Frazier immediately rushed off without a good-bye. When Nathan turned to face her, his gaze was guarded, his face weary. The thought that she had caused him pain made her ache.

Nervously, she licked her lips. "What did you say to him?"

"I asked him if he preferred to die now or tomorrow. Apparently, he prefers tomorrow," Nathan drawled in a ruthless tone.

She so desperately wanted to talk to Nathan without such a large barrier between them. She wanted nothing more in this moment than to hear the truth from his lips and tell him the truth in return. As noise and people swirled around her, she swallowed hard. She didn't care about her pride at all. She would give up her pride and every worldly possession she now owned if it meant the happiness she had glimpsed with Nathan so long ago could be theirs again.

Looking up into his implacable, unrelenting gaze, she flung her pride to the wind. "I never slept with Mr. Frazier."

His scorching gaze searched her face, and it felt as if he were delving inside of her.

She swallowed her fear and continued. "I've never slept with any man but you. I've never even kissed another man but you."

If she'd not been searching for a sign of hope, she wouldn't have noticed that his eyes widened ever so slightly. She wanted to swoon with relief. She was getting to him. She hoped. "I died inside when I thought you were gone forever, and then later when I learned you had lied to me and betrayed me with that woman Marguerite, I wanted you alive so I could kill you and hurt you as you had hurt me. So I set out to destroy my love for you and the memory of you that was imprinted on my soul."

He reached out and smoothed back a tendril of her hair that had fallen into her eyes, tucking it behind her ear. The gesture was so intimate, so loving, she could not suppress the cry that escaped her lips. His eyes widened another fraction, and he took her hand in his and peeled her glove off. She trembled as he splayed her fingers out and interlaced his with hers. Her heart exploded as his strong, rough hand curled around hers and he drew her close.

He leaned in and whispered in her ear. "And did you succeed?"

His hot breath fanned over her neck and made goose flesh cover her body. "It's an impossible task." Her voice shook as she spoke. "I love you. I didn't mean what I said before about no longer loving you. I was hurt and angry."

His lips parted at her statement, and then his eyes, which had been like granite, softened and filled with a glint of wonder. "Are you offering me your love again?" Disbelief filled his voice.

She nodded. "I am. I am offering all I have to give, But only if you love me, too."

Without saying a word or releasing her hand, he turned on his heel and tugged her up the stairs toward the exit. As they went, several people attempted to talk to Nathan, but he kept on walking as if they did not exist. Unsure what was happening, whether she was being dragged away for love or to be sent packing and back to isolation, she pasted a smile to her lips and mumbled greetings to the people he'd snubbed.

A coachman she didn't recognize was waiting in front of the home, and he hopped down from his perch and opened the gleaming, lacquered door of Nathan's carriage.

She pulled back on Nathan's hand and scanned the carriages for Mr. Burk—the stable master had insisted on staying while she went inside—as he was following Nathan's order to not let her go anywhere without him. "Mr. Burk brought me."

"I know," Nathan replied, his impassive tone not giving the slightest hint to how he was feeling. "I dismissed him."

She gasped and tugged her hand out of Nathan's. "You cannot dismiss Mr. Burk!"

Nathan cracked the first smile she had seen since he had risen from the dead. "I didn't *dismiss* Burk. I sent him home for the night. I knew you would be leaving with me." He held out his hand to her. "Now that we have settled that, please get in." Though there was no mistaking that he was commanding and not really asking, a subtle softness that she had not heard in over a year underlay his steely tone.

Her heart constricted with hope. Once they were settled inside the carriage and Nathan instructed the coachman to take them to the Mayfair townhome, she breathed a little easier knowing at least Nathan wasn't forcing the man to drive to St. Ives tonight.

For the first few minutes that the carriage was rolling through the starlit night, Nathan looked out the window and didn't speak. She began to worry that maybe he was never going to talk when he finally turned and looked at her. The light in the carriage was just enough that she could see that his lips were pressed into a grim line, and the little bit of hope that had wiggled back into her heart faded.

She struggled to fight her tears as he yanked on the cravat he wore and finally succeeded in pulling it all the way off. He tugged at his shirt until the front hung open, and then he offered her a rueful smile. "After a year of not wearing a shirt, I can hardly stand this thing against my skin." He held up an arm. "Let alone the damn cravat, which I hated well before I was enslaved. Now the material wound tightly around my neck reminds me of the manacles that bound my legs and ankles."

She held her breath for a moment, afraid to say anything. He was sharing how he felt with her! He was showing her a weakness in his unshakeable strength, which was so unlike him.

He tugged a hand through his hair. "When I was first kidnapped, all I could think about was you and what you might think when I didn't come back to you. I knew there was no way you could know I loved you, because I had never told you."

She fisted the material of her gown in her hands to try to stop herself from crying out her joy at his admission. He needed to talk and she was going to let him, even if it drove her mad. What she couldn't hold back were the tears of happiness. They ran down her face in warm tracks, and she watched him as he stared at her.

"Later, when I awoke from the first beating, all I could think was that I'd been such a coward not to take the love you had offered me." He didn't blink or break his eye contact with her. "I'd been so afraid, you see, that you would take back that love once you knew the real me."

"Never," she promised and bit her lip on the realization that she had tried to do exactly that.

He arched a sardonic eyebrow, as if his thoughts echoed hers. "I can only imagine that gossip brought you to the conclusion that I betrayed you with Marguerite, and based on some rather odd things Amelia said to me tonight, is it safe to conclude you believed I had planned to keep Marguerite as my paramour in London?"

Sophia nodded. "Except it wasn't gossip. Marguerite told Ellison you had slept with her the night you went to see her in Lincolnshire and that you told her your relationship with her would continue as always so she should go back to the townhome in London."

"And why, pray tell, did Ellison impart these lies to you?"

His voice sounded as though it could be used as a sword to lop off a man's head. Not that she felt overly fond of Ellison at the moment, but she did believe he had been simply trying to help her. However, he could have picked a much better time than her birthday dinner to tell her that Marguerite said Nathan had slept with her.

"Don't be angry with him, Nathan. He didn't know Marguerite had lied to him, and he thought he was helping me. He was afraid I would go out amongst the *ton* and continue to drone on about how honorable, and true, and wonderful you were. He said he did not want people laughing at me."

Oh dear! That did not sound good at all.

"It's good to know Ellison thinks so highly of me. How did you come to believe in me and not the lies? This seems a change from our previous reunion."

She averted her eyes for a moment, shamed to her toes that she hadn't had enough faith in him, but then she forced herself to gaze at him once more. "I ran into Marguerite earlier outside of the townhome you apparently just kicked her out of...again. Things she said made me realize she'd lied about the two of you."

Nathan was visibly shaking as he looked at her. "Never mind. I don't give a damn how you came to believe it," he said in a choked voice.

Sophia's heart splintered in a way she had not thought it had the capacity to do anymore. She gripped her chest at the pain. "Nathan, please..."

In a blur, he was across the carriage, scooped her into his arms, and deposited her on his lap. He cradled her against him. "No, darling, shh." He brushed his lips to the hollow space between her collarbones, where her pulse was hammering. "You misunderstand me. I love you, too, and I don't care how you came to believe in me again, only that you do."

She moaned in response, and he brushed his lips to hers once more. "I am not good, but I vow, God as my witness, I am true and I do try to be honorable. And I never slept with Marguerite after I met you, nor did I have any desire to do so. Marguerite is a vindictive witch who likely was still angry with me, even when she thought I was dead, that I had ended our relationship, something I should have done long ago. I think I stayed with her because I thought a man like me deserved no better than a woman like her."

"Oh, Nathan!" Sophia pressed her lips to his, savoring his warmth, his taste, and the promise of his love. "I believe you! I believe you were true to me. And I'm sorry I ever doubted it. I'm sorry I tried to hurt you by saying those awful things the night you came home, and I'm sorry I tried to take back my love."

He cupped her face and kissed her forehead, her nose, and then her lips. "I'm glad you didn't manage it, but I want to tell you now of my past so you will know the worst of me."

"You don't need to do that!" she exclaimed.

His gaze locked with hers. "I do need to, Sophia. I need to know that you can hear all the terrible choices I have made and still love me. Still want me."

She nodded and laid her head against his chest. He talked while stroking her back.

As the carriage rumbled toward the townhome, then eventually arrived, the carriage door was opened and then discreetly shut with a look from Nathan to the coachman. And during that time, Nathan told her of his addiction to laudanum that started with his accident with his parents and ended with waking up in Marguerite's bed with the taste of laudanum in his mouth, and her smiling and telling him he had drank it off her. He told Sophia of being a member of the Order of the Dark Lords and of the learning that his onetime friend, Ravensdale, was robbing people in their carriages. He told her of turning Ravensdale in, quitting the Dark Lords, and trying to pick up the pieces of the life that had been shattered long ago by his mother's cruelty and his father's desire to avoid conflict.

After he told her all his sins, he finally told her again the one thing, the only thing she really wanted to hear. "I love you, Sophia. It was my love for you and the promise of the life and happiness we could share that kept me alive this past year. You saved me the day I met you. And then you saved me again every day that I was held prisoner. If you still want me, I'm yours, bruised body and battered soul."

"You are all I ever wanted," she said. "Even before I knew it. Now, come, let's go upstairs and have a proper welcome home."

As they alighted from the carriage and walked hand in hand up the stairs and to his bedchamber, her heart expanded and filled with exquisite happiness. Once he undressed her with care, she started to undress him but he stilled her hands. "One moment." He bent down, fumbled near his ankle, and came up with a dagger. "I never go anywhere without this now. I didn't want you to be surprised."

Her heart ached for the ordeal he had been through. She understood all too well the need to feel protected. Once they were both undressed and standing face-to-face in his bedchamber, Nathan asked her to stand still so he could look at her. She agreed, though she felt a burning shyness that he, so beautiful even with his scars, was examining her, who paled so in comparison.

He traced his fingers like a feather over her breasts, her belly, her hips, and down her legs. He kneeled before her and ran his hands up her calves, her thighs, and over the rounded curve of her bottom. Then his hands clasped on to her flesh and his fingers curled into her skin as he tugged her to him and kissed her stomach and then lower still to the secret space only he had ever been.

The pleasure he brought her was so intense that it danced on that razor-sharp edge of torment and delight. Between long, lavish strokes of his tongue to her sensitive bud, she lost her ability to stand, but he caught her as she crumpled and lowered her gently to the ground. He gave no quarter to her need and brought her all the way to the pinnacle of desire until she screamed her demands that he take her. And this time, though the savage still dwelled within him, all his touches, kisses, and strokes in and out of her were filled with tender love that made tears come to her eyes.

Together, they climbed toward the happiness that had almost eluded them, and as his mouth worshipped hers and his body rocked in time with hers, she clung to him with shaking limbs and savored his strength while offering him her softness. When he withdrew almost to his tip, his eyes locked with hers just before he drove back inside her, and sparks of ecstasy spiraled from her core to every space in her body. She clenched around him with her own release as he stilled, crying out his, and then, utterly exhausted and satisfied, they lay on the floor, wrapped in each other's arms and slept.

Hours later, she awoke and stared at her sleeping husband. He was perfectly naked and perfectly beautiful, inside and out. As she was gazing at him, his eyes opened, and he turned his head to look at her.

She rested her chin on his chest and smiled. "Did I wake you?"

"No. I think it's the floor. I've been unable to sleep in a
real bed since returning, but suddenly I find that I want only
soft things in my life." He traced a finger over her breast and
circled it around her nipple with a lascivious smile on his lips.
"I want a soft bed and my soft wife, and I think I'd like to stay
there for several uninterrupted days."

"Then we shall!"

Giggling, she scrambled up and into the bed where he
joined her. And for two days they got out of bed only to take
long baths and eat the hearty meals that the blushing maid
served them.

During that time, the news of the Duke of Scarsdale's rise from
the dead spread like wildfire through London. During their
self-imposed exile from everyday life, hoards of visitors and
well-wishers came to the townhome until Nathan, finally, on
the third day, dragged himself out of his wife's arms and their
warm bed and set about putting his affairs in order so they
could retire to Whitecliffe, where they both agreed they very
much wanted to live year-round.

For an entire day, Nathan was holed up in his study with
his solicitor, Aversley, and Harthorne as he made decisions
about different business happenings that had transpired while
he was away. That night, Sophia and Nathan dined casually
together and then tired each other out with their lovemaking.

When she awoke the next morning, she was blissfully
happy, except for one thing. Ellison had been notably absent
yesterday, and when she had broached the subject with
Nathan he had admitted he was putting off seeing his cousin
because taking everything that went along with the dukedom
away from Ellison made Nathan feel awful. She didn't want
the sole person in his family who Nathan had cared about to
slip away from him, but she was unsure what to do.

As she was sitting there thinking on the matter, the butler
brought her a note with nothing but her name written on the

outside of it. For a moment, she wondered if Mr. Frazier was so daft as to write to her, but she quickly discarded the idea and unfolded the note, scanning first to the bottom where she saw Ellison's signature.

She drew her gaze up to the top and read the short note:

Please come to see me but don't tell Scarsdale. I'm in a very bad way and truly feel awful about my part in unknowingly hurting you. I'd like to beg your forgiveness and seek your advice on what I should do with my life. The thought of being dependent on Scarsdale's charity once again is intolerable to me. I've rented some rooms one block from the two of you, as I want to stand on my own two feet. Here is the street and number if you decide to come see me.

Sophia folded the letter and pondered what to do. She should tell Nathan, but then again, he was in meetings and would probably be in them all day. She could easily walk to the address Ellison had jotted down. She'd seen that street yesterday on the way here.

Her heart wrenched a bit for Ellison and how he must feel, must have always felt, rather unimportant next to Nathan, though she knew that was not because of anything Nathan had intentionally done. It was simply fate. Nathan was the duke. He was handsome, magnetic, and sophisticated in contrast to Ellison's dull looks, rather listless charms, and stilted, often almost-bumbling personality. She knew what it was to feel inadequate.

She'd go to him and see if she could help him while also helping to mend the fracture she saw developing between him and Nathan.

It was easy enough to slip out unnoticed. The servants were busy packing the trunks and preparing for her and Nathan's departure for Whitecliffe tomorrow. The walk was quick, and she had no trouble finding the place Ellison had rented. She knocked on the door, and when Ellison answered it himself, she hid her shock with a smile.

His face tinted red as his gaze locked with hers. "I cannot afford servants if I am to remain living on solely what is mine and support my mother, as well. She has a rather lavish lifestyle she wants to maintain and she does not appreciate the fact that I no longer want Scarsdale to help me."

Sophia linked her arm through Ellison's. "I think you are marvelous for wanting your independence, but I know Nathan would never think to deny you anything you needed."

Ellison gave her an odd look, but then he smiled, though she could tell from its tightness that it was forced. "Come in and I'll get you some tea."

She nodded and followed him into the sparsely decorated house. Truly, it looked as if he did not even live here. Frowning and suddenly feeling slightly uneasy, she slowed her pace and almost considered leaving, but then she shook the nonsense away. He was probably loath to settle into surroundings that were so meager compared to what he was accustomed.

After he showed her into the parlor, he went to get them some tea. As she sat on the light-blue threadbare settee, she glanced around the room. One painting decorated the wall. Two men were in the painting, one whom looked very much like Nathan.

Ellison came in as she was looking at it. He closed the door behind him and walked over to where she sat and handed her a cup of tea. He took a sip from his own and then glanced at her as if urging her to do the same, so she did. The tea was very bitter and she fought the urge to purse her lips in disgust. She made to set it down, not overly thirsty anyway, and he laughed.

"I'm terrible at making tea. Such a simple thing, too. I cannot do anything right, I suppose."

Sophia's heart twisted in pity, and she raised the teacup back to her lips. "It's delicious, truly. I was just giving it a moment to cool, but my!" She took another sip. "It already has cooled."

"You are a very sweet liar."

"No!" she gushed and drank the entire bitter cup down.

Ellison pointed to the painting and said, "The man on the left is my father and the one on the right is Scarsdale's father. Did you know they were twins?"

She shook her head and frowned. Her head felt very strange, heavy somehow.

Ellison didn't spare her a glance, thank goodness. He continued talking as she struggled to concentrate. "They never looked alike," Ellison said, his voice sounding odd to her.

Sophia squinted at the picture as her vision had suddenly become blurry. The awful feeling was familiar and reminded her very much of how she'd felt the night she'd gotten sick at Whitecliffe. Her gut twisted with fear.

"Ellison," she choked out, finding it hard to talk because her tongue felt numb.

He kept talking as if he had not heard her. "Everyone always said that from the moment they came out of the womb, Scarsdale's father was the golden child, just like Scarsdale. I had a nanny that told me my father was actually born first, but the last duchess made everyone say Scarsdale's father was eldest because he was the most handsome and, therefore, would make the best duke."

"Ellison!" she said sharply, as the room around her started spinning.

He stood abruptly and looked down at her, then strode across the room toward a desk in the corner. As he walked, it hit her that he was not limping, and the uneasy feeling exploded into something more like suspicion. She licked her dry lips, even as her throat screamed for water. "You're not limping."

The smile on his face when he turned chilled her to the bone. "It's been gone for years, but I had to keep up the pretense as the poor, fat, crippled cousin until Scarsdale was dead."

She pressed her sweaty palms to her hot forehead. "I don't understand."

"I'm happy to explain it to you, Sophia, since you will soon be dead yourself." Panic filled her chest as he went on, not giving her a chance to speak. "Years ago, I became sick and tired of listening to my mother put me down and complain about how I should have been the duke, how she should have married Scarsdale's father and not mine because then she would have been duchess, and I decided to do something about it."

Sophia's ears were ringing so loudly it took great effort to hear, let alone comprehend, every word.

"Instead of sitting around as I had been and letting my life pass me by, I formed a plan, and the first part of the plan was to see if I could walk without a cane so my mother would quit calling me a pathetic cripple. Imagine my surprise when I started walking with no limp at all. It was two years' worth of excruciating exercise that made me toss my accounts, but I did it."

Sophia tried to get up to run but her legs would not work. "Ellison, what have you done to me?"

He smiled again and the coldness of it made her almost certain he had gone mad.

"I've poisoned you so you wouldn't give me any fuss."

"*What?*" Her head was reeling, her heart hammering.

"Mother wanted me to kill you right away. I promised her before she left for Bath yesterday that I would. But *I'm* doing all the dirty work, so I will do it my way for once. And I want to kill you with Scarsdale watching, and then I will kill him."

Sophia clutched at the side of the settee, but even her fingers felt weak. She started to slump over, but Ellison reached out and steadied her. His face came near hers. "It's not personal, Sophia. In fact, I rather like you, but you stand between me and the dukedom." He placed a hand on her belly. "I know Scarsdale well, and I'm quite certain you could be carrying his child."

She glanced down and moaned.

"Finally, Scarsdale will know what it is to feel helpless and weak compared to me."

"You're mad," she whispered, unable to make her voice come out any stronger.

He shook his head. "No. Not mad. A madman would have rushed. I took my time. I knew I didn't need to rush because Scarsdale was not rushing into marriage, and frankly, he was making me a lot of money with his business decisions. Well, technically"—he grinned in a way that made her skin crawl—"he was making himself money, but I knew I would eventually inherit it. Plus, when people rush, they become careless. Don't you agree?"

He was beyond mad! She couldn't even speak now. Tears began to leak from her eyes.

"Oh dear," he said on a sigh and swiped at her face. "I hate to see a woman cry. Mother cried when we did not succeed at killing Scarsdale that first time. The bumbling man we hired botched the job. All he had to do was run Scarsdale over with a carriage and the fool missed him. So we thought quickly, and Mother, Ravensdale, and I put our heads together, and we decided to ambush Scarsdale. But then you came along, you little minx, and you helped Scarsdale escape his fate once again." Ellison sighed loudly. "Mother was not happy, but when her poisoned wine did not do you in, I thought she might just make a fatal mistake. I tell you, I fretted day and night until I managed to come up with a new plan. It should have worked." Spittle flew out of Ellison's mouth. "I thought it did work."

He released Sophia, and she slumped over on the settee. Her mind screamed but nothing else would cooperate. Not even her eyes would stay open. The settee creaked as Ellison got up. He circled his hands around her waist and hauled her up and threw her over his shoulder. She flopped there and fought back the encroaching darkness.

"Everyone has his own agenda, it seems."

She jostled as he carried her out of the room. "Ravensdale said he wanted Scarsdale dead as much as I did, but he lied. He wanted to torture him. If Ravensdale were not already dead, I'd eagerly kill him for how he has made me work even more for what should be mine. What is rightfully mine. His foolish desire almost lost me everything because your damn husband refused to die. I suppose it will be rather poetic in the end. It seems I'll be much like kings of the past. I have to take my throne by force. And then I will have earned it."

Sophia could not hold on any longer. With a ragged exhale, the darkness claimed her.

Twenty-Seven

Nathan finished his meeting with Sir Richard, Aversley, and Harthorne around dusk and sat at his desk long after they left. He stared out the window into the darkening sky and contemplated what Sir Richard had said. He'd not had any good leads yet, so Nathan simply had to be patient. They'd spent all day going over every detail Nathan could recall of Ravensdale's crew, and Sir Richard had vowed to double his efforts.

Feeling tired and tense, he went in search of Sophia to find comfort in her smile and her arms, but thirty minutes later, when he had combed the house and not been able to locate her, he started to become concerned. He paced the floor, trying to think. Maybe she had gone to see Amelia? No, the carriage was still at home. He racked his mind, and just as he was about to get in the carriage to search the streets for her, a knock came at the door.

Nathan brushed past the butler and footman and swung open the door. "Ellison," he said, trying to hide his annoyance that it was not Sophia. "Now is not a good time."

Ellison clapped him on the shoulder. "I have a confession."

Nathan frowned. "What is it?"

"I sent a note to your wife earlier to come see my new townhome and take tea with me. I wanted to beg her forgiveness."

Nathan fairly shoved Ellison out of the way to get out the door, expecting to see Sophia there, but the street was empty. Not even Ellison's carriage was there.

"Where's Sophia?"

Ellison grinned. "She's at my home. I came to fetch you so we can all have dinner together. I've a new French cook and I talked Sophia into staying, so what say you? Will you come? If you won't, I vow Sophia will be disappointed. I'm trying to be more independent, Scarsdale."

"So it would seem," Nathan agreed. "How far is your home?"

"One block. Close enough for the two of you to walk home on a beautiful night like this. If a cripple like me can walk it, you can."

Nathan frowned at Ellison's self-deprecating remark but decided not to comment, and without a parting word to the staff, they left.

They walked in silence most of the way, but when they neared the townhome Ellison indicated was his, he paused and faced Nathan. "I'm sorry," he said simply.

Nathan cocked an eyebrow. "For what?"

"For being churlish about you giving me the townhome the other night. I think what has happened is good. I need to learn to stand on my own without any help."

"If you wish it. But I never minded sharing with you, Ellison. You are my family."

Ellison smiled as they went to the door, and he let them in while explaining that he was in the process of interviewing for a footman and butler.

"Welcome to my home," Ellison crowed and clapped Nathan on the left shoulder, in the exact spot he had been shot so many months ago. Nathan flinched, and Ellison laughed. "Sorry. Did I hit the old bullet wound?"

"Yes," Nathan replied, shutting the door behind him, and then frowning, as he stared at his cousin's back, confused. "But I never told you which shoulder I was shot in…"

Ellison stopped and turned slowly around. He had a pistol pointed at Nathan. "No, you didn't, but that bastard Ravensdale did."

Nathan's heartbeat pounded in his ears as his blood surged

through his veins. His cousin had been conspiring with Ravensdale? "Where's Sophia?" he ground out.

Ellison pointed to the parlor. "Waiting for us in the parlor. She's all tied up, so I'll take you to her."

"If you've hurt her—"

"You'll what?" Ellison demanded as he shoved the pistol against Nathan's chest. "I have the upper hand now. I'm the king. I'm taking the throne."

Ellison had lost his mind. Nathan considered the dagger tucked in the sheath sewn into the side of his boot. He only needed one second while Ellison was distracted and then he could get to it.

"You'll never get away with killing us," Nathan said, for he had no doubt Ellison planned to kill Sophia, too. Otherwise, it made no sense for him to have gone to the trouble of bringing her here.

Ellison stared at him with flared nostrils. "I will. Once you two don't return home, I'll tell the investigators that I last saw the two of you when you were walking home from dinner at my house. They'd never suspect me. I'm a poor, helpless cripple. Now, get going." Ellison stepped to the side and motioned Nathan forward.

With the pistol shoved in his back, Nathan had no choice but to bide his time.

Sophia struggled against the ropes that bound her hands behind her back, and she nearly whooped with joy when she got her right hand free. The sound of footsteps coming near made her hands, which were already slow from the drugs that had not totally worn off yet, unsteady and her pulse erratic. She fumbled to free her left hand, uncertain what horror Ellison might be bringing to her.

Once she was free, she bent to untie her ankles but only got one undone before the door opened. She shot upright and pulled her hands behind her back as Nathan stepped into the room with Ellison behind him. For a moment, her mind fumbled to understand why Nathan wasn't fighting his cousin, but when Ellison moved forward and stood beside Nathan she saw the pistol that he pointed at her husband.

Ellison directed Nathan to the chair directly in front of the one to which she had been tied. "Sit there, Scarsdale. That way you will be nice and close when I slit your wife's throat."

Nathan didn't move.

Sophia feared he would snap and get himself killed trying to save her. "Don't worry, darling," she murmured, her words slurred from the lingering effects of the drugs. "Remember how I saved you before? You'll find a way to save me. Won't you?" She slid her gaze to his ankle, then back up to his face. Their eyes locked, and understanding that only came with hope and faith passed between them.

"Yes," he said. "I'll find a way, if you'll help me?"

She nodded and glanced purposely behind her and down toward her hands, as Ellison shouted, "Silence!"

Nathan was quiet. She saw his muscles flex, and when he gave her a sharp nod, she pushed up with her one free foot and launched forward to crash into Ellison. He cried out as she snaked her hand around his ankle, and in a blur, Nathan had Ellison on his back, very near Sophia's face, with his boot planted on Ellison's chest. Nathan gripped his dagger in one hand and Ellison's pistol in the other.

"Do you prefer to die by pistol or knife?" Nathan asked in a lethal voice.

Sophia quickly untied her other foot and stood. She stepped beside Nathan and placed her hand on his arm. He flinched at her touch, and then she could feel the muscles in his arm relax. She willed him to listen as she spoke. "You're not a killer, Nathan. Let others dole out the justice, and let's you and I get on with our lives. There is so much hope and promise in our future, darling."

After a moment, he nodded. She sighed with relief as he sheathed his knife without taking his gaze—or the pistol—off Ellison, who stared back in stony silence.

Nathan took her hand with his now-free one and gave it a gentle squeeze "Are you all right?"

"Yes," she whispered hoarsely, raising Nathan's hand to her lips. "As long as I have you, I'm perfect."

Epilogue

Two Months Later
St. Ives

Sophia stood hand in hand with Nathan in the warm air, made all the warmer by the bonfire that Nathan had built. It roared in the pit before them, and she didn't speak because he didn't. She was certain that when he was ready to talk, he would. Her cheeks burned from the heat, but she didn't want to look away. As the bright-orange flames engulfed yet another one of the portraits of Nathan that Sophia had helped him drag from the attic, the death grip Nathan had on her hand loosened a bit more. She smiled inwardly. With each painting that burned, Nathan's torturous past was destroyed a bit more. His aunt and cousin were gone, cut-off and sent to make their own way in America, and life was finally settling into peacefulness.

They stood for hours, Nathan's arm slung over her shoulder, as the sky turned from twilight to full dark. The fire and stars illuminated the night around them, and a cool breeze finally blew. Wood popped and crackled as the last of the portraits disappeared into the flames, and a log shifted sending sparks dancing into the air.

Nathan turned to her and cupped her face. "It's done."

She nodded.

He traced his thumb over her upper and then lower lip, and he smiled. "That was my past."

"Yes, it was," she agreed, her heart singing with joy.

The fire danced in his dark eyes as his gaze held hers. He

leaned down and brushed his lips against her mouth, and the touch of her husband's kiss sent goose flesh racing across her skin as it always did. He intertwined their fingers and brought her hand to his heart, where he pressed their palms, as one, against his beating chest. "You are my future. Together, we will make a family that will be filled with love."

She smiled slowly, gripped his other hand with hers, and laid it against her stomach. "We've already made a family, my darling. And it will most certainly be filled with love."

Dear Readers,
I hope you enjoyed this book. I invite you to try the first chapter of My Enchanting Hoyden, A Once Upon a Rogue, Book 3.

Prologue

The Year of Our Lord 1820
New York, United States of America

*M*iss Jemma Adair could count the number of things she regretted on one hand. Of course, if she counted the things she knew she *ought* to regret but simply did not, she'd likely have to use two hands, but before today, she'd managed to stick to just the one. Yet now, as she leaned against the counter—upon which sat the containers she was *supposed* to be filling with her mother's freshly baked lemon tarts—her stomach roiled, filling her with unease. Giving her innocence to Will three nights prior may have been the thing to make her list of regrets overflow from one hand to two.

She stared at the large wooden door that led from the street into their family bakery and imagined Will breezing through the threshold with his rich-chocolate hair and coffee-colored eyes, as he'd done for the seven years he'd worked here. He'd taken a better job several years ago so he could afford to attend law school, but from his very first day at the bakery, he had always stopped at the counter, set down his delivery sack—empty after transporting orders—and popped a tart into his mouth as he winked and complimented first her sister, Anne, and then her.

Any boy kind enough to pay Anne such positive notice—

she'd been born with a lame leg and was usually teased rather mercilessly—was a boy worthy of Jemma's admiration. At the age of eleven, she'd given that admiration to him without pause. Then, at the age of twelve, when he'd knocked out Stephen Smith's tooth after he'd criticized Anne, Jemma had given her heart to him, as well.

She poked a finger into one of the lemon tarts and sucked off the bitter jam as she wished for the jingle of the bell to announce Will. Even though he'd not worked here in a while, he'd not failed to come by every day before the bakery opened. Her stomach clenched. Except he had not come by in the last three days, not since—

The bell clanged, causing her to jerk and bump one of the tart-filled trays with her elbow. She grabbed it when it began to slide and set it to rights as her heart raced ahead in hope, even as her mind registered the fact that the door hadn't moved the smallest iota. Understanding and disappointment filled her as she turned and glared, first at the bell above the door that led from the kitchen into the main bakery, and then again at her mother when she glided through the doorway.

Her brown hair had escaped her loose bun and a smear of flour covered her right cheek. She huffed as she balanced a tray filled with a combination of berry and lemon tarts. Jemma's stomach growled, and she scrambled toward the door to help her mother with the heavy-laden tray. When she reached her mother, Anne struggled through the same doorway holding a tray fairly bursting with trifles. She tripped with a gasp, and the tray dipped sharply to the left. Jemma lunged forward and caught the tray just as two chocolate trifles slid to the ground and plopped onto her only pair of decent slippers. She frowned down at the dark lump on her pale shoes, the mess very fitting for her mood.

Without a word, she took the tray from her sister, who was grimacing and tilting to the right, favoring her good leg. "Did you hurt yourself?" Jemma asked.

Anne shook her head, her lovely blond curls swinging as she did. Jemma eyed those curls, wondering, as she often did, how they could be twins when they looked absolutely nothing alike. Jemma had flaming-red hair with too-tight curls and eyes neither green nor blue but oddly both. Anne, however, was a classic beauty with lovely blond hair and clear blue eyes.

Their mother slammed her tray on the counter, making Jemma jump. "Honestly, Jemma. You've been moping around the bakery for three solid days, not even doing your job. Don't think I haven't noticed your sister covering for you. But it stops now. Anne cannot carry these heavy trays, and you know it as well as I do."

Anne huffed and opened her mouth to protest, but Mother's quelling look silenced whatever she had been about to say. Jemma tensed when her mother's gaze locked on her. "I could not help but notice that William hasn't been around to the bakery in those three days. Did you two have an argument?"

"No," Jemma said slowly, a mental picture of Will's naked body filling her mind and heating her cheeks with embarrassment. Not shame. Never that. Despite the fact that she hadn't meant to give Will her innocence… Frankly, when her heart had quit pounding, her ears had stopped roaring, and her body had cooled off, she could scarcely believe what she had done. But it was done. Besides, she loved Will, and she was sure he loved her in return. He had told her that he would be very busy with his studies for the next few days, after all. She was being silly. Selfish, really. They were going to be married just as soon as he had enough money saved to move out of the room he rented and purchase a home for the two of them.

She squared her shoulders and shoved back the doubt that had been plaguing her since she'd succumbed to her desire. "Will has exams and is studying."

Mother pressed her pale lips together for a moment, and Jemma prayed that would be the end of it. She knew how her mother felt about Will—all men really. Jemma did not need yet another reminder. Her mother turned as if to begin putting the tarts in the case, and Jemma exhaled with relief, but that relief was short-lived.

Mother swiveled back around and eyed her askance. "William always managed to come by during his exams before."

Leave it to her mother to point out the painfully obvious without blinking an eye. Fresh doubt battered Jemma's heart, but she refused to show it. "This is his last year, *you know that.* These exams are the hardest and the most important."

Her mother snorted. "That's not a good excuse. If you ask me—"

"I didn't," Jemma reminded her.

Her mother shot her a glare. "Don't be disrespectful. You don't know everything at eighteen. And you know I understand a great deal about *gentlemen.*" Her mother said the word with exaggerated derisiveness, as usual.

"Mother," Anne said in a tiny, hesitant voice. Jemma gave her twin a grateful look, but one quick reproachful glare from Mother and Anne fell to silence once again, dashing Jemma's hope of being rescued. Really, she couldn't believe they were twins. Yes, they were born on the same day—two minutes apart with Jemma coming first—but they may as well have been born in different time periods for what they shared in personality, as well as looks. Anne was obedient and sweet, and Jemma... Well, she did *try* to be obedient, but it was very, very hard when she felt she was in the right.

"I warned you," Mother continued, as if Anne hadn't interrupted her, as if she hadn't said these exact same words hundreds of times before. "I warned you that men are deceitful, self-serving rakes. You're better off possessing a bakery as I do than trying to possess a man's heart."

Jemma felt as if there were a tight band inside her, stretching and stretching. She curled her hands into fists and fought against speaking her mind. It wouldn't do. It really wouldn't. But that band stretched further and snapped, and really, she simply could not help herself. She had to defend Will.

"Will is not Father. He will not abandon me as Father did you. Will does not want me for my money." She slashed a hand through the air. "We have none! We barely get by! Will wants me for me."

Out of the corner of her eye, Jemma saw Anne frantically

shaking her head for Jemma to stop talking, but Jemma's blood roared in her ears. She'd endured her mother's tirades about men for years. Now, when she needed a kind word, she had to tolerate more hatred. A voice in her head reminded her that her mother didn't know Jemma needed comfort and reassurance, and some of her mounting anger slipped away.

"Mother," she started, prepared to simply apologize so they wouldn't argue.

"He may not want you for money as your father wanted me and abandon you when you're with child and he realizes no money is coming, but mark my words—" Mother huffed "—he will break your heart in his own special way. All men do."

"Will is not like Father," Jemma said, finding a calm, firm voice, though a tempest swirled inside her. "He will never abandon me."

"I hope not," her mother said so quietly and in such a small voice that Jemma knew she'd hurt her mother's feelings.

Shame washed over her in unbearable waves. "Mother, I'm sorry."

Her mother shook her head. "Just don't go losing your senses until you're good and properly married."

Jemma's stomach knotted, uncoiled, and plummeted to the ground. It was too late for that warning. She'd lost every ounce of sense she'd possessed when in Will's arms three nights ago. Staring at her mother, she longed to confide her fears, but Mother's heart was so hardened to men that Jemma feared she'd immediately march to Will's lodgings and demand a marriage take place posthaste. That wouldn't do. Will was going to marry her, but she certainly preferred to know it was his choice and not something he did by guilt or force. Besides that, as Jemma stared at her mother she noticed dark smudges under her eyes and that Mother's skin looked almost sallow.

"Mother, do you feel all right?"

Her mother nodded, even as her hand strayed to her chest and rubbed it. "Just an ache here. But that's nothing new," she said in a hard voice.

The bell at the front door jingled and all three of them jumped at once. It wasn't quite time for the bakery to be open, so that had to mean...

"Will!" Jemma exclaimed, rushing past her mother and Anne, and stopping just short of flinging herself into his arms. He had on tan breeches, a dark coat, and a crisp white shirt with a light-blue cravat he'd recently taken to wearing. She eyed the cravat, still feeling as if he'd not been truthful about his parents purchasing it for him, but she shooed the doubt away, knowing it was surely her own insecurity making her feel thusly.

"Where have you been?" she blurted, then bit down on her traitorous tongue. Hadn't she told herself repeatedly that when he finally came around she would act wholly unbothered by the fact that he'd not come by in three days.

So much for that plan.

When he didn't answer, she stepped toward him and gazed into his eyes. "Were exams that difficult?"

He opened and shut his mouth, while his face turned a deep-crimson color. Pity filled her and determination to make him feel better drove her forward to grasp his arm. "Oh, Will, don't worry. We'll think of something. Could you take the exams again?"

He shook his head, still not speaking.

Jemma squeezed his arm. "That's all right."

"I passed with top honors," he blurted, a bead of sweat dripping down his face.

Jemma wrinkled her brow. He seemed very nervous for someone who'd passed with honors. "Then what is it? I don't understand."

Will's gaze darted from her, to her mother, to Anne, and back to Jemma. "Might I speak with you in private?"

The bell chimed again, and Jemma glanced at the longcase clock, then stifled the curse on the tip of her tongue. Eight o'clock. The bakery was open and the first customers had arrived, and by the looks of them, they would not be patient. Wealthy people so rarely were. Jemma would bet her left arm that this young lady and her companion—no, actually, likely her father by the similar eyes and mouth—were grossly rich. The girl was beautiful with her china doll skin and large blue eyes, but she was made even more so dressed as she was in an exquisite emerald-green gown. Her father had peppered hair, covered partially by a shiny top hat, and he wore an overcoat made in a deep, rich burgundy with large, gleaming stones set into the sleeves.

They strolled through the door, and Jemma pasted on a smile as her mother and Anne, both a heated mess from baking in the kitchen, scurried away to tidy themselves. She turned to greet the customers when Will jerked her back around to face him. "Jemma, I must tell you—"

"William," the girl said in a sweetly chiding voice that made Jemma's stomach flop. "You said five minutes. Father timed it, and we've been waiting five minutes and twenty seconds. Haven't we, Father?"

The man gave a curt nod. "The ship is waiting," he said, flicking a dull gaze over Jemma. His eyes widened for a moment before he locked his gaze on Will. "The ship leaves for London within the hour. We must depart now."

"Two minutes," Will said firmly.

Jemma's mind froze on the word *we*. *We*. As in *Will*, or as in the two strangers? She rubbed her suddenly sweaty palms against her cotton skirts and swallowed. "Will?" She cringed at the shaky sound of her own voice.

"Really, William," the woman snapped. "Tell your cousin good-bye. We must leave."

Will nodded. Jemma blinked, but her eyelids felt heavy as stones. *Cousin?* The word rippled across her mind, slow and languid, like the undulation of the water when she swirled her toes in it. *Cousin.*

She snapped her eyebrows together. "I'm not—"

"Two minutes," Will repeated, interrupting her and stepping in front of her so her view of the strangers was blocked.

"No more than that," the woman replied. "We don't want to miss boarding." With that statement, she swiveled away, and within seconds the bell chimed once more, leaving only silence and Jemma's screeching mind. She eyed the door to the kitchens, certain any minute her mother would burst through it.

Her mind whirred, uncertain what to ask and afraid to ask anything at the same time. Yet she had to say something. Ask something. "Who was that?"

Will shuffled his feet. "Lady Jane."

"*Who* is Lady Jane?"

Will tugged on his cravat, and something clicked in her mind. It was a dreadful something that made her skin prickle. "Did Lady Jane give you that cravat you've been wearing?"

He let out a long, rattling sigh and then nodded. The prickling sensation spread over her entire body and became more pronounced, like tiny beestings. She licked her lips and tried to order her thoughts, but they spun and spun until she felt slightly dizzy. "How do you—"

Will grabbed Jemma's arm. She would have jerked away, but she thought she might just topple right over if he released her.

"I never meant to hurt you," she thought he said, but his voice sounded as if it came from down a long tunnel.

"Hurt me?"

"She has a cousin from America in school with me, and well, I've known Lady Jane for quite some time, but I never thought—She's an heiress to a shipping empire. She lives in London and only visits twice a year. I never imagined she'd want *me*, not even a lawyer yet."

Jemma spoke, though her tongue didn't want to form the words. "Want you?" Of course, she'd want him. He was intelligent, handsome, and wanted to change the world for the better. *And* he was a liar. From somewhere within, Jemma managed to yank her arm out of his hold and remain standing. The victory was small and pathetic, but she clung to it. "Who is she to you?" Jemma demanded, her voice now coming out loud and strong.

He blew out a breath, his cheeks puffing and then deflating. Her heart deflated right along with them. "She's going to be my wife. We're to be married. That is—What I'm trying to tell you is—"

"I know what you're trying to tell me!" she bit out, the sting of her nails as they curled into her palms making her wince. "I'm not an imbecile, just a blind fool."

He moved as if to touch her, and she jerked back, her skin rippling with revulsion. "I gave you my love," she whispered, feeling broken. "I gave you my *innocence*." As she said it, a horrified thought stuck her. Marriage was lost to her forever; no man would want a wife who wasn't innocent. She clenched her teeth. She didn't care. She never wanted to be in love again, so there was absolutely no point in marrying. Dear God! Mother had warned her repeatedly never to give a man her trust, yet she'd not listened. "How long have you known you would be marrying her?" The bitter words stung as they left her mouth.

He shifted from foot to foot again, and though she didn't think it was possible to feel worse, with each dart of his gaze, her humiliation deepened until her body was burning with regret.

"Two weeks," he finally said.

"Two weeks?" She could hardly believe her ears. Anger and mortification warred within, anger winning the battle. She shook her fists in his face. "You are a disgusting pig," she snapped. "We were *together* three nights ago." Her heart hammered so that her chest ached with the force.

"I came to tell you everything and say good-bye."

"*Everything?* There's more? What more could there be?"

He jerked his hands through his hair. "She's with child, Jemma."

Jemma's mind flashed back to the night they'd been together and he'd used what he'd called *protective measures*. Dear heaven! Had he used them with this Lady Jane and she'd gotten with child?

"Did you—" She gulped, not believing she needed to ask this. "Did you use—"

"No," he interrupted, shaking his head. "I didn't know of the measures one could use then."

"Well"—her voice cracked and she willed herself to be strong—"I suppose you've learned more than the law in school," she said dryly.

Will's shoulders slumped forward. "Jemma, I'm sorry."

"You are *that*," she agreed, feeling nauseated.

"I did love you. I still—"

By all that was holy, she couldn't take anymore. "Get out!" she demanded. "Get on the ship for England, and good riddance to you."

"Jemma, please forgive me."

"Forgive you?" Blood pumped through her veins like a raging river. Forgive him? She looked wildly around the room and picked up the only thing near her that she could use to harm him. Waving the half-empty tray of lemon tarts at him, she screamed, "Go now! Go or I'll bash you over the head with this tray and you can leave for the ship with a split head and covered in jam filling."

When he stood there gawking at her, she snapped. She hurled the tray at his head, and he deflected it with his arm. Tarts flew through the air as the tray went crashing to the ground with a loud rattle. Dual bells jingled, at once announcing someone entering the shop and either her mother or Anne coming out from the kitchens. Jemma expected to see Lady Jane appear in the door, but two men dressed in dark suits stepped into the bakery. A gasp came from behind her, and she whirled around to see her mother, white-faced, staring with huge eyes at the men. What little blood was in her mother's face drained away, leaving even her lips blanched.

Jemma shoved at Will's back. "Go, you cad," she whispered fiercely.

Will stepped around the men and departed out the door, and Jemma didn't even have time to spare a thought for her broken heart. The taller of the two men handed her mother a piece of paper. "Payment for the loan wasn't received, so I believe you know what that means."

Jemma could see the paper her mother now held, trembling in her hands. Her mother licked her colorless lips and nodded. "Yes. Please go."

The man gave a curt nod. "You've two months to either pay the loan in full or leave the premises. The bank will repossess the property in exactly sixty days."

"I understand," Mother said in a shaky tone.

Jemma's mind whirled with disbelief as the men departed. She stared at her mother, who was rubbing her arm and then her chest, clearly unsure what to say. Jemma swallowed and voiced one of her suddenly numerous fears. "Will we lose the bakery? Our home?"

Her mother forced a smile. "Don't be silly. I'll simply swallow my pride and write to my father. He *owes* me. After all these years, it's time he paid the debt of driving your father away from me." Her mother shuffled over to the tray Jemma had thrown at Will's head, and as she bent down to grasp it, she let out a muffled cry and crumpled to the ground. Jemma raced to her mother's side and turned her over.

A short gasp came from her as she clawed at her neck. "Can't breathe," she choked out.

Jemma's skin tingled and her muscles tensed as she yelled out for Anne while pulling her mother's head into her lap. She glanced wildly around the room. "Anne!" she shrieked again as Mother's eyes rolled back in her head and her mouth fell open.

Anne came through the door singing a song. She stopped mid-tune and screamed before staggering over to Jemma and Mother. "What's happened?"

"I don't know! One moment she was standing and the next—Never mind! Take her head while I run to fetch the physician." Anne nodded as Jemma slid herself out from under her mother, whose eyes had shut. Anne took Mother's head in her lap and started speaking to her immediately. The last thing Jemma saw as she raced out the door was her mother's hand lying unmoving against the ground.

Jemma raced down the block to the physician's office and found him with a patient. It took what surely must have been only a second, but seemed forever, for him to gather his bag, and the two of them set off running back down the block to the bakery.

She burst through the door with the physician on her heels and dropped to her knees. She took her mother's slack hand in hers and patted Anne, who was crying incoherently. The physician barked an order for them both to move, and Jemma had to physically drag Anne away. They hovered above him as he worked for a few minutes. All sound around Jemma faded, save the physician's sighs and muttering.

The smell of lemon tarts swirled around her and made her stomach roil. Sweat dampened her brow, her hands, and under her arms, and the cotton of her gown clung to her, making her horridly hot. Then, suddenly, she shivered with cold.

The physician sat up and turned to look at them. His eyes held Jemma's for a moment as he shook his head. "She's gone."

Sound crashed in, the loudest tick of the longcase clock. Her thoughts scrambled in her head as her mind raced to latch on to one. With a sharp intake of breath, she repeated what the physician had said. "She's gone?"

He nodded as he stood, walked to the door, turned the lock, and then moved to the windows to pull the curtains closed. Anne's sobs once again invaded Jemma's awareness. For one brief, selfish second Jemma wanted to scream for Anne to stop it. Instead, she inhaled a deep breath and wrapped her arms around her sister. In shock, she clung to her, hardly able to believe Mother was gone. Memories of her mother flashed before her eyes and the pain twisted through her. She wanted to shut it all out, but she couldn't. The bakery and their home would be gone, too, if Jemma didn't take immediate action in her mother's stead. Someone had to take care of them. Someone had to shelve her grief until the dark hours of the night. Jemma glanced at her sister. Mother had always taken special care of fragile Anne, and now it was up to Jemma.

She moved through the rest of the day in a numb haze,

alternately soothing Anne and making burial arrangements. Very late that night, as Anne slept fitfully, whimpering in her bed, Jemma, with bleary eyes and a pounding head, forced her shaking hand to foolscap and wrote her first letter ever to her grandfather, the cold Duke of Rowan. Would he even read it? She worried her lip. Had the years softened his heart and made him regret disowning Mother after she had disobeyed him and married Father? She cried silent tears as she told her grandfather of Mother's sudden death and the impending foreclosure on the bakery that was also their home, and finally asked him if he would send enough money to pay off the loan for the bakery. She knew, from Mother's talk of his wealth, that it wouldn't even nick his vast fortune to send that amount.

Jemma's eyes burned and blurred as she sealed the letter. When she was finished, she laid her head on her mother's desk and sobbed as quietly as possible so as not to wake Anne. She wanted her mother back. She wanted to apologize for acting as if Mother knew nothing. She wanted to take back every snide comment she'd ever made. Jemma rocked back and forth in her chair. Mother was gone. Gone.

She wanted more than anything to tell her she was sorry and that Mother had been perfectly correct. Now she would never get the chance. She would gladly sit for hours listening to her mother rant about how men were *not* to be trusted, how they were callous and careless with the hearts they captured, how they would bruise, batter, and destroy the delicate organs, if only she could have her mother back. At this moment, it hurt far greater that her mother was gone than the fact that her mother had been right about men all along.

She wanted to apologize for scoffing at her mother, for arguing with her, and for making her life more worrisome. Perhaps it was the worry from the bank loan that had made Mother sick, or perhaps it was Jemma's constant squabbling with her that had made her unwell. Jemma's heart twisted as hot tears coursed down her cheeks and wet her hands. Before she fell asleep, she said another prayer to God that he would instill forgiveness and generosity into her grandfather's heart.

He was all they had now.

Time had a way of flying by in a blur when one worked ceaselessly to run a bakery. One night, just as Jemma was heading to the door to lock it, the bell jingled and the door swung open. In marched a serious-faced gentleman with tan breeches, shining black boots, and a long overcoat of a dark, superfine material. He wore a cravat of rich red, tied expertly and touching his chin, and a hat that appeared to be lined with some sort of luxurious brown fur capped a full head of silver hair. The man was tall but not lanky. He was solidly built and carried himself with the pretentious air of a duke. She knew at once it was her grandfather, even before her gaze locked with his.

The shape and color of his eyes matched her mother's. A pang of sadness reverberated through Jemma, and she swallowed. Before she could properly introduce herself, a line of two men and a lady entered the bakery, filing in behind her grandfather in mute silence.

As she stared at them, it belatedly occurred to her that Grandfather had traveled across the ocean to meet them. Surely he was bringing good tidings and the money she needed to save the bakery! The burden of the last couple of months seemed to lift a little, and hope filled her. If he'd traveled all this way, he must care for them. She felt her cheeks pull into a smile.

"Are you the Duke of Rowan?" she asked, though she was fairly certain the answer was yes.

He nodded. Relief, weariness, and joy overcame her at once. She'd not held much hope he'd respond to her letter, let alone appear here as a caring grandfather would.

She rushed to him and hugged him, so very glad, for once in her life, to be wrong. "I'm your eldest granddaughter, Jemma."

She felt him stiffen underneath her touch as he extracted

himself from her arms, stepped back, and patted her awkwardly on the shoulder. "I'm very sorry about your mother. I'm not sure what she told you about me..."

Jemma couldn't stop herself from wincing, and his eyes immediately narrowed. "I see. I'm not surprised." He flicked a dismissive hand behind him. "This is my valet, footman, and your new tutor, Mrs. Young." His voice did not hold the warmth of a loving grandfather but the formalness of the man her mother had always described.

Jemma bit her lip as Mrs. Young curtsied, and Jemma simply gawked while everything her grandfather had just announced bounced around in her head.

"You must curtsy," the woman chided.

Jemma stared the woman down until the tutor blinked, then snorted in contempt. Mrs. Young clicked her tongue and moved to Jemma's grandfather's side. "This will take at least six months if the young ladies don't even know how to curtsy." The woman's voice was snide and her look condescending. Jemma knew very well how to curtsy, but something warned her to keep the information to herself for now.

Jemma's grandfather gave a brief nod of acknowledgment to the tutor before assessing Jemma. "You look healthy, Granddaughter."

Was that a compliment? It had the slightly warmer tone of one but was a rather pathetic attempt to start a conversation with a granddaughter he'd never met. "Thank you," she managed. "I don't understand why you brought a tutor, however. I don't need a tutor—only money."

Grandfather raised his silver eyebrows. "You are mistaken," he snapped. "If you are to secure a proper husband, you most definitely need a tutor."

"Marry? I don't want to marry!" She never wanted to give her heart to another man to destroy again. Never mind that she was no longer innocent.

"Don't be silly," he replied. "You are eighteen. You cannot possibly know what you want. You and your sister will return to England with me."

She clenched her teeth until her temples throbbed. When she released her jaw, she had to move it back and forth before speaking. "I don't wish to return to England with you, and I'm sure *my sister*, Anne, will not, either."

When her grandfather stared past her, Jemma knew Anne surely must have been standing there. She turned to confirm it. Anne was in the doorway, white-faced and with eyes open wide.

"Tell him, Anne," Jemma insisted. "Tell him you don't wish to go back to England any more than I do."

Anne's lips parted, and her forehead creased with a deep frown. She said nothing, but the silence was louder than a piercing scream. Anne wanted to go. She didn't trust that Jemma could take care of them. Jemma deflated. "Oh, Anne."

"I'm sorry!" she blurted.

Grandfather simply nodded. "At least one of you is sensible." He pointed at Jemma. "You need to come to your senses, as well. Whether you want to go to England or not, it's the only help I'm offering you. Without it, you'll be homeless. Is that what you want for your sister or yourself?"

The years clearly had not made Grandfather any less cold or controlling than Mother had described him. But what choice did Jemma have? She bit the inside of her cheek as she thought. She needed time, which was something she had none of currently. If she went to England, she could buy herself some time and formulate a plan for how to afford to buy another bakery and take care of herself and Anne, if Anne wished it.

"What will be required of me *if* I return to England with you?" Jemma was not quite ready to admit defeat to this man.

"That's simple. You shall do as I say or I vow you'll meet the same fate your mother did."

Jemma inhaled sharply. He was threatening to disown her if she disobeyed him as Mother had dared to do. Whatever hope she had briefly held of his loving them disappeared. She despised him, and she'd just met him. "Do you care to give me some insight as to what requirements you might have of Anne and me?" she asked through clenched teeth.

"I'm pleased to do so," he replied, motioning to Mrs. Young. "You will follow all Mrs. Young's instructions, as will your sister. Mrs. Young will ensure you're both proper ladies in six months' time." He paused and looked sideways at the tutor who nodded. "At the end of the six months, as the eldest, you will marry. I took the liberty of setting up a suitor for you."

You've done what? she wanted to shout. She clenched her teeth once again, until she felt she could speak without screaming. "How very kind of you." Now was not the moment to defy him with nothing to her name. That would come when she had saved enough money to go off on her own. But how did one save money when one didn't earn any?

"Think nothing of it," he said and actually smiled. "Lord Glenmore is my neighbor's son and heir. He will be a fine match for you."

She felt her nostrils flare. It was just as Mother had said. Grandfather had cared more about a man having wealth and a title than Mother having love, and now he was trying to do the same thing to Jemma. Would he disown her if she told him now that she wasn't an innocent so his plans to marry her off were futile? Her head throbbed with uncertainty. She couldn't chance how he might react when she had no one else to turn to and nowhere else to go.

"All you have to do is learn to be a proper English lady, and I feel positive Lord Glenmore will be pleased to take you as his wife. He's already agreed to court you. Six months should be plenty of time to learn the rules of etiquette so you'll not do anything to drive Lord Glenmore away."

Drive Lord Glenmore away! The words reverberated through her head, and a plan was born.

One

England, 1357

*F*aking her death would be simple. It was escaping her home that would be difficult. Marion de Lacy stared hard into the slowly darkening sky, thinking about the plan she intended to put into action tomorrow—if all went well—but growing uneasiness tightened her belly. From where she stood in the bailey, she counted the guards up in the tower. It was not her imagination: Father had tripled the knights keeping guard at all times, as if he was expecting trouble.

Taking a deep breath of the damp air, she pulled her mother's cloak tighter around her to ward off the twilight chill. A lump lodged in her throat as the wool scratched her neck. In the many years since her mother had been gone, Marion had both hated and loved this cloak for the death and life it represented. Her mother's freesia scent had long since faded from the garment, yet simply calling up a memory of her mother wearing it gave Marion comfort.

She rubbed her fingers against the rough material. When she fled, she couldn't chance taking anything with her but the clothes on her body and this cloak. Her death had to appear accidental, and the cloak that everyone knew she prized would ensure her freedom. Finding it tangled in the branches at the edge of the sea cliff ought to be just the thing to convince her father and William Froste that she'd drowned. After all, neither man thought she could swim. They didn't truly care about her anyway. Her marriage to the blackhearted knight was only about what her hand could give the two men. Her father, Baron de Lacy, wanted more power, and Froste wanted her family's prized land. A match made in Heaven, if only the match didn't involve her...but it did.

Father would set the hounds of Hell themselves to track her down if he had the slightest suspicion that she was still alive. She was an inestimable possession to be given to secure Froste's unwavering allegiance and, therefore, that of the renowned ferocious knights who served him. Whatever small sliver of hope she had that her father would grant her mercy and not marry her to Froste had been destroyed by the lashing she'd received when she'd pleaded for him to do so.

The moon crested above the watchtower, reminding her why she was out here so close to mealtime: to meet Angus. The Scotsman may have been her father's stable master, but he was *her* ally, and when he'd proposed she flee England for Scotland, she'd readily consented.

Marion looked to the west, the direction from which Angus would return from Newcastle. He should be back any minute now from meeting his cousin and clansman Neil, who was to escort her to Scotland. She prayed all was set and that Angus's kin was ready to depart. With her wedding to Froste to take place in six days, she wanted to be far away before there was even the slightest chance he'd be making his way here. And since he was set to arrive the night before the wedding, leaving tomorrow promised she'd not encounter him.

A sense of urgency enveloped her, and Marion forced herself to stroll across the bailey toward the gatehouse that led to the tunnel preceding the drawbridge. She couldn't risk raising suspicion from the tower guards. At the gatehouse, she nodded to Albert, one of the knights who operated the drawbridge mechanism. He was young and rarely questioned her excursions to pick flowers or find herbs.

"Off to get some medicine?" he inquired.

"Yes," she lied with a smile and a little pang of guilt. But this was survival, she reminded herself as she entered the tunnel. When she exited the heavy wooden door that led to freedom, she wasn't surprised to find Peter and Andrew not yet up in the twin towers that flanked the entrance to the drawbridge. It was, after all, time for the changing of the guard.

They smiled at her as they put on their helmets and demi-gauntlets. They were an imposing presence to any who crossed the drawbridge and dared to approach the castle gate. Both men were tall and looked particularly daunting in their full armor, which Father insisted upon at all times. The men were certainly a fortress in their own right.

She nodded to them. "I'll not be long. I want to gather some more flowers for the supper table." Her voice didn't even wobble with the lie.

Peter grinned at her, his kind brown eyes crinkling at the edges. "Will you pick me one of those pale winter flowers for my wife again, Marion?"

She returned his smile. "It took away her anger as I said it would, didn't it?"

"It did," he replied. "You always know just how to help with her."

"I'll get a pink one if I can find it. The colors are becoming scarcer as the weather cools."

Andrew, the younger of the two knights, smiled, display-ing a set of straight teeth. He held up his covered arm. "My cut is almost healed."

Marion nodded. "I told you! Now maybe you'll listen to me sooner next time you're wounded in training."

He gave a soft laugh. "I will. Should I put more of your paste on tonight?"

"Yes, keep using it. I'll have to gather some more yarrow, if I can find any, and mix up another batch of the medicine for you." And she'd have to do it before she escaped. "I better get going if I'm going to find those things." She knew she should not have agreed to search for the flowers and offered to find the yarrow when she still had to speak to Angus and return to the castle in time for supper, but both men had been kind to her when many had not. It was her way of thanking them.

After Peter lowered the bridge and opened the door, she departed the castle grounds, considering her plan once more. Had she forgotten anything? She didn't think so. She was simply going to walk straight out of her father's castle and never come back. Tomorrow, she'd announce she was going out to collect more winter blooms, and then, instead, she would go down to the edge of the cliff overlooking the sea. She would slip off her cloak and leave it for a search party to find. Her breath caught deep in her chest at the simple yet dangerous plot. The last detail to see to was Angus.

She stared down the long dirt path that led to the sea and stilled, listening for hoofbeats. A slight vibration of the ground tingled her feet, and her heart sped in hopeful anticipation that it was Angus coming down the dirt road on his horse. When the crafty stable master appeared with a grin spread across his face, the worry that was squeezing her heart loosened. For the first time since he had ridden out that morning, she took a proper breath. He stopped his stallion alongside her and dismounted.

She tilted her head back to look up at him as he towered over her. An errant thought struck. "Angus, are all Scots as tall as you?"

"Nay, but ye ken Scots are bigger than all the wee Englishmen." Suppressed laughter filled his deep voice. "So even the ones nae as tall as me are giants compared te the scrawny men here."

"You're teasing me," she replied, even as she arched her eyebrows in uncertainty.

"A wee bit," he agreed and tousled her hair. The laughter vanished from his eyes as he rubbed a hand over his square jaw and then stared down his bumpy nose at her, fixing what he called his "lecturing look" on her. "We've nae much time. Neil is in Newcastle just as he's supposed te be, but there's been a slight change."

She frowned. "For the last month, every time I wanted to

simply make haste and flee, you refused my suggestion, and now you say there's a slight change?"

His ruddy complexion darkened. She'd pricked that Mac-Leod temper her mother had always said Angus's clan was known for throughout the Isle of Skye, where they lived in the farthest reaches of Scotland. Marion could remember her mother chuckling and teasing Angus about how no one knew the MacLeod temperament better than their neighboring clan, the MacDonalds of Sleat, to which her mother had been born. The two clans had a history of feuding.

Angus cleared his throat and recaptured Marion's attention. Without warning, his hand closed over her shoulder, and he squeezed gently. "I'm sorry te say it so plain, but ye must die at once."

Her eyes widened as dread settled in the pit of her stomach. "What? Why?" The sudden fear she felt was unreasonable. She knew he didn't mean she was really going to die, but her palms were sweating and her lungs had tightened all the same. She sucked in air and wiped her damp hands down the length of her cotton skirts. Suddenly, the idea of going to a foreign land and living with her mother's clan, people she'd never met, made her apprehensive.

She didn't even know if the MacDonalds—her uncle, in particular, who was now the laird—would accept her or not. She was half-English, after all, and Angus had told her that when a Scot considered her English bloodline and the fact that she'd been raised there, they would most likely brand her fully English, which was not a good thing in a Scottish mind. And if her uncle was anything like her grandfather had been, the man was not going to be very reasonable. But she didn't have any other family to turn to who would dare defy her father, and Angus hadn't offered for her to go to his clan, so she'd not asked. He likely didn't want to bring trouble to his clan's doorstep, and she didn't blame him.

Panic bubbled inside her. She needed more time, even if it was only the day she'd thought she had, to gather her courage.

"Why must I flee tonight? I was to teach Eustice how to

dress a wound. She might serve as a maid, but then she will be able to help the knights when I'm gone. And her little brother, Bernard, needs a few more lessons before he's mastered writing his name and reading. And Eustice's youngest sister has begged me to speak to Father about allowing her to visit her mother next week."

"Ye kinnae watch out for everyone here anymore, Marion."

She placed her hand over his on her shoulder. "Neither can you."

Their gazes locked in understanding and disagreement.

He slipped his hand from her shoulder, and then crossed his arms over his chest in a gesture that screamed stubborn, unyielding protector. "If I leave at the same time ye feign yer death," he said, changing the subject, "it could stir yer father's suspicion and make him ask questions when none need te be asked. I'll be going home te Scotland soon after ye." Angus reached into a satchel attached to his horse and pulled out a dagger, which he slipped to her. "I had this made for ye."

Marion took the weapon and turned it over, her heart pounding. "It's beautiful." She held it by its black handle while withdrawing it from the sheath and examining it. "It's much sharper than the one I have."

"Aye," he said grimly. "It is. Dunnae forget that just because I taught ye te wield a dagger does nae mean ye can defend yerself from *all* harm. Listen te my cousin and do as he says. Follow his lead."

She gave a tight nod. "I will. But why must I leave now and not tomorrow?"

Concern filled Angus's eyes. "Because I ran into Froste's brother in town and he told me that Froste sent word that he would be arriving in two days."

Marion gasped. "That's earlier than expected."

"Aye," Angus said and took her arm with gentle authority. "So ye must go now. I'd rather be trying te trick only yer father than yer father, Froste, and his savage knights. I want ye long gone and yer death accepted when Froste arrives."

She shivered as her mind began to race with all that could go wrong.

"I see the worry darkening yer green eyes," Angus said, interrupting her thoughts. He whipped off his hat and his hair, still shockingly red in spite of his years, fell down around his shoulders. He only ever wore it that way when he was riding. He said the wind in his hair reminded him of riding his own horse when he was in Scotland. "I was going to talk to ye tonight, but now that I kinnae..." He shifted from foot to foot, as if uncomfortable. "I want te offer ye something. I'd have proposed it sooner, but I did nae want ye te feel ye had te take my offer so as nae te hurt me, but I kinnae hold my tongue, even so."

She furrowed her brow. "What is it?"

"I'd be proud if ye wanted te stay with the MacLeod clan instead of going te the MacDonalds. Then ye'd nae have te leave everyone ye ken behind. Ye'd have me."

A surge of relief filled her. She threw her arms around Angus, and he returned her hug quick and hard before setting her away. Her eyes misted at once. "I had hoped you would ask me," she admitted.

For a moment, he looked astonished, but then he spoke. "Yer mother risked her life te come into MacLeod territory at a time when we were fighting terrible with the MacDonalds, as ye well ken."

Marion nodded. She knew the story of how Angus had ended up here. He'd told her many times. Her mother had been somewhat of a renowned healer from a young age, and when Angus's wife had a hard birthing, her mother had gone to help. The knowledge that his wife and child had died anyway still made Marion want to cry.

"I pledged my life te keep yer mother safe for the kindness she'd done me, which brought me here, but, lass, long ago ye became like a daughter te me, and I pledge the rest of my miserable life te defending ye."

She gripped Angus's hand. "I wish you were my father."

He gave her a proud yet smug look, one she was used to

seeing. She chortled to herself. The man did have a terrible streak of pride. She'd have to give Father John another coin for penance for Angus, since the Scot refused to take up the custom himself.

Angus hooked his thumb in his gray tunic. "Ye'll make a fine MacLeod because ye already ken we're the best clan in Scotland."

Mentally, she added another coin to her dues. "Do you think they'll let me become a MacLeod, though, since my mother was the daughter of the previous MacDonald laird and I've an English father?"

"They will," he answered without hesitation, but she heard the slight catch in his voice.

"Angus." She narrowed her eyes. "You said you would never lie to me."

His brows dipped together, and he gave her a long, disgruntled look. "They may be a bit wary," he finally admitted. "But I'll nae let them turn ye away. Dunnae worry," he finished, his Scottish brogue becoming thick with emotion.

She bit her lip. "Yes, but you won't be with me when I first get there. What should I do to make certain that they will let me stay?"

He quirked his mouth as he considered her question. "Ye must first get the laird te like ye. Tell Neil te take ye directly te the MacLeod te get his consent for ye te live there. I kinnae vouch for the man myself as I've never met him, but Neil says he's verra honorable, fierce in battle, patient, and reasonable." Angus cocked his head as if in thought. "Now that I think about it, I'm sure the MacLeod can get ye a husband, and then the clan will more readily accept ye. Aye." He nodded. "Get in the laird's good graces as soon as ye meet him and ask him te find ye a husband." A scowl twisted his lips. "Preferably one who will accept yer acting like a man sometimes."

She frowned at him. "*You* are the one who taught me how to ride bareback, wield a dagger, and shoot an arrow true."

"Aye." He nodded. "I did. But when I started teaching ye, I thought yer mama would be around te add her woman's touch. I did nae ken at the time that she'd pass when ye'd only seen eight summers in yer life."

"You're lying again," Marion said. "You continued those lessons long after Mama's death. You weren't a bit worried how I'd turn out."

"I sure was!" he objected, even as a guilty look crossed his face. "But what could I do? Ye insisted on hunting for the widows so they'd have food in the winter, and ye insisted on going out in the dark te help injured knights when I could nae go with ye. I had te teach ye te hunt and defend yerself. Plus, you were a sad, lonely thing, and I could nae verra well overlook ye when ye came te the stables and asked me te teach ye things."

"Oh, you could have," she replied. "Father overlooked me all the time, but your heart is too big to treat someone like that." She patted him on the chest. "I think you taught me the best things in the world, and it seems to me any man would want his woman to be able to defend herself."

"Shows how much ye ken about men," Angus muttered with a shake of his head. "Men like te think a woman needs *them*."

"I dunnae need a man," she said in her best Scottish accent.

He threw up his hands. "Ye do. Ye're just afeared."

The fear was true enough. Part of her longed for love, to feel as if she belonged to a family. For so long she'd wanted those things from her father, but she had never gotten them, no matter what she did. It was difficult to believe it would be any different in the future. She'd rather not be disappointed.

Angus tilted his head, looking at her uncertainly. "Ye want a wee bairn some day, dunnae ye?"

"Well, yes," she admitted and peered down at the ground, feeling foolish.

"Then ye need a man," he crowed.

She drew her gaze up to his. "Not just any man. I want a man who will truly love me."

He waved a hand dismissively. Marriages of convenience

were a part of life, she knew, but she would not marry unless she was in love and her potential husband loved her in return. She would support herself if she needed to.

"The other big problem with a husband for ye," he continued, purposely avoiding, she suspected, her mention of the word *love*, "as I see it, is yer tender heart."

"What's wrong with a tender heart?" She raised her brow in question.

"'Tis more likely te get broken, aye?" His response was matter-of-fact.

"Nay. 'Tis more likely to have compassion," she replied with a grin.

"We're both right," he announced. "Yer mama had a tender heart like ye. 'Tis why yer father's black heart hurt her so. I dunnae care te watch the light dim in ye as it did yer mother."

"I don't wish for that fate, either," she replied, trying hard not to think about how sad and distant her mother had often seemed. "Which is why I will only marry for love. And why I need to get out of England."

"I ken that, lass, truly I do, but ye kinnae go through life alone."

"I don't wish to," she defended. "But if I have to, I have you, so I'll not be alone." With a shudder, her heart denied the possibility that she may never find love, but she squared her shoulders.

"'Tis nae the same as a husband," he said. "I'm old. Ye need a younger man who has the power te defend ye. And if Sir Frosty Pants ever comes after ye, you're going te need a strong man te go against him."

Marion snorted to cover the worry that was creeping in.

Angus moved his mouth to speak, but his reply was drowned by the sound of the supper horn blowing. "God's bones!" Angus muttered when the sound died. "I've flapped my jaw too long. Ye must go now. I'll head te the stables and start the fire as we intended. It'll draw Andrew and Peter away if they are watching ye too closely."

Marion looked over her shoulder at the knights, her stomach turning. She had known the plan since the day they had formed it, but now the reality of it scared her into a cold sweat. She turned back to Angus and gripped her dagger hard. "I'm afraid."

Determination filled his expression, as if his will for her to stay out of harm would make it so. "Ye will stay safe," he commanded. "Make yer way through the path in the woods that I showed ye, straight te Newcastle. I left ye a bag of coins under the first tree ye come te, the one with the rope tied te it. Neil will be waiting for ye by Pilgrim Gate on Pilgrim Street. The two of ye will depart from there."

She worried her lip but nodded all the same.

"Neil has become friends with a friar who can get the two of ye out," Angus went on. "Dunnae talk te anyone, especially any men. Ye should go unnoticed, as ye've never been there and won't likely see anyone ye've ever come in contact with here."

Fear tightened her lungs, but she swallowed. "I didn't even bid anyone farewell." Not that she really could have, nor did she think anyone would miss her other than Angus, and she would be seeing him again. Peter and Andrew *had* been kind to her, but they were her father's men, and she knew it well. She had been taken to the dungeon by the knights several times for punishment for transgressions that ranged from her tone not pleasing her father to his thinking she gave him a disrespectful look. Other times, they'd carried out the duty of tying her to the post for a thrashing when she'd angered her father. They had begged her forgiveness profusely but done their duties all the same. They would likely be somewhat glad they did not have to contend with such things anymore.

Eustice was both kind *and* thankful for Marion teaching her brother how to read, but Eustice lost all color any time someone mentioned the maid going with Marion to Froste's home after Marion was married. She suspected the woman was afraid to go to the home of the infamous "Merciless Knight." Eustice would likely be relieved when Marion disappeared. Not that Marion blamed her.

A small lump lodged in her throat. Would her father even mourn her loss? It wasn't likely, and her stomach knotted at the thought.

"You'll come as soon as you can?" she asked Angus.

"Aye. Dunnae fash yerself."

She forced a smile. "You are already sounding like you're back in Scotland. Don't forget to curb that when speaking with Father."

"I'll remember. Now, make haste te the cliff te leave yer cloak, then head straight for Newcastle."

"I don't want to leave you," she said, ashamed at the sudden rise of cowardliness in her chest and at the way her eyes stung with unshed tears.

"Gather yer courage, lass. I'll be seeing ye soon, and Neil will keep ye safe."

She sniffed. "I'll do the same for Neil."

"I've nay doubt ye'll try," Angus said, sounding proud and wary at the same time.

"I'm not afraid for myself," she told him in a shaky voice. "You're taking a great risk for me. How will I ever make it up to you?"

"Ye already have," Angus said hastily, glancing around and directing a worried look toward the drawbridge. "Ye want te live with my clan, which means I can go te my dying day treating ye as my daughter. Now, dunnae cry when I walk away. I ken how sorely ye'll miss me," he boasted with a wink. "I'll miss ye just as much."

With that, he swung up onto his mount. He had just given the signal for his beast to go when Marion realized she didn't know what Neil looked like.

"Angus!"

He pulled back on the reins and turned toward her. "Aye?"

"I need Neil's description."

Angus's eyes widened. "I'm getting old," he grumbled. "I dunnae believe I forgot such a detail. He's got hair redder than mine, and wears it tied back always. Oh, and he's missing his right ear, thanks te Froste. Took it when Neil came through these parts te see me last year."

"What?" She gaped at him. "You never told me that!"

"I did nae because I knew ye would try te go after Neil and patch him up, and that surely would have cost ye another beating if ye were caught." His gaze bore into her. "Ye're verra courageous. I reckon I had a hand in that 'cause I knew ye needed te be strong te withstand yer father. But dunnae be mindless. Courageous men and women who are mindless get killed. Ye ken?"

She nodded.

"Tread carefully," he warned.

"You too." She said the words to his back, for he was already turned and headed toward the drawbridge.

She made her way slowly to the edge of the steep embankment as tears filled her eyes. She wasn't upset because she was leaving her father—she'd certainly need to say a prayer of forgiveness for that sin tonight—but she couldn't shake the feeling that she'd never see Angus again. It was silly; everything would go as they had planned. Before she could fret further, the blast of the fire horn jerked her into motion. There was no time for any thoughts but those of escape.

Series by Julie Johnstone

Scottish Medieval Romance Books:

Highlander Vows: Entangled Hearts Series

Regency Romance Books:

A Whisper of Scandal Series

A Once Upon A Rogue Series

Lords of Deception Series

Danby Regency Christmas Novellas
The Redemption of a Dissolute Earl, Book 1
Season For Surrender, Book 2
It's in the Duke's Kiss, Book 3

Regency Anthologies
A Summons from the Duke of Danby (Regency Christmas Summons, Book 2)
Thwarting the Duke (When the Duke Comes to Town, Book 2)

Regency Romance Box Sets
A Whisper of Scandal Trilogy (Books 1-3)
Dukes, Duchesses & Dashing Noblemen (A Once Upon a Rogue Regency Novels, Books 1-3)

Paranormal Books:

The Siren Saga
Echoes in the Silence, Book 1

About the Author

As a little girl I loved to create fantasy worlds and then give all my friends roles to play. Of course, I was always the heroine! Books have always been an escape for me and brought me so much pleasure, but it didn't occur to me that I could possibly be a writer for a living until I was in a career that was not my passion. One day, I decided I wanted to craft stories like the ones I loved, and with a great leap of faith I quit my day job and decided to try to make my dream come true. I discovered my passion, and I have never looked back. I feel incredibly blessed and fortunate that I have been able to make a career out of sharing the stories that are in my head! I write Scottish Medieval Romance, Regency Romance, and I have even written a Paranormal Romance book. And because I have the best readers in the world, I have hit the USA Today bestseller list several times.

If you love me, I hope you do, you can follow me on Bookbub, and they will send you notices whenever I have a sale or a new release. You can follow me here:
bookbub.com/authors/julie-johnstone

You can also join my newsletter to get great prizes and inside scoops!
Join here: https://goo.gl/qnkXFF

I really want to hear from you! It makes my day!
Email me here:
juliejohnstoneauthor@gmail.com

I'm on Facebook a great deal chatting about books and life. If you want to follow me, you can do so here:
facebook.com/authorjuliejohnstone

Can't get enough of me? Well, good! Come see me here:
Twitter:
@juliejohnstone
Goodreads:
https://goo.gl/T57MTA